1971

W9-ACP-448

3 0301 00034302 6

BOOKS BY P. M. PASINETTI

L'IRA DI DIO
VENETIAN RED
THE SMILE ON THE FACE OF THE LION
FROM THE ACADEMY BRIDGE

FROM THE ACADEMY BRIDGE

FROM THE ACADEMY BRIDGE

A
NOVEL
BY
P. M. PASINETTI

RANDOM HOUSE   NEW YORK

LIBRARY
College of St. Francis

First American Edition

Copyright © 1970 by P. M. Pasinetti

All rights reserved under International and Pan-American
Copyright Conventions. Published in the United States
by Random House, Inc., New York, and simultaneously
in Canada by Random House of Canada Limited, Toronto.
Originally published in Italy as *Il Ponte dell'Accademia*
by Bompiani, Milan.

Library of Congress Catalog Card Number: 77-85572

Manufactured in the United States of America
by Kingsport Press, Inc., Kingsport, Tennessee

TO ALBERT AND MARISA ERSKINE

853.9
P252f

58942

58942

FROM THE ACADEMY BRIDGE

CHAPTER ONE

GILBERTO ROSSI:

That stretch of the Pacific Highway which runs southward from Palos Rojos to Bradley in the direction of the Mexican border, has on the inland side an unbroken chain of mountains with colors that go from that of burnt earth to that of fog, while on the outside it has a series of beaches, very narrow and slanting at some points while at other points they are smooth, white and wide like piazzas, under the heavy sun.

So the coastal highway stretches on, glittering between beaches and mountains, four lanes north–south and four south–north. To climb up to our Institute you can turn from the highway into any of the three canyons between Palos Rojos and Bradley: Palos Rojos Canyon, Bitter Canyon, Bradley Canyon. I almost always choose Bitter, whether I come from the north or from the south; it is the narrowest and stoniest, nearly always deserted between precipices. In that abandoned silence the squirrel jumps, the lizard moves jerkily forward, blazed;

and every now and then you discover bushes of flowers with colors of a blinding intensity.

It is rather tortuous and at first it is all caught between steep walls; then as you go on climbing, the landscape opens up, like an immense dry flower revealing petal by petal the successive layers of mountains, the nearest ones brown, the farther ones bluish, and every once in a while, sudden and very, very far down below, slabs of ocean water. Bitter Canyon at some point joins Palos Rojos Canyon, larger and more important, all nicely paved with asphalt. Three quarters of a mile from this crossing there are wide plateaulike spaces which have been obtained by sawing off a few mountain tops. Various new university buildings have been placed up here, while in the small town of Palos Rojos down in the valley there is still the university center, the old campus, white stucco and brick-colored tiled roofs, little cloisters and patios among the palm trees.

Up here, instead, a prevalence of glass and steel: the Center for Business Statistics, with its own telephone exchange and the latest in electronic computers; the Subtropical Horticulture Station; and, of course, our Institute, the Institute for Language and Communication Analysis.

From the time when, having obtained my immigration visa for the United States, I accepted the offer of employment extended to me by director Alphonse Rossi, this has been my office address; to make the proper impression it should be typewritten, single-spaced, on an oblong envelope:

> *Mr. Gilberto Rossi,*
> *Palos Rojos Institute for Language and*
> *Communication Analysis,*
> *University of Palos Rojos,*
> *Palos Rojos, Calif. 92099.*

Occasionally I type that address all by myself on an envelope or on a white piece of paper and then I keep staring at it with stings of astonishment.

So here I am, I, born at Portogruaro, raised in Portogruaro and Venice, graduated from the University of Milan a couple of years before the war, obtaining 102/110 points (a very undistinguished grade), variously engaged in the common political and martial sufferings and in modest cultural professions between

[*4*]

youth and ripe age—here I am now on the Pacific Coast, being part of one of those study centers where "the world of yesterday and of today is being analyzed to prepare for the world of tomorrow," or some such key phrase; I am rather nicely settled in a small house among subtropical vegetation; I have a wide view of mountains and ocean from my bedroom window; I also have a comfortable office at the Institute and a small metal desk reserved at the library; sufficient salary; abundant research tools: all of this to analyze documents of history of the last fifty years, particularly Italian. Theoretically, in my area, I should also decide about problems to be programmed for the electronic computer which Business Statistics allows us to use for some segments of time.

The Opportunity to come to the Pacific had presented itself when my life in Italy seemed silently and unobtrusively to be falling apart. I suddenly noticed that we were racing toward the end of the twenty-year period from the conclusion of the war; in our office at the Di Gaetano publishing house (myself and two other employees), I was the only one to notice that. I also realized that there would be, after that, another period of twenty years, much quicker than the first one, so as to pass almost unobserved. And that would carry me, in terms of age, close to seventy. For all practical purposes, I felt I was as good as seventy already.

My military service during the Second World War, I would tell myself, casting glances over my past and attempting recapitulations, was perfectly indistinguishable from that of millions of others; the first postwar twenty-year stretch has been ninety-five percent dull. What am I, I would ask myself, Gilberto Rossi, as a human fact, as a unique and unrepeatable event? And consequently, what am I as a social individual, as a citizen? I am a democrat, in the broadest sense of the term. Backed up by a passable education and carried on by my natural disposition, I have become a professional of culture. What do you mean by that, Gilberto? Well, let's say—a man who attempts to express and divulge, in one way or another, certain particular visions of what he considers to be the truth. Or something of the sort. I would tell myself this, and then I would think that for about twenty years I had been an obscure and hardly influential employee at a publishing house, one day on top of the

[5]

other, one day on top of the other, with brief hopes and long frustrations in my work; pleasantness and disheartenment, love and egotism in my private life. So I had accumulated these twenty years and had now come to see the clear necessity for a renewed contact with myself, a jolt, a crisis.

I saw in my past professional life only two brief periods that had been slightly out of the ordinary: that academic year, at the beginning of the war, when I taught Italian at a German university, and that solar year, at the beginning of the postwar era, when I was a member of a little jazz band in Venice.

First thing, I went to see Ceroni. I had taken my university degree in Milan before the war under his direction; some years ago he moved to Rome, where he also has a position as consultant for Cultural Relations with Foreign Countries. I indicated my aspiration to cultural employment outside of Italy.

"What's the matter with Italy, Rossi? Now that there is so much to be done?"

I started on my usual wrong foot: "There certainly would be a lot to be done, to straighten out the situation of the disinherited, of those who have had few or no chances at the start, but I haven't chosen the political profession, lacking any aptitude for it, so I have neither the capacity nor the power to do anything for them, except give my loyal, if passive, support, while despising the holders of power when they prove to be not only inept but mysteriosophic as well."

"Mysteriosophic?"

"You know what I mean. Besides, I have come to the conclusion that the Italy of the economic miracle and of affluence really doesn't concern me. Let them all gorge themselves. I have nothing to do with it." It would have been difficult to find a worse way to broach the subject.

Indeed Ceroni was silent for a long while. Sensibly then he said, "You're no longer a boy. How old are you now? Forty?"

"Long past." I look younger, so the smiling and nonchalant tone of my admission was visibly crushing him. "I have a small salary at the publishing house and I may even get a raise," I went on, from bad to worse. "I'm a bachelor, I could become engaged tomorrow if I wanted to, I have a charming and affectionate girl friend, an American."

Here I was lying. But if, at the opposite extreme, I had told him that I wanted to leave Italy because things with Mary were not going as well as before, and that she had another man, I would have been an even worse liar.

"Hm," Ceroni said.

"About these cultural positions abroad, do they or don't they exist? To me, holding one of those would be fascinating, because I could then also acquire a certain perspective on Italy, for when you live in it, this country turns out to be, at the very least, incomprehensible. Now, I was told that we have Italian cultural institutes even in Nigeria, or Indonesia. Just for instance."

Ceroni confirmed that the positions did exist; he talked about them at length, in his lively Tuscan manner, with a wealth of details, and in conclusion said that those positions were given to young men of outstanding merit. "As a philologist you are no good. After taking your degree, which was a colorless performance, you were busy with jazz. What else?"

"I was *Universitätslektor* in Germany, at Göttingen, the university of the great mathematician David Hilpert, and of that basic figure in modern physics, Max Planck. I happen to be a serious, meticulous man. And I have published some rather unusual articles."

"I bet you they were all about jazz."

"Oh, no. My jazz period was unfortunately very brief. But I knew all about jazz. I've read everything on the subject. When I set my mind on something, I read all about it. Di Gaetano, the publisher, actually hired me because, among other things, I was a specialist on jazz. You know—for the . . ." My breath failed in the anguished effort to make myself clear.

"For the what?"

In the ministerial office, high-ceilinged, white, air-conditioned, I studied Ceroni, in his shiny fresh summer suit, his hair also shiny and well combed, not at all professorial, but looking, rather, like an elegant gentleman traceable to the thirties. He kept his metallic, blond man's eyes fixed on me, but he had already practically ceased to listen. Wasting his time humiliated me. A topnotch scholar. His favorite pupils, all of them well placed in university chairs. Very attractive to women, too.

". . . for the *MME*," I completed.

"What is that?"

"That's the *Modern Musical Encyclopedia.*" That was my usual vice at the time—pour it out, babble on incessantly: "Later, Di Gaetano even planned a whole series of little volumes about jazz, but instead of letting me edit the series, he didn't even mention it to me. He put me to work on some historical series, and I would sweat blood to promote ideas, which he never accepted; then naturally I worked on other things, too, like handbooks on administrative techniques, which I hoped could contribute to the reform of certain bureaucratic systems, for instance in our public libraries and in the mechanism of civil service examinations . . ." My talk was completely out of place. "As for jazz," I resumed, because I am a man of precision and go back to a question when the person who has asked it has already forgotten it, "as for jazz, the man who was put in charge of that section would come to me to have me translate English texts and to get explanations. This fellow even went to Di Gaetano several times and asked him, 'Why don't we use Gilberto Rossi too on the jazz series?' But Di Gaetano answered every time, mysteriosophically, 'No, no, not Rossi.' "

"Mysteriosophically?"

"You know what I mean."

But by now Ceroni had really switched off all contact with me. "Pity," he said, "pity, because the subject I gave you for your thesis was rather nice, and you with your Venetian background could have got quite a bit out of it."

I recognized his allusion to a philological subject chosen in the very early days, later abandoned in favor of a totally different one. Ceroni, understandably, had forgotten all about me. In other words, the years had had this peculiarity: though not concretely existing, they had gone by anyway, producing effects. I took my leave. Good-bye, foreign appointment under Ceronian auspices.

But I was among the few who had never lost contact—I won't say with jazz, but more generally, with the American dream. I have always known the personnel of American cultural agencies both in Rome and in Milan, not to mention the fact that my friend Mary was employed by one for a while. They would invite me to films, lectures and concerts, and I would relish attending them. Mary spoke Italian too well for me to impose the obsession of my English upon her, so what I knew of spoken

English I owed to films in the original, seen wherever I could find any and nearly always seen again two or three times. As for written English, what I had of it was mainly from reading books about jazz and also books by the American New Critics, which fascinated me.

In my small entourage, almost everybody at that time was against America, the only exceptions being myself and some militants of the extreme left like Corso Gianfranchi, who knew America well, went there often and had friends by whom he was very well liked. Di Gaetano himself took a trip of three weeks to New York and Chicago; he came back full of disdain for the food and everything.

I saw, after Ceroni, other powerful people; I sought out contemporaries of mine from the Venetia region who had achieved university chairs or other important positions, like Gabriele Crocetta; from the point of view of age and everything, they looked closer to Ceroni than to me. They were important, i.e., their specific gravity was different from mine, even physically. I had allowed years to go by during which the others had acquired new mannerisms, in their gestures and behavior, and had woven alliances which at the moment of my crisis appeared thoroughly unbeatable. All of the influential people with whom I spoke were avid readers of the magazines where some excellent articles of mine had appeared; however, they literally did not seem to have perceived my articles; I myself, in the presence of those people, under their looks, had the feeling of being transparent.

Things had reached this point when Corso Gianfranchi uttered the magic phrase one evening, "Why don't I have you meet Halleck?" This meant to me the opening of the great and bewitching panorama of American foundations. Which happen to be gigantic legacies, transformed into institutions for the financing of culture.

James Audubon Halleck wore a bow tie and an olive-colored gabardine suit; he may have been sixty but looked twenty years younger. The reason why he had preserved himself well must have been that he was small: he had always easily held all of himself well under control. A compact and coherent little man, starting from his measured voice down to his beautifully shined shoes. He was a kind of globe-trotting representative for the

[9]

Newton Ash Foundation, and that gave him happiness and total fulfillment, so he told you quietly whatever was on his mind, looking at you without reservation.

At dinner in the Roman *trattoria* Dal Pignolone, in the old Piazzetta del Cordaro, where Halleck himself took us (he knew Italian very well, and all the regional dishes and specialties), Corso Gianfranchi, who was an old friend of Halleck's (he called him "Jim" and Halleck in turn called him "Corr-so," proud of his *r* rolled *all'italiana*), spoke about me in such embarrassing terms as to make me blush and want to leave. In fact, I would have left, but Halleck, turning to me, switched from Italian to English, and I realized that this was a kind of examination. Soon he was saying that my English was all right, and he was already calling me "Gilberr-to." Then, total change within me: pride and a desire to talk, like an urgent watering of the mouth. Much variety in my talk: historical views, semantic analyses, jumps into autobiography. The *spaghetti all'amatriciana* came and Halleck was proved right: it was superb. Roman cuisine had never pleased me so much. The idea of not having brought Mary to this meeting—in fact, of not having even considered the possibility of bringing her—now gave me tears of remorse. At that time there were already tensions between Mary and me, the other man had already entered into her life, an Italo-American psychologist named Ottorino. Seeing that I struck up such a successful rapport at first sight with a cultivated and influential American like Halleck would perhaps have contributed to her drifting back toward me, I thought.

Halleck knew Italian history rather well. When, during the *abbacchio,* I told him of a project I had presented years earlier to Di Gaetano (who had received it as a frivolity on my part) of doing for the historical paperback series a little book on the former Italian royal family, to be called *Semantics and Literary Style of the House of Savoy,* Halleck smiled and said that my approach interested him. We imagined, in fact, a whole possible series to be prolonged and extended in all directions, *Semantics and Literary Style* of some of the popes—Mastai-Ferretti, Sarto, Pacelli; of the British queens; of the last Austrian archdukes; of the Southern generals in the American Civil War: it became a free-for-all. We would quote Great Historical Sayings. We agreed that in a speech or in a historical document one should seek out the key phrases and then subject them to up-to-date analyses; and that the ideal thing to do then would be to publish the results of the analyses in simple language in inexpensive little volumes accessible to populations that have been obfuscated by millennia of verbal swindles.

"In the area of language and communication," he said nonchalantly, "the Newton Ash Foundation has done quite a bit. The Palos Rojos Institute has been largely financed by us." While fresh fruit was being brought, he was already suggesting, "Why don't you meet Alphonse Rossi, who will be in Italy presently? Meanwhile, send him your publications." And he gave me a short description of the man who is now my boss, promising that he would arrange a meeting.

Three weeks later I found Alphonse Rossi in his hotel apartment. He received me in the bedroom in shirt sleeves, energetic and debonair, oozing authoritative charm; from the nearby living room one could hear his wife and daughter, who were playing games. Alphonse gave me a gin and tonic. He urged me to talk; the whole time we were together he did nothing but that. He spoke with a Bologna accent. "Go on, go on," he said if I stopped for a moment. He walked up and down the room while his large ears absorbed my random autobiographical talk. We understood each other from the first moment, achieving a kind of rapport which I have not yet fully analyzed.

When I came out I was drunk, not from the gin but from the prospect that Alphonse had opened for me of a year to be spent on this Pacific Coast. I started living in a state of frantic joy. After he left Rome, things speeded up: there were exchanges of letters, meetings with important Americans in Italy. When finally the letter with the formal offer arrived—I carried it around with me for days, wearing it out by reading and rereading it—it did not actually produce a great change in my mood, so high was the degree of tension I had reached, anyway. I have always liked hamburgers, American breakfasts, even American coffee, and bourbon whiskey: in that period I ate or drank nothing else. I was being carried upon the crest of the Pacific wave. Passing through the bureaucratic mysteries to obtain documents and visas, I was never deserted by the most complete and irresponsible sense of euphoria. As if accompanied by ballet music,

I allowed them to vaccinate me, draw blood, do anything.

I flew from Italy direct to the Pacific Coast, without changing planes. From the moment you entered the jet, you were already in a transatlantic atmosphere: the crashing noises and jolts of Mediterranean life were being replaced by swishing noises, well-oiled gestures, calm—in other words, the main American characteristics. In comparison, for example, with a Roman street, these motions and noises made you feel as though you were living under water.

The first person who took care of me was Alphonse's factotum secretary. It was she who had typed my appointment letter, which at the bottom bore the double formula *AR/dp*. *AR* for Alphonse Rossi, and her name was Diane Peck. I say "was," because her last name is different since her marriage to a young scientist. In the first few days, for several hours every day, our */dp* took me around in her convertible, helping me find a place to stay and make domestic purchases. In our thoughtlessness in those first days up these canyons, we exchanged a few kisses which now, seen from the present perspective, appear wholly unreal to me, as they must to the young lady who meanwhile has married this astrophysicist of Polish origin.

What I shall finally accomplish here naturally remains to be seen. I work a lot; I always involve myself deeply in the things I do. At the present rate of exchange I earn perhaps a third of what, for example, Ceroni does, but never mind, I hope to live a more original and droll life than he has. He is considered one of the two top Petrarch scholars in Italy; as long as I was in his presence, this fact used to paralyze me, but now I am beginning to see it with greater equanimity. The day I found the right lodgings and made them mine with a regular lease, I sent Ceroni an impulsive post card, a view of this coast in vivid colors, with palm and cactus trees; as a text I chose that nostalgic line of the patriotic Italian poet Carducci in which, dreaming of his youthful love, he says: *"Marrying you, fair Maria, would have been better,"* only instead of "better" I wrote "worse," signing it simply "Gilbert." Infantile stupidity on my part? Will I regret this some day? Well, that's too bad.

"A fish," my late Uncle Bartolomeo, and not he alone, used to say, "starts stinking from the head." Let us then attempt a pocket-sized biographical sketch of the director of the Institute, who, as everyone already knows by now, by pure coincidence is called Rossi like myself.

Alphonse Rossi was born Alfonso Rossi in Bologna in the last days of the nineteenth century and was educated there; he received his degree in philosophy with a dissertation in experimental psychology on Freud and Leonardo da Vinci. I believe this was in 1928, which makes it later than usual; for a few years he was one of those older students wearing beards, walking the streets at night, his voice sonorous under the arcades of his city, a great habitué of whorehouses. Only the most attentive observer can detect traces of this past in the Alphonse of today—a handsome gentleman, electrically shaved, with the right degree of silver in his hair, who speaks English with an accent rather closer to British than to American, is chummy with presidents of foundations, heads of governments, celebrities, senators.

Let's follow his European past for a moment. Not long after taking his degree, around 1930, we see him, hardly a lover of the Regime, slip unobtrusively out of Italy into France, where he was to remain until the mid-thirties.

In Paris he became Alphonse, he perfected his French to the point of writing it with ease. He was active, he was industrious, he was esteemed: Alphonse Rossi is the plodding type. He enjoyed the confidence of editors of specialized reviews, of publishers unknown to a large public, with roots sunk in the most ancient and well-shaded cultural soils in Paris; he dealt with subjects like the history of education, the history of rhetorics, the new techniques in verbal communication; he even compiled educational statistics. My director has never been a trifler, not he; in fact, let's face it, his writing is on the ponderous side. Even now. Now, however, his books and reports do not appear, as they did in Paris, in thick, uncut paperbound volumes and his name soberly given as *A. Rossi*. Now his books are clothbound, and on the back of the dust jackets Alphonse appears photographed with a pipe, against a background of white shelves full of books.

Among other merits, Alphonse Rossi also has that of being a born convention man, and he was among the first Europeans fully to appreciate the panel system, the idea of putting five or six gentlemen on a stage to reason things out urbanely; I

[13]

haven't the slightest doubt that Alphonse will pass as one of the great moderators of the century. Why? Because, I say, his voice carries his native vibration through the world, the resonances of the nocturnal Bologna arcades, of the interminable peripatetic dialogues into the wee hours, his mind serene and lucid after the visit to the whorehouse.

When, in the mid-thirties (both of the century and his own) Alphonse Rossi left Paris to cross the ocean, there were already American universities and foundations that offered him Opportunity. In America, in the cultural world, he revealed his organizational abilities; he mastered English as he had French; he held chairs; for a period of time he was dean of a small college; he achieved a certain influence; in an election year he would entertain relations with the more intelligent of the two presidential candidates; he was called for consultation by government committees in Washington; he married for the second time.

His first wife, dead in an accident at twenty-six, is buried in Montparnasse; even now, if you mention her to him, Alphonse bites his lower lip, frowns, looks at you confused and defensive, as if to say, "Why do you have to do this to me? What have I done to you?" His second wife is the very popular Doris.

Not tall, she has wonderful legs and hips, eyes both sweet and sly; she oozes likability and a need for action. Their association undoubtedly developed on the basis of sex, too. She does the driving for him; Alphonse cannot drive a car. He sits next to her in the Buick and looks like a Cabinet minister being transported from home to the ministry, or from the ministry, home. Doris has always been a marvelous hostess. She dresses elegantly —that is, simply—wearing one or two jewels of little value at the most. The Rossis know lots of people—for example, the governor and his wife—and they extend and receive many invitations. "The Alphonse Rossis are very social," says our electronics technician, Budd Rotondi, translating the sentence literally into Italian and making it sound like perfect nonsense. They go quite often to New York and Washington, besides going to Europe; they have been guests at the White House. Sometimes the Rossis give dinners with butlers and maids, cooks and bartenders, all of them hired for the occasion; they arrive in their long automobiles brandishing the tools of their trade and carrying large trays of food.

[*14*]

It must be clear by now that the destiny ruling the life of Alphonse Rossi could hardly have been more different from the one which directed the life of Gilberto Rossi. Roughly fifteen years older than I, he left Italy, quite well equipped with a degree, in the eighth year of the Regime, while I was still in school; in fact, around that time I joined the GUF (abbreviation for the Regime's student organization, Gruppo Universitario, et cetera), and it occurs to me now that to render the pronunciation in English, you would have to spell it *Goof*. I joined the Goof when I was still in Venice, before going to study at Milan. When I went to apply for membership I was accompanied and supported by the most influential friend I had then, Gabriele Crocetta, who held a position in the cultural affairs office. I can still hear his somewhat dark and throttled voice and the touch of mysteriosophic hierarchical haughtiness he put in it when he said "our Venice Goof."

I wrote a few short articles for the Goof magazine, but I never achieved any visibility either there or at school. My university grade points were very pallid, and I have already mentioned my degree under Ceroni at Milan. I also mentioned the culminating point in my academic life: in 1940 I was a teacher of the Italian language, furnished by our government to Germany along with about fifty other teachers, who were distributed around that country, then larger than it is now. *Lektor für italienisch!* Göttingen! Planck! The Planck of the quantum theory. My official bureaucratic title was, roughly translated, Supplementary Teacher Appointed by the Royal Government; that was next to the last; lower than that there was only the Supplementary Teacher Employed Locally, like Signora Mingazzini at the Italian Cultural Institute in Berlin, a city where she has remained throughout all that has happened, and where she still lives, eighty-six years old.

As I said, mine was a very different destiny from that of Alphonse, one can see that even from the few sketchy data I have given. Not to mention the war. Alphonse spent a war period chronologically almost coincident with mine, on a Washington job that had to do with breaking codes, cryptography; we are in the area of counterespionage, something important, very impressive as a conversation subject.

On the other hand, it must finally be admitted that Alphonse

Rossi and I have some important characteristics in common besides our surname, and I am sure that he offered me this position because he had scented them. I am a man of little success, but I am not a little man. I do not possess the talent to be oppressed, humiliated & wronged. Besides, I am a real worker. I set out to do a job, and I do it. I budget my time well, I am punctual, and I do all of this by choice, for my own comfort. Then I have another very important trait in common with my director—curiosity. About everything, especially people. Individuals, historical and private, present and past. Their problems. Their moral sense. And mainly, their language. Their syntax. Their semantics.

Unlike Alphonse, however, I carry the burden of all the difficulties and the fundamental lack of timing of the shy & introverted, whereas he is one of the creators of the very concept of Human Relations. In the most ordinary human relations, things have never gone too well for me, especially in Italy. I always appear as an intruder in initiating conversations and as a bore in carrying them on, the type of man that people in Rome look at with growing impatience and disdain, finally asking themselves, "What the hell does he want?" Here in the United States, things have been going much better for me because people are better mannered, and then perhaps because until now I have had much greater solitude and fewer temptations to break it, let alone the natural inclination to keep silent as one grows older. Not to mention my famous verbal blocks. And altogether skipping any mention of the initial deficiencies in my English.

But when I was in Italy I used to cause perplexity and annoyance by talking insistently with, for example, impatient and theologically rather unprepared priests, with telephone operators, with newspaper vendors. It occurred to me to mention newspaper vendors because during my last months in Italy there were various newspaper strikes, in support of the just demands of typographers. Well, every time I came close to a newsstand and examined the two or three newspapers that had been published, alone and meager in the general void, I would look quizzically at the newsdealer and the customers, and then I would say things like "Well, let's buy this one. Right? After all"—I would be pointing to the Italian counterpart of the *Wall Street Journal*—"after all, newspapers of this sort, generally unacceptable in terms of politics, are often good from an information point of view. Don't you agree? But, wait, there is the *Carlino*. Perhaps . . . What?" The newsdealer would ask me, "Well, which paper do you want?" He would look at me with stupefaction, then with spite.

I have always wanted to discuss, to intrude, without being cut out for the role. For example, I have a friend, Fiorenzo Bocca, who is partner in a water-tap factory. In Italy they have factories where they just make faucets. Well, every time I saw him I would start telling him things like this: "Fiorenzo, the hot and cold water in the installation in my house, and in many homes of friends, never mix right. The water comes out completely cold, then it suddenly comes in hiccups, steaming hot like espresso coffee, then again ice-cold. Why?" In such cases I'd become insistent, even anxious. At first Fiorenzo would keep silent. I would insist, with my crushing faith in the word, "Explain it to me, you who are running such a factory. *Let us talk about it.*" Evasively, but with his eyes already beginning to pop out of his head, he would say that he handled only the business end of the operation, and that they produced only water taps, anyway, and that therefore all problems of pipes, hydraulic pressure, etc., were, after all, not theirs. I would laugh, overwhelming him with new argumentation: "But I *am* talking about the water tap. It doesn't take long for the hot-water faucet to become so blistering hot that you can't even touch it, let alone regulate or shut it." He would mumble phrases containing key words like "managerial," "sales curves," with mysteriosophic allusions to problems which he considered to be outside my sphere of competence and interest. I would say, "Do give me some specific informational material that I may study the problems." Nothing doing. I would raise my voice: "I know only one thing—I do not tolerate incompetence. It gives me nausea. I have a craving for competence."

So I often acquired the reputation of an incoherent, out-of-phase speaker, but the truth is that I face even the problem of faucets with sincere interest and with a desire to look into it clearly and come to conclusions. Perhaps I am not helped by the fact that always in my life too many things have interested me. Examples: Besides jazz, there were times when I was quite an expert on certain sports; I could have been the winner in any quiz on the history of prize fighting. I have never been in Paris for longer than a week at a time, yet through maps and other materials I know its topography and its town-planning history so well that I could be a guide or a cab driver there. It is symptomatic that on an infinite number of occasions in my life I discovered that I was laughing all by myself. On the other hand, my intrusions and suggestions appeared obscure or were mistaken for levity. Hence, as the years went by, I had to tighten up my self-control in the presence of other people, so that in the end I must inevitably talk to myself or put autobiographical notes on paper. Fiorenzo Bocca and such people (mind you, quite a few among them are not simply entrusted with the care of faucets but perhaps of human souls, or of the national government) camouflage their incompetence under mysteriosophic phrases, while I have to stick to my scorching-hot water taps. Or rather, I had to. Here in the United States, such things generally work well—which is simply their duty, so one doesn't notice them.

My failures in rapport with other people, and generally in my everyday life, can perhaps—I say perhaps—be related to the fact that to a certain extent I have always identified myself with a puppet; add to that my tendency to see others from a similar point of view. As a child I was a maniacally compulsive talker, and my mother, grabbing me in midair while I was doing a ballet around her, would squeeze me and suffocate me with kisses, saying, "You keep quiet, you puppet." There were no threats or anything (I had a good life then) ; in fact, she would grow a bit emotional, there were tears in her laughter. She and I could engage in matches of mutual tickling, torturing each other to the point of ecstasy.

Besides, for years and years, in our house at Portogruaro and later in Venice (when my father transferred his legal practice there) we had puppet shows produced by myself as leader of the group, by the two sons of my late Uncle Bartolomeo and my Aunt Luciana, and by others temporarily engaged. I am not interested at this point in evoking our tragedies (they were costume plays in vaguely defined settings, as in Calderón or Shakespeare) ; each show, however, would be concluded by a sketch based on contemporary events, taken from either the domestic or the national scene, where present realities were transformed by us into art. We would put characters onstage which were taken from life, both private and public: Uncle Bartolomeo himself and his wife, Luciana; Mother and Father; the generals of the Great War; our family friend Signora Lezze-Adorno and her son, Oliviero; the cardinal patriarch of Venice; and that famed war hero, D'Annunzio the soldier-poet; our family doctor, Giulio Levi; and of course ourselves. I have given examples at random. As I said, my job here at the Institute implies the study of certain phases of Italian history; well, very often it occurs to me that even contemporary national events involving the beloved country, the Regime, the Black Shirts, the pocket-sized king of my green years, and so forth, have a tendency to come back to my mind as they were echoed in homemade versions which would later be stylized by us and artistically transformed into puppet shows.

When we witnessed a noteworthy event or when one was even simply reported at the dinner table, my cousins and I used a conventional signal, a raising of the thumb, which meant "booked up"; whoever made that gesture first acquired a kind of copyright, was authorized to stage the event with puppets. That meant cutting it down to essentials, focusing on a memorable phrase, like the one uttered by the patriarch of Venice one evening in October 1922, when according to a report by Oliviero Lezze-Adorno to my father seated at the dinner table, he had thanked the Lord from the pulpit and had exhorted the faithful also "to thank Him for having held the heart of the king in His hands." Often the key phrase was in the semivernacular of Venetians accustomed to speaking the dialect but trying to sound lapidary, as was the case with a phrase famous in our domestic chronicles: "Paola, is one permitted to salute? Long live Ee-tally!" The words were thrown as a challenge, with devouring irony, at her friend Signora Perigotto, a foe of the Regime, by Signora Lezze-Adorno, fanatically favorable to it. They had been uttered by Signora Lezze-Adorno in Venice, in the *salone* of the Perigotto home with windows on the Grand Canal, in the very act of leaning out of one of those windows to salute with outstretched Roman arm some of the early exemplars of Regime chieftains, macabre and fatuous, gliding in a gondola along the canal, on the occasion of the royal regatta of 1923, or perhaps it was 1924.

A spring gadget was introduced into the arm of Signora Lezze-Adorno presented in a black outfit (the servant maid of the puppets minus white apron) so her salute from the window would be particularly vibrant and dashing. Thousands of such gestures and phrases I have stored up within myself; they are now like useful formulas to be developed in the computer of my mind or like the abbreviated titles of volumes deposited in the archives of memory.

That's why so many times up here, in the evening, I see ghosts caught in the cactus trees—ghosts of forty years ago and more: Oliviero Lezze-Adorno, a white death's-head embroidered on the front of his black shirt, waving his black mane (in later years it was to be flattened by many-splendored brilliantine), standing next to my father, who listened without looking at him and weighed with mistrust that phrase which had first resounded in St. Mark's Basilica and was now being quoted by Oliviero, having the patriarch as its speaker and as its subject the Creator, who had "held the heart of the king in His hands."

"This phrase should be saluted!" Oliviero cried. *He* had quoted the phrase to us; he was writing his own script. And in fact there he stood, a solitary militia man, a one-man ceremony, in our small dining room, his arm outstretched, his lips tightened, his face ecstatic and grim. No one felt like following his example. Then he looked at us, not with reproach or threat, but with approval: it was right that he, a priest of the new mysteries, should have a monopoly on the ritual gesture.

Meanwhile the metaphorical language had long since been decoded, the patriarch's allusion had been understood (by my father, mother, uncle and aunt; not so much by myself, since at that stage of the game I was eight years old): the heart of His Majesty, sustained by its Creator, had dictated within His Majesty the counsel to abstain from proclaiming a state of national emergency, a measure which would block the possibility of crowds assembling in the streets, demonstrations, mass movements; and this royal measure, or rather, this royal nonmeasure, would present opportunities for mass gatherings, marches and the eventual establishment of the Regime in His Majesty's country, the *patria* which was also, incidentally, our own.

A year or two go by and there she is, jumping into view, Oliviero's patriotic mother, Giuseppina, wife of Armando Lezze-Adorno (a simple soul, holder of a war bronze medal, an excellent insurance company employee), on our usual stage, representing this time the *salone* of the Perigotto home in Venice. We have been invited from Portogruaro to watch the yearly boat race, the royal regatta.

Among the flowery summer dresses and straw hats and delicate ribbons worn by Signora Perigotto and by my mother, Aunt Luciana and the other ladies as well, Giuseppina Lezze-Adorno has appeared, isolated and yet as if in marching order, her shirt and skirt both black, a nun in the New Order. Let us look at her as she marches to the gilded cardboard window from which, her head rigidly turned toward her hostess as if she had a stiff neck, she hurls at her that passionate, sarcastic, severely admonishing challenge: "Paola, is one permitted to salute?" Naturally, before adding her "Long live Ee-tally!" she does not wait for any reply, reaction or comment; the spring mechanism is already being activated, her arm is stretched out stiffly toward a Grand Canal which remains unseen but is rather cleverly rendered through a pocket flashlight directed from backstage toward the inside of the *salone* in fluid motions imitating the reflections of water.

And now, alone up here, I see everything: instead of the Pacific I see the Grand Canal down below, with all the boats. From the windows of the Perigotto home during the regatta one could twice enjoy the fleeting sight of the racing boats, the magic, slim, speedy little gondolas, bearing numbers and painted in different colors. The champion gondoliers would pass under the Perigotto windows, the first time rowing with fresh strength and routine oar strokes, and then they would return on their way back, widely spaced, panting. In fact, from the Perigottos' you could even see the finish post, a big barge known as The Machine.

We are now waiting for the magic vessels, the very water holds its breath, immobile golden barges are placed in front of the palaces leaving a free passage in the middle: a lane of water, perfectly still as you never see it in reality but only in ancient pictures, a well-brushed rolled-out carpet. While this water carpet is all ready for the lightning-quick racing boats, now an official procession of personages appears on it instead, rocking idly along, perhaps being transported to The Machine at the last moment to avoid discomforts and sunstroke. In a gondola containing deluxe military uniforms with spun-glass panaches, there is also the king himself. From the palaces, hail of applause. Finally among the parade flotilla, the gondola of the new chieftains is recognized; then several of our mothers utter a suffocated cry of admiration mingled with terror.

It should be recalled that gondolas are always black to begin with. So now the question is: those who have chosen black as their flag, mourning as their uniform, the absence of color as their color, how will they acquire visibility, avoid camouflage? It's all right with the shirts, duly funereal and terroristic, but how will their parade boat become identifiable, if all other boats are black as well? The answer is under our very eyes: the other gondolas are as usual coated with varnish and sparkle in the sun; the gondola of the new chieftains is painted a flat, lackluster, opaque black. The cry of the new patriot goes out to that vessel blacker than black, to that unique instance of gloom; and with her gesture, rigid and disciplined, yet passionate and self-offering, toward the first apparition of that shadowy cockroach on the waters of the Grand Canal, the lady really seems to validate and celebrate, ecstatically, death.

Those very distant times continued to offer us, in our small circle, material for brief sketches, but from the recollection I have of them I know that their tone was less and less joyful; Signora Lezze-Adorno's voice, bitter and ominous, after all, had drained our scenes and key phrases of simplicity and mirth. In fact, examining things from the present perspective almost forty years later, I think I can safely say that during that period of the Cockroach Gondola, as far as I was concerned, childhood ended prematurely. It was also then that my father got into the habit of leaning on my shoulder (perhaps because that came naturally, considering our respective sizes), thus creating a wordless but important and unforgettable confidence between us. He never said much, but he always understood everything about me, including my shyness and mediocrity.

Neither did Olivicro, with that skull embroidered on his chest, offer a much more hilarious spectacle than the one given at the Perigottos' by his mother, the more so because not long after the revelation of the Cockroach Gondola, every time he came to see us he started pointing at me, saying mysteriosophically to my father, "This child should sign up. Look at Sergio and Gianluigi"—key phrases which were duly registered by our puppets. Indeed, the two sons of my Uncle Bartolomeo (a war "interventionist" since 1914, quite the opposite to my father, and a stalwart Alpine Corps officer in 1915–1918), although smaller than myself, joined the organizations of the Regime much earlier than I; there was a between-lines suggestion that joining the Regime's forces indicated a strong potential of virile efficiency—an indication which Sergio and Gianluigi, for that matter, fully confirmed by becoming, in due time, inveterate ladies' men. Not always, however, was there a strict concomitance between early membership in the Regime and a taste for women, or conversely, between opposition to the Regime and austere intellectualism. My father never said anything. The fact, however, is that when Oliviero Lezze-Adorno, who incidentally had had a very strict Catholic upbringing, walked to the altar at twenty-two, he was suspected of still being a virgin and later became an impeccably faithful husband; whereas a completely unobtrusive man like my father, though married to a woman of considerable beauty, had mistresses, nearly always foreign, one or two of whom discreetly emerged from darkest secrecy when he prematurely became a widower.

Father, Father. Fernando Rossi, attorney-at-law. Who knows what kind of thoughts this Fernando Rossi may have had, ten years or so before the Cockroach Gondola, shaving in the bathroom, while I, in the matrimonial bedroom, was being born. The midwife had been with my mother for several hours, but they all had the impression that it was still a little bit early. Nothing could be more true to my father's style than to jump on this chance to put up a studied display of strictly routine behavior. So to conclude, he was shaving in the bathroom when I was born. His principle was never to get excited, never deviate. "Consistency, that's all." It's a principle which has always made him take unpopular stands. Just at the time of my birth there had been, in the very distant and improbable Bosnia-Herzegovina, the assassination of the archduke and his wife; the world crack-up was beginning; Italy, however, was out of it during three quarters of the first year of conflict. But even when during that three quarters of a year the voices of people who were hot on "interventionism" grew ever more deafening, my father remained a neutralist. Without ever being polemical or anything. (Only much later, years after the end of the war, when he got into the habit of drinking much wine after dinner with my Uncle Bartolomeo, the two of them would spend the evening in long debates about the war, on which in fact we based several sketches like the one, technically very complex for us, representing the military ceremony of the Decimation.) I imagine that Fernando Rossi's very manner of speech—sober, soft, even though at bottom unshakable—made him a hundred times more irritating than if he had indulged in convulsive gesticulations or fistfights with his opponents. I have heard that some people mysteriosophically accused him of being pro-German, i.e., pro-barbarian and anti-Italian, because at some point in his young age he had studied in Austria, a country to whose women he later remained very much attached. Through my research on the period before the First World War I have known of some others, also Venetians, who seem to have had ideas similar to my father's during those historical moments of half a century ago—people like Luigi Fossà, like Marco Partibon; but those two were huge full-blooded men, the first one with a large socialist beard, whereas Father probably created antipathy also because he was blond, small and dry, with a slightly nasal voice and that kind of finicky attitude which I have so successfully absorbed.

He and I actually understood each other from the first moment. The scene with him in the bathroom, the morning I came into the world, reached us through family tales and became part of our repertory, with its regular key line: "Tell him I'll be there in a minute." The puppet's cardboard hands reproduced the motion of lathering and shaving. As a puppet, Fernando Rossi wore a lawyer's gown even in the bathroom. At some point, while he was shaving and humming a tune, a messenger, looking like something between a male nurse and a yokel, came in announcing with a rustic accent, "Boy already born." While he completed his shaving, Fernando gathered information:

[24]

"And how is he?" With his goitrous voice the messenger immediately remarked about the extraordinary blackness of the newborn. Actually at birth I struck everybody with the fact that I looked very dark; later I slid rather quickly toward the present middle tones of both my hair and my skin. "Darrrk, darrrk . . ." the yokel kept saying. Fernando, wearing his gown, moved a little toward the proscenium to utter the phrase distinctly: "Tell him I'll be there in a minute." Tell whom? Me. There is no other possibility. At any rate, now I feel as though I had heard that phrase with my own ears, and that, borrowing the poet's words, it was the best way for him "to start consoling *me* for being born." Besides, his composure was also a tribute of confidence in the splendid strength and independence of my mother.

The Portogruaro years remain rather outside of history. Little history was being made even in Venice. Rome was at the other end of the world. A couple of years after the Cockroach Gondola had made its appearance on the Grand Canal we moved to Venice. It was my mother's city. She was a native Venetian, a descendant of tugboat captains of the Venice port. A little over three more years went by; and in her very city my mother, who was still so young and witty, suddenly died; one has never been able really to get full awareness of such a totally cruel and rapid event. When she died she was twelve years younger than I am now. From then on, Father started wearing either all white or all black. Though unfaithful as a husband, he was perfectly sincere in the feeling that his life was now definitely broken. From then on, he adopted a special smile, which I understood very well. Particularly in the few months after her death, he would urge me to try and live in the Italy of my time (with key lines like "Go on, Gilberto, my boy, participate, sign up"), but as far as he was concerned he seemed curiously relieved at the idea that the recent blow and his present emptiness liberated him from the problem of whether he should come to an arrangement with the new climate of the country; all he wanted was to make enough money to see me complete my studies and get settled, and then he would abandon not only Italy but the world in general. In doing precisely that, this unobtrusive but basically inflexible man later showed an extraordinary sense of timing.

58942

LIBRARY
College of St. Francis
JOLIET. ILL.

He did not see me being born, I did not see him die. The last time I saw him alive, his friend Giulio Levi was sitting in the room with him. This was during the time of foreshadowings preluding the Second World War. Dr. Levi was leaning forward, his elbows on his knees, looking at the face of my father in bed. By now everything could be inferred, all diagnoses had been made, there was absolutely nothing more to be said. Also as far as he, Giulio Levi, was concerned. Although for his detached manner in alluding to the degradations recently inflicted upon him by the Regime, he must have felt he was at that moment one of the most nobly dignified figures in the world, he must also have guessed that that dignity was something gratuitous, wasted, without purpose or echo. My father, his voice soft but firm as ever, at some point expressed the desire to be left alone, so I accompanied the doctor downstairs.

We lived in Campo San Vidal, near the Academy Bridge. I went with Dr. Levi to the top of the bridge. He still wore tails, a cutaway; in such a costume, we had put him onstage several times as a puppet. He was looking at me with not much affection, and our parting had the tacit air of an ending; I saw him go down the steps on the other side of the bridge, disappear into the Alberetti as into the wings on a stage; he made his exit, leaving me alone; nor did I feel I had any right to share his sorrows. I lingered awhile on top of the Academy Bridge, as I sometimes did, gazing absently at the flowing water. Then suddenly I went back home as though following a distinct call, and as soon as I entered the room I realized what had happened. With my two thumbs I shut lawyer Rossi's now motionless eyes.

He appeared to be the most fortunate of us all, lying there with his perpetual smile, which looked particularly firm and secure now that he had left the puppet show for good. I could have been saddened by the thought that he had not been sorry to leave me, but even in that extreme situation, as from the very first moment of my life, we understood each other perfectly: he had thus left History, the Country, the National Blood as well; he had left the Regime which, however unreal and fictitious, nevertheless managed gloatingly to breed a concrete reality of misfortune, ignominy, butchery: the bovine, macabre, calamitous Regime. Heavy adjectives. Others have come to some sort

of compromise with their memories, but on that score I am becoming less and less flexible as the years go by. Even a secondary
citizen like my father, think how many things he missed, having
to live like that. And as for his life, his courage, no one has any
memory of that.

Alphonse Rossi, not exactly the first time we talked up here
at the Institute, but undoubtedly during our first important
conversation, scratched his forehead and said that of course he
remembered having known Fernando Rossi. "A man of the old
school, a good Socialist; certainly I remember him." The most
he could have remembered was what he had heard from me
during my autobiographical talks at his hotel in Italy. Instead
he thought he had actually met him, and from this I realized
how Alphonse was warming up to me: with entreaty rather
than complicity in his eyes he was inviting me to pretend that I
believed him.

Perhaps in order not to endanger that moment of pleasant
connivance, he abandoned the theme, went over to problems of
work. Our Alphonse, for that matter, is always a great manipu-
lator of themes. Meetings with him are like symphonies; themes
emerge at the right moment, they float over the wavy poly-
phonic waters as long as necessary, then they go down again to
re-emerge later with another side exposed, like rigatoni in boil-
ing water, till at the end one has dealt with all themes without
realizing it and has established a Human Relation with Alphonse.

One of the themes that time was the use that the Institute
made of machines—from tape recorders to electronic computers. He had already touched on those subjects when we first met
in Italy; now I suspected that he might be coming back to that
in order to prevent my objections—that he might suppose I was
one of those fanatically Old World types who say things like
"Our old humanistic tradition" or "True research is done with
a piece of paper and a pencil." I decided to free him from any
embarrassment by treating the subject with familiarity. "In
Italy," I said, "computers are referred to as 'electronic elaborators' and I find the expression more precise."

From the way he looked at me I realized my suspicions had
been baseless; in fact, the contrary seemed to be true; namely,

that he might be afraid I could mistake *him* for a fanatic conservative. He knew, among other things, that to come here to see him one has to go through the anteroom-office, with pastel wall-to-wall carpeting, walls painted in different tones of pastel, metal desk and filing cabinets, pastel as well; what I mean is that after you passed through this room you were even more impressed by the décor of Alphonse's office, ostentatiously pre-electronic: Early American desk, brass lamp with green glass cupola, even wood panelings and leather. I myself was seated in an old leather armchair, dark red.

He made me get up, and keeping me under surveillance with his dark shrewd eyes, he said, "Come, let's go have a look at the electrolibrary."

His private office was really what is known as an oasis; immediately as we went out through the door we were walking noiselessly over the carpeting along bluish corridors bathed in fluorescent light. He was walking ahead, piloting me; navigating in that conditioned air, we would coast along light-gray metal doors with the names of the office occupants in small plastic frames. Then we sailed along a wide plate-glass window and behind that we saw, as in an aquarium, beautiful young women who looked like ordinary typists, except that the machines they were operating, streamlined and of delicate colors, were sublimations of typewriters: they produced rectangular holes on cards, in other words they were translating texts into the electronic language that would feed the "elaborators." In that aseptic manner they were copying writings and speeches by historical figures, among the most pernicious and contaminating in our century.

When we stopped at a metal door much larger than the others, Alphonse said, "Here we are," and we came into the electrolibrary. Both corridor and electrolibrary are air-conditioned and light-conditioned to exactly the same degree: every cubic inch of air is of identical quality, including acoustic effects. Speaking in such ambience you feel as though you had a microphone in your throat. A perfect microphone. Voices kept at the right temperature.

There appeared in front of me, as far as the eye could see, a long perspective of walls with built-in metal cases, of different sizes according to the type of material preserved in them: miles of microfilm; magnetic tape, miles of that too; and thousands of texts transcribed into minute rectangular frames on interminable and well-ordered files of perforated cards. The electrolibrary is kept in beautiful order. Alphonse pointed to places where the writings and speeches of recent historical figures were arranged, transferred to the various electronic languages.

"There, for instance, we have all of So-and-so, there we have So-and-so." He was citing the names of particularly notorious historical Europeans of the last fifty years. "In that file over there, if I'm not mistaken, there is a lot of stuff by So-and-so."

"Until now," I said, exaggerating a little, "the only perforated texts of that kind which I have seen are electricity and gas bills." The last So-and-so he had mentioned was the Italian. "Luckily those perforations don't work the same way as on player-piano rolls, otherwise we'd have to listen to him all over again," I said, on the whole rather stupidly, since that personage is abundantly present among our audio-visual material as well.

Alphonse, as a matter of fact, looked rather surprised and said to me, "We have a lot of stuff on film and tape, you know. For example, last year a German scholar here at the Institute did some work with our own Harold Epstein on the auditory aspects—I would feel rather funny calling them musical aspects—of political oratory in his country from 1933 to 1945. He did not reach very illuminating conclusions, to tell you the truth. Our own Epstein is very clever, but he also finds it difficult to establish criteria that have a minimum of objectivity and universality."

With my mind's ear I could still hear the roarings of the dictators who obsessed our youth; here they were now, being treated like anatomical pieces at a deluxe morgue.

"Speaking of microfilmed material"—Alphonse indicated a distant wall with one of his imposing gestures, somewhere between a baseball player and a Roman emperor, his statuary arm horizontally extended—"there you'll find things that will interest you. We have, for example, complete yearly collections of Italian newspapers from 1914 on, for our research program on the First World War."

I could already see myself, seated in a cubicle, like a film cutter watching on a small screen all of that stuff which is part of my country's history. I was here on the Pacific Coast for this incredible and precise reason. *The ancient walls, the arches, the simulacra and the solitary towers of our ancestors,* as the poet puts it, all here among these canyons. What delight. What horror. What tension. I looked at those metal boxes: more than six thousand miles from the scene of the crime, they contained just about everything, including Oliviero Lezze-Adorno's dark nonsense, including my Uncle Bartolomeo, stalwart Alpine soldier climbing his country's First World War emblem, bloody Mount Grappa.

Alphonse went on talking, beautifully tall and senatorial above me. I should add that I always feel affection and loyalty toward Alphonse, even when he pontificates about the obvious: "So, you see, my dear Rossi, I am not in the least opposed to mechanical help, not at all, not at all."

He was lost in his thoughts for a while, then he began to flitter around: "In much more general terms, I'm convinced that only with the aid of machines can one effectively do good works. But let me add a basic rule: Don't ever be boastful about it. Helping the underdeveloped is all right, but never assume a superior attitude, like that of moralizing missionaries. A strictly technical operation, in other words. At any rate, quite obviously the performer of good works is unthinkable without the machine." He shrugged. "And then if you are recognized in your own country as that kind of operator by a sufficient number of people, or to be exact, by fifty percent plus one of the electorate (by now I have a two-party-system mentality), you may even become, let's say, President. But such a cataract of power wouldn't suit me, I wouldn't know how to use it."

His large bright eyes were reading my thoughts. "Of course," he said, answering them, "even maintaining a position like my own here implies, in its small way, exercising power. And I'll tell you something else: in doing so, I show what may seem considerable ability and shrewdness. But actually it's only common sense."

End of flight; he settled again on the theme of the machines: "Budd Rotondi, the electronics technician at Business Statistics who does a little work for us, too, looks in adoration at the machines, he caresses them, he pampers them—'Here is my 840 X, there is my 920 W'—I'm inventing the numbers, I don't even remember the real ones. He's at opposite poles from those who are horrified by the machines, yet it looks to me as though he and those others are all in the same boat. The machines, I say, are useful and they are machines—beautiful, vital, sometimes surprising. Of course they don't *think*. It was I who convinced the Newton Ash people to make arrangements so we could use one of those computers every now and then—pardon me, 'elaborators'—for some of our work. Not much so far but done the way I want, with what I like to call 'sublime' diligence."

He took me by the arm and bent his large handsome head toward me—silver mane, tanned face, full lips moving with gusto —to whisper, "What have we always been doing here at the Institute?" Having deposited that question in my ear, he straightened up, still holding my arm, his intense look still on me. Almost immediately he proceeded to answer himself: "As object of our study we have taken men"—here he let go of my arm and started to punctuate every other word in his speech with a bladelike movement of his right hand, as though he were slicing each phrase to make it sharper, or even slicing the men he was referring to, to make them easier to digest—"men/who have had/decisive influence/in the history/of their countries/and of their times. And what have we been studying about these men?" Now he stared into empty space and softened his muscular voice, remarking almost casually, "We have studied them through their language." He added, "That, as far as we are concerned, is their way of existing." He was quoting. Quoting himself, to be sure. "A man's vocabulary is his view of the world." He shrugged his powerful shoulders. "Et cetera, et cetera." He took me again by the arm. "Ergo . . ."

I murmured, "Concordances?"

He nodded, lowering his eyelids; he was now a scientific luminary savoring a disciple's answer. "Say that one of our preliminary operations," he went on, "is the search for key words and phrases and of their contexts in the speech of a given individual or of a given period and environment—well, let's keep in mind that the processing of texts and compilation of lexicons, concordances, et cetera, which would take months or years for a human amanuensis, is a matter of seconds for the electronic scribe."

I skip over other instances of how obvious Alphonse's remarks can be. But I want to recall that during that long conversation we had that day I was informed of an event remote in time but essential in the life of my director—namely, that he had lost his older brother Carlo in the First World War. On the Isonzo River in 1917. Which meant that among those billions of words on microfilm or punch cards, there were also those of the "period and environment" in which his brother, twenty-two years old, had been killed. "That was almost a half-century ago," Alphonse himself said quickly, "and I don't know about you, but I certainly wouldn't be able to tell what the word 'country'—fatherland, *patria*—meant to Carlo Rossi."

On that occasion I also made note of some of Alphonse's key phrases. "The word: the elements which form a word. The essence of meaning. Difficult, arduous, like studying the composition of living matter; more arduous, perhaps." There he got lost for a while, speaking to himself in a low voice. "History, after all . . . our own business . . . there wouldn't be so much alienation in our lives . . ."

But Alphonse always picks up the loose threads of his syntax. "At any rate, it was I who acquired these working tools for the Institute. And many others, mechanical or not. To mention what I might call a picturesque example, did you ever see our collection of posters and propaganda material from the First World War? *I* put it together. The most complete in the world. It involved a fantastic amount of work, not to mention money. The trustees of the Institute and the Newton Ash executives go along with me in everything. Never turned down an appropriation I have suggested. I pilot them with my common sense; the only thing I would never be able to convince them of is that they no longer need me." He repeated, "With my common sense. Which is one and the same as sensuality, the simple sensuality of my native city of Bologna. This thing is hard to grasp unless you do so intuitively; some people, I among them, seem to possess what you may call the carnal presence, the warmth, I mean the actual physical warmth of the persuader." Here we became silent for a long while. "They won't get rid of me, not so much because I have tenure but because they are fond of me."

"What is 'tenure'?"

"Permanent employment for life." That was another thing I

[*32*]

learned that day. Dreamily he added, "Only death can take me away from here."

"Death?" I repeated mechanically, but with a certain curiosity.

"I had cancer of the bladder. There, you see, Gilberto"—here he started calling me by my first name—"you see that I'm using the past tense? As if I referred to an event concluded in the past? You see?"

I am sure I cannot effectively describe that moment, but I know it was overwhelming. I felt that subconsciously he must have given me a position at the Institute so that we would come to this moment. That I might share his optimism. I could have hugged him, I could have offered to bear his cancer for him, because I got a sense of delight from understanding him so clearly. I stammered, but in a very high-pitched voice, "In my own way I had deep affection for Fernando Rossi, but I can't help feeling somehow that perhaps I should have had a father like you, Dr. Rossi." Now I no longer recall whether it was during that first interview that I said this.

"Don't talk nonsense," he said. "And call me Alphonse."

Dozens of meetings of the kind, in the course of months; meanwhile I have settled down in my research work and also in my teaching. Within the so-called interdepartmental programs of the university I have been put in charge of a course in cultural history, or *Kulturgeschichte,* on modern Italy. Preparing my lectures cost me great physical & moral effort but I have had great satisfaction from them. Also because, once I got the assignment and a classroom was provided, no one ever bothered about me any more, I am under no control, and every time it is like taking the students along with me on an excursion wherever I please.

Alphonse has several times consulted me on hiring new people for the Institute. Then, out of a drawer in his Early American desk he pulls one of those folders they here call Manila, with the papers of the applicant on which he asks my opinion. Generally they are Europeans who want to come to the Institute for a period of time financed by their governments or by the Newton Ash or other foundations.

Naturally, therefore, one evening while the sunset light was falling with beautiful violence on the dried-up moors out here, on the glass and steel of the buildings, and on the Pacific down below, partly blazing and partly in the shadow with large bands of fog, Alphonse showed me the Manila folder with the documents and correspondence concerning Ruggero Tava, Jr.

About that evening I would remember everything with a certain vividness and tension, also for other reasons. It was a somewhat particular evening. I had just bought my car. It is a three-year-old Dodge, the first automobile in my life. We had stayed on at the Institute later than usual, practically alone, Alphonse and I; it was decided that I would drive him home in my Dodge and I was invited for dinner at his house. "The Pickfords will be there too," he had said.

Louis and Nadine Pickford. They had invited me to dinner several times, and I had found myself the only guest, so we ate in the kitchen—superb food prepared by him. The impression, even for a man like myself with little social experience, was that the Pickfords were planning to adopt me, which would mean offer me a good position among their vassals. People like them usually hand-pick their vassals and then work on them one by one. Listening to the Pickfords with half an ear, alone like that, the three of us in their kitchen, I realized that they had a whole series of observations and jokes about Alphonse stored up in the busy workshops of their malevolent and extremely well informed minds.

There I go, using an adjective like "malevolent," which would never occur to me in their presence. I sit with them in that beautiful kitchen full of conveniences: the garish icebox, the smooth and immaculate woodwork, the refulgent steel, the window curtains Nadine had made herself and kept like little girls' Sunday dresses; or else we sit in the spacious, low-ceilinged, asymmetrical living room, in the blond light of table lamps and of the rich flames in the fireplace, and I allow myself to be overwhelmed by relaxation, I forget everything. Louis Pickford pours a drink for me, and his lean red face, with the pepper-and-salt diadem of his short hair, the face of a slightly wine-flustered Indian, finally seems to me not only friendly but even childishly innocent. Suspicions and worries about the Pickfords begin the moment you no longer have them around you.

That evening I also wanted to observe how they behaved in

the presence of Alphonse, whether they would administer poison to him. For several reasons, then, I was experiencing curiosity and nervousness as I was getting ready to drive my Dodge with Alphonse aboard for the first time, and then to spend the evening at the Rossis' in the presence of these potential poisoners, when before we left his office Alphonse got that Manila folder out of the drawer, glanced at the papers it contained and passed it on to me across the desk: "See what impression you get of this Ruggero Tava."

He must have seen at once that something was happening to my face: violent pallor or violent flush, I imagine, distressed eyes. Perhaps he asked me, "What's happening to you?" My ears were buzzing and I was speechless, paralyzed in silence and astonishment.

"Who is he? Somebody you know? Is this Ruggero Tava somebody you've already heard about?" Et cetera. Naturally, he was asking questions like that. Meanwhile I was beginning to leaf through the papers, more or less hypnotized.

The first thing I said was also the most natural: "I knew his father."

"Really? What does his father do, who is he? Tell me."

"I knew his father," I repeated. "In fact, this name here, Ruggero Tava, is not his legal name." With my chin I indicated the paper. "It's his father's."

Alphonse was looking at me with interest and a great desire to help. Seeing that I did not move, he filled the silence by himself, as when a radio station improvises a neutral music program while an important bulletin is expected imminently: "There are some very good young men coming up now; that one, for instance, looks rather phenomenal. We had a Frenchman or two just like him—solid background, sharp minds, magnificent linguists." Then he attempted delicately: "What do you mean, that's his father's name and not his own? Can't they both have the same name? The father is Senior and this one is Junior, why not?" I didn't answer and he resumed his musical interval, raising his forefinger: "The kind of young men who do very well when they come to us. Background, both in history and linguistics . . ."

All of a sudden I began to realize who—what we were discussing. That is, I saw clearly my friend Ruggero Tava again, dead now over twenty years. I even had to do some mental arithmetic. At some point I burst out laughing. How confusing. I repeated Alphonse's words "this one is Junior." But I completed: "Senior, however—his father—was not too bright. He never graduated from the university. We were in school together. I helped him many times with his homework. During the finals I wrote a large part of his Italian essay." Alphonse was listening with all the receptiveness of his benevolence and curiosity.

My heart was galloping. This occasionally happens when certain memories suddenly emerge here and capture me.

I went on, "At seventeen I went to the University of Milan and he left too, he volunteered for early military service. Then he served as a second lieutenant in the reserve, at Bergamo; he came to see me in Milan every now and then, or I would visit him. Then he got married and almost immediately after that he died. Tava was literally one of the first five or six Italian officers to fall in the Second World War." And I felt the muscles of my lips, with an independent jerk of their own, tensing in laughter.

A cloud passed briefly over Alphonse's face but he continued to watch me with deep attention. He pointed cautiously to the papers: "And do you know the son well?"

Again I laughed. But Alphonse knew that in important and tense moments I am likely to start laughing like that. "As for the son," I said, "I never saw him in my life." Long silence. After a new brief spurt of my laughter, I added, "His father never saw him either."

Alphonse murmured, "There he is, look at him."

Among the papers there was indeed a picture of Junior. Did he look like his father? It was hard to tell. If I met Tava now, my own Tava, as he was then, I wouldn't recognize him. The dead have their own way of existing, of growing. For that matter, even if he had survived in the normal sense of the word, I would have difficulty recognizing him. At this point my mind started operating on its own, inventing a scene.

In this scene Tava, absurdly and criminally sent to his death, had nevertheless not been killed under fire from a French blockhouse in the western Alps in June 1940. They shot at him continuously, but crawling, he managed to reach the blockhouse alive. Tava had relatives in France, so that he was now in a familiar milieu. He survived. Years went by. And after the war, having opted for France, he was there, a well-settled Parisian.

I meet him on the rue de Rivoli, under an arcade vaguely resembling the St. Mark Procuratie. He wears a camel's-hair overcoat, a beautiful scarf, he has become rather bulky.

He recognizes me first and then I ask him, "I beg your pardon, weren't you dead?"

He smiles, pointing to himself, his overcoat, his bulk, and then a bit apologetically he utters his line, his key phrase, "Well, this is the way things turned out."

Enough of that. I shook myself awake. I had to come back to the Pacific, facing Alphonse Rossi. I said to Alphonse, "I remember when I heard the news that Tava had died. At that particular point, in late 1940, I was in Germany as *Universitäts-lektor.*"

Gabriele Crocetta had come to Germany on a cultural mission from the Goof, and casually, in the course of our conversation, he told me that Tava had died. We were standing in Town Hall Square at Göttingen, looking at the statue of little Lisa with the goose, the "Gänseliesel," with a bit of snow on her small head. "As a matter of fact, died several months ago," Crocetta added. In other words, that piece of news had little freshness or interest for him, and as always happens in such cases, the story now came adorned with successive encrustations, which had become *de rigueur* among the well-informed: essential among these ornaments was the smile with which Crocetta alluded to the unusual state of affairs which Tava had left behind —two pregnant girls, one of them his wife. Even this had lost freshness for them, but Crocetta brightened up a little because he had found me still intact, virgin ground; I asked him, countering his smiles with one of my bursts of laughter which are certainly no smiles, "Did he know that they were pregnant?"

"He knew about his wife, he hadn't found out about the other one."

There I was again, letting my mind run loose along my own thoughts; staring stupidly at Alphonse, I spoke Crocetta's phrase out loud: "He knew about his wife, he hadn't found out about the other one."

"What are you trying to tell me, Gilberto?"

[*37*]

By now it was getting dark outside; here we have quick sunsets, almost tropical.

I said to him, "He not only didn't ever get to see this son of his, he never even got to know of his potential existence." I spoke calmly, slowly. I wanted Alphonse to understand me well. I needed somebody to understand me well. Or at least begin to understand. "Leaving for the Alps and his death, he knew about his pregnant wife but not about the girl he had loved from the time they were children."

"I see," Alphonse said. He got up. His attitude was not indifference, he only wanted to let time pass until things would open up for me and it would be natural for me to talk about them. "Let's go now." He raised his finger. "At any rate, that looks like an excellent young man."

In the car I forgot about everything except driving. I watched Alphonse sideways every now and then to see if he had any remarks to make. I dance and drive very badly but I like both things enormously. Alphonse just lies stretched out in his seat, perfectly seraphic, as if he were in a gondola. At one point he said, "Wait a minute, Doris asked me to get some whiskey."

We stopped at a liquor store, a kind of huge hut that looks like a customs house at some mountain border, and got two bottles of whiskey. Perfumes from the surrounding vegetation fused in the evening air with the odor of meat broiled on charcoal or wood from nearby shrubs.

When we came to the Rossis' house, the Pickfords were already there. Nadine was helping Doris to cook and to set the table. Louis Pickford had assigned himself to the bar. He would prepare even the simplest and most usual drinks as if they, manipulated by him, were something exceptional; he would hand you the glass, his black eyes sparkling through half-closed eyelids as if through embrasures, meaning: "Up to this moment in your life you have never known what a real whiskey and soda is." As a cook, however, he is really excellent. In fact, the reason why he had assigned himself to the bar was that he doesn't want to have anything to do with the preparation of food except in his own kitchen. And by the way, between the Pickfords and the Rossis there was an atmosphere of great mutual affection. Warmth. Casualness. Years of training.

Other people came later on, and this is another reason why I shall always vividly remember that evening—I met Beatrice Clinton for the first time. The name, as it happens, never stirred up the obvious evocations in me; for that matter, the way the name is pronounced here would in my native language be written down something like *Bitris;* and what we designate by the name Clinton—that is, a simple and slightly crazy wine with a vague flavor of cherries—in its true home, the Venetian countryside, is pronounced "cleento" or even "creento."

I am trying to recall exactly what Beatrice looked like to me that first time and I realize that from the very start her image was the definitive one. Very blond hair pulled back from a serious, pensive forehead—the forehead of a child, but of a child looking already like an adult; watchful and shrewd eyes and smile. I noticed at once that her forehead and hair formed one round blond whole; behind it one irresistibly imagined erotic thoughts, much more so than if she had been the Mediterranean black-and-olive type. Daughter of Walter F. Clinton, famous professor of English literature, now retired and around eighty-five; she is twenty-six, so she was born of a father already around sixty. There she was, observing everything, moving very little. She sat next to me at the table. She had been to Europe several times. She had evidently had a first-rate education, yet she placed her elbow on the table and her cheek on her closed fist, somewhat in the posture of a man at a tavern, and every chance she had, she picked up food with her fingers. She encouraged me to talk; I had the impression I was being given a kind of examination. The conclusion was that toward the end of the evening she announced that one of the next few days she would take me to some of her friends.

I am trying to say that an evening of that sort, even if nothing extraordinary happens—in fact, for that very reason—has the power of dissolving previous thoughts, which meant in my case the thought of Ruggero Tava. Or at any rate, such thoughts are set aside, postponed. You find yourself in the midst of a variety of people with thoughts too different from the ones that occupied you. And these people accept you, you feel identified, you take part. New scene, new puppets.

The only exception was Alphonse, who still remembered our conversation at the Institute. I could see it deep in his eyes when he looked at me. At some point he and I were alone, and to tempt me he said something like "That will be interesting for you, seeing the son of one of your school friends."

I replied that the new Ruggero obviously could know nothing about me, almost without doubt did not even know that I existed. "If he comes here, I suppose I shall not even mention his father." I repeated to myself the line I had attributed to my own Ruggero, the Ruggero who had not died young in the war, who had in fact become a sedate middle-aged man: "Well, this is the way things turned out." Perhaps I alone in the whole world know how much that phrase is in his style. Truer than life; something heartbreaking.

"Some memories had better be cut out once and for all," I said. I would have liked to add that memories here can be something unbearable, a violent flash, a blowup.

CHAPTER
TWO

From his room at the hotel a young man, not tall but well proportioned, his shoulders round, his manners courteous, with chestnut hair and a very healthy complexion, was calling the Milan office of *Roma Sabato,* asking for the editor in chief, Perineschi, who should be in Milan on an organization-and-inspection visit from Rome. He had to go through only one secretarial voice and then the head of the Milan bureau, Tranquillo Massenti, was immediately on the other end. "Look here," he said, "I don't remember exactly whether the super editor has just arrived or whether he has just left; at any rate, *he isn't here."*

"The super editor?"

"Perineschi. Don't you know anything?"

"About what? No, I don't know anything." The young man's voice was pleasant, alert.

"I should have had a tape made, a kind of electronic circular letter." Massenti's voice recited flatly: "At any rate—from being head of the Milan office, I'm going to become editor of *Milano Sabato,* the new weekly which will be partly the same as *Roma*

Sabato and partly adapted for local consumption or, as the super editor says, using the English word, *adjusted*—"

The young man interrupted softly, "But I know all that."

"Then why did you ask?" Now Massenti's voice sounded amused. "Who are you? Yes, of course—Ruggero Tava; the secretary told me. Excuse me, Tava. Tell me . . . tell me something about yourself." There was a long silence. "You *are* Tava, aren't you?" the voice asked, again amused.

"Yes. Or at any rate, that's the way I sign my articles."

"I've got the picture. Talk to me. In fact, you are coming to the office, aren't you?"

Ruggero made a brief pause. Then he said, "I'll be there in twenty-five minutes."

"Good Lord."

Ruggero selected a necktie. Even without using a mirror he obtained a perfect knot, with the two ends of the tie absolutely even. In addition, the colors of the tie were so satisfactory that they vividly reminded him of something his mother, Elena Partibon, had said years earlier, "A well-chosen color can be exhilarating." He put on a coat and ran out of the room. Since his last visit to Milan two weeks earlier, the hotel had completed the installation of a new elevator; the inside was equipped with plastic panelings and indirect lighting; you barely touched a button and your command would be transmitted softly to the door, which closed with a slow pneumatic swish.

Passing through the lobby, Ruggero left his key with the concierge, who interrupted his conversation with a lady to smile at him. A waiter from the bar appeared at the door, smiling too, not obsequiously but friendly.

Outside, Ruggero found a Milan day of light haze resplendent with sunshine; he breathed that air deeply, drawing energy from it, and a desire for action; deep in it he also discovered an agreeable aroma of toasted bread. He walked through streets that looked both sober and opulent, their sumptuousness well hidden under a gray patina. Through tall portals he glimpsed courtyards with inner gardens, well-swept pavements, concierge booths with old, shiny glass doors, sparkling brass doorknobs.

He turned into a street of shops as diligently kept as those booths, finally entered a café which was all mirrors, and in a corner he immediately saw Irene; she got up as if she were receiving him in a parlor. She was small, solid, with intense hazel eyes.

He stooped to kiss her on the temple, holding both her hands; Irene's grasp was as strong and secure as his own. They sat looking at each other in silence.

Then Ruggero asked, "And how is Kuntz?"

"Not well. But he pretends it's nothing. He talks. He plays. He is very much alive."

Ruggero listened intently. He smiled and whispered, "Kuntz has seen worse crises."

"He likes the way I play," she said softly. "I have never seen him so happy as he was this time. He was really happy. Kuntz is rarely happy, but this time he was really very, very happy. He accompanied me himself on the piano. I had called him to let him know I was coming and he insisted that I bring the cello, then he sat at the piano in his dressing gown."

"Really?" Ruggero seemed dazzled with delight. "And how is he?" he asked again, as though facts could now have changed. Irene shrugged.

Ruggero looked at his watch. "I can only stay ten minutes," he said. "We'll meet at your house later."

"My father and brother left together this morning; they are always together now, especially since father—"

"I understand. So I'll come up." They repeated things they already knew; they were still holding hands.

"Father has left his dog with me; now that poor animal is at home with Natasha but later on I'll take him out."

"Good."

"I very much want to be with you today." Irene was having tea with milk and melted cheese on toast.

Ruggero had ordered *caffelatte* and was sipping it slowly. He swallowed and said, "I'm going to see Massenti at *Roma Sabato*."

Irene's eyes were following his every gesture, she was examining his hands, his lips. "If you make an arrangement with *Roma Sabato*—which, after all, means both *Roma Sabato* and *Milano Sabato*—get them to pay you a lot. Apparently they received a bundle of money recently." When Ruggero looked at his watch and started to get up, she said, "You go; let me pay."

. . .

[*43*]

As had been the case every time lately, once he entered the offices of *Roma Sabato,* Ruggero felt as if he had chanced upon a moment of exceptional upheaval and crisis. Before getting to the receptionist, he passed several empty offices where a few workingmen were slowly painting the walls white. From the windows he saw bulldozers at work, and from a distant room a voice was repeating with a certain amount of despair: "Hello, Rome, hello, Rome."

In the receptionist's office he found a number of people coming and going, and in their midst, like a buoy in an agitated sea, was that usual fixture, a time waster, looking as if he knew all the answers but deprived of any useful function. There was always someone like that in the reception room: not a doorman, not an editorial employee, not even a waiting visitor; rather, a member of the household, but like an impoverished unemployed uncle. This time he was a dry man in his fifties, with a few gray hairs planted one by one on his shiny head browned by the sun, mobile like blades of grass in a breeze.

After Ruggero had given his name to the receptionist—under the Perineschi regime the English word *receptionist* was used— informing her that he had an appointment with Tranquillo Massenti, the unemployed uncle started looking at him with frenzied curiosity until Ruggero, to simplify matters, nodded at him and said invitingly, "Good morning."

The man pointed with his thumb over his shoulder toward a closed door behind him. "You too," he whispered, "are jumping on the bandwagon with the other climbers?" He fixed his blue, hallucinated eyes on Ruggero's face as if to see his words penetrate there; then abruptly his own face became relaxed, and without waiting for an answer, as if moving on to a serious, adult subject, he offered Ruggero his hand and said, "I am Francalancia."

"Tava," Ruggero replied, smiling with curiosity.

"Don't tell me—I guessed right!" Francalancia said at once. Still studying the other's face and acting feverishly, he patted Ruggero's arm. "You are young, Tava, you write well, you are a handsome young man, *mens sana,* you really turned out very well." He concluded, "Twenty-five years ago I knew your mother in Venice." He was silent for a long while.

Ruggero was silent in turn, with his serene smile.

"Remember that for a man of my age who knew that world a little bit, you would be noteworthy if only because you are the son of Elena Partibon. At that time, beauty was still in fashion —just by existing, as a gratuitous spectacle. Some students at Padua used to call her simply and, let us admit, rather obviously, the Fair Helena. Later on, sticking to Homer, and perhaps with a trace of mockery, somebody called her Andromache. Oh, I remember. Venetian friends of that period. Giorgio Partibon was Elena's brother. And who else? Eugenio Testa, Gabriele Crocetta, Nuto Pancini . . ."

"Gilberto Rossi?"

"Who is he?"

"I don't have any exact data but I thought he too was a Venetian from that time. I'm going to America to work at an institute where I know this Gilberto Rossi is working too."

"Hm. Well, maybe. Gilberto Rossi. Who knows? He may be in it too. In the *giro*—I mean, the coterie of people who are in circulation. World-wide nowadays. Two or three thousand people. And those two or three thousand people, they all know one another. Perhaps they are even fewer than that. Good-bye, Tava. Look, the door of the powerful is opening for you."

Indeed, the door was being opened wide and Tranquillo Massenti appeared framed within it, large, smiling, inviting Tava.

When they were closeted in his office, Tranquillo Massenti greeted Ruggero, patting him on the side in a theatrical, Brazilian-style embrace. "Hello, Tava. When are you leaving?"

"I'm going to Venice to see my mother this evening or tomorrow morning, then I'll go to Paris—perhaps by car if the Camentini boys give me a lift and if they let me do the driving. In Paris I'll also see my Uncle Giorgio, and then I'll just take a plane to America."

Massenti scrutinized him in silence, as if he sensed a hidden meaning behind the young man's words.

"Who is Francalancia?" Ruggero asked. "A man who is waiting outside?"

"That's it—he's a man who waits outside." Massenti smiled and shook his head. "Francalancia! Well, every now and then he writes a little article for us."

Ruggero registered Massenti's smile and could place it immediately. It was like finding electronically, at exactly the right place in his brain, the Massenti index card with the facts already processed: Tranquillo Massenti, the all-round journalist, the former heavy drinker, now for years the head of the Milan office of *Roma Sabato,* and soon behind that same desk, the editor of *Milano Sabato;* married to a Swedish woman who before their marriage had lived with him for several years; a champion of Milan against Rome; a refugee from the Roman swamp, whereas here in Milan "two plus two makes four," even the climate is corroborating, and so on and so forth; no point in reading the rest of the mental index card. Or to give one other example: Massenti would go with his Swedish wife every Sunday to the soccer game, and would enjoy it with fanatic partisanship. Ruggero placed the Massenti card back in its place.

He resumed in his equanimous tone, "I asked who Francalancià was because he told me that many years ago he knew my mother."

"You don't say."

Ruggero spoke as if dictating a note into a tape recorder: "Particular things he remembered about my mother."

"What did he remember?" Massenti interrupted with a reporter's peremptoriness, but without interest.

"Some nicknames they used to give her."

Massenti did not answer. He went around his desk and sat down, with Ruggero facing him. "I hear that you'll write for us from America," Massenti said. "Perineschi wants something about this institute for sociological semantics, or whatever it is, where you will be working. If you want to write lively articles, you're handicapped by the fact that you will be in America for a whole year, which is too long."

"No, it's one academic semester, plus a little traveling—five and a half months altogether."

"You are so exact. You are one of these exact young men that there are now. Let me look at you. Well, at any rate, try to preserve imagination in your articles, inventiveness, the neomythological. You may speak about American cultural institutions, following Pereneschi's directives, but don't let his anguished desire for facts influence you too much. Of course, American universities—Hello, Paleona," Massenti interjected when he saw

Paleona come in like a silent, watchful cat without having knocked. "American universities are capable of anything."

"You can say that again," Paleona commented. "Paleona," he said, offering Ruggero his hand.

"Tava," Ruggero said.

"I was in America as a boy," Tranquillo Massenti went on. "I use the term 'boy' in a relative sense." He darted a significant look at Ruggero, as if he were giving the interviewer a juicy piece of news. "I—have—had—the—American—mania. I'll be fascinated now to hear your point of view. Many of my contemporaries are bogged down in a love-hate situation with no exit. I have been in America fourteen times. I would take any excuse —inauguration of new airline, world premiere of the mammoth film *Caligula,* Soviet Premier's visit, even visits of Italian Cabinet members."

Encouraged, Ruggero asked, "Have you ever met the President?"

"The president of what?"

"Of the United States."

"No, I've never had the opportunity," Massenti replied. Ruggero's seraphic air confused him a little. Evidently a serious young man, with chestnut hair properly cut and well combed, the round, intent shoulders of a young scholar, yet with those large oval clear eyes, incapable of ambiguities, and those cheeks full of vitamins.

"Why, have *you* met the President of the United States?" Paleona asked with a whiff of laughter from his nostrils, to annihilate the boy.

"No. That's why I was asking." The young man's eyes passed with detached curiosity from one to the other of those two middle-aged journalists, who now were looking at him with suspicion. To break the silence he remarked, "One evening in Venice years ago my mother found herself at a dinner party where she was too—the wife, I mean."

"Whose wife?"

"The President's." Ruggero shrugged his shoulders almost imperceptibly, and changing register, he turned to Massenti and said, "May I ask what the neomythological is?"

"Well, it's a term coined by Federico, who is now the most

important of the young critics." Massenti pressed the palms of his hands against the edge of the desk as if to push it away, and as he rose he continued, weighing heavily upon each word, perhaps to charge it with irony, "Federico—Velluti—our—literary —critic." He started to walk up and down the room. "What I meant to say, my boy," he resumed, "is that when, for instance, I used to send my stuff from America, the Perineschis among us found it a little outmoded because my pieces would start off something like this: 'Flocks of grasshoppers lay dead on the sides of the very wide road, a wind swollen with oil carried them in the direction of Ponca City,' and so forth, but with things like that, I gave you Oklahoma much better than all of your statistics. Perineschi has always thought that he wanted American-style reportage and for over twenty years now he has casually been using English words like factual or *hard-boiled*. But never mind, you let yourself go with confidence into the neomythological. Besides, Perineschi no longer reads what he publishes, and even if he did, it would be easy to make him believe that his own directives had been followed; you see, he never knows exactly whether he says what he is saying."

Ruggero continued to listen to Massenti with polite curiosity. Extraordinary how people of that age and type went on performing their roles to perfection, with quotable coined phrases and all. Paleona weighed Massenti's talk with the wariness of a competitor. Both professionally grown up in Rome. Closely allied, though affecting a certain amount of mutual contempt in speaking of each other.

"Do you get the idea, Tava?" Massenti asked, satisfied.

"Quite. Actually, I wanted some information from you. How much do you think they plan to pay me? A friend of mine, Irene Berlocchi, told me that you just got a bundle of money."

"A bundle of money," Massenti echoed without commenting. "Berlocchi?" he asked, raising an eyebrow. "Wasn't that name mentioned in connection with the scandal—"

Ruggero interrupted, "You're right; her father is implicated." Then immediately: "You see, before I decide whether I want to contribute to your publication, I must have some exact figures. If doing it yourself bothers you, why don't you let me talk directly with Perineschi, or even better, with somebody in the business office?" He made a motion to get up, looking around quickly toward the four cardinal points as if to ask where the business manager was and ready to fly off and then perch himself upon him.

Astonishment and admiration appeared on Massenti's face; he smiled. "Cool off, I can tell you myself: thirty or thirty-five thousand lire for the shorter pieces, sixty thousand for the more substantial ones."

"Sixty thousand . . . that's slightly less than one hundred dollars," Ruggero said, and he let his clear, well-rested eyes linger awhile first on Massenti, then on Paleona. Spiritedly, "You know," he said as if announcing a jolly piece of news, "I don't believe I'm interested in writing for your magazine."

"Do you know that our rates are among the highest anybody pays?" Paleona exploded.

"Oh, I believe that," Ruggero replied affably. He turned to Massenti. "You've got a beautiful office," he said, pointing around the room. "I like it. Has it just been redecorated? Nice color. I like that one." His finger stopped on the table lamp. "Listen, by the way," he went on without a pause, "do you happen to know someone called Gilberto Rossi?"

"No, who's he?" Massenti asked with a somnambulist's glazed stare.

"He works in the same place that I'm going to. He's been there for about a year, but before that he was in Italy, in Rome and also here in Milan."

"No, I don't know him. But wait a minute—yes, Gilberto Rossi. Do you mean that obnoxious character who used to work for Marcello Di Gaetano?"

"Di Gaetano kicked him out, so he ended up in South America," Paleona volunteered.

"No, not South America," Ruggero said. "Who told you that he went to South America?"

He looked alternately at Paleona and Massenti, coming to the conclusion that they were inaccurate and trivial; once more he shrugged imperceptibly. There was a long, heavy silence on the part of the other two. Massenti broke it: "Tell me, Tava, if you don't mind—how much would you like to be paid per article?"

"One hundred thousand. Which is just over one hundred and

sixty dollars at the present rate of exchange. While I am over there, I'll write four articles for you, or let's call it a long essay which you will publish in four installments. If not, I'll publish it whole in the *CSI Review*—the *Centro Studi Informazione*—which is specialized, and somehow or other I'll scrape together the money you'd be giving me. Right?"

The expression of curiosity on Massenti's face was now mixed with revulsion: "You are a well-organized young man." There was also the shadow of a threat. He paused and then repeated more flatly, with a kind of hopelessness: "You are a well-organized young man."

He went back to his desk and sat down, his eyes turning away from Ruggero. "Look, Tava," he resumed, "this is how things stand: the super editor, for reasons of his own, which are unreal, since there is no connection between Perineschi's thought and his actions"—here he exchanged a smile with Paleona as if to check on the brilliance of his own remark—"is very keen on your doing these articles for us from America. You do them the way you want, but be sure they are long, massive, and you'll see that they'll pay you what you're asking, one hundred thousand each." Again he checked with Paleona: "That's the same as they paid for Miss Trentinaglia's pieces on legalized abortion in Japan."

"You see? Bravo, Massenti!" Ruggero exclaimed as if Massenti had just found a brilliant solution to some problem of his own. Observing slight confusion on the man's face, he asked, "Or do you want me to go to Perineschi directly?" as if offering his own help in Massenti's present difficulty.

"No, Tava, there will be no need for that. Don't forget that I'm going to be the Milan editor."

"We're all set. And by the way, congratulations."

While Ruggero got up to take his leave, both Massenti and Paleona stared at him, torn between indecision and astonishment: Was this young man a simpleton or was he a monster of shrewdness? But whereas Paleona continued to act superior and guarded, in the end Massenti gave him a fatherly send-off: Tava was so young and pink-cheeked, a sturdy boy from a mountain village—except that his solid, stooped shoulders indicated a fastidious scholar and he had that permanently self-assured way of looking at you, his mind always obsessively lucid. "Good-bye and bon voyage. Say hello to America for me. Who knows whether I shall ever go back there? At any rate, not soon. I am sending you. Right?"

"There is an eight or nine percent element of truth in what you say, Massenti, since you're going to pay for my articles that way. Then, I still have something coming from my work on a documentary film, and the rest is provided by the Newton Ash Foundation and a little bit by the CSI."

Once more Massenti embraced Ruggero in the Brazilian manner. Paleona looked at him with dulled, suspicious eyes, offering a limp hand which Ruggero shook with vigor. From the threshold the young man turned back to wave at the two men, smiling at them knowingly.

He was hardly out of the room when Paleona asked Massenti in a tone of quiet fury, "Who *is* he? Can you tell me where you manage to pick up bastards like that? And why are you laughing? What's so funny?"

"I am laughing because Tava *is* a bastard. In the real, technical sense of the word."

Ruggero went slowly on his way, observing all shop windows and house doors. He drank through his eyes. At a bookstore he noticed new bindings and dust jackets of his favorite Italian publisher; for a long time he had thought he would give him his first book to publish, a concise and practical little handbook which he would entitle *A Brief History of Information*. Writing articles would also be good training for the book. He could already see the articles, clear, lined up in an orderly manner, like his one hundred and sixty-five imminent American days, or like these house doors, of a color close to that of the blond wood of motorboats in his native city, Venice, or even of the seasoned and precious wood of musical instruments, of Irene's cello.

So his thoughts turned freely, unhurriedly, to Irene, toward whose house he was walking. The visit to Massenti had been practically the last business visit before his departure for America; he had completed everything at the American consulate and at the clinic where he had gone through a general checkup. Everything was also in order with the CSI people and with the producers of documentaries on urban problems who had paid him four hundred and fifty thousand lire for the narration, both Italian and English, on Venice: his work had been pronounced excellent. So now he was looking forward only to casual and unscheduled leave-taking visits: Irene first of all, later Kuntz; and in Venice his mother, his Partibon grandfather, and Fassola, in whose law office he would certainly also meet his Uncle Giuliano, who went to see his friend there every evening; later on, passing through Paris, he would see his Uncle Giorgio. Everything would be relaxing, familiar; even going to Irene's was like going back home. He had homes everywhere. He was always camping in one place or another. Considering that her father and brother were away, he might stay the night with Irene; but more probably he would leave for Venice that evening in the soft, huge automobile of Piero Camentini, who was a kind of honorary uncle.

Projects and thoughts were loosening up, like his limbs; he perceived an actual pleasure in his head as he felt his mind physically stretching out. The sun had pierced through the silvery haze. Traffic was very lively. He was hungry. He smiled because he was sure that at Irene's he would find his old friend Natasha, the woman who went there every day to cook and clean.

And as a matter of fact, when he got to the Berlocchis' apartment, Natasha came to open the door. She said immediately, "How well you look," even before greeting him. At the very bottom of Natasha's voice there was still the guttural harshness of the mainland Venetian, like an atavistic memory of peasant choirs, of loud calls in the fields. "Irene isn't back yet, you know," she warned, walking ahead of him, leading the way into the large living room with its well-kept furniture, recently upholstered armchairs, freshly polished tables, objects which immediately revealed themselves not as family heirlooms but as purchases from art dealers, embalmed and alien precisely because they possessed indisputable certificates of authenticity: it was a house furnished all at once and then rarely inhabited.

"Would you like me to fix you something to eat while you wait?" Natasha asked in her now-domesticated peasant's voice. They were standing face to face in the middle of the living room; Ruggero leaned down, and taking her hands in his,

[52]

pressed his cheek against hers; so they exchanged a caress with their faces.

"How are you?" he asked, straightening up but still looking at her. "Do you still come here to work every day? What else do you do? Did you vote? Do you vote here or in Venice? Or at Dolo?"

"I vote here in Milan. Come, I'll fix you an omelette." She led him toward the kitchen. Halfway, Ruggero stopped at the bathroom. Natasha went on alone to prepare the food.

At her birth thirty-three years earlier in a hamlet near Dolo, in one of the most beautiful and rustic sections around the Lagoon of Venice, where the industrial smoke of Marghera brushes against the first encountered Palladian villas, she had been baptized Natalina. But later, all over Venice—from the Giudecca to the Misericordia, from Cannaregio to Castello, and even in the outlying rural areas from Fusina to the Lido, from San Donà di Piave to Malamocco, there had sprouted the Sonias, the Sergias, the Nadias, the Mirkas, even the Kiras, and then she had regarded herself as the most daring of them all by changing her own Natalina to Natasha; it was like replacing a silly little twinkle with the crack of a whip. A friend who was now working with a shipping company, formerly in the merchant marine, had learnedly told her sometime later that it was just a different way of saying the same name.

The change had occurred when she was fifteen, and from that age to thirty, Natasha—bold and self-sufficient, though always surrounded by men who wanted her—had been employed as a servant by Ruggero's mother, Elena Partibon, during the long periods of time that Elena had spent in Venice. Natasha was therefore part of Ruggero's childhood and adolescence, a dozen years older than he, but not motherly, not a nurse, not even the maid-mistress, yet always with a place of her own so distinct and precise that there was no need for it to be observed, defined; thus, even now that they saw each other only when he came to Milan, with every encounter and look exchanged between them, the presence of memories was immediate and total.

Now Natasha was breaking fresh eggs into a red bowl. When she heard the cascade of water from the bathroom, she put some butter in the pan. Walking into the kitchen, Ruggero found her beating the eggs for the omelette.

"What kind of wine do you want?" she asked. "If you want white wine, get it out of the refrigerator, otherwise there is—"

"White is all right, Natasha, thank you." Ruggero got a long green bottle out of the refrigerator, uncorked it, poured wine into two glasses. He drank at once one half of his own, murmuring, "Very good."

"Is it good? That's the wine that Mr. Berlocchi, the wretched man, got from South Tyrol."

"Very good. Try it too, won't you?"

"I'm not in the habit of drinking between meals."

"Then eat something, won't you?"

"I've eaten already. I made an omelette for myself, too."

"You always did make fabulous omelettes."

Natasha nodded. "And this time," she said, adding a last touch to Ruggero's omelette, "I have the impression I have surpassed myself." The phrase was recognizably Irene's—of the moments when the satisfaction with a job well done, like a good performance on the cello, put a sort of intense and restrained frenzy into her eyes.

Natasha looked at him while he ate in silence. She felt the pleasure of taste along with him. Then she turned her back, turned on the water in the sink and let it run over the red bowl she had used for the eggs.

"Do you really believe," she asked, "that Irene's father may have to go to jail?"

Ruggero finished the last mouthful of his omelette, drank the last drops of wine, dried his lips. "I don't have any specific information," he said as he got up.

"Would you like me to make you some coffee?"

"I wish you would." He went on, "In Venice I'll talk with some lawyer friends, and I'll get their picture of the situation. Arturo Fontana. Or more exactly, in Fontana's office, Enrico Fassola, whom you know well."

"They are good."

"You know how it is, lawyers are all more or less alike."

"Fassola is also very human."

From behind, Ruggero put his arms around her shoulders; again he touched her cheek with his own. "Would you be sorry if Irene's father really went to jail?"

Holding her elbows tight at her sides, Natasha freed her

[*54*]

hands and forearms, gesturing as she spoke. "Well, don't you think it would be painful, and very sad?"

"Really?"

Natasha turned around and looked him in the eyes; she found the usual expression—cherubic yet alert, courteous but hard. She knew Ruggero's ways so well that she could only accept them. There had really never been any need to understand him. Or rather, understanding meant precisely this: looking at each other, without having to explain. She said, as if double-checking on some information, "You don't worry at all about Irene?"

"Why should I worry?"

Natasha nodded; she took Ruggero's plate and let the hot water run over it.

"I'll write or phone you from Venice if I have any significant information," Ruggero said as he took the rinsed plate from Natasha's hands; he dried it while she finished washing the glasses and the silver. Ruggero dried those too. They went out of the kitchen, leaving it in perfect order.

In the hall Natasha said, "I'm leaving now, you know."

"Have you got other work to do?"

"No, I'm going to rest a little. I'm not feeling very well, so I've got into the habit of taking a rest for an hour or two after lunch until I recover my strength."

"That's smart."

Ruggero accompanied her to the door; on the threshold he asked her, "Do you want any cigarettes?" He offered her a package.

"Give me only one." She put it immediately between her lips; Ruggero lighted it for her. Natasha opened the door. "So you're going to America," she said. She put her hand on his arm. With her other hand she took the cigarette out of her mouth to give him a kiss, quick but solid, something she was planting on that cheek and leaving there. She started smoking again. "Perhaps next time I'll come to America with you," she said in a burst of laughter and smoke. When she laughed she hardly moved her face—that round, red, shiny face which had changed so little through the years.

"Yes, that's a good idea, perhaps. Meanwhile, I'll go ahead and see what America is like."

After going down a few steps, Natasha turned around. "Say hello to your mother. Is it true that the doctor has ordered her not to drink wine any more?"

"No, Natasha, that's not true."

"Say hello to her for me."

"Of course. She asks about you first thing every time I come from Milan."

Natasha stopped halfway down the stairs, turning back to look quizzically at Ruggero. An old story went that it was she, Ruggero's mother, who had "sent Natasha away" from Venice. And now Natasha was there, motionless halfway down the stairs, smoking pensively, looking at Ruggero with a steady, scrutinizing gaze through the cigarette smoke.

For fifteen years, every time Elena Partibon came back to Venice after long visits abroad, she had been certain that she would find Natasha ready to come to her. It seemed as though with the instinct of a dog or a bird, Natasha had sensed those returns like a climate mutation. Then she would immediately leave the house of the noble and obtuse old ladies, the Dall'Olivos, mother and daughter, where she was staying during those absences, and go back to the Partibon house. Elena's old parents, Vittoria and Paolo Partibon, occupying the ground floor in the same house, would have liked to "keep Natasha" during the periods when their daughter and their little grandson were away; but she preferred to go and work for the Dall'Olivos, those perfect strangers, with whom she entertained a very sour relationship; their sarcasm and recriminations she countered with her hearty, raucous laughter. They tolerated her because those who used to be maids were lured away by industry, and because this particular servant was clean and very efficient; however, they accused her of thinking of nothing but men, they pronounced her "too much of a thief" in her handling of household expenses (a margin of theft, according to their particularly offensive theory, was taken for granted, but Natasha was overdoing it), and they called her a streetwalker, or rather, Venice being the city, a *calle*walker.

Rather than putting up a direct counteroffensive, Natasha would look at those old ladies with a kind of dark and victorious glee. But with Elena it had been completely different. Because Elena, without doing anything, had vanquished her; simply by her example she had made her understand what a woman could be in life, what she could get to enjoy, to suffer, to realize. While Natasha's feeling toward the authoritarian and basically weak old ladies, with their harsh and livid air of reproach and their tense, cold lips, had focused on a single wish (to crush them, or even better, to see them die by the slow fire of inexorable liver ailment), toward Elena there had been only admiration, without qualification and without envy; Natasha simply would have liked to resemble her.

Then there had been the "trouble," and with it, her disentanglement from Venice and everything.

One afternoon two policemen camouflaged as visitors had caught Natasha by surprise with other young women in a house evidently set up to accommodate quick and fierce love rendezvous, in the industrial Venetian mainland. Through the solicitous concern of Ruggero, then eighteen, there was the patient and very able intervention of Enrico Fassola, the Partibons' old friend, a former diplomat and now a lawyer in the Venetian firm of Arturo Fontana. The suggestion that Natasha had been in that house only to do the cleaning was introduced, elaborated on and accepted. So after a period of dark uncertainty Natasha found herself freed from everything, like the wind on the Lagoon bridge; and by that very bridge she left Venice, after saying good-bye to Elena.

Some people had gone on speculating whether it was she who had left Elena or whether instead, somehow, Natasha had been chased away, perhaps through a tacit agreement, by some telepathic device, not only without words but even without gestures; the first tangible sign had simply been Natasha's suitcase, beautiful, new, probably a gift from Elena herself, already packed, placed on the terrazzo floor in the vestibule.

Elena had said, expressing not even vaguely a command, but rather acceptance and consent, "Yes, Natasha, you had better go to Milan." And with a twinkle in her eye she added, "From all points of view, you know."

"Madam!" Natasha's eyes, reflecting that twinkle, had in turn lighted up with ribald and histrionic irony, as if Elena had hinted at something very different from the expulsion from the places where Natasha had had her "trouble," places which happened to be Natasha's native country, the rural and industrial extensions around the Lagoon of Venice, from which, as a maid, or "domestic help," she had arrived, fifteen years old, in the island city itself, to work in its houses and palaces—not the punitive exile from all of this, but on the contrary, the opening up of greater opportunities in a city considerably more profitable, with widespread and rich love nets. "What are you saying, madam? From what points of view?"

But those women, the thirty-year-old Natasha and her paragon, the forty-year-old Elena, both knew that that wry allusiveness was nothing but a game; they understood each other completely in their last exchange of knowing looks, in a final outburst of laughter. It was as if they were telling each other that Natasha was strong, that she would do something to better herself. In Milan she had married a merchant. She had left him almost at once. He continued to want her and help her. She had no other men.

She dressed with care, more and more tastefully. She liked going to the movies rather than watching television. She bought many magazines and phonograph records. These were things she had done with Elena and for her. She studied with minute curiosity, silently, the faces of women, their gestures. She spoke with a voice more tenuous than before, but she had not dropped her Venetian accent or acquired any trace of the local one.

"And by the way, please give my regards to Mr. Fassola," she said from the staircase. "Promise."

"Yes. And I'll write to you. I'll write to you from America too."

But Natasha was following her own train of thought. "Mr. Enrico Fassola is a just man," she said with authority. This was no longer the Natasha of the "trouble"; her judgment was free, superior. "He is a man one can really trust."

"You're right, Natasha." They exchanged one last smile. Ruggero closed the door.

Alone, he went to Irene's room. As he always did, he studied the place with a critical eye. He took off his coat, draped it over the cello and started moving the furniture around; he replaced a chest of drawers with a small sofa, and vice versa. He put on his coat again and adjusted his tie in front of the mirror. Many photographs were inserted between the mirror and its frame:

one of Irene's father; another showing three girls, Irene in the middle, wearing skiing outfits and standing at attention, with faces sunburned and rigid, almost terrified. Then there was a picture of Kuntz in his early youth, taken in Switzerland before the First World War. And there was one of Ruggero himself standing on the poop of a gondola, rowing; with a pen he drew a long and thin mustache on the face. He found a little comb of Irene's, and a nail file; he combed his hair, he filed his nails. He put the books in order, almost all of them English, French or German. He looked for letters in the drawers; he found very few. Irene had an idea of order which consisted in throwing away as many things as possible, especially papers.

Ruggero knew very well, for he had noticed them the moment he came into the room, that there remained for him to examine certain documents which would provide glimpses of his immediate future, in the form of booklets which Irene had left on her tiny desk—the same desk she had used from the last year of grade school on.

There were three copies of the same bulletin. At the top of the cover, in small type, was the inscription UNIVERSITY OF PALOS ROJOS; and underneath, in larger type and in five languages, four of which were comprehensible to Ruggero, but not the fifth, which was probably Arabic: INSTITUTE FOR LANGUAGE AND COMMUNICATION ANALYSIS: PURPOSES, ORGANIZATION, RESEARCH ACTIVITIES.

Irene knew her way around American cultural agencies; as soon as she found out Ruggero's exact destination she had evidently gone to ask for information, just as she would go to a tourist office and ask for maps before leaving on a trip. Even though this was not her trip, she had undoubtedly gathered that material for her own information rather than to help Ruggero; in fact, if she had found him leafing through those booklets, she would have taken them away from him, sighing, "Don't bother, you already know all about it, and anyway, you are going there, aren't you?" At his question "Then why did you get three copies?" she would say, "In case some get lost," or some other, similarly inappropriate and disarming remark, like "They got them especially for me, so I might as well ask for three of them."

Ruggero composed Irene's answers in his mind, and the certainty that they were perfectly in character gave him a pleasant thrill, like the correct solution of a puzzle. In fact, the attachment between Irene and himself consisted also in being able to foresee each other's reactions. Irene would also provide herself with maps of the region where Ruggero was going to stay in America, and she would do that not in order to follow him with nostalgic feelings, but rather to exploit as much as possible the experience that Ruggero was going to have and in which she neither could nor wanted to follow him.

Ruggero knew very well that Irene did not want to go to America or anywhere else. Too many things detained her: music, with the help of Kuntz; the prospect of a rather good job as a translator and interpreter; also some new and interesting acquaintances with whom she had recently overcome her exclusiveness in regard to himself. He had encouraged her in her cello practice, and she had also met Kuntz through him. Besides, he had directed her to a school for interpreters, later keeping an eye on her while she prepared for her written, oral and simultaneous-translation exams. Ruggero knew that he was almost bilingual in English and that she was better than he in German; in French they were even.

He took one of the three American booklets and on the cover he did a simplified line drawing, a caricature of himself grown much older, bald but with huge sideburns; he wrote underneath: *Roger de Tava, Directeur Général.* He started leafing through the booklet, discovering and appreciating its order and the precision of its language; a useful name index was included at the end. Ruggero looked up the name *Rossi, Gilberto,* with two page references: one in the list of staff members, where he was referred to as Research Associate; the other in the long list of "Work in Progress at the Institute"; here the name *Rossi, Gilberto,* appeared coupled with that of a *Blatt, Hugh A.,* and the projects on which these two were collaborating were listed in small but clear type:

1. (PS) Updating of Equivalences in Political Terminology (Ital.).
2. (H) Key Words and Key Phrases in Italian Public Speaking 1914–1924.

[60]

3. (H) Religious and Mystical Elements in Patriotic Oratory (cf. Lebournet, 2).

Caught in the game, Ruggero followed the reference and found a *Lebournet, Paul,* followed by—

1. (CT) Rhetorical Patterns in the Television Commercial (cf. Palmerston, 1–2).
2. (H) The Reference to the Godhead in the Patriotic Peroration (cf. Rossi-Blatt, 3).

With the help of an Abbreviations Index on page 4, Ruggero could confirm, as he had guessed, that *PS* stood for Public Service and *H* for History; he then discovered, with disappointment because he had not been able to guess that too, that *CT* stood for Communication Techniques. Continuing the game, he followed the reference to the name Palmerston, and under *Palmerston, Charles,* he found four titles, the first two concerning TV communication, and the others, in the PS category, having to do with Updating of Equivalences in Military Terminology. There were, in their turn, references to other names, like *Epstein, Harold; Pickford, Louis* . . .

At this point Ruggero was already settled on Irene's bed, his back pressed against a doubled-up pillow. He went on leafing through the booklet, bouncing from reference to reference, from name to name; he alternated between this occupation and some rather prolonged moments during which he closed his eyes and allowed himself to get lost in light but pleasant sleep.

When he heard Irene's steps he got up from the bed, gave a last few touches to his own caricature on the cover and placed the pamphlet back on Irene's desk.

Irene came in with the dog in her arms—a gray poodle, still very small, who let himself be laid on the carpet with the passivity and lightness of a powder puff. Clearly she had noticed the furniture displacement and the caricature on the American booklet, but she spoke only about the dog, a bit aggressively: "He insists on going out, and then he is dead tired." From down below, disheveled and exhausted but with shiny, intent eyes, the dog followed her talk. "I always have to take care of him and he isn't mine, he isn't mine; he's my father's."

"But right now, you should understand . . ."

"He is a wretched creature, a wretched creature," Irene said with exasperation while the dog looked at her with lost eyes. On his own mental recorder, Ruggero noted: Identification dog-father. She went on, "Abandoned like that, he makes you sorry, and you finally take him out, but you have to be careful, otherwise you become his slave." More soberly: "He's a very intelligent dog. He talks."

Both Ruggero and Irene leaned over the dog to listen. "Can you hear this mumbling? You will admit, Ruggero, that this has nothing to do with ordinary dog-barking. This is a voice."

"I know that. I was the first to make you notice."

"You're always the first to get everywhere, you always know everything, don't you?" The exaggerated animosity in Irene's voice showed up her fatigue. She took off her jacket, under which she was wearing a black turtleneck sweater; coming close to Ruggero she continued with barbed sweetness, "Isn't it true, dear? You always know everything before anyone else does."

There were moments, Ruggero noticed, when Irene looked forty. *Quick mental note:* Every woman has the age of her gestures, of the things she does; even her face now looked withered. And her hair was a mess. "Sit down, relax while I go make some tea for you." Irene nodded and let herself collapse in an armchair; her head bent backward; immediately the dog jumped up on her lap; with closed eyes she stroked his head.

Ruggero lingered a long while in the kitchen; when he came back with the tea he found Irene still reclining in her armchair but now drowsing; her cheeks were pink; her beautiful regular breathing seemed to be rhythmically nourishing her. Ruggero walked on tiptoe and delicately placed the tea tray on the table next to her. The dog was now on the floor, calm and watchful at the foot of the chair as if standing guard. He seemed to ponder the choice of the right moment; finally, twisting his neck, his muzzle pointed upward, he opened his mouth wide and barked three times distinctly and loudly. He shut his mouth and became perfectly still and composed again.

Irene coughed without stirring or opening her eyes.

"This dog doesn't breathe enough oxygen," Ruggero said. "He ought to be in the country."

Without moving, her eyes still closed, Irene said, "My father will have to sell the country place."

"Yes, probably."

"Oh no, I'm quite sure of it." Irene shook herself awake and rubbed her eyes with her fists. "Please pour my tea," she begged while she stretched herself methodically, as if to resume possession of all her joints one by one. While Ruggero poured the tea, adding milk and one spoonful of sugar, she followed with her eyes every detail of his movements, savoring that service which was being rendered her. When he offered her the cup, Irene took it but put it on the table to stretch both arms out to him. "Hello, Ruggero," she said, "how are you? Come here."

She made him sit on her armrest and held his hands tightly in her own. She hid her face in the hollow of his arm, breathing deeply and pressing herself against him, smelling the wool of his jacket. She freed herself abruptly, so that Ruggero lost his balance and fell on her lap, sinking between the arms of the chair.

Their faces met, now very close. He seemed to be rediscovering Irene, completely revitalized after her sleep, the delicate veins under her transparent skin, each tiny straw shining in her hazel eyes, her small short teeth. "You can always fall asleep like that, on command," he said.

"Are you kidding? You're much better than I."

"Not always," Ruggero said, pondering. "It depends, rather than on anything else, on my work schedule. For example . . ."

Irene studied him with interest: even on a subject like this, he always had to give a full answer with all the data in the right place. She didn't allow him to continue; clasping his neck strongly, she started kissing his mouth.

In the past, Ruggero's clarity and precision, his capacity to dive to the bottom of himself, with a minimum of forewarning, and come back to the surface with the right definition, had given her a sense of desperate surprise and exhaustion. She had grown up practically alone, she had never really had any girl friends. For over a year now Ruggero had given her life its very form. Lately she felt she had changed. She experienced a sense of gratitude, and at the same time, of detachment. Earlier, finding herself in bed with him or in a boat during the summer, at the very moment when she had possessed him, embraced him, held him with certainty within herself, she had never really dominated him, because her attraction for him had ultimately had a tender, sticky, debilitating quality. Now there was balance between them instead; in one year she had become considerably stronger and freer. She had even felt she had an advantage over him; in physical joy she had realized she was making ever more intense discoveries, leaving behind herself Ruggero, who by comparison now seemed tepid and too easily contented.

"Wait," she said, "you're in such a hurry," thus underlining the motions of his fingers along her side—blindly and rather casually he moved them up the metal nervature to reach the little hook and open up her skirt. "Get up, let me go." When she had him standing straight in front of her, she looked deeply into his eyes, whispering, "Stay there," and walked toward the bathroom.

In the course of their friendship, Irene's preparatory sessions in the bathroom had become longer. A few years earlier in a similar situation in Venice with a friend of his mother's who had seduced him, finding himself abandoned there, alone, to undress and wait in a large bedroom on the Grand Canal, he had experienced such tension and finally such total sense of alienation as to fear that at the reappearance of the woman back from the bathroom he would not be able even to recognize her, let alone satisfy her; only the blind, always available vigor of his eighteen years had finally dissolved all uncertainties.

In the case of Irene, however, Ruggero lived through those moments of solitude in the bedroom, enjoying a sense of relaxation which bordered on beatitude. He took his time to undress, folding his clothes carefully so that later he would find them not only ready to wear but in even better condition; as he got into bed he would look around, in the white light of the room where he still saw so many objects which had belonged to Irene's childhood, a period which had ended, one might say, only a few years earlier. From the thought of having contributed to making her become a woman and identify in herself ever more clearly the strengths and pleasures of that state, Ruggero derived a profound and completely conscious feeling of satisfaction. From the time when he had met Irene, then eighteen, things had developed in the right direction; her practical and useful activities seemed to him to be clearly headed toward success, and this increased his desire to be useful to her.

Irene had left her tea untouched on the table; this too was one of her habits: she liked it lukewarm. When she came back she was wearing a nightgown, and before getting into bed, she leaned over the table to take a few sips of tea. She took off her gown, and snuggling up to Ruggero, she said, "You always smell wonderful. You are tremendously healthy."

"I just went yesterday to get a complete checkup."

"And what was the verdict?"

"Very, very good."

"There you are—see?"

They were awakened by the telephone when the room was already pitch-dark. Irene got up, put on her gown and went barefoot to the corridor where the telephone was; from there she cried out to Ruggero that the call was for him, but then, as if that didn't matter, she continued to speak with the person at the other end of the line, nor did Ruggero seem to move—instead, he settled himself more comfortably on the bed, placing two pillows behind his back and lighting his pipe with much care and preparation.

Back in bed, Irene grabbed his arm possessively, rested her cheek on his shoulder. Ruggero was now smoking busily.

"You know who that was on the phone, don't you?"

"Piero Camentini. He wants me to go to Venice with him in his car tonight. What do you think of that?"

"I think you'll go."

"I thought you might want me to stay here tonight."

Irene pressed herself against him, their hands interlaced under the sheet. She raised her head to kiss him on the cheek, then placed her head on his shoulder again.

"All things considered, Irene," Ruggero said, "you should marry me."

Irene ignored his remark and resumed, "The Camentinis are great fans of yours, they're always offering you hospitality and all kinds of means of transportation. Why? But of course others do too. Well, that's understandable, perhaps."

Ruggero looked into her eyes; he liked seeing her eyes as they were now, lively and brightened, yet transparent and calm. "Do you believe you'll miss me in the next months?"

"Why, of course."

Ruggero repeated, "After all, you should marry me."

"Married to a man like you, I think I'd go insane."

"That's not necessarily true."

There was a very long silence, then Irene spoke abruptly, continuing her own thoughts aloud, "My father did everything wrong—I mean, his life in general. At least this is the impression I have. Don't you agree? Everybody always thought he was having a wonderful time; on the contrary, he never got any pleasure from anything."

Another long silence, then she went on in the same tone, "To tell you the truth, Ruggero, a basic reason why I'd never leave Milan is because Kuntz is here."

"That I understand."

"Lately, you know, Kuntz has been talking to me more and more about his life. He comes up with some of his own very distant memories, rather intimate things, and so right." She detached herself from Ruggero, laced her hands behind her head, looking at the ceiling. "As a very small boy, Kuntz always had great fears—of squeaks in the night, of huge cockroaches he thought he was seeing, of people he thought were going to hit him from behind. That's how he became so strong very early."

Suddenly she sat up and jumped out of bed. "We must go if we want to pay a visit to Kuntz and then meet Piero Camentini." She was already in the middle of the room, serene, dressing slowly, mumbling, "Pie-ro, Uncle Pie-ro . . ."

"Where did he say he would meet us?"

"At the usual place—you know?"

Camentini had to wait for the two young people for quite a while; however, he did not feel any impatience, only curiosity and pleasant anticipation. Meanwhile he stared fixedly at young people dancing.

Piero Camentini was a journalist and an author; he wrote literary articles for a Venice newspaper and volumes of prose published by houses with small editions. However, the dilettantish air about him was not particularly due to the quality of his writing, which, for that matter, few people were aware of, although in Venice he was a familiar and extremely well-liked figure; it was due to the fact that never in his life had he had to do any of his literary or newspaper work for a living. His father had owned a few apartments in Venice and some land at Campagnalupia, his mother a villa at Preganziol. The reverberation not only of economic comfort but of actual opulence had decidedly brightened Piero's image ever since the time when, about twenty years earlier, his brother Giovanni, then slim and very vibrant, one of the major Venetian lovers in his generation, had married a great confectionery fortune, becoming later, on the death of his father-in-law, titular head of the firm.

For Piero Camentini all comfort, all pleasures of life—in fact, all human experience—had no meaning and interest if he could not share them with other people and particularly with the young. Both he and his brother had married girls who enjoyed delicate health; tender and sweet but at the same time endowed with congenital and very deep-seated egotism, not very remunerative emotionally, and with little aptitude to savor life robustly.

With the passage of time and with the decline of his celebrated aggressive virility, Giovanni Camentini had filled the emptiness of his life with work for his candy factories, crowned with considerable success internationally as well. Piero's life had been different. The two brothers each had a son; but while in the case of Giovanni Camentini that had been sufficient to fulfill his paternal needs, Piero had maintained even on his face, in his look, a lost air of permanent and querulous dissatisfaction. He always seemed to be looking for something to lean on, for occasions to practice a sort of possessive generosity. Although for that purpose he had managed to captivate for himself his brother's son, a young man who was much closer to his uncle than to his own father, that was not sufficient for Piero's demands. Over the years he had therefore been directing his scarcely noticed affection toward some of his son's and his nephew's friends. For a long time Ruggero had been one of them.

Incapable of jealousy, Piero had at once accepted, without reservation, the fact that Ruggero appeared to be rather more promising than his son, Silvio, and his nephew, Riccardo. Even as adolescents he had told them, "Boys, Ruggero is someone who will go very far—he's serious-minded, and very simpatico. Follow his example, my boys, try to be like him."

With the arrogance of early puberty and the first glimmer of beard and sex, Silvio had one day asked his father, out of genuine stupidity rather than malevolence, in the nasal singsong of the boy who would ask a question in class not so much to satisfy curiosity as to waste time, "Why, Father, should we try to be like Ruggero, follow his example? Perhaps because he is a bastard, Father?"

Piero Camentini had restricted himself to looking at his son for a few moments with a calm, almost affable smile; then he took the correct stance, like a sportsman, like a pigeon shooter, and still without a word, placed a stupefying slap on his son's face.

For, indeed, Piero Camentini belonged to those people who had never considered the illegitimate birth of Ruggero an object for shame but rather the praiseworthy result of an act of love, and courage on the part of the mother. Camentini had not known Elena Partibon in his youth, but had always associated that name with vague images of dash and nonconformism. He had not known Ruggero's father even by sight and had no feelings of any kind, not even curiosity, toward that young man about whom he knew only that he was not from Venice and that although married to somebody else, he had made Elena Partibon pregnant too, and that shortly thereafter he was killed in the war. For that matter, in the city at large—what with the war, and then with time trotting on with inexorable normality —the Partibon-Tava episode had been almost entirely absorbed and dissolved. As for Piero Camentini, the potent slap in his son's face, and a few barkings punctuated by some eloquent profanity directed at particularly bigoted and malevolent meddlers, had been his only acts of violence necessary in dealing with that subject.

Meanwhile, the generation of Silvio and Riccardo, and of Ruggero himself, had decidedly come on the scene, taking full possession of Piero's heart.

In the club where Camentini was waiting for Ruggero and Irene there was, first, an entrance with a checkroom, then an enormous hall simply furnished and lighted; the general style of the place and the furnishings, unlike those of old, mysterious night clubs looking like crypts, rather recalled a Swiss or American college gymnasium.

Piero Camentini was already seated with a couple at a table; while he waited for Ruggero and Irene to come, he followed the band and the dancers with an immobile but pleased smile on his face. He saw boys and girls generally even younger than Ruggero and Irene, clean and scrubbed, wearing sports outfits; Christlike hairstyles and beards, not infrequent among the boys, seemed to be fresh with shampoo. The dancing took place on a platform at the far end of the hall; in the middle of the platform the band played with dazzling competence, yet always managing to convey, by the style of the individual players, and by the expressions on their faces, a feeling of improvisation and enjoyment. The amalgam of dancers and musicians was complete, not only because they all looked as though they knew one another like experts in a sport they all practiced, but also because the couples were not in each other's arms; each dancer, functioning in isolation and therefore occupying less space, could easily thread his way between players while with raised head and half-closed eyes he followed and savored an interior rhythm of his own.

"Ruggero, Irene—how are you, my dears?" Camentini asked in a booming voice when he finally saw the young couple appear. He got up and kissed Irene's hand; with Ruggero he exchanged a half embrace. He had provisionally ordered an after-dinner grappa for himself and had taken a sip or two; now he suggested, "How about a drop of champagne? Let's celebrate Ruggero's successes. What's-his-name here was telling me." With his head he indicated the back of his table companion, who had turned his chair around to drink in the spectacle of the dancers and musicians on the platform. At this, the man turned; it was Tranquillo Massenti, and the lady seated between him and Camentini was Tranquillo's Swedish wife, dark and strong, with long bones. Ruggero noted that it was typical of Piero to get him and Massenti together, as there was a business relationship to be kept alive. Superfluous solicitude. Ruggero had discussed everything with Massenti. When he was introduced to Irene, Massenti murmured, "Oh, Berlocchi," and kept his eyes fixed on the girl while his wife, perhaps to cover what may have seemed brazen curiosity toward a girl whose father was considered to be very close to a trial and a prison sentence, asked her, undulating her vowels, as a Swede would, "How is it going, my dear, with your work as an interpreter of languages?"

"*Mycket bra*," Irene answered, using the only two Swedish words she knew. Camentini moved his possessive gaze from her to Ruggero, then back to her. Irene was seated next to him; he put his hairy hand on her own, soft and warm, whispering, "Irene, my dear, how is it going with your father? We are all, all on his side."

"Why?" Irene asked. Then, feeling Massenti's look as a weight upon her, she turned to him. "Are you the one who will do *Milano Sabato?*"

Massenti raised his hand to stop her. "Yes, but at this hour of the night I'm off duty." He started to suck busily on a large fruit drink through a straw.

"You people are very stingy, it seems." Irene left him alone with this statement and turned again to Camentini. "Excuse us, Piero, for being late, but we went by Kuntz's. Ruggero wanted to see him and—"

"How *is* Kuntz?" Piero interrupted eagerly, immediately annexing Kuntz, too, for himself while he raised his hand and snapped his fingers to order champagne.

"He was sleeping. He had fallen asleep toward evening. And, of course, we didn't want to awaken him, so we waited a couple of hours, but he went on sleeping, which, after all, is a very good thing, except that Ruggero couldn't talk to him before leaving; he only caught a glimpse of him from the door."

"He was snoring," Ruggero completed. "Kuntz is a first-rate snorer."

Massenti asked peremptorily, "Who is this Kuntz?"

Piero Camentini waited for Ruggero and Irene to answer, but the two of them sat completely still, with blank faces. He encouraged them warmly: "An extraordinary man, Kuntz is, isn't he?"

Irene's little face remained motionless; Ruggero frowned for an instant as if he had not understood the question. When he saw them so impenetrably sure of themselves, Piero's love for them, a sort of inexhaustible desire, became lacerating. Champagne was being poured. He raised his glass and said in a low voice, "This is to Kuntz."

Irene and Ruggero exchanged looks, then formally joined the toast.

"And to your trip," Piero added. They drank bottoms up.

Irene said to Ruggero, "Ask him about Gilberto Rossi."

"Right. Piero, did you ever know somebody called Rossi, Gilberto, and do you know exactly what he does and whether he is any good?"

At first Camentini looked bright and friendly, but when the memory of Gilberto Rossi visibly hit him, his face darkened and he mumbled, "Yes, vaguely—he used to write for the little magazines. In Venice before the war. Even before you were born. I must have seen him once or twice here in Milan, too, in more recent years."

"And do you know what he was doing?"

Piero was almost aggressive: "I barely remember him, I'm telling you. A person of no relevance."

But on the contrary, now he remembered him well. He hardly knew him, but he remembered him. The few times he had met him in the street in Milan, they had not said hello but had only looked at each other, and at least once Rossi had laughed in Camentini's face. A tense, sour kind of laughter. The impression it had left in Piero's memory was like that of an unpleasant dream. In this dream the much dimmer image of Rossi in Venice had also re-emerged (he must have lived somewhere near the Academy Bridge) , a character whom the present Camentini could certainly not think of annexing to himself. And yet that character was part of his life. He felt guilty, exposed. It was like looking at himself in the mirror, dark bags under the eyes, flabby jowls. He felt the eyes of the two young people upon him and he knew he must look suspicious, frightened. He perceived something like a suppuration of nostalgia, nausea, remorse emerging through the layer of buried years. A brief moment; the suppuration was soon reabsorbed.

No, he certainly could not annex that phantom, Gilberto Rossi, to himself. He, Piero Camentini, felt younger now than he had then. Well established in the cultural world, in a niche which he very much liked. Avant-garde men of letters were his friends, he was recognized by "in" people. A clean, modern life.

Wasn't it? He sought Massenti's eyes, but he did not come to his assistance. As if to exorcise Gilberto Rossi's laughter forever, he laughed in his turn; what he produced was a flabby, somewhat buffoonish laughter which uncovered the cleavage between gums and false teeth. "A man of no relevance," he concluded. "A bit crazy, too."

Irene got up, took Ruggero by the arm and dragged him to the dance platform; it looked as if the two wanted to avoid an embarrassing spectacle.

They stayed in a corner of the platform and were one of the few embracing couples. Holding each other very close, they barely moved; breathing on his lips Irene whispered, "This is it. Now we say good-bye. You'll go to Venice with Piero; I won't see you to the car; I'll stay here, I've seen some of my friends."

"Good, good. *Arrivederci,* anyway."

Coming back to the table, they found Camentini in a perfect state of repair, again in excellent form. They listened to him for a while. He was speaking vivaciously about the modern novel and particularly about the "Joycean break" to Massenti, who was reacting aggressively and ineffectively.

Although maintaining an average speed of ninety miles per hour on the highway, Piero tried to conduct a conversation with Ruggero, but he had little success. At Sesto San Giovanni the young man was already beginning to make some intermittent descents into sleep. As far as Brescia he still managed to provide minimal replies.

". . . very tight literary structures, and at the same time, very free. Don't you agree, Ruggero?"

"Why, of course."

". . . Well, that's exactly where I see the *engagement,* the lively existential contact. Don't you?"

"Right."

". . . Frankly, Ruggero, I'm a little afraid of this institute where you're going to work. They make lists of what they call 'important ideas,' don't they? They think through machines, don't they? I'm horrified by these intrusions of the terrible robot into cultural life—hm, into the very tissue of humanism." But he seemed to want somebody to change his mind for him.

"How are you fixed for money?" he asked cautiously, almost bashfully.

"What? Oh—well, well."

There was a more definite period of total sleep, then again some intermittent reactions. They had already reached eastern Vicenza when Piero delicately touched on the subject of Irene's father: "Infinitely sad . . . More bad luck than guilt . . . Moralizing public life, that's easily said . . . We must help Irene, be near her . . ."

"Near what?"

"Irene."

"Sure." Ruggero seemed to be talking and snoring at the same time. He closed his eyes. "I'll get the facts from Enrico Fassola."

He almost regained consciousness as they neared Venice, recognizing half in a dream the pungent air of industrial smoke and saltiness. Natasha's native country. He breathed deeply, deciding to wake up enough to carry him home; in a sudden flow of dreamily uttered words he apologized for his dozing and lack of attention to Camentini, who maintained his pleasant, brotherly mood. Like a very happy somnambulist, Ruggero reached the motorboat which Piero's brother had sent to fetch them.

Ruggero disembarked at the Academy, and after a light-footed run he arrived at the Partibon home on the Zattere. He found the house in complete silence. He remembered that he hadn't had any dinner and went on tiptoe to the kitchen, found a cold veal cutlet in the refrigerator and ate it holding it between his fingers like a sandwich. In nearby and upstairs rooms his grandparents and his mother were asleep. Tomorrow, in a holiday spirit, he would listen to their farewell discourse at his leisure, and then fly alone via Paris toward the Pacific.

CHAPTER
THREE

There was the usual plastic-sounding buzz, very short; from the lighted button on the intercom Enrico Fassola saw that his partner was calling from his office nearby. He picked up the phone. "But of course, Arturo," he said, "send him in. I'll see him, with pleasure." He replaced the receiver. "I'll see him . . ." The formula had stuck with him from years of government service and it was so out of place that it made him laugh.

Enrico Fassola's working day at the office was over, his desk was clear; in his briefcase were some papers which he wanted to look over again after dinner. Through the window, mild autumn air carried the sound of bells, as always at the beginning of the evening; there were steps and voices in the little square below. In moments like this, Enrico Fassola felt how satisfactory his life had become lately, how comprehensible and well proportioned. Now Ruggero's visit struck the perfectly right note.

When the younger man entered, Enrico thought he had grown a little taller. There was no athletic ostentatiousness about him, rather, he seemed to affect a certain gravity, in contrast to his extreme youth. He sat down at once, solidly, crossing his legs and pulling out his pipe. While he started to prepare it with ritual slowness, smiling in silence, he observed Fassola, well settled behind his desk.

Ruggero's eyes, Enrico was noticing, were decidedly Partibon, not so much in their color as in their shape—large, oval and set rather far apart; they suggested a capacity for stable and ample vision.

"Arturo had to see a couple more people," Enrico Fassola opened, "so meanwhile you and I here . . ."

After using several matches in succession, Ruggero had blown life into his pipe to the safe point; he obtained a first rich mouthful of smoke, blew it all out at once and interrupted Enrico, "I can use our meeting. I wanted to put three questions to you—partly business questions."

"I see."

"First, Irene and Natasha think very highly of you and would like to have your legal opinion on the situation of Berlocchi, Irene's father."

"I see," Enrico said again, but more darkly. He rested his chin in his hand, shook his head. He muttered offhandedly, "We're not his lawyers, you know."

"Yes, yes, but anyway," Ruggero said, pointing with the stem of his pipe at the walls covered with books, "you're in a position to give an opinion, aren't you?"

"It won't be long now before the trial starts, but the defendants, either under arrest or on bail, are numerous. It will go on forever. If you want my personal opinion, Berlocchi will get a two-year sentence, possibly a little less but not more."

Ruggero was smoking quietly. He measured Enrico with his look. Clearly this was the most one could obtain from him. He filed the few data at the proper place in his mind.

Enrico asked cautiously, "What about Irene? How is Irene?"

Ruggero took the pipe out of his mouth. "Quite well. She has passed her examinations brilliantly, Kuntz is happy about the way she plays, and then, in a general sense, Irene has made a lot of progress lately. I mean in self-assurance, in getting involved in the things she does. I've asked her to marry me but she doesn't want to. And what about you?" Ruggero pointed at Enrico with the stem of his pipe. "Are you still happy? That feeling of euphoria you had, is that still going on?"

"Well, what can I tell you—yes, I believe resigning from the foreign service was the first right thing I ever did in my life. What was I doing there? At any rate"—Enrico inserted a little smile—"I don't believe diplomacy is missing me much."

Again Ruggero pointed at him with his pipe. "Do you believe diplomacy is useless?"

The way Enrico shrank his shoulders and opened his arms was sufficient for Ruggero to know the answer already: present speed in communications; immediate contacts between governments, while once upon a time an ambassador really meant something; conversation with the local king by a palace window during a court dance. He let Fassola speak for a few moments, then he nodded and said, "Listen, Enrico, I have another question. Did you ever know someone called Gilberto Rossi, who used to live here in Venice many years ago? Rossi. Gilberto. Does that ring a bell?"

"Gilberto Rossi. Let me think a moment. Why are you interested?"

"I've heard about him in Milan. He's working at that institute in America where I'm going now."

Enrico studied Ruggero's face; he did not understand the young man's approach to facts and people, his very relationship to other men, especially since he, Ruggero Tava Partibon, had now become a man. But Enrico had known him from the time when he was a round, golden baby, and this image was a kind of safety valve even in front of the man of today, it was something more important than mere understanding.

"You know what, Ruggero? I'm almost sure your Gilberto Rossi is actually the son of a lawyer here in Venice. Yes, I really believe the Rossi I have in mind was called Gilberto. An only child, and wait a minute, what was his father's name? Alfredo Rossi. No—Federico Rossi. No—Fernando. That's it, I have a feeling it was Fernando. Fernando Rossi, attorney-at-law. A minor figure. Pale. I say 'pale' perhaps because he really had a pale face or perhaps because he wasn't very prominent in the city." Now Fassola, talking, adopted the manner of an old Venetian—the inexorable chatter, the spinning wheel, the piercing drill, set in motion by a taste for the long, aimless chronicle. "If my father were still alive he could tell you. My father was a

[76]

prominent lawyer, with a nationwide reputation, yet he remembered the life, career and fortune of every Venetian, even the professional small fry. Not that my father was a great lawyer, mind you. At the office his partner did everything. On the contrary, that Fernando Rossi may very well have been a man of the first order. But there are people who live in obscurity. Good for them. But I'm boring you. Sorry I can't tell you much about your Gilberto Rossi."

"That's all right, go on."

"So you'll be close to another Venetian in America. Well, Venetian . . . these definitions don't matter much now. Do you consider yourself a Venetian? Or what? In America there must also be a relative of yours, a Partibon who is an art dealer. I don't know whether you'll see him, I believe he lives in the East. He did some business with your grandfather Paolo Partibon, at the time when Paolo went through his art-dealing mania. Did you know that?"

"I suppose so. At any rate, this Rossi is about your age—like my Uncle Giorgio?"

"More or less. Apart from the fact that your Uncle Giorgio is younger than I—there is a five-year difference. You'll stop and see Giorgio, won't you? Perhaps he remembers Rossi."

"I'll ask him."

"For that matter"—Fassola's wheel resumed its spinning—"five years younger or five years older . . . Giorgio . . . Your Gilberto Rossi . . . Do you want to know what we all are? We are the men of 1945. That means nothing to you, but it does to me. 1945. The void. Free road. Starting from scratch."

Ruggero, still smoking, nodded rhythmically, with well-intentioned thoughtfulness, but without managing to get involved.

"Too many hopes, altogether too vague. Perhaps if a modest person like myself had said at that time, 'I'll settle in my city and try to practice law with the greatest possible honesty and competence . . .' Hm. At any rate, now I'm not doing badly and I'm not entirely useless to my fellow citizens. Then, toward evening, some old friend comes to pick me up here at the office —your Uncle Giuliano, for instance; he'll turn up here before long, you'll see; we usually have a drink, often we have dinner together; then I go home early and look over some office papers while my mother sits there in her armchair reading her books and magazines."

"So you're all right, you are happy, aren't you? And listen—third question. Couldn't I simply write my name 'Ruggero Tava' in my passport?"

"Ruggero Tava in your passport? No, you couldn't."

"That's the way I sign everything I write and publish; it would be very convenient if there was a way for me to—"

"Arturo Fontana knows your background better than I do. From the strictly legal angle, of course, not from the human one. I think the Tavas once wanted to adopt you. I'm sure Arturo can tell you."

Ruggero looked around as though he expected to see Fontana suddenly come in, now that he wanted to talk to him.

"He'll be here in a moment, he too wants to say good-bye to you."

"Really? Good. I can stay here another thirty or thirty-five minutes, then I'll visit with my grandfather, whom I like a lot, and tonight I'll go out for dinner with my mother; she and I alone."

"How is she?"

"Usual. You've seen her lately, haven't you?"

"Four or five days ago. There was some business trifle, papers to sign, so I had to see both her and her father. In your grandfather Paolo you can still see the Partibon spirit at its purest. Complete detachment from life and at the same time total immersion in it. I don't know how they do it. I spent my early youth trying to understand that. Your grandfather is the only old man I know who gives you the impression he is using a wheelchair as an altogether enjoyable means of transportation. But since we mentioned your mother's health—I might as well tell you that I insisted she have her heart thoroughly examined, perhaps by Aurelio Moscato, who is a friend and who after all is the most—"

"How did she react?"

"I'm sure you can imagine that; you know the way your mother talks." At this point it was impossible for Enrico to refrain from mimicking Elena Partibon's voice, a voice which he had had in his ears for over forty years: " 'For centuries our family has been in Tullio Moscato's power; he's an uncle of our contemporary Aurelio Moscato. Now, Tullio was never permitted to examine us thoroughly; he had a tendency to reduce everything to 'nervous phenomena.' But my heart ailment is real, and if anything, it's my nerves that keep me more or less going.' Is that an answer? A convincing talk? No. Yet the idea of going for a cardiogram is filed away indefinitely."

"Actually, you know, she did have one taken once. And what about my grandfather? I haven't seen him yet. Yesterday when I came he was asleep, and when I got up today he had already left. Occasionally he goes to the country."

"In a wheelchair?"

"No, he still manages to drive a car."

Fassola sighed deeply.

"What does that mean," Ruggero asked, "that he has had accidents? In fact, I believe they took away his license, but he goes anyhow. He obviously enjoys it. How old is he now—about eighty?"

"A little more than that, I guess."

"By the way, in his old age he has started to believe in medicine. He gets complete checkups all the time because he has a lot of friends at the hospital and they do it for free. But here comes the Prince of the Law Courts"—Ruggero raised his voice —"so now we can submit my question to him."

Arturo Fontana was at the door. Fontana's demeanor managed to appear very serious and at the same time profoundly ironical. He stood still, looking, expressing nothing. Visitors to his law office always found him like that, neither inhospitable nor welcoming. All that he did seemed to be the result of a decision taken at the beginning of his career—the decision to see men's actions and problems with total and arid equanimity. He had gray eyes, he wore a very well-cut gray suit. A very thin and obviously very costly gold chain was draped across his waistcoat. The immediately perceptible aroma of the cigar he was smoking proclaimed its excellence. He greeted Ruggero with a cordial, motionless smile, a smile which even before the greeting had already been there on his large, soft lips surmounted by a bushy gray mustache.

Ruggero usually found his visits to Fontana satisfactory; he was one of the few Venetians with whom he could establish meaningful communication; procrastinations and embellishments were rare.

"Before leaving for the Pacific Coast," Enrico Fassola said, "our Ruggero is paying a series of visits. We all give him something, a memory, a word to take along. You, Arturo, with a little bit of know-how, could on this occasion have given him his final identity, his name and surname."

"He's already got those on his passport, hasn't he?" Fontana's voice was not high, but rough, penetrating. His accent was very Venetian. His smile now moved a little. He had not yet finished his day's work but was consciously allowing himself a pause; sometimes he remained in the office until midnight.

He walked over to the leather sofa at the other end of the room, sat down and crossed his legs. He recited a bit somnolently, "In a case like that—mother's surname, mother's surname. As a matter of fact, Ruggero, what your mother did when you were born"—he laughed briefly and soundlessly—"was rather clever: your first name is Ruggero Tava, just as mine is Arturo Edoardo. But then, for legal purposes, your Partibon is my Fontana." He coughed. With his middle finger he scratched his head vigorously, seeking a precise point on the scalp under his short, very thick hair.

Enrico Fassola was looking at him without interrupting; he hoped Fontana would go on talking. Ruggero's desire was clear to Enrico—a practical measure, like asking the telephone company for a number easier to remember. But he, Enrico, unlike Ruggero, also had his memories of a distant past, and Arturo Fontana's opaque voice was confirming to him how well those memories were now settled, pacified, within the new order his life had found here, among these walls, in his city. The distant torments—Ruggero's illegitimate birth in March 1941; and Ruggero's mother, whom he, Enrico, had desperately loved and who had always rejected him; the lacerations; the years of deep wounds—all of this now seemed placated and made plausible by Arturo's voice. It was not a voice that invited tempers to cool off, filling the void with innocuous facts to avoid explosive ones; rather, Fontana spoke that way because to him all facts, whether innocuous or explosive, had the same weight and temperature and were registered with an even, medium grayness.

"Pity," Ruggero said. "That three-name technicality is long

for communications purposes. Luckily I've always corresponded with that institute in America signing myself simply 'Ruggero Tava,' and they don't seem to care. I'll point out to them that in things like passports and visas there's the other name too."

"My Fontana is your Partibon," Fontana resumed, "no way to get out of that. Actually, at one point some members of the Tava family did make some exploratory and rather inexpert moves to see if there was a way to adopt you. Then your mother came to me . . ." In a rare moment of histrionic abandonment, even Fontana tried to imitate Elena Partibon's contralto: " 'Now really, Mr. Fontana'—we were not on a first-name basis yet—'don't tell me that an adoption is impossible! If *you* try?' In this discourse, the element that a stranger would have had some difficulty in discerning was that your mother did not want that adoption at all. But knowing her, I was perfectly aware of this from the very beginning. Someone might ask, 'Then what did she want?' Well, only to keep things in motion—families, lawyers—but in the void, as it were, to expose the vanity of it all. Then her father—your grandfather Paolo Partibon—came out very violently against this adoption fantasy, shouting the way he does; and then your mother joined him, in an offhand way, implying that nobody could ever have given serious thought to such an absurdity." The lawyer looked around while he took three or four quick puffs on his cigar, like big avid kisses. "At any rate," he resumed, "the Tavas were hardly suitable for the purpose. I would rather have seen that Englishman, your mother's husband, adopt the boy but then he died too, and anyway, I don't believe that Elena—"

"How could you expect this to mean anything to her?" Enrico erupted. "With her own flesh and blood, this golden creature, this rosy, fat, palpable creature?"

"What creature?" Fontana inquired. "Oh, you mean him . . ." He pointed with his thumb toward Ruggero, who sat there smoking quietly.

But Enrico was overwhelmed by visions which he alone in the room possessed; he looked into empty space, with a half smile: "As a child Ruggero must have been rather irritating. Perplexing. For instance, at three he already spoke in perfectly formulated sentences. And when, at four, he began to write, he apparently never made a mistake in spelling. Besides, although people here at the time certainly did not have much to eat, he managed to grow up nice and plump even on rations."

"Imagine," Fontana murmured.

The present twenty-one-year-old Ruggero listened to Fassola's evocations with a polite smile, neither engaged nor detached.

"His mother never spoke of him, either for or against. I imagine there was too much of a symbiosis between the two. Instead, it was his grandmother Vittoria Partibon, a woman I have always adored, who spoke out clearly. I remember very well. She would look at him and ask, 'Do you suppose there is a danger he may grow up to be a bore, a pedant? And then,' she remarked rather correctly, 'one hears of children who do well at school; but who has ever heard of a child who does well at kindergarten? There is no such thing.' It seems to me that since birth, Ruggero's main purpose in life has been to put words and sentences together and then enunciate them distinctly. In our time this is a weapon, one of the foremost. But when he was a child at home nobody paid much attention to him; there never was even the slightest danger of that nauseating kind of jig which families dance around their precocious offspring."

Enrico went on rambling: in the city, according to him, the Partibon family had few friendships, but very intense; it was the friends, not the relatives, who would talk among themselves, spinning out theories, concluding that in the case of Ruggero "the spark of the Partibon spirit" had entered a "solid, orderly, scientific head"; innumerable ancestors of his father had been military people or civil servants. From such crossings Ruggero had sprung, a new phenomenon. The Partibon family had allowed him to grow up very much on his own, and as for the Tava family, one might say it did not exist any longer. A solitary, pensive and happy childhood. Illegitimate child, too, a blessed outlaw. "And the curious thing is, Ruggero, that you were born and spent the very first years of your life entirely in time of war. Your grandfather once told me that they were afraid you might be deaf."

Indeed, the child had lived through periods when the Venice area was bombed by the Anglo-Americans; from Mestre, from Marghera, came the sound of explosions, roaring over the island city thick with houses; but Ruggero clearly gave the impression of hearing absolutely nothing. Great-aunts and friends of the family, but not his mother and grandmother, would circle around the child, stoop over him; the question "But don't you hear the bombs?" was put in a solicitous, caressing tone, to which he replied only with smiles. Finally his grandfather Paolo Partibon would elbow his way through that circle of women and ask matter-of-factly, onomatopeically, "Don't—you—hear —this—noise—*boom, boom, boom?*"

"*Boom, boom,*" the little cherub would echo with the air of simply wanting to please that jocular old man.

"You can see that he hears," the grandfather said, "when he wants to hear."

"My feeling is he's pulling your leg," said one of the great-aunts.

"Not at all; this is a boy who does not and never will pull anybody's leg." And actually, even when the boy made everybody burst into laughter with his unexpected quotations from the adult language which he had absorbed, his act bore no trace of mimic caricature; he maintained himself serious and courteous, intent only on the exactness of his enunciation. " 'Don't speak to me about hot-water bottles,' " he said one day out of the blue, scanning each word clearly, with a perfect rendering of the tone of one of his mother's friends; " 'in my bed I will only tolerate human warmth.' "

His grandmother said, "There, he keeps silent so long you begin to think he's deaf and dumb, then when he opens his mouth it's to utter a *bêtise.*

"Don't fool yourselves," she went on, "this boy is already perfectly aware of the fact that he has beautiful eyes." According to widespread opinion, the child had an extraordinary ability to captivate people and persuade them to give him what he wanted. His mother's friend, the one he had imitated, said, "This child already looks promising—he has, from all points of view, the right temperature."

Others would say, "This is a child who seldom laughs, and yet he never makes you sad. And as a presence, as a companion, he is already quite rewarding, like some very intelligent animals." Someone even ventured: "I believe he understands we are living in terrible times and that's why he doesn't want to bother people by adding his own lamentations."

His great-uncle Marco Partibon, who had been given a long

prison sentence for political reasons, had shortly thereafter been smuggled out of jail; before going into exile in Switzerland, he had spent his last clandestine Venetian moments holding in his arms that child, that flesh: "Let me touch him once more, this is a living good-luck piece."

After the war, when the daily routine and the food situation had returned more or less to normal, new perspectives opened up for the boy's health and popularity. One day his grandmother Vittoria said, "I hope he doesn't develop into what is known as an *attractive* man! That, to me, is always a rather repulsive type. At any rate, so far the main product of his talent for charming people has been to leave unpaid bills at all the ice cream parlors in Venice."

"He already acts like an adult," some people said. Later on he was rather slow compared to his friends, in starting to smoke, going, however, directly to the pipe; and about the same time his mother's friend, the young lady who had decided he had the right temperature, also initiated him. All these people were on such confidential terms that the friend herself reported sometime later to Elena, "Perfectly casual, imagine, he came to bed announcing, 'All aboard! We're off!' And even the first time, he acted as if it was just a routine matter."

Elena's reply: "Well, it may have looked that way to you, but on the contrary, whatever he accomplishes is the result of determined effort. It was the same way with languages." Already as a very small boy, his mother explained, Ruggero would raise his finger in imitation of his great-aunts, his eyes popping out, shouting distinctly, " 'Ro-ger! *É-tu-dier!* " This may have seemed like a buffoonish act, but at the same time he was working hard on his French and finally knew it quite well. As for English, Elena's marriage to an Englishman had lasted long enough for Ruggero to become practically bilingual, thanks to his long visits to England, "but you should have seen him," Elena reported, "the way he made mental collections of words, or repeated and analyzed sentences. That's why more than once here in Venice and elsewhere he got jobs as an interpreter during international conventions."

"In other words, a phenomenon, a genius," the friend said with a warm, cordial touch of animosity—for after all, from her affair with Ruggero she had expected more, both physically and emotionally.

Elena looked at her friend as if those words—"phenomenon," "genius"—struck her as rather offensive. And she replied in the rather incoherent manner in which both she and her mother would sometimes close conversations, "Ruggero, my dear, can draw enjoyment even from trifles."

It was generally agreed that he had not changed much over the years. Ready now to leave Venice and fly over practically half the globe to go and spend some time on the Pacific Coast, he appeared serene as usual in his loneliness; he listened to Enrico Fassola's farewell not so much for his own sake as to please the lawyer, now fiftyish, an old friend of the family's, a well-settled Venetian. However, in order not to prolong the event, he carefully discouraged the themes to which Enrico was most passionately attached, first of all Enrico's own ancient love for Elena; Ruggero had heard him harp on it more than once, also with expressions of the utmost openness and banality, such as "You will probably never understand how much, and in what way, I have loved her." And even when she was thirteen years old, everybody knew she had rejected him, with a kind of desperate and sarcastic lucidity. It was hard to tell whether she had thus ruined his life, his twenty years, or whether she had perhaps created it, giving it a sense, a temperature.

One day Enrico, abandoning in midair a generic talk about families and about the rapport between different generations, and assuming a new, passionate, last-will tone, had said, "Remember, Ruggero, that when I say I despised and detested my father, it was not because of his moral weaknesses, not because I saw in him the big opportunist whom I considered guilty of having corrupted me, too—no, Ruggero, I detested him because he never understood or respected my love for Elena Partibon, for your mother as a girl. My Uncle Ermete was much more of a big shot than my father, much more deeply compromised with the Regime and everything. But I preferred to live with him in Rome, just because the few times he mentioned Elena he did it with kindness and chivalry." He had continued, more brokenly and incoherently, "There is now a tendency to believe that at that time only public sorrows and nuisances existed . . . We place everything in a historical frame, coldly . . . Oh, it's easy to talk about it now."

Actually Enrico Fassola's talk tended at some point to assume the quality of icebergs—most of it remained under water, and from the emerging tops it was hard to gauge the size of whatever remained immersed, unsaid.

Now, looking at Ruggero, he resumed, "So you'll spend half a year in America; I don't know if I envy you. But of course everything is so easily within reach these days . . . For example, Arturo here, he not only goes to Rome every other minute, he goes to London, to Prague, sometimes to Canada . . . I went to London the first time when I was eighteen . . . I even made a trip to India . . . Now I stay here instead. I don't know if I envy you, even though you are twenty, or just over . . . places filled with good-looking women, for instance . . . However, on the whole this is a more serious time—less tragic, but more serious. In my time crises, tensions were much more—how shall I put it . . . Even patriotism, love . . . Sticky things . . . The men of '45 believed they were starting from scratch, but instead it's you who . . . When I think of what we used to call politics, history . . . But then, in the last analysis, I have the impression that it is you who, in your own way . . . You don't hate, but you don't admire anybody, either . . . I know these things; I'm a bachelor but many of my friends have intelligent children who have turned out all right . . ."

Through the windows the sound of nearby church bells was coming in, impetuous and shrill. This was an inner section of Venice; no canals ran under the office windows; there was the gray stone pavement of the little square, with the hard sound of people's steps, and cats lying stretched out in dark corners. Ruggero and Fontana heard Enrico's voice like background music accompanying their thoughts, and it seemed as though they were sucking up these thoughts, one from his pipe and the other from his cigar.

Enrico's icebergs kept floating by: "You are technicians . . . I've read somewhere about translating machines . . . Perhaps you'll have more luck . . . I remember just before the Second World War broke out . . . diplomatic nightmares . . . conferences among ectoplasms, monsters of the imagination . . . And there was an English friend of mine who thought he could sum

[*86*]

it all up simply by saying, 'People who haven't made things clear to one another.' He ended up by committing suicide; an English poet . . . used to spend long periods of time in Venice."

Simultaneously Fontana's and Ruggero's heads turned toward the door, where an ash-blond man was standing. He had an abundant, soft, drooping mustache, a luminous smile on his half-closed lips, eyes wide and clear. "You're talking about Arnold, poor fellow; I knew him too." The newcomer's rubicund face was shining with affability.

The two lawyers did not get up but turned to him with monosyllables of recognition—"Hm . . . Look . . . Giuliano"—; all exchanged smiles.

Remaining on the threshold, the newcomer had hung his thick Malacca cane on his arm; now he grabbed the handle again, pressed the point of the cane heavily on the wooden floor and started to limp toward Ruggero, who had got up to greet him. In the middle of the room he again placed the cane on his arm; with his free arm he drew Ruggero to him and kissed him on both cheeks. Ruggero returned the greeting. "How are you, Uncle Giuliano?"

Pointing at Ruggero, Giuliano turned to Enrico. "Did you hear that? That's the new style."

"What style?"

"In our house," Giuliano explained, gesturing with his free hand, "the new generation used to call everybody by their first name, even grandparents—Paolo here, Vittoria there. Well, during a family reunion more or less *au grand complet,* my sister, Elena, turned all of a sudden to my brother Giorgio's two girls, and to my own boy and girl, and said, 'Listen, this way of calling us by our first name is silly. Anybody can do that now. Do me a favor, call me Aunt.' " Again Giuliano pressed his cane to the floor; he was a massive man but he carried himself with agility; with a kind of final pirouette he sat down on the leather sofa, where Fontana made room for him. Ruggero sat down too; they all looked at one another, smiling, saying nothing, happy. Since the bells had stopped ringing, there was now the sound of steps and chattering voices from the little square below.

Giuliano turned to his nephew. "I hear you're taking her out tonight."

"Yes, I'll take her to dinner."

[*87*]

"When she goes out to dinner, she eats and drinks too much."

"Elena drinks?" Fontana asked.

"Wine. A lot of wine," Enrico intervened. Elena Partibon, the tormentor of his youth, now had a lot of gray hair, and that heart trouble. And "Elena's drinking" was a popular subject of discussion between friends meeting on the street or chatting over the phone. If Elena herself happened to be listening, she had an air of curiosity, as if they were talking about someone else. Enrico knew well that she had followed many events in her own life with the same detached air—even great difficulties, even heartbreaking sorrows. It seemed as though according to Elena's rules, the more vexing a thought was, the more one should keep it under wraps and take care of other people's problems instead; and this should be done not with ostentation, but with a solicitous, maternal attitude—which seemed to him somewhat histrionic, a humorous imitation of some of her aunts' ways.

There they were, out of his past, those vocal intonations, those gestures, frownings, whinings which could have been either lamentations or the beginning of laughter . . . And suddenly, like water bursting forth, a vision flashed into Enrico Fassola's mind—of a distant afternoon under a violent rain, in a southern English village called Penhill, where Elena's English husband had recently died in that large country place which was locally referred to as a castle, a solid brown structure full of windows once well protected by double windowpanes with sturdy locks, but now neglected, as was evident not only in such details as rattling doorknobs, or the dust and the cracks in the glass of cupboards which sheltered amputated collections of books and china, but also in more obvious and basic signs which suggested abandonment rather than neglect—vast dark rectangles on the walls indicating vanished paintings; the floor of what had been a small music room, now broken through at various points and never repaired; deserted passages with stucco flaking from the ceiling; and then, former bedrooms choked with furniture, with frames without paintings in them, like eyelids without eyes; chipped porcelain washbasins with bucolic blue vignettes; primitive mechanical objects, such as old radios and sewing machines—all of this piled up in the heterogeneity and moldy smell of attics, in an old, still, humid air.

Enrico had passed through many rooms like these to reach Elena, finally finding her in a veritable oasis—a room with bright-colored armchairs, a Venetian desk, an old, stark gray marble fireplace with flames sparkling in it; even the brown dog was shiny, perfect, stylized—like a coat-of-arms animal.

They had taken each other's hands, studying each other in silence. They hadn't met in years. She had looked away first, already self-possessed, without surprise, as if reality to her immediately acquired perspective, becoming memory as it developed before her eyes, which could appear at the same time secure and lost, abandoned and resolute. And of course she had been the first to speak; freeing her hands, she had touched his hair with her fingertips, then his coat with the back of her hand; after a brief spurt of laughter she had used a regional Venetian adjective: "You're *bombo*—drenched. How crazy of you not to take shelter." Inside, the driving rain was only a soft, steady murmur which mixed with that of the fire. "You're crazy. How did you happen to come? Were you somewhere around here?"

"I came to see you. I've been in England for quite a few years, you know, in London. Now I'm about to leave . . . Perhaps I'll even resign . . . I've been watching you from a distance, but until now—"

"And why did you come just now? To offer your sympathy?" She wanted to help him, disentangle him. "My husband has been dead for over two months, did you know?"

"I knew. I knew. And you were with him day and night."

"Well, at the end he suffered terribly."

"Mutual friends, visiting Italians, told me that. I mean, that you were close to him day and night, while in the past"—Enrico laughed briefly, tensely—"the very same people would tell me that your marriage wasn't a success at all, that you were not very happy . . ." He was questioning her by his tone of voice, his glances.

But on Elena's part there had been no reaction; she evidently considered it impossible to explain situations abstractly, through words—in fact, futile, frivolous. Enrico, pressingly: "All your life you've been cultivating what is here called self-control. All of you—a little bit—in your family. Perhaps that's why your English husband attracted you?"

"Well! I never thought of that." She busied herself with Enrico, making him sit comfortably, preparing hot *caffelatte* for him. Standing straight behind his chair, she watched him drink it; then, putting a hand on his hair, caressing it rapidly, she said, "Poor darling, you've remained a bachelor." She left his side to walk over to the dog, bending down with some effort because she was "full of aches"; she picked up the dog and sat down in a chair with the dog in her lap. "The dog is still whining. They loved each other very much."

She too, Elena later admitted in answer to Enrico's insistent questions, she too was on the verge of leaving the country, of going back home. Yes, all things considered, home meant Venice. "Ruggero is there already. He's staying with his grandparents, which means he could just as well be living alone—he has total freedom. You wouldn't recognize him; he is big, ruddy, less serious than when he was a small child. He'll probably end up being a happy man, don't you think?"

"Come with me. Let's leave together. I'm leaving before Christmas."

"Me too, just about."

That abandoned house, in the Nordic winter countryside. The rain beating on the windows. The whining dog. "Elena, you can't stay on here all by yourself. Come away with me now."

"You arrive at the last moment and want to take me away. But you must realize, Enrico, that *you're* the one who can't take it; you feel a lump in your throat, not I."

She had persuaded him to return to London and met him there later, agreeing to stay for a few days in his apartment. There were trunks everywhere, already packed; most of the furniture he had brought from home had already been shipped back to Italy. Elena looked around and made one of those remarks of hers which always sounded incongruous yet very appropriate: "This is the end of the postwar period." One of the first things she had also said there was: "You must have a lot of excellent wine. In your profession, don't you get wines at a low price?"

They went out for dinner the first night, coming back tired, retiring early, each in his room. The second evening they had dinner at home, eating things he had bought, ransacking what was left of his cellar. Toward the end of the dinner he grasped her hand firmly, and after having held it for a long while, he asked her, as he had so many times in their young days, to marry him. Elena did not even answer, she simply looked at him with her famous smile—tender, curious, detached—as if Enrico had been referring to two other people, perhaps two invented characters. She made him talk about the most diverse subjects while she rose from the table and inspected the half-deserted apartment with minute interest, eliciting explanations about what furniture he had had there, how it had been arranged; she asked for details about his life, his activities and duties. "After all," she said, "yours is a horrible profession."

After building a fire, Enrico sank down next to her on the sofa; he put his arm around her shoulders, pulling her close to him. They exchanged secret thoughts and memories in a low voice— she listening to his projects and giving him advice; he nodding his assent—like husband and wife in the night. Then, looking at each other, they stopped talking all of a sudden, as if they had just discovered each other's faces; they kissed, something they had not done in fifteen years, since the prehistorical, even prenatal time before the war; they had kissed without either reticence or anxiety, studying each other with a conscious, adult curiosity.

It was she who got up first to lead him to the room where she was camping. "Come," she said, "I'll give you a Christmas present." So, far away from Venice and on her decision, the love was consummated which for Enrico Fassola had had its beginning in the very distant years of adolescence.

A couple of days later they left. They spent Christmas in Venice, without seeing each other. They met much later, each settled in separate parts of the city, when Enrico's decision to enter law practice in Venice had already been put into action. Not long after that, Arturo Fontana asked Enrico to take care of the Partibons' affairs; there wasn't much to do, but it was a sort of tradition—Enrico's father and grandfather had done the same.

Lost in his memories, Enrico Fassola had missed the others' conversation about "Elena's drinking."

"Well, all right," Ruggero was saying, "I'll take her to a place behind the Riva degli Schiavoni where they have an excellent Barolo."

Giuliano, huge, heavy, tense, was holding on to his cane handle with shaking fists: "Then you'll see, she's going to drink too much."

Elena's son looked at his watch and jumped to his feet, announcing that he had to leave. His Uncle Giuliano and the two lawyers got up to embrace him one by one and kiss him on both cheeks. After holding him in his arms longer than the others, his uncle looked at him searchingly, trying to think of a way to detain him. "You're going by plane, aren't you?" he asked, unable to find anything better.

"Well, yes. That is, I might accept a ride with the Camentini boys to Paris, then from Paris there's a direct flight."

"The Camentinis are very fond of you," his uncle said, opening his clear eyes wide as if just discovering that fact with surprise. Then to himself, mechanically: "They have a frightful amount of money."

Arturo Fontana's low, woolly voice was heard: "Ruggero here is a boy who'll get farther than anybody else. Deservedly, of course." A bachelor to the age of fifty, Fontana had then married a widow with a son already at the university. "Whereas my wife's son, for example," he added, "is still infantile."

Again Uncle Giuliano: "Don't forget that sending baggage by air is very expensive, and you'll certainly have some overweight. Leave some of your stuff here; I'll have a box made at the factory and we'll ship it to America for you." He was employed in the business office of a glassworks. "Our people ship stuff to America all the time."

Ruggero was already at the door. "I have nothing to ship"— he waved his hand in a final good bye—"everything is taken care of."

Moments later the three middle-aged men were standing by the window to catch a last glimpse of him—he was crossing the small Venetian square, getting away from them toward America with a quick step, his shoulders stooped, his fists clenched. They said nothing; there was nothing they could do for him.

Ruggero Tava Partibon's maternal grandfather, Paolo Partibon, spent many hours of the day in his armchair or preferably in his wheelchair; and he maintained a continuous and avid curiosity about world events. He felt involved, even though he did nothing for other people to become aware of this. In fact, he confused people's impressions of him, giving credence to the hypothesis that he was mainly an oddball, undoubtedly senile and perhaps insane. These notions were not shared by Ruggero, who communicated with the old man through short but satisfactory lines of dialogue.

Ruggero found him in his room, which was cluttered with paintings and assorted pieces of furniture, including two radiophonographs and a massive, antiquated television set. He was seated at the far end of the room in his wheelchair near a balcony, a reading light shining on his large round silvery head; when he saw his grandson, he took off his glasses and let the French newspaper he was reading slide down across his knees as if for some time he had prepared and kept in store various tricky questions to put to him.

It was already dark outside and the fog was rolling in; a boat's moan came from the Giudecca Canal, then the long sound of the fogbell from the ferryboat landing.

"I hear you're going to America for some advanced study. But do you know the language?"

"You came to that peace congress to see me at work as an interpreter and then you praised me very much."

"I don't know the language. How could I judge?"

"That's your problem, Grandfather."

"You're going all the way to the Pacific. I don't remember who told me that—young Fassola, I think. How long will it take you to get to the Pacific by plane?"

"About twelve hours from Paris."

"Hm, that's rather long."

"It's a direct flight."

"Unless you stop at Winnipeg. At any rate, what will you do there on the Coast?" The grandfather's eyes showed sparkles, immediately subdued, of curiosity and envy.

"There is an institute where I am interested in working for a while. I've always been interested in problems regarding information."

"Information about what?"

"Clearly formulating and transmitting news, data."

"Glad to hear that," the old man roared. "Very glad indeed. Let's hope that when you come back you'll manage to get things changed." He raised his fist and shook it threateningly in the direction of the TV set.

Every news program, interview, political conference engendered a stubborn dialogue between the old man and the pictures. During a recent election his exchange of ideas with that screen had meant an uninterrupted series of insults, sneers, grimaces on his part. His sisters had intervened, deciding to turn off the set for good and declare it out of order. Paolo had accepted that fiction, sensing that his involvement with the national political struggle, and his obstinate dialogue with the shadows of public men he faced in the dark, could damage his health, of which he took the most scrupulous care.

He took two deep breaths to put oxygen into his system, blew his nose, and after accurately folding his huge red handkerchief and pocketing it, he pointed at his grandson, ordering, "Tell me all about the Berlocchis."

"Irene is well. I've asked her to marry me."

"Good. That Berlocchi child is beautiful—very, very well formed. And what's new about her father?"

"Very little. Enrico Fassola predicts he'll have to serve a couple of years. That's his opinion."

"A couple of years in jail?"

"That's an opinion, Grandfather."

"But if he goes to jail, then various other people must follow him, including some of those gentlemen, am I right?" He indicated the now-blind TV screen.

"At any rate, so far all we can obtain is hypotheses. How was it in the country?"

"Splendid. Yellow shades of color. Brown. Did you see Natasha?"

"She sends her regards."

"Beautiful woman. Type of beauty that I have always found deeply moving. What about Kuntz?"

"He had another crisis; now he's well. We went by his house last night but he was asleep and we didn't wake him up."

"Wise idea. I always have very vivid images of Kuntz, of the time when he made a living here in Venice as a piano tuner."

"Listen, Grandfather, does the name Fernando Rossi mean anything to you? Somebody who used to be a lawyer here in Venice?"

The old man frowned, then immediately his forehead was smooth again; he smiled. "Thin fellow. Yellowish complexion. Alpine cheekbones, thick lips. Bit of mustache. Ladies' man. Died of pulmonary emphysema. They used to live near the Academy Bridge."

"How do you always happen to have this kind of data? What are your sources?"

The grandfather stared at him with his large, clear, childlike eyes wide open. "I *see*."

"Well, then, do you know a son of that lawyer, one Rossi, Gilberto?"

"He must have been one of those boys who came up shortly before the last war and then left, almost all of them. Won't you be seeing Giorgio in Paris? Ask him. Giorgio himself was one of those boys."

"I'll ask Uncle Giorgio."

The old man became distracted. He cupped his large ear. He was hearing sounds from the next room, at least four or five voices, predominately feminine, each of them very authoritative and independent. He pointed toward the door: "Your relatives are coming."

Ruggero rose to receive the group. The first to appear was his great-uncle Marco, followed by the two great-aunts, Ersilia and Delia; they were all very robust and very old, with tears in their eyes from all that laughing and yelling. There was Uncle Giuliano again, from whom Ruggero thought he had taken leave sufficiently in the Fassola office. His grandmother and mother followed at a distance. Ruggero and his mother were the smallest of all. If he just bent his head, Ruggero could catch the resounding noise of his great-uncle Marco's voice directly from his chest, as from a huge soundbox.

Marco Partibon was wearing a red-and-black checked shirt and on top of it a corduroy hunting jacket. His body structure and face pattern, with the thick nose and eyes set far apart, made him resemble his brother, Paolo; the difference was in their eyes, in their gaze. Large and sky-blue, Paolo's were most often absorbed by inner visions; Marco, on the other hand, with dark-blue eyes sparkling behind gold-rimmed glasses, could take aim at precise points even from a great distance, and since he could avail himself of a strong and penetrating voice, he managed to get across a sentence or two even during family conversations, which generally amounted to a chorus of monologues.

"Stop reading *Le Figaro,* here comes the millennium," he announced to his brother at the other end of the room, and looking around, he exacted a smile of recognition from everybody for that line which was already well known and by which he meant that their ages added up to a thousand years. "The millennium in full force." It was the first and last isolated line uttered by the group.

Grandfather Paolo, leaning on his sisters, got up so that the vibrations of his voice would be carried at the same level as the others'. Ruggero felt curiously unnoticed—curiously, because the talk was all about him. They were discussing, each on his own, his future. So the young man chose a corner chair, in the Renaissance style with a high, elaborate back, and sat down. With his elbow on the arm of the chair, chin resting on clenched fist, he calmly contemplated the panorama of relatives towering over him like a chain of high mountains. Crossing above his head, those agitated voices were expressing generally unfavorable opinions on his impending trip.

Ruggero was able to disentangle some rather well-known themes. Great-uncle Marco: "Hm. Leaving and then settling in one spot. Shutting himself up in a scientific institute. Anyway, at this particular time I would rather have gone to Africa or to the Far East."

Great-aunts Delia and Ersilia, dissociated, without realizing that they were both expressing the same idea: "Whether it's sailing ships, like in the old, old days, or whether it's these jet planes, it amounts to the same; distances don't change." Grandmother Vittoria: "One of the very first things one hears about that country is that they excel in the field of surgery. But why should *he* ever need an operation? Haven't we always agreed that there hasn't been such a healthy Partibon in centuries?" Grandfather Paolo, perhaps intentionally cryptic: "We are not, but he is already in America even if he is here."

Ruggero's mother came close to him, brushed his hair with

her hand, saying in a low voice, "Actually, the work he will do there is rather serious, I believe."

Taking her hand, Ruggero raised his eyes toward her. "You're having dinner with me, aren't you?"

Surreptiously Elena motioned with her eyes toward the door —an invitation to escape. Ruggero pressed down on the arm-rests, rising slowly, trying to pass unobserved. He took his mother's hand again. So, almost imperceptibly, the two smallest members of the family slipped through their relatives toward the door.

In the foyer Ruggero helped his mother put on her coat. The relatives' talk continued undisturbed in the next room. "Put this one on too." Ruggero wrapped a scarf around Elena's neck. "We're going to ferry across the canal at the Customs Point, and the evening breeze is rather cold by now."

At the restaurant which Ruggero had chosen, they antago-nized the waitresses—old friends, incidentally—by ordering red wine with fish. The Barolo was brought immediately. After her second half-glass Elena announced, "I don't feel chilly at all any more. I really feel well."

At intervals they would just look at each other, saying noth-ing. The fish came; it had the dark silver colors of old spoons and forks, but with beautiful vibrations of light over it—a per-fect result of the encounter between scale and flame. The taste, they found, was also magnificent. They savored it slowly, with pauses.

Ruggero talked about his encounter with Francalancia in Milan, about the nicknames Elena had been given as a girl.

"I never heard of them, but anything is possible."

Ruggero asked his mother whether by any chance she remem-bered one Gilberto Rossi.

Elena answered immediately, "He was from Portogruaro. When you're in Paris, ask your Uncle Giorgio. I'm almost sure he went to Portogruaro with him once. Gilberto Rossi. When he met me in the street he never spoke; he just stared, very tense. I remember him very well. If I saw him I would recognize him at once, with those wide-open eyes, and that tension. You know, the tense-young-man type? Especially at that time; nowa-days you young men are different, much more relaxed. But that

[97]

young man was very tense; I can see him now, as I did once or twice then, standing on top of the Academy Bridge in the wind; and then, when young men behaved like that, I became tense too, I felt I was growing hostile. It was like that with several of them. Perhaps also because I and your Uncle Giorgio always acted on the assumption that people disliked us."

CHAPTER
FOUR

GILBERTO ROSSI:

First of all, I had better settle a few problems within myself. If I read over again what I was writing sometime ago, I can see that everything finally converges on one person: Ruggero Tava. There was a shock when I came upon that name, and I stopped. Of course, I am referring to the father, to my dead friend, not to the son, who is due to arrive among us one of these days. I probably won't even let him recognize me—if recognize is the word.

I'll admit that when I started jotting down some notes, I did it following a perfectly natural, and for that matter, irresistible impulse. I had the impression I was entering the most interesting period of my mediocre existence. Besides memories, which here have a way of crowding in on you, claiming to be set in order, there was also the desire to put on paper, while they were still hot, the affectionate image of Alphonse, the ambiguous description of Louis and Nadine Pickford, the intriguing portrait of Beatrice Clinton. Et cetera, et cetera. But when Tava's image came onstage it gave me a shock, and for some time I couldn't write anything.

I must analyze that shock, get to the origins of my Tava trauma. Actually there is no need to be mysteriosophic. Let's look at the facts: suddenly I hear that Ruggero Tava's son, a grown-up man by now, will arrive, and this news has an upsetting effect on me. Well, of course. If I observe, e.g., that the death of Ruggero Tava, Sr., furnished an excellent example of all that has been unjust and abominable in the history of Italy, I certainly do not feel that I am making a shocking disclosure; I am, rather, stating the commonplace at its most obvious. Besides, Tava was my friend, one of the few people I ever got along with. He was a sturdy fellow, full of laughs but never malicious or mocking; eyes without double bottoms; blond and pink, for some time almost chubby. Then during his military service he grew a mustache, and somehow his skull also became visible, his cheekbones pronounced. He had a lot of style, but in an entirely spontaneous way. Less intelligent than I but much more natural, incomparably more likable. And they sent him to his death because there was a need for a certain number of tokens—i.e., of dead bodies—to play with at an armistice table. But let's cut off these usual historical references and stick to private lives.

Well, then, evoking Tava necessarily means also evoking a Venetian family which I never knew well, the Partibons. I seldom encountered these Partibons, but I recall them vividly, in their physical appearance as well. The elder brother, Giuliano, was an unpretentious good fellow, and actually I remember him less clearly, but as for his younger brother and sister, Giorgio and Elena, I can still see them, always managing to look intensely serious and scatterbrained at the same time.

Friends of mine from Venice who knew them better than I did considered them intolerably affected. At some point she just left school. Elena Partibon. Known also for her beauty. Who knows? Good-looking, no doubt. Asymmetrical. Actually she didn't move well, her arms hanging straight like sticks, and she walked with her legs wide apart and looking a bit like sticks too. But when you saw her in the street and she looked at you in turn, in a particular manner both desperate and mocking, you had to take this thing into account, this emotion. Over the years I met her face to face more than once, in the Mercerie or in St. Mark's Square, or on top of the Academy Bridge, where I used to linger to meditate; I would nod but it wasn't clear whether her way of looking at me was a reply to my greeting. As a matter of fact, I could never really be sure that she knew who I was.

I knew Giorgio a little better. By mere accident we once spent twelve uninterrupted hours together. In fact, a little more than twelve. From three in the morning to the afternoon of New Year's Day—I can't tell whether it was '37 or '38. The first part on a train, the second at Portogruaro in my Aunt Luciana's house. I was traveling from Milan that night to spend New Year's Day at Portogruaro.

Train almost empty, needless to say; who would ever dream of taking a trip on New Year's Eve? But at the Padua station at two or three in the morning a lot of noisy people came aboard; first their muffled voices were heard through the shut windows, then they were in the corridor, along with gusts of freezing wind. Finally, as if he had been conjured up, I saw Giorgio Partibon standing rigidly on the threshold of my compartment, wearing a tight dark topcoat. He was not with the noisy company outside. He was alone like me. He came into the compartment, empty except for my presence, shut the door behind him with the motions of a mechanical puppet, sank down in the seat across from mine and whispered, "So we can sleep in peace." This is no joke: a quarter century has passed since that night, yet I feel that whisper as if I were touching it. Giorgio Partibon, uncle of Ruggero, Jr., was more or less the age Ruggero, Jr., is now.

"Rossi," he said; I was surprised that he recognized me, the more so since his eyes looked dilated and lost; and without any greeting but with a vague idiotic smile he pointed at me and spoke in an exaggerated style of mock formality, something like: "Pray tell, Rossi, has it not been rumored that you pursued your university studies in Milan and then settled in that metropolis? But wait—I recall someone telling me that you had even ascended to the glories of Rome."

"I'm coming from Milan now."

He looked at me with a kind of exultation. "Which means" —he tapped on the crystal of his wrist watch, "that at midnight you were here on this train alone."

I nodded. Now we were looking at each other with the electrified and unreasonable curiosity one can still feel at that age.

He settled back comfortably in his seat, his head sinking between his shoulders. He looked at me cheerfully. "Clever," he said, as though I had told him about a practical joke played on somebody, "here, far from the world, alone on a train. Clever." Now when he spoke I became aware of his thick tongue, his drooping eyelids.

"And where have *you* been?" I asked.

"Me? I went to a party in Padua." He laughed senselessly, his eyes were closing, he mumbled something between the soft lips: "A veddy big thelebration." He emitted a couple of grunts, which might have been an expression of either horror or voluptuousness, then he became silent and began to breathe with an even rhythm, finally snoring softly.

To this day I haven't been able to figure out whether I purposely failed to inform Partibon about the mistake he had made. It must have been absolutely clear to me that he had taken this train to get back to Venice. But I knew that a large section of the train, including the car we were in, would not go to Venice. It would make a short stop at Mestre; then, instead of making a round trip across the Lagoon bridge, it would proceed in a northeasterly direction.

And there he was, asleep. At Mestre the train stopped for a couple of minutes. Perhaps the fact that immediately after this stop the train resumed its run in a very efficient and self-assured manner, made me neglect the thought of Partibon, who in turn was so totally occupied with his purring: a man sleeping with such conviction clearly was doing the right thing.

I observed him closely for a long while. He was not particularly large or tall, he had a rather childish face, and he must have been shy, yet he had a reputation for being a boy who easily came to blows. One of the stories about him also was that he made love with his sister, Elena. He wrote articles which, however, he did not have published. He must have been a nuisance as an individual, though in a different way from me.

Once he had stopped me in the street for the sole purpose of making a long speech, out of the blue, on some ideas he had about the teaching of Roman history in our schools. I suggested his name to Gabriele Crocetta as a possible contributor to the Goof magazine. "No, no," Crocetta said at once, rather mysteriosophically, if I remember correctly, "let's leave Partibon alone." Then in an affable, chummy tone of voice: "A pain in the neck."

Finally the conductor woke him up. He stretched, rubbed his eyes, listened with curiosity to the regular rhythm of the wheels, looked at his watch. "What's going on?" he asked me.

Meanwhile the conductor, seeing his Venice–Padua student pass, informed him that the car we were in did not go to Venice, stopping only at Mestre, now far behind.

"So where is this train going?"

"It's going to Hungary."

Partibon produced a long and complicated smile. "Apart from all other considerations," he said slowly, with a nasal voice, "I do not possess a passport. Nor is it an easy matter for us to obtain one." In other words, he was the kind of person that took advantage of even the most banal occasion to remind himself of how enslaved we were. He sighed and asked, "How are we going to solve this?"

The conductor waived the payment for the extra distance (anyway, Partibon told him that he didn't have a penny "either in my pocket or at home in Venice") ; as he went away he simply announced, "Portogruaro next stop."

Partibon pointed at me: "Your town."

I nodded. We burst out laughing. He did not go back to sleep and went on repeating, "I've never been to Portogruaro and I know it's wonderful." He also said, "Pity that my sister isn't with us." His sister. The little girl whom in past years I had seen cross the Academy Bridge, the future mother of Ruggero, Jr., who will soon appear here on the Coast . . .

But the future father, the senior Ruggero, I had seen in Milan only a few days earlier. Since he was doing his military service in Bergamo, we got together quite often, either in Bergamo or Milan. We would go to the movies, then talk and talk for hours, mostly about silly things that amused us. In some corner of my mind there was at the time the awareness of the fact that Elena Partibon had been the great love of his childhood and adolescence; he never mentioned her. He was not then on speaking terms with the Partibons; this, however, I learned much later—actually, I think, from Gabriele Crocetta after Tava had died, unknowingly leaving Elena pregnant.

I am trying to say that a fact, a human event, is never fully grasped, never entirely understood, and this simply because *it goes on happening*. Even that night on the train becomes meaningful, the memory of those hours expands in all directions. Facts continue to develop in memory. Each fact is like a birth, it begins to exist only *after* it has happened; that is, after it has come into the world and entered into circulation, into the whirlpool. Et cetera, et cetera. All obvious.

I said to Giorgio Partibon, "I used to see your sister in the street. How is she? What is she doing?"

He answered that his sister—like himself, for that matter—was waiting. Waiting for what? I asked. In answering that, he did not use any of the glib generic phrases "collapse of the Regime," "general crack-up") ; instead, he began to lecture slowly and didactically. At first he sounded rather tedious, but in the end I became interested: you could see, from the way he spoke, he was truly suffering; you could read the pain in his eyes, in his tense lips. Looking at him, I laughed several times. He also sounded like a man who has long been in isolation and then, suddenly finding somebody to hook on to, to talk to, doesn't let go.

He actually made rather extreme and dangerous statements, but you became aware of this only after listening to him for a while because he spoke without ever changing register, in a tone that was not at all polemical, rather as if he had discovered that your ideas were not very clear and he wanted to straighten you out with a sort of aggrieved kindness. "You see, the violent elimination of the President of the Council of Ministers"—that antiquated title sounded bizarre or mocking to begin with, but Partibon used it with the utmost naturalness—"apart from the immense technical difficulties, would doubtless be a spectacular action, but it would be only falsely decisive. I'll grant you," he conceded, even though I had made no objection, "that if you were offered the unbelievable chance to perform that operation, you would perform it. But think about it for a moment, Rossi: what would your act of courage essentially amount to?"

That's the way he spoke, more or less (in fact, almost exactly: my capacity for recollecting key phrases and speech patterns is no less than frightening) , and after giving his little discourse he would settle his gaze on you and leave it there. Naturally you would wait until he answered his own question: "Your act of courage, Rossi, would be like a light stroke of the scalpel, which would fallaciously suggest healing but would leave the important and deep tumors intact. First among these is the very idea of the nation, of the fatherland, which today can only be considered from one standpoint—complicity in crime. Those are the tumors you have to reach and cut into."

Actually, Partibon lived in the world of reality even less than I did. The key word in his rambling night talk is "courage." He looked increasingly excruciated and naïve. He kept saying, "Believe me, this is a very important point: this vanity, this humiliation, this bottling up of our courage. This fact of always being confronted with a choice between two different forms of ignominy."

And then all of a sudden, as though he were my Uncle Bartolomeo, he started listing names from the Great War, names connected with Legendary Feats performed with the Courage of a Lion.

"Big deal, I'm telling you," he commented. "Take, for instance, our Ermete Fassola, dear Enrico's uncle, I'm sure you know him. Well, you see, Rossi, if a man like Ermete Fassola had died, had fallen, decorated with a gold medal, in '16 or '17—thus, incidentally, depriving us of his presence now in eminent posts of the Regime—what kind of death would that have been? Try to imagine, try to create for yourself a vision of those deeds."

I've always tried to. Then, and even now here on the Pacific Coast. Besides, I always have within myself the voice of my Uncle Bartolomeo, with his memories; and here now, in their antiseptic thecae, I have the microfilms, the punch cards, the audio-visual material for Alphonse's many study programs. And then, above all, as far as I am concerned, there is the night, during which I am alone, and as usual I see, I see: in the night, outside, caught among the cactus trees, I see also the ghost of Ermete Fassola, in fact, the ghost of a ghost, reverberation of a reverberation: Ermete the adolescent war volunteer, or anyone like him, already promoted to the status of a legendary vision when he was proposed as a heroic example by the patriotic schoolmistress and by the Alpine-soldier uncle. "I'm sure you know him!" Partibon's voice surges toward me over this quarter century from the Portogruaro train. Of course I know Ermete Fassola. Actually he is still alive, even in the conventional sense of the term. He must be sixty-two or sixty-three.

Rather like a midget in size but lots of guts. Come on, Fassola! March on, boys! The leap out of the trench at dawn. Chest forward against the barbed wire. And if at some point there is no more ammunition, then you throw any kind of object against the enemy—canteen, cartridge box, mess tin, your own heart, your plentiful guts, your glass eye—before you jump on him and strangle him with your bare hands.

No. Hold it. Fassola was with the air force. Even better, then. A volunteer at sixteen, against the explicit will of a banker father, concealing his departure from Mother, leaving an already heroic letter for her on handmade Fabriano paper, conspicuous on the eighteenth-century desk, with fluid lead-gray reflections from the Grand Canal water, in the penumbra of a Venetian early dawn. A pilot. One of the very first. An idol, both to Signora Perigotto and to Signora Lezze-Adorno. A thrower of bombs and of defiant messages over enemy cities, from aboard troglodytic flying machines made of canvas and wood, closer to kites than to jets.

"You will understand, Rossi"—Partibon's lecture goes on with the rhythm of the night train—"that if a man like that had fallen in the war, his death, compared to the deaths that are in store for us, would have been a privileged death, *a deluxe death*. What courage did it take to face *a deluxe death?* Anyhow," he said with a tense half smile, "he escaped even that, and now he is one of *them,* one of the powerful. And as if that were not enough, his nephew, our dear Enrico, wants to marry my sister, Elena."

This thought of Enrico Fassola wanting to marry his sister seemed to crush him with bitterness. When he spoke about it he produced a homemade, very Venetian accent. "It seems to me that in every possible situation, private as well as public, all of us are only given a chance to choose between different forms of shame."

[*106*]

He added, "Even this enormous desire to live that I have, that too weighs upon me as a shame."

This Partibon showed incisiveness and naïveté at the same time. Total hopelessness and total vitality—that's the kind of people who will last. I was overwhelmed by one of my moments of prophetic folly which normally go unnoticed. "What the hell do you care about Fassola?" I shouted. "You are the men of to-morrow, you have got the real stamina. Compared to you, the Fassolas are ephemeral vaudeville characters, whereas you will last, you will endure."

This time he looked at me in astonishment and I took advantage of that to elaborate: "Everybody now identifies the Fassolas with power, while it is you Partibons that will eventually conquer Italy. By then maybe your name will no longer be Partibon, nor will there be any talk of Italy, and no one will recognize the thing as a conquest, you least of all, but that's the way history works, isn't it? So now, you stop thinking of death, whether deluxe or third-class. Besides, don't you see you are bursting with lust to live?"

I spoke to him with a lashing voice. He blushed. Neither I nor he could understand why, but the fact is that he blushed. Quite visibly too. There we were, the two of us alone in a compartment on that train running through the Venetian night, through the most beautiful countryside in the world, now invisible; he could have been twenty at the most; all in all, we were both in a rather bad fix, as people of that age were in that time and place; evoking our images there in the darkness, I even feel a slight lump in my throat.

But when we got off the train at Portogruaro, sensory impressions caught us immediately. "It's so cold, I feel I could chew it," Partibon said. He was crazy with pleasure. There was some snow with sparkles in the gray-blue penumbra. Under the arcades of my town, more beautiful than ever, we met little girls with white embroidered dresses, carrying lighted candles; there were men inside the café, in the hazy smoke interrupted by the glimmering of the espresso machine with its nickel eagle on top: everything beautiful, bewitched, in the chill of early dawn. Bits of canals between old houses, with trees bending over them, still, stopped cold. Orchards behind the houses, icy and motionless too, beyond dark entrance halls, beyond tall portals. "I knew it was a marvel," Partibon said, increasingly frenetic. We drank glasses of wine at five in the morning. We thought we were flying. And my Aunt Luciana, always intuitive and slightly magic herself, looked as though she had felt us coming. She received us standing by the open door of old, light wood, well polished and domestic like a cupboard.

Sooner or later I'll have to organize my thoughts about the women in my life. Only Norma, I'm afraid, will always be excluded from the possibilities of language & communication. Meanwhile, at any rate, it's all right to begin with my Aunt Luciana, who was essentially my first love. Somehow all that I write sounds to me, deep down, like a long letter to her. She is my mental control. For that matter, I write her frequently, and before mailing the letters, I contemplate with pleasure her name and address on the outside, written by me in an intentionally old-fashioned style. I am quite a fanatic about this sort of thing.

Gentilissima Signora Luciana Strigato,
Via Cavour, 23,
Portogruaro (provincia di Venezia),
Italy

She is fifteen years older than I. About Alphonse's age. Aunt Luciana's elder son, Sergio, was born when she was nineteen. Indeed, Sergio and Gianluigi were smaller than I, and when we used to give our puppet performances, fashioning the day's realities into artistic form, my two cousins functioned mostly as my attendants, especially in the early days. At six or seven both of them were already husky, with thick voices and lively eyes, ever ready and quick.

Aunt Luciana is my aunt by marriage. She is a native of Portogruaro, daughter of a certain Angelino (Lino) Marcon, a very tall man with a beard who owned land around there, though not much. Above all he had dignity, style. Aunt Luciana was a university student of what used to be called, in a rather haughty tone of voice, *belle lettere.* The fact that she had been a student of *belle lettere,* in a family which my father, with smug injustice, used to define as "practically illiterate," immediately turned Luciana into something singular and visible, against the background of Portogruaro, a beautiful town small enough to make exceptional people very conspicuous.

Her husband, Bartolomeo Strigato, was from Venice, but in order to find the right woman in his life he had to come to Portogruaro, where his sister lived, married to Fernando Rossi, attorney-at-law: my mother, Adriana Rossi, née Strigato. There, now it's beginning to look as though I were filling out a form: I am onstage, an actor hit by a spotlight or a puppet by the beam of a pocket flashlight, in front of an immigration official or a judge, in the act of requesting residence or citizenship privileges and therefore intent on providing the host-country authorities with details of my pedigree. This is a scene which often takes shape in my mind. Even more often than the one, for example, in which I am dragged out at dawn onto an old soccer field to be shot. I have a whole repertory of scenes like that, quite varied.

Your Excellency, Your Honor—as I was saying, my mother was born and died in Venice; there were tugboat pilots among her ancestors, and her brother Bartolomeo was always rather proud of that heritage, as well as of his being part of the Alpine Corps. With the Adriatic port on one side and the mountains on the other, he must have had the impression he was holding the whole Venetia region in his hands, so to speak. Whereas Fernando Rossi, my father, must never have had the impression he was holding in his hands anything at all. He wandered here and there before stopping at Portogruaro, where I was born, and in Venice, where he died. His death occurred shortly after the visit of an intimate friend, Dr. Giulio Levi, a very stable Venetian, born in Venice and with a permanent home there (in San Vio near the Academy Bridge), a suicide when the nefarious masters proclaimed him an alien in the very place where he felt he had such deep roots. And my father, who died a natural death, must never have felt he had roots anywhere.

He was born at Auronzo, up in northern Venezia, where his father, Gilberto Rossi, Sr., and his grandfather Aurelio Rossi were lumber merchants. There was, in fact, a certain woodiness in their appearance, and that's perhaps where the puppetlike components in my personality and my *Weltanschauung* come from. New paragraph.

Here in the new paragraph, let's get back to Aunt Luciana. When my Uncle Bartolomeo, on leave from the bloody Carso front, first loved her, and they got married in a mutual flash of decision the moment they met in his sister's house (i.e., in our house), I am sure that the very name, Luciana, must have carried with it an exceptional phosphorescence and a great feeling of class. Some of that phosphorescence had stuck to it even in the years when I was a child. Imagine, then, what it must have been when Uncle Bartolomeo was a young man. The idea of being loved, respected, obeyed, protected, pampered, taken seriously, kissed, hugged by somebody called Luciana. And then she was very blond, with soft, flowing hair. But no aestheticism, no Pre-Raphaelite mysteries and swoons. In fact, she has always been a very resistant woman; she has always been, and is even now, an excellent shot. Even better than her husband. Without any fuss, she would bag eight pheasants in the time it took him to bag four.

But she thought it was right that the dog should be more fond of him than of her, because it's the man who must guide and have influence over his helpmates. Nevertheless, when Uncle Bartolomeo died, for a long while she went on treating the dog as if he were a real orphan, with key lines of this type: "Without Bartolomeo this dog doesn't do anything any more." "Well, I'm exaggerating," she would correct herself, shrinking her shoulders and throwing her neck out rhythmically, laughing in short, hard jolts; "he does know me and actually brings me the pheasants, but I don't know, it isn't as if he gave the birds to me personally, it's just that by nature he's a dog that doesn't want game to go to waste. But with Bartolomeo, he gave them to him personally."

I would say, "Aunt Luciana, you have no personal rapport with the dog because shooting is to you, as it is to me, something that gives one a chill, a nightmarish feeling, throwing a sinister light on the country itself, on the whole landscape." I would embrace her, but she would become gloomy and look at me in silence.

When the new scientific discoveries became fashionable everywhere, like penicillin or polio vaccine, not to mention artificial kidneys and nylon arteries, she would weigh the information on the subject and then be perfectly capable of opening a discussion with a preamble like this: "As a woman married for so many years to a man of science, I . . ." The spectacle of this loyal and blind attachment to my Uncle Bartolomeo, to the point of calling him "man of science,"—an elementary, workaday doctor absolutely closed to any scientific speculation—compelled me to embrace her and kiss her red, unsmooth cheeks, exclaiming in a kind of ecstatic lamentation, "Dear aunt, dearrr . . ."

For that matter, throughout his life Uncle Bartolomeo gave her equal or even greater loyalty and blindness in return. Aunt Luciana, not so much because she had been a *belle lettere* student as because her head is constructed in such a way that it can contain vast reservoirs of curiosity and sharpness, has always read a lot and shown intelligence and discernment in her choices. I have a vivid memory of some newspapers which she subscribed to in the years between 1920 and 1925, seriously cultural and therefore vigorously opposed to the Regime, which actually, later on, prohibited them; she kept those old newspaper collections around the house for a long time and finally donated them to me. "Keep them, they are true gold mines," she said as she placed them in my hands.

Uncle Bartolomeo respectfully lowered his sky-blue eyes. One should keep in mind that he was a patriot, in favor of the Regime in its role as official protector of Italy's claims after the so-called Mutilated Victory of 1918; yet at the same time and without seeing any connections, he respected her cultural—i.e., anti-Regime—values and was proud of them. He wore his wife's merits like a boutonniere, without ever having examined them closely.

Aunt Luciana had decisive importance for me, beginning at least with my crisis at age fifteen. Each of us has crises at some points in life; I've had about one every five years, and the first, perhaps the most memorable because it was the first, occurred when I was fifteen. I was finishing the first year of *liceo*, and I don't know exactly when—but there must have been a precise moment, while from the top of the Academy Bridge, where I had lingered to meditate, I was watching a fine rain fall on the Grand Canal, needling its green, unquiet water—suddenly the crisis erupted. A revelation.

Just to mention one thing: I felt as if I did not know anything or anybody any more. The canal beneath and the boats were no longer a concrete reality but at most an image from some old motion picture showing an Indian river. I saw people cross the bridge and they were perfect strangers; I did not understand how I could ever have thought that they spoke the same language as I, wore the same type of coat, of shoes, proceeded more or less in the same manner, right leg forward, then left leg forward, then right again, et cetera. At first I said to myself, "The reason must be that no one I know happens to be going by; tomorrow morning at school it will be different, among friends and teachers."

Actually it was even worse. I didn't know anybody there, either. I felt completely excluded, obscured, vilified, mutilated, deaf and dumb. Not only that, but I felt as if that situation had always existed; now it had revealed itself to me, but it had always been there. It was like discovering on one's body a malignant though invisible lump. And even if I had been able to relate my discovery to others, I knew the least they would do would be to chase me away and scorn me. So I didn't open my mouth. At any hour of the day or night, the moment I was alone I wept with rage and fear. I find it difficult now to understand how that was; I cannot very well reconstruct my own self of that time. But evoking now that fifteen-year-old boy in a crisis, I also hasten to add that I feel the greatest respect toward him.

We had already been living in Venice for a couple of years, and Aunt Luciana often came from Portogruaro to visit us. That time she only glanced at me for a moment, then immediately said, "Giberto"—she has always pronounced my name that way, skipping the l—"Giberto, I don't like the way you look."

She brought me back with her. It was the beginning of the Easter vacation. We arrived at Portogruaro in the evening, with the lights already on in the shops under the arcades, and on bicycles. Aunt Luciana got some sleeping pills from Uncle Bartolomeo and made me take two at once. She put me to bed and I fell asleep without even having had the pleasure of absorbing the silence, which along with the cool night breeze entered from the surrounding countryside, threading its way into the streets and canals of my native town.

The next morning, waking up toward noon and discovering that I had slept fifteen hours in a row, I was extremely annoyed. On top of my depression, or rather, of my total incapacity to establish any rapport with reality and with people, there was now added my rage at having been blocked by that enormous, debilitating, useless sleep. When Aunt Luciana came in with a cup of coffee I told her, "Why do you bring me coffee? Go, let me sleep on; perhaps sleep on forever, which would be the best solution."

She was not a person to be enticed by melodramatic phrases. She said, "Well, no coffee then; let's call a mortician."

But she looked at me, very serious. She set the cup with its untouched coffee on the chest of drawers and sat in front of me on the bed; she began by asking, "Tell me, Giberto, what have they done to you?"

"Nothing, of course," I replied. "Anyway, who? Whom are you talking about?"

She shrugged.

"Whom are you talking about?" I insisted. "Don't you understand that as far as I'm concerned, no one exists any more? That as a matter of fact, I have realized that no one has ever existed?"

She nodded as though she had always known that.

As a matter of principle, so to speak, I stayed in bed that whole day and the following one, too, with her seated in front of me to make me talk. Isolated sentences, maybe with intervals of a half-hour between one and the next. Every now and then Uncle Bartolomeo, coming up from his office on the ground floor, or my cousins Sergio and Gianluigi, would stick their heads through the bedroom door, but Aunt Luciana waved them away, whispering that I shouldn't be disturbed while I was "steaming off"; a rather absurd expression in appearance, considering the desultory manner of my talk, but on the other hand substantially correct.

My steaming off consisted mainly in a panoramic observation of the people and places which had had sharpest evidence during my life, and had now ceased to exist in the same way that I had ceased to exist for them.

Aunt Luciana listened to me closely because she realized perfectly well that this was no longer one of those moments of petulance, sadness and rage which I had had as a child, when I felt that the whole world was against me, all men were enemies, and when there had been repartees like this between us:

"But is it possible," she would ask, "that everybody is so rotten, filthy, wicked, fake?"

"They all are, they all are," I would reply in a kind of reassuring tone, "all of them, dirty rascals from beginning to end."

Obviously such an outlook on life and mankind couldn't hold; my rage was just childish nonsense. I'll grant that it might also have been my intuitive way of feeling the historical moment in which we lived, so rich in iniquitous and senseless crimes. Anyway, now the thing was different, it was no longer merely a historical but rather a cosmic phenomenon. I tried to describe to my Aunt Luciana the revelation I had had on the Academy Bridge, which was one of the most familiar places in my life; I used expressions like "the void" or even more pretentious words like "unreality" and "anguish," although I felt they were inadequate; I tried to make myself clear by saying that in all the visions I had, streets and canals, people and objects, it was as if their usual components had been replaced by others, with which I had no relationship; as far as I was concerned, the very system by which the world was run and presented itself to me had been totally changed.

It is curious to note that my Aunt Luciana was then nearly twenty years younger than I am now. To me she displayed only an image of maturity, calm and wisdom, but she must also have been a beautiful girl, vivacious, well made, desirable. She listened to me for a while, then she placed her hand on my arm to stop me, indicating that she had now gathered enough data to be able to formulate a conclusion.

She explained very soberly what, in her opinion, had happened to me. She said I had discovered something fundamental in life—solitude. To have discovered solitude, she went on, was good because now I could discover love, too, which, without the premise of solitude, could never be discovered. Now I was ready for love, I needed it. Those persons and things which I felt did not exist any more had actually been all alike, a two-dimensional spectacle, and that was why now they had suddenly revealed to me their flatness, the impossibility for me really to capture them and be captured by them in turn—a state of affairs which I had defined with words like "unreality" and "the void." On the other hand, with the discovery of love, tridimensional persons and things would begin to exist for me—individualized, important, relevant, intrusive, committing. Aunt Luciana gave me to understand that she herself—many years earlier, of course—had made a similar discovery. There were certain words, she said—"love," "being in love"—which were nothing much, but since they did exist, one might as well use them to some purpose. Well, she concluded, if those expressions had to have a meaning, then, to give the obvious, immediate examples, she loved my Uncle Bartolomeo, my cousins Sergio and Gianluigi, and me.

She spoke for quite a while. I looked at her with a feeling that I was discovering her. My heart was galloping. Strange, but even with my crushing verbal memory I wouldn't be able exactly to reconstruct her talk. It was rather a general sensation which enveloped me wholly and forever. This was clear to me: she had elevated me to her own level, turning me into a man, as it were.

Toward evening I ended my two days in bed and came down to the dining room, received by everybody with the greatest casualness. "You know, Aunt, you did well, giving me those sleeping pills," I told her. "I feel tranquilized and at the same time rather strong."

Years later my aunt also played an important part in making me decide to go to Milan to complete my university studies. We planned that, without speaking about it to anyone else. Actually I was a bit disappointed at the way my father accepted the idea at once: "You're right, there is more circulation over there. Don't bury yourself here." He seemed to be in a hurry for me to leave.

Let's go back to Aunt Luciana that morning when I arrived at Portogruaro with Giorgio Partibon. Her first form of greeting was to smell us: "You reek of wine, both of you." To offset the effect of the alcohol, but also because it was the perfect choice anyway, she gave us fried polenta with milk. As for Partibon, she treated him rather like a big bumbling child: "A bit absent-minded, aren't you, Partibon? Imagine missing trains like that." She also said, confusing him, that she had heard about him but had imagined him completely different. Taken a bit off guard but at the same time rather flattered, Partibon asked how she had imagined him, then, but got nothing out of her other than "Well, I don't know—different, sort of."

We asked Aunt Luciana how come she had got up so early, and she said that at four in the morning she had warmed some milk for Uncle Bartolomeo, who had left for the mountains to spend the day with friends, as he often did on holidays.

"Oh, a patriotic gathering, no doubt," young Partibon remarked, tightening his lips in a stiff little smile.

"Whether it's patriotic I don't know. Anyway, they were going to Mount Grappa."

Meanwhile my cousins had turned up too, Sergio and Gianluigi, embracing and kissing me, then hitting me in the belly with the back of the hand; and what with the idea that Bartolomeo was on Mount Grappa, and one thing and another, at some point one of them idly started to hum the obvious tune, "Mount Grappa, You Are My Homeland," and from that it was a short step to other Alpine battle songs and community singing.

Before long, even the wine *fiasco* appeared, and Giorgio Partibon seemed to welcome the straw-covered bottle with particular interest and pleasure. He was a steady and systematic drinker; that is, he drank slowly but without missing a beat; as he drank, his mind seemed to grow more lucid. He still had the didactic tone and the undercurrent of suffering which had attracted me during his talk on the train. Now that Sergio and Gianluigi were there, listening to him too—big boys but considerably younger and simpler than myself—I was wondering how they would react. At first, when Partibon started harping on the same thing, the idea of doing away with "the President of the Council of Ministers," my cousins literally did not understand whom he was talking about; later, when they not only understood who it was but also realized that Partibon was discussing the theory of violently eliminating the character in question, they shrieked with laughter, as if he had snapped out a piquant practical joke.

My Aunt Luciana was more serious, and after listening quietly, she said only, "Look, my dear, you live with your head in the clouds, you know."

Aunt Luciana has always been endowed with the crushing

type of common sense, and actually that's the only way to describe Giorgio Partibon's expression now: crushed. Back in line. Cut down to size. Ready to ask for advice. In the end she consoled him: "Don't worry; now you feel unhappy, but you're the kind that will always muddle through, fall on your feet."

That prophecy was basically not very different from the one I had made on the train. I forget now who later told me, quite a few years ago, that Giorgio Partibon had married someone from northern Venetia, hence probably full of vitality and tenderness, and then I also heard that he lived with his wife and two daughters in Paris, well established in one of those international agencies which also have to do with culture. In fact, at the time of my twenty-years-after-the-war crisis, the idea of looking him up must have crossed my mind but it must also have left it immediately, once I considered the difference in way of life and specific gravity between myself and those of my contemporaries who were already established, associated, organized, settled—arduous people for me to deal with.

Ruggero Tava, however, is settled only in my imagination; and I settle him, curiously enough, in Paris too. I meet him there, a middle-aged bourgeois rather than a boy killed in the war, and almost apologetically he tells me, "Well, this is the way things turned out."

It just may be that I have sometimes felt a great need to listen to him again, and have therefore resurrected him for my own use to made him talk. For Tava meant friendship to me, and friendship reaches its apogee when it is all beautifully expanded, given freely, dispersive, with big empty spaces punctuated by colorless, commonplace remarks, repeated a thousand times at comfortable, irregular intervals. Et cetera. In other words, a friend is the opposite to a historical figure with great lapidary phrases, fossilized from the start. Tava was admittedly a bit average and plain, and that is what made him rare and very precious. He never paid attention to himself. At the time of my crisis when I was fifteen, we were already classmates but not very close friends yet, although he used to come to my house to get help with his homework. He came when I returned from Portogruaro after being cured by my aunt; I took him to the top of the Academy Bridge and tried to explain to him what I had felt in those days. I tried to describe my sense of alienation and exclusion from the people who passed by and he said, "You know how it is, they have their own troubles."

In the end he simply commented, "Well, thank goodness you got over it." It wasn't clear what he had understood. Yet he had the power to make me feel slightly histrionic. Tava was a man who seemed to accept everything. Sometimes I tried to talk politics with him. You can't say he was a slavish conformist; if anything, he gave the opposite impression. But I couldn't tell what my impression was based on.

Commemorating the dead—what does that mean? Honoring their memory? Having loved somebody? Even wishing oneself dead with them means nothing. This occurs to me because during the war, deep down, I envied Tava, who had got out of it in the very first days, who had reached, one way or another, the end of his life at the very start of that era of calamities which were obviously going to mark us forever.

And now I see Giorgio Partibon and myself at Portogruaro, walking under arcades or along canals, drinking wine and "chewing the cold," mad with well-being. And then the polenta, the harmony singing, the wine bottles. Aunt Luciana fixed a midday dinner which seemed never to come to an end. Giorgio Partibon, glowing like a street lamp, drank and chewed methodically, repeating at regular intervals, "pity that my sister Elena isn't here too."

And where was Tava? To tell the truth, he was dead already. I mean that for all practical purposes, to us it was as if he were already gone, excluded, retired, eliminated. And for that matter, only a couple of years later he was fatally shot, in the Alps, by the French. He, who even had relatives in France; Tava had an aunt who could speak only French. In memory, all levels intermingle, all time is present time. While Tava gets killed by a relative I am there at Portogruaro drinking wine with his phantom brother-in-law, Giorgio Partibon.

To sum up: Is it or is it not true that of the whole "private and public" mess, he somehow has been the victim? That is the stabbing question. That is my Tava trauma. That is the unhealing wound.

My rumination of memories had reached this point when Alphonse Rossi called me to his office to talk about Ruggero, Jr., and about his imminent arrival: "Give him a little guidance. Take him under your wing a bit."

"No, Alphonse, I'd rather not."

He looked at me with his usual robust and all-embracing affability. I said, "Let's hand him over to Hugh Blatt. In many ways he knows Italy better than I do; he's been working on Italy for years—political lexicons, Great War collections, electrolibrary . . . Now, to put it a little pompously, let's say that this Tava, Jr., comes here to bring the contribution of his generation to our studies on Italy. And quite a while ago already, Italy was chosen by the Institute as the guinea-pig country."

"Right," he said absent-mindedly. "Or rather"—he picked himself up immediately—"wait a minute. Let's see. His generation. Which generation? It seems to me that these new young men—we had some excellent people from France and also, for instance, from Pakistan—don't feel about this generation business the way perhaps you and I do. Years ago . . . I don't recall where, I don't recall who did a research study on the visual representation of time in people of different ages and cultural backgrounds, arriving at conclusions like these: those who have had an education, roughly speaking like yours or mine, possess in their mental make-up something like a line, a lineal structure of some kind, projecting backward; and thereon they hang, or they place as in so many niches or set up in some other equivalent manner their visions of the various periods of the past—styles, personages, what have you. Now, the new young men examined by this researcher—who *was* he? I can't remember, maybe it was just some fool—not only do they not carry this lineal structure in their heads, but apparently they live perfectly well without it. As to the case at hand, I'd be very surprised if the son of your poor friend Tava will understand what you're talking about when you tell him that he comes here to represent a generation."

"Of course. And, anyway, I have no intention of talking to him beyond the necessary minimum."

Alphonse went on without having heard me, "I'm coming to your second subject—Italy as guinea-pig country. From the point of view of public relations, an unfortunate choice of words. I don't know who came out with that definition first, but I suspect it was you and Blatt, possibly without knowing what

[*119*]

you were doing. An even less felicitous notion was the one promoted, I suspect, by Louis Pickford, or whoever it was that said Italy had been chosen as our special research area because it represents 'an interesting stage between an underdeveloped and semideveloped country.' One of the last times I was in Washington I had the impression that the Italian ambassador was cold-shouldering me; fortunately we are old friends and we laughed the thing off. Not to mention the usual threatening letters from members of Italian colonies in North and South America, in the Imperial Rome, Columbus, Michelangelo vein." He drew a deep sigh, a kind of warm-up before the new sprint of oratory, his face glowing with the pleasure of his own eloquence, like that of a baby suckling: "And then the most mistaken rumor of all is that I forced the trustees' hand to gather so much Italian material and declare Italy a special research area. Oddly enough, the opposite is true. I mean, one of the reasons why I was called to succeed Horace Buterweg as director of the Institute is precisely that it had partly acquired this Italian coloring. But you know that very well. You've read the reports of the special areas committee."

In the same way that even when we speak Italian here we refer to the "Institute" rather than *"Istituto,"* so we say "committee" rather than *"comitato"* or *"commissione";* we speak hybrid. All of the work here is organized, distributed, regulated by dint of committee. Immediately after I arrived I heard that word "committee" being continuously used, and from the way it was pronounced, I made up for myself an exaggerated mental spelling of it: *kamiri.* I have these exaggerated mental spellings. So it is from key lines like "I'm sorry I can't make it this afternoon, I have an important committee meeting," that my exaggerated mental spelling derives: *kamiri miri.* It has become common usage among some of us even in writing. It can well happen that I find on my desk or in my mailbox one of those yellow forms used for interoffice memos, with a note from Blatt: "Sorry. Can't make it at three. Kamiri miri." Another word much in use is "tenure." It means "engagement for life," "guarantee of permanent employment." For the word "tenure" my exaggerated mental spelling was immediately *tenia,* which of course means "tapeworm." When you have this tapeworm they can dismiss you only on the grounds of incompetence or of proved acts of high immorality, which the regulations describe as "turpitude."

Alphonse doesn't know about these exaggerated mental spellings, so when he says, "You've read the *committee* reports" in Italian, he uses the English word.

"But of course," I assured him. "And then, just think about Blatt, who was here at the Institute even before you came and who has always had Italy as his principal mania. So"—I went back to the starting point—"Blatt is made to order to take care also of this Ruggero Tava, Jr., whether or not the latter belongs to a generation and possesses visual images of time." I tried to formalize my speech lest my Tava trauma catch me again, in which case I might become emotional and incoherent.

Let's linger awhile on dear Blatt, my main friend and collaborator here. Hugh A. Blatt. Hugh Alexander Blatt. He has a crew cut and a straight, neat profile, and he moves with athletic precision. Considering that he is, besides, a man of great sensitivity and gentleness, capable of letting himself be carried away by feelings, a man with alert and solicitous sky-blue eyes, caressively attentive to ladies, occasionally victimized by them and divorced from a tyrant, it will be easy to understand that I saw in him a ballroom waltzer of the pre-Great War period and that I have dubbed him Hugo von Blatt, placing him mentally onstage as a young Austrian, later sent to fight against an impersonation of myself on the Isonzo River in 1917.

Putting people together to work in tandem or in a group is part of Alphonse's concept of organized research. So, shortly after I arrived here, Alphonse sent Blatt to my office for us to get to know each other. Courteous and agile, he sat down, crossing his legs; and already that first time, as so often thereafter, we conversed for several hours, discovering points we had in common both in the area of reality and in the realm of fantasy.

My encounter with Blatt had been preceded by a few lengths by Louis and Nadine Pickford's attempt at making me their vassal during long and exquisite dinners in their model kitchen. My meetings with the Pickfords had always left a margin of perplexity within me, and not only because of their allusive needling of Alphonse.

Pickford is the son of a former American professor of Romance philology; this accounts for the fact that he was born in

Paris, about fifty years ago (of a mother originally from Arizona), and christened Louis. At first glance I immediately saw European seeds in him, cultivated in vitro, as it were, and partly fed on mysteriosophic substances. For example, he would talk to me a lot about Dante, in a way that turned out to be entirely incomprehensible and awesome to me. It was like having studied the usual arithmetic since childhood and now having an entirely new system presented to you, with different numbers and symbols. In such cases I can stay awake all night, deceive myself into thinking at some point that I have mastered the new numbers and symbols, and feverishly prepare answers and objections to be presented in daylight. But the next time I saw Pickford I would let myself be overwhelmed again; I would just nibble at and ruminate the wonderful foods that he and his wife gave me, and I would let him do the talking.

Pickford has another favorite theme—Germany. In the postwar years he went repeatedly to Germany to watch some of the trials conducted against the nefarious masters of major and medium grade who, at the most, were sentenced to die by hanging. From his experiences as an observer, our Pickford culled material for a volume written with considerable elegance, which first appeared in installments in one of the chic magazines, devoted to a study of those creatures not so much from the historical as from the subtly human and psychological angle. This book, entitled *The Monsters Day By Day*, has always produced a slight feeling of nausea in me. Yet every time I met Pickford after I had prepared my nocturnal verbal analysis of that nausea, and he started to talk, the objections I had prepared remained, as it were, shrouded in night darkness, refusing to come out into the light of day. Not even by accident did I manage to use some of the memories I had from the year I spent in Germany as *Universitätslektor,* gathering by my own lights vitally interesting observations and experiences. I felt my brain becoming paralyzed, blocked, constipated. A hunk of arid matter incapable of producing any sound. Am I changing now? Am I getting rid of these verbal paralyses? Is perhaps the third large wave of eloquence in my life opening up? Controlled eloquence, this time, well ordered, listened to? I shall come back to these questions, which present themselves to me in daily life, especially during certain kamiri miris and also when I am asleep and live through oneiric encounters and exchanges with the publisher Di Gaetano, with Professor Ceroni, or with the two of them fused into one, and I try at least partially to rectify my last conversations with them.

Now let's stick to Blatt. Alphonse put me to work with him on the Updating Service (Ital.) of Current Parallel Terminologies in the Areas of Politics and Cultural Industry. Besides that, he assigned me, again with Blatt, to Concordance and Analysis of Languages and Lexicons (Italian Section) from 1914 Onward. I have produced accurate little studies of words of the greatest variety, as, for example, "freedom," "enemy," "heart," "blood," taken alone and in context, with due consideration to the particular sauces and condiments with which they are dressed by leaders in their oratorical texts, et cetera, the manner of communication, et cetera. When you come then to words like *patria* ("fatherland"), "nation," "people," "war," "God"— well, these are like large, iridescent, highly privileged flies to whose study, in their different contexts, a great many linguist-entomologists are contributing. I personally have other jobs besides these: for the university I am giving my interdepartmental course in modern Italian *Kulturgeschichte;* then I am a member of the kamiri for relations with the science departments, whose chairman is Beatrice Clinton's octogenarian father; in fact, at the very beginning that's where I experienced some of my highest moments of cultural & human satisfaction.

Alphonse's recommendation had been: "You and Blatt should feel your way around a bit, see that you establish your own *modus operandi.*"

Blatt immediately jumped into the middle of things, telling me that in his view the most useful work the Institute had ever undertaken was that on the Verbal Origin of Wars.

"Wars have never been studied from the point of view of language, of lexicons; international treaties, press campaigns, speeches by politicians and agitators, et cetera, et cetera, examined from an L & C [Language & Communication] point of view. It's Columbus' egg; yet I believe we are the first to devote ourselves systematically to this kind of research."

When he is through with a little talk like this, Blatt lowers his head with a jolt, as if placing a stamp on his own words. This, however, does not irritate you, because afterward he raises his head and looks at you with questioning, naïve eyes.

"I'm happy to be working with you," he complimented me at the start; "you devour the material, you get your bearings immediately, you look as though you had been with us for years." There was nothing I could reply to that. I have always known that I am an assiduous, finicky worker, if only I am allowed to follow my methods and schedules.

"Our work is useful," he went on, debating against the air, "even when we prove points which may already be well known."

"What points?"

"For instance, that men went to war to get themselves killed because they were inspired by speeches from politicians and war poets which, linguistically, were almost incomprehensible to them. Budd Rotondi has attempted some computer programming in this area. From a mass of material furnished and processed by us, including letters to relatives, et cetera, it has been possible to reconstruct a substantial lexicon of the average 1915–1918 Italian soldier. Using this worldbook as a reference, it has been calculated that the soldier's capacity to understand the official language (regulations, bulletins, patriotic poems, orations, et cetera) inciting him to go to battle and to his death, could be established at approximately thirty percent."

I mumbled, "Perhaps the percentage was even lower than that."

Blatt's talk was rather interesting but it didn't really excite me. This average soldier whom he placed before me in my house here by the Pacific didn't mean much to me. I offered him something to drink; he chose wine and began to loosen up. He knew Italy practically mile by mile. He spoke in detail about Orvieto, Bergamo, Rimini—about a certain fish soup at Rimini. The vision of Bergamo naturally recalled for me that of Ruggero Tava, whose son's existence had never been known or even suspected by him; but for that matter, the image of my dead friend would remain closed within myself.

Blatt reminded me that the Institute's studies on Italy and the Great War had begun years earlier as a common project with young professors from the history and economics departments of the university. The title of the project was "The Hypothesis of a Neutral Italy in the War of 1914–1918." Later the historians and economists disagreed, which means they didn't see eye to eye on the best way to distribute the financing provided by the Newton Ash people and by other foundations.

Alphonse, with his infallible Bologna spirit, authoritarian and debonair, got all the money he needed and displaced the main bulk of our research to cover the Verbal Aspects of History. The relationship between Word and History. How Words have influenced History. Analysis, examination, discussion, lexical cataloguing, et cetera, of the largest possible number of relevant texts.

My first encounters with Blatt confirmed what I had already understood from my talks with Alphonse. I mean, I had understood the nature of my destiny here on the Coast. I had come to realize that the life of my mind here must develop on two levels at least. On one level there are the vast resources of the Institute, well ordered, catalogued, dehydrated, electrified; and on the other there is, for example, Bartolomeo Strigato, my uncle, descending to Portogruaro after months spent on the front line in mud and filth, to join the blond princess of *belle lettere;* there he is, ready to leave on his furlough to get married, walking once more the whole length of the trenches ("Allgoodwishes Lieutenant." "Thanks boys see you soon") . The boot sinking in mud and water gets caught in rotting matter, vegetation, corpses, but Bartolomeo's face remains friendly and firm, his eyes self-assured, clear. When these images were transmitted years later to me and to his sons Sergio and Gianluigi, it was difficult for many reasons to pay homage to him with our puppets. A very complicated production: how could we render that *ploff* noise of dead water, or the shooting in the distance? And what about the Austrians? Who could take the role of the Austrians? Now with Hugo von Blatt in front of me, things would become a little less difficult.

With Blatt I first placed the figure of Bartolomeo Strigato in a bare minimum of historical perspective: "The Hypothesis of a Neutral Italy in the War of 1914–1918 never occurred to my Uncle Bartolomeo. My father, though, just at the time I was being born . . ."

I was astonished at Blatt's interruption: "I know of your father's neutralist position. You talked about it to Alphonse when you met in Italy. He mentioned it in his report about you to the kamiri for appointing research associates, which then chose you. In fact, I think that item about your father was processed through the electronic computer along with your other particulars and with the data of all of the other candidates for the position."

This idea that my pedigree and my curriculum vitae had been put through electronic computers interested me but I thought then that Blatt was being funny. On the contrary, Blatt had spoken the sober truth, as was confirmed to me when my course on modern Italian culture was first being discussed.

One afternoon, after the suggestion had been made to me through Alphonse that I give the course, I was summoned to the old campus down the hill by the head of the university kamiri in charge of interdepartmental instruction. Chalk-white cloisters with nice wide arches, palm trees and flowers, and the buildings, chalk-white too, with nearly Venetian-red tiled roofs. Above all of this, large fragments of an absolutely spotless sky. Low buildings. The office I was going to was on the ground floor. Warm dry air, so the door to the office under the cloister arches was open. You just had to open the screen door and you found yourself in the presence of the secretary, a puffy elderly lady all rose and silver. The door to the inside room was wide open too, and I immediately saw my man seated at his desk, holding the phone tightly between shoulder and ear; with his right hand he was signing letters, with his left he invited me to come in.

He was a man in his sixties but still with a full head of short and vigorous red hair, marvelous false teeth, huge glasses in slender frames: everything on his face sparkled. My file was already on his desk. For inevitable and partly subconscious reasons I was trembling from head to foot, also perspiring profusely. To calm down I said, "Well, here I am," with a smile that must have looked rather silly.

Having completed his phone conversation and his signatures, he was now concentrating on my papers, which he had started to leaf through, raising his eyes at me every now and then as if to say, "I'll be with you in a minute." Finally, with satisfaction, he found the paper he had been looking for and tapped on it with two fingers, like a policeman on a suspect's shoulder. He temporarily suspended action on that sheet of paper to put an introductory question to me: "You have filed a request to be permitted to establish a new course, entitled 'Aspects of Modern Italian Culture,' haven't you?"

I experienced one of my most complete verbal blocks. *They* had requested me to teach the course; actually the idea had put me in a rather understandable state of shock, considering that to me it meant making an attempt at objectifying myself as an intellectual, moral and—I was almost going to say—historical person, all of these thousands of miles away from my original background, in front of perfect strangers. These thoughts had meant insomnia for me, but I had finally accepted and was ready to carry on the task with my usual concentration.

I didn't manage to tell him any of this, and he went on talking: "I am happy to announce that your request to establish the course has been accepted by the kamiri for interdepartmental courses."

"Thank you," I said, which was neither here nor there.

Now he pressed his elbows on the desk, grasping the sheet tightly by the margins so that the paper would be spread out flat before him. For an instant I saw his brown eyes behind the huge lenses rise above the sheet to watch me; he said, "Let's see, who will be the instructor for this course? Will it be you?" Luckily he nodded to himself; I didn't have to say anything. He went on, "That being the case, we'll have to fill in a few data on you here. This is the list of your academic and bio-bibliographical qualifications. Like those of other candidates for the research associateship which you now hold, they were processed at the proper time by the various human and mechanical methods in use here. The final result came out in your favor, and there you are—you now occupy the position."

There we were. "By the various human and mechanical methods" included data-processing machines. But let's be clear on this point: electronic opinion is not decisive, for the good reason that it is not an opinion—it is a mechanical device used by people to perform on it such exclusively human acts as expressing opinions and making choices. Or am I wrong?

He proceeded, "Now, besides being a research associate, you want to become a course instructor. For your appointment as instructor to become operative, we have to fill out a few blank spaces here on this form. This concerns the evaluation of some of your linguistic abilities. Grade one hundred represents the absolute ideal. Keeping this in mind, how many grade points would you allot to your knowledge of Chinese?"

This datum on my Chinese, like the one on my father's being a neutralist during 1914–1915, had originated in my rambling autobiographical talk with Alphonse in Italy. Now I saw it turn up here on the Coast, to be evaluated by various human and mechanical methods. Very interesting. Agitated by memories, I felt a sudden urge to talk.

"Oh, my Chinese," I said. "Well, over twenty years ago, when I was *Universitätslektor* at Göttingen, I sometimes got together with my Chinese colleague, Teh, in the evening, and I would get some explanations on the way his language works. He brought me just to the point where I could grasp some ideograms and understand an elementary sentence or two, if sentence is the word, and to pronounce them intelligibly. Teh was a dear friend. I often think of him. I'm told that he's a librarian in Peking. About Chinese I've learned one fundamental thing: you must devote your life to it, otherwise there is no point in even starting. So, imagine, I persuaded a German pupil of mine, a skinny young man by the name of Hans Friedrich Steyr, who was secretly opposed to that regime of nefarious criminals in his country—well, I persuaded this young man to devote himself to learning Chinese. I have it on good authority that Steyr is now a Sinologist of some eminence." I went on for quite a while at the same pace.

Suddenly I burst out laughing: I could just see Ceroni's face if I had subjected him to such gibberish. My present interlocutor, however, was listening to me amicably and with deference. He had placed the form sheet on the table and kept the point of his pencil hanging over it, ready to fill in the blank spaces. He waited for me to finish, then asked, "How high shall we grade your Chinese, then?"

"Zero."

He shook his head. "That's impossible." He smiled. "How does two out of a hundred strike you?"

I shrugged, but not out of indifference. It was rather, an emotional reflex, upon which all sorts of things impinged: my distant life at Göttingen and my present life here, Teh in Peking, and generally, the history of the world, lived by me in apparently marginal but intensely significant ways.

Meanwhile my man was marking down that 2/100 score and went on to say, "The evaluation for Italian is missing too. The maximum ideal score is still one hundred. The secretary has tentatively marked down ninety for Italian."

"Ninety?" I shouted.

"It does seem high. What would you suggest?"

"One hundred and twenty."

"That doesn't exist."

"It would convey an awareness that I am someone who widens the existing areas of the language. With Italian, if I apply myself to it, I do incredible things, in vocabulary, syntax, semantics, et cetera."

He raised his hand toward his mouth, and placing his forefinger on the tip of his nose, he pensively stroked the underside with his thumb. We all have our idiosyncratic movements while meditating; that was his. All in all, a very likable man. But I couldn't let him do silly things, put down data which, incidentally, would later go through the computers, and which did not reflect reality. At my suggestion of a 120/100 score, he concluded his meditation by shrugging, and shook his head. From that moment on I stopped talking to him, although I had enjoyed our conversation. After all, you can't pretend that an accord exists when, on the contrary, it is impossible.

"Let's postpone a decision for the moment," he said. "The course, as I told you, has been approved, but our kamiri will now have to vote on confirmation of your name as instructor. Even though the regulations do not request it specifically, the practice of our kamiri is always to seek unanimous decisions."

I got up, made a little bow and left with a maximum of dignified urbanity. I haven't seen him since. I was sure the idea of the course would be shelved, and I was already experiencing a feeling of disappointment and at the same time of liberation when a few days later, from another remote office, I received directions about my weekly schedule and the room where I was to meet my class.

The first time I entered that room, after a sleepless night, I thought I wouldn't find anybody there. Eighteen pupils were present, at least five of them excellent. The second week I had twenty-seven. A couple of months after the opening of the course I received a letter from the kamiri for interdepartmental courses, signed by my man, instructing me to open the course. Through Alphonse's secretary, our well-known /dp, who uses the efficient information net at the secretarial level, I learned later that my score for Italian had been established at 85 points. New paragraph.

Here in the new paragraph, I'll hook up again to the Blatt line. From the very beginning, Blatt has been helping me with everything. He is thoroughly familiar with all problems, including administrative & bureaucratic matters. He explained the reason why my insignificant Chinese past had created attention. It is this: for a long time the Institute has been debating the problem of guinea-pig languages. The plan is to offer a model of the perfect method of teaching languages, using one of them for intensive experimentation; and Alphonse has no doubt that this language should be Chinese. There is a special kamiri to deal with the problem.

At first it seemed as though agreement had been reached on a duet, Arabic and Italian, but then the promoters of Arabic left as a consequence of political complications in their countries, and with Italian the kamiri ran into difficulties because the head of Romance languages at the university, Bassinelli, refused to collaborate, in fact instituted a sort of undeclared boycott. For a short while, then, it became fashionable to suggest English as a guinea-pig language, in which case foreign guinea-pig students would be used.

At any rate, the kamiri dealing with the problem is getting nowhere and meets but rarely; meanwhile Alphonse doesn't budge from his Chinese idea, and since several kamiris object to it on the grounds that the difficulties in finding an adequate Chinese staff are insurmountable (it takes people who know how to handle electronic teaching aids, and who are up to date, according to the general rules of the Institute, on the current and ever changing language of the government class of the country in question), he countered with a key line: "We'll take care of it ourselves with some new Chinese." And with his usual mixture of pragmatism and perfunctoriness he asked if I would try to get my friend Teh over from China, with a group of young men of his own; unfortunately, at this time the success of such a project seems to be, quite literally, more improbable than going to the moon.

"The logical choice," Blatt said, "would have been Italian, but Bassinelli is an extremely nervous individual, and his pupils, who could be utilized as instructors, tend to be very nervous too. Besides, we need native Italians for the experiment. And here at the Institute we certainly have no Italians to spare on a pedagogical experiment." Here he winked at me with a significant smile.

For, indeed, as I have already noted, Blatt is fanatical about Italy and rather given to excesses in his praise. He doesn't confine himself to exaggeration at the level of single individuals, he extends his views to matters of a general character, to historical perspectives.

Individual & human level: "You are the most interesting acquisition the Institute has made lately. I've always said that we would need a dozen Italians here on a permanent basis."

National & historical level: "You Italians are considered braggarts, whereas you are enormously self-critical and self-derogatory."

And then off he goes: "To illustrate by an example from one of our study areas, let's take your defeat in the fall of 1917, known in this part of the world especially through Hemingway's sentimental novel, *A Farewell to Arms*. To study an elementary case of the way you handle your own affairs, national disasters in particular, all you have to do is analyze, from the L & C point of view, the original texts concerning that famous rout, starting from the king's first dramatic message to the nation. I'll confine myself to a technical detail: the message had already reached the foreign press before the men who had actually drafted it realized the advisability of eliding at least the most lugubrious and masochistic expressions from it."

It should be noted that Blatt is apt to talk like this when he speaks Italian, including the use of *elidere* for "delete" and the last pair of adjectives. He went on like that for a while, raising his hand to his chest to mimic the king saying, "My heart as an Italian and as a king." (According to Blatt, "heart" is one of the most insidious words in existence.) He did a bit of semantic analysis, mixing contained passion with cold objectivity, meanwhile drinking a California mountain wine we are both fond of.

It was then that I pointed at him, suddenly and irreversibly announcing that I had recognized in him the young Austrian, Hugo von Blatt, and asking him, "And what about you, Von Blatt? As a young Austro-Hungarian officer on the other side, what was your impression?"

He understood me at once. Actually, in such cases, either there is immediate identification or nothing ever comes of it.

Together we see Leutnant von Blatt, former student, former visitor from *Mitteleuropa* to Italy *en touriste* in the celebrated years of bourgeois bounty before the Great War, with no need of a passport and on beautiful *art nouveau* trains, now instead put into uniform, in the incipient autumn of 1917, stopped at the Austrian (Slovenian) border with Italy (the Hypothesis of a Neutral Italy did not hold), blocked there—and, to be sure, not by ordinary customs officials but by several army corps—crouching for weeks and months in the subhuman discomfort of the trenches, vis-à-vis myself, Bartolomeo–Gilberto Strigato–Rossi, in my turn lying in the subhuman discomfort of a trench about forty yards away from his; and for him it was my Caporetto in reverse: the wide break, the sudden rush down the valleys.

"Did you rejoice as you once more invaded the garden of Europe? Did you feel the 'proud security' mentioned in our last war bulletin? Did you alternate the rhythm of a waltz with the tempo of 'The Radetzky March'?"

"Descending into Venetia, naturally we had to negotiate various obstacles, even numerous corpses of men and animals. Italians in retreat. Open road in front of us. Free road. Freedom, meaning also: the void in front of us. For me it also meant: panic. For me perhaps it also meant: the beginning of the end."

"You really chose the right moment to feel *Angst*."

He looks at me for a long while in silence, with wisdom in his blue eyes, and irony. Then he suggests, "At any rate, you won in the end."

"Who did?"

"You. All of you. All past events, even the most sordid, finally come in handy when you have a parade to the sound of fanfares under an Augustan triumphal arch, the generals on horseback out in front, with plumage on their hats." And he went on at the same trotting pace.

Extraordinary man, Blatt. You feel you've known him since childhood. He grasps your ideas at once. He contributes to the production. There they are, in fact, the puppet-generals rushing onstage, the commanders in chief commanded in turn by Rossi (Gilberto) and Strigato (Sergio and Gianluigi), the illustrious dramatis personae belonging to ancient families from the Alpine foothills who are very close to the royal family, all of them bearing magnificent surnames with splendid nobility appendages: Carlo Alberto Sbalzi di Temperatura, who is totally incomprehensible to the lower classes but a firm and intrepid commander; Gian Astolfo Limitati di Risorse, the one who by a few monosyllabic vernacular words of exhortation, hissed through his mustache impregnated with cigar smoke, manages to lead his Sardinians, his Apulians to impossible exploits . . . "But tell me now, Blatt, who gave a damn that those people won?"

"Obviously, if they won, your neutral father won too, all relatives and friends did."

"And what about Tognon? Did he win too?"

"Who is Tognon?"

"He's the one who grasps a bare thirty percent of the lexicon. He's the yokel-messenger who announces to Fernando Rossi, during his morning shave, the birth of his son Gilberto, a very dark little boy. Tognon . . . the one who survives, since he has drawn number nine, thus finding himself lined up elbow to elbow with number ten, who is executed."

I no longer knew whether I was dialoguing with Blatt or with myself, whether he was doing it with himself or with me. The Decimation scene had always been one of our most arduous war-horses. With puppets, we could allow ourselves strong emotions, a lump in our throat.

"Decimation," from Lat. *decem*. A kind of collective shock treatment. Reinvigorating the troops by shooting soldier number ten and all of his multiples. On that occasion the word itself, "decimation," which had not belonged to the well-known thirty percent of the lexicon, became part of it.

Tognon draws number nine. His immediate neighbor, number ten at the count, starts shaking epileptically. Like a tooth he is pulled out of the row of comrades in arms. From that moment on, just like an extracted tooth, he is, for all practical purposes, already dead, but all divine & human attentions are showered upon him until that final moment of the fusillade and of his crumpling in a pool of blood, while Tognon, a tooth next to a gap, is there, standing at attention, in safety, astounded, relieved, liberated, forgotten.

"All past events," according to the Blatt formula, "finally come in handy." So Tognon, number nine, has won the war too? And number ten himself, hasn't he won too? In fact, which one of the two has won more?

Number ten undoubtedly; he is the chosen one, the representative, the identified, the raison d'être for and the focal point of the show, inserted into History.

Only rarely during our numerous encounters did dialogues between Blatt and me thus branch out into the metaphysical. From the very beginning we have consistently spoken about our work and about the Institute. Blatt is excellent at giving you the picture of a situation in lucid form.

"It seems to me you are deceiving yourself a little, as far as Alphonse's fortune and power are concerned. Actually Alphonse is in rather a mess."

Surprise and frowning on my part. On his part, crossing of legs and a little cough, as a prelude to summary explanation. "Macrocosm and microcosm," he opened. "As in the country in general, so at the Institute you can detect a two-party pattern."

"Meaning"—I tried to hurry him—"that there's one party for Alphonse and another against him."

"Don't get the idea that it's something like a Western, with our people on one side and the black hats on the other. In real life, whether macro or micro, things are much more fluid, there's more chiaroscuro. As a matter of fact, I can tell you that the Institute will one day represent a very sensitive model of a political structure in miniature, with possibilities and subtleties that would get lost in a macroorganization."

I stopped his abstractions: "Tell me something, Blatt. I suspect that one of those who'd like to hang a rope around Alphonse's neck is Louis Pickford. Am I wrong?"

"An excellent example. The answer is precisely: yes and no.

Pickford is quite a big shot at the Institute and such a man hardly goes in for direct political action; he maintains himself superior and Jove-like, provided that the Jove image will fit in the case of a thin, dark-skinned man like Pickford; at any rate, he acts politically through devotees who—this is the point—may represent varied and even opposite currents. Ambiguity, for that matter, has always been one of Louis' principal assets. See his book, *The Monsters Day By Day*. Is that a denunciation? Is it a defense? Or an explanation? Perhaps we can't even pose the question."

"Oh yes, we can," I said sotto voce. That time I was still fresh from one of my periods of verbal paralysis in front of Pickford. At first Blatt paralyzed me a little bit too. I talked and I already felt insomnia awaiting me, when in the dark I would look for the right questions to put to him. There were moments in the dark when I felt I had really entangled myself for good, coming to the Pacific and accepting this position. Then I saw with my mind's eye the large reassuring face of Alphonse. I said, "Blatt, your metaphors about fluidity and chiaroscuro basically mean that a clear and organized opposition to Alphonse doesn't exist. And as a matter of fact, why should it?"

"Well, listen—if you really cornered them for an opinion, everybody from the president of the Newton Ash Foundation to the last of our part-time secretaries would ultimately have to admit that an opposition exists and they would point to at least one leader, Chuck Palmerston—a devotee of Alphonse."

Charles W. Palmerston, commonly called Chuck Palmerston, is someone I've seen more than once at meetings of the kamiri for relations with the science departments, whose chairman, as I have said already, is Beatrice Clinton's aged and robust father.

When he (Palmerston) sees me, he is quite capable of inflicting upon me compliments of this sort: "Our Institute has become too important not to be used against the present and potential adversaries of our country. Do they or do they not practice brainwashing? Well, we have here with us some of the finest minds in the West, ready to organize a counterwashing. We have tremendous resources. Let's use them." From the way he looks at me and shakes my arm, his readiness to recruit me as Tremendous Resource is clear.

Aspects of Palmerston's personality and style have always confused me a little, but that may well be because I am new to this place. Chuck Palmerston, just to give you some idea, has very intense nationalistic visions, and yet he flaunts his cosmopolitan acquaintances. He is an embattled public speaker, and a cordial, shoulder-patting fellow in individual relationships. Being, as I believe also, an advocate of the theory expressed by such key phrases as "Showing our teeth to the enemy; taking full advantage of our crushing superiority as long as we've got it," years ago he was awarded a nickname, "Ultimatum," which some still use, shortening it to "Ulty," although most people call him "Chuck." One of his ideas is that the Institute should compile a "definitive polyglot war lexicon (cold and hot), to be furnished as a weapon to all our men overseas."

Alphonse's reaction to the idea was one of his routine lines, "A lexicon is always the opposite of definitive," and the matter was shelved.

A similar exchange between the two occurred one time in my presence at the Pickfords', not during one of their kitchen dinners but during a reception for many people. Chuck and Alphonse, standing, were looking at each other, clutching their tall drinks, and they were like two seasoned actors at a rehearsal, detachedly repeating lines too often recited. Since I was there too, Chuck hung on to me, jabbing me in the chest as if to say, "This is up your alley; as a European, you can understand me."

To make me realize what high-ranking people he had rubbed elbows with in the Old World, he engaged in some name-dropping—names of characters belonging to that world, names which were either unknown to me or, if known, obnoxious. I wish I had asked him, with a high-class, flutelike modulation of my voice, "Do you know Count Limitati di Risorse?" But instead, needless to say, I found myself verbally blocked.

One reason for my perplexity in front of Chuck is that I rather tend to associate his type of mind with people who are physically quite different from him: men with slick hair combed back, straight parting and profile, well-kept skin, perhaps even starched white collar and certainly double-breasted blue suit. Palmerston, however, is obviously the outdoor type, who usually wears checked shirts and denim pants clinging skin-tight to his buttocks and thighs; his own skin is like hard leather, scorched by sun and wind; his hair is gray and disheveled, copious and curly; and even when he is in a room he always speaks as if he were in the middle of a prairie.

The first time Blatt talked to me about Chuck Palmerston he raised his didactic finger at me: "As a European, more particularly as a Renaissance Italian, you will smell nepotism, since Chuck married the daughter of the former director of the Institute, Horace Buterweg."

"I didn't even know that. And anyway"—I drew a bit heavily on the few data I had—"I know Buterweg paid relatively little attention to the Institute. Only with Alphonse did it begin to flourish."

"All the more reason why Buterweg, who is now, among other things, executive secretary of a large foundation, should want to draw the Institute back into his own orbit." He shook his head, waving away the subject with his hand. "At any rate, these are secondary considerations. The main fact is that the Institute is an interesting property. A struggle to get hold of it is in the making—a struggle for power." A short cough, and he stopped.

"Go on," I said.

"The two stages, or platforms, are set, as ever in a two-party system. Now an Issue is needed. And it's taking shape."

"Go on," I insisted.

He stretched out his hands, palms up. "There are these two fixed stages. Here"—with his chin he pointed to his left hand —"you have the one reserved for Alphonse and his people, and here"—chin pointed to his right hand—"you have the one for the opposition. Two stages with a panel table on each. Now what you need is the Issue."

"I see you're placing Alphonse on the left. That's significant in itself."

"As a nineteenth-century European you're full of right and left, as though they were magic fluids impregnating the very wood the stages are made of. No. There are just these two little theaters. Ordinarily the groups occupying them would form and then scatter; there would be a continuous rotation of faces and comings and goings from one stage to the other, according to the particular current issues concerning immediate, practical problems. But in time of a struggle for power, you'll see how all of that will change. Just as in wartime, commercial planes are converted into bombers, so the two stages will be converted for war purposes, and it will be necessary to inflate artificially a great Issue dividing them, suspending work at hand until the struggle for power is decided in favor of one side or the other."

"Yes, yes, I understand you," I said quickly the first time I got this kind of lecture from Blatt. I found him quite brilliant, but he was also acting the pedagogue with me and I didn't want to give him too much satisfaction. "I have my reservations, but in a sense, what you're saying may be quite correct. Now it remains for you to tell me: What will the Issue be? Or to put it more clearly, What machinery will they use to hang a rope around Alphonse's neck? You objected when I came out with ideas of left and right but I thought it was all sufficiently clear, however ancient and vague those terms may be."

I must admit that although I had raised the question about the Issue, when he started to answer me I didn't let him go on. I didn't give him a chance to interrupt me. If somebody touches certain nervous centers, I flare up immediately and nobody can stop me. I even gesture effectively. Now I hammered the air with my fists, as if to nail each word down firmly: "It was all clear from the moment you instinctively assigned the left side to Alphonse, while everybody's visceral feeling is that people like Chuck and Pickford represent those opposed to him. And these are the kind of people who are perfectly capable of telling me, winking and smiling, that the heroes and protagonists of some of the defunct European regimes were not all bad . . . pity, however . . . nevertheless . . . in retrospect . . . this and that, et cetera, et cetera."

Blatt was probably about to open his mouth and utter something like what's-this-all-got-to-do-with-it, but my peroration was going on. "Let it be very clear, Blatt"—I felt my cheeks getting red—"that anything smelling even vaguely of those defunct Regimes, under which I undeniably lived and functioned in my youth, gives me total physical and metaphysical nausea, will always be opposed by me systematically, absolutely, down to the slightest detail."

My conversation with Blatt remained more or less suspended at this point. I remember that I left for home immediately and went to bed with a feeling of panic, usually a prelude to insomnia. But I fell asleep rather quickly and dreamed of Di Gaetano, my former publisher boss. Actually this significant figure in my dream was not only Di Gaetano—at some point it became Professor Ceroni as well; I talked, listening to myself as if I were a third person. "You may conduct yourself whichever way you want," this Gilberto Rossi was saying to this Di Gaetano-Ceroni, "but remember that I, for one, as far as my life under the defunct Regime is concerned, am ashamed about everything. I assume the weight of this shame. And I wish to do all I can in order not to see it repeated in my lifetime."

"You are naïve."

"But of course. That suits me. Look—I'm naïve."

"The usual Rossi, the usual Rossi."

The wave of oneiric eloquence was carrying me on its crest. "Now I understand why I left your firm. First of all, of course, I left it because I'm not a masochist. In the past thirty or forty years there has been a whole lot of masochistic literature showing the little employee oppressed by a devouring Boss. It doesn't concern me. But what is more important, what really embraces the whole situation, is that between you and me there was, at bottom, this grave moral contrast. And permit me to add that all of you have made the mistake of considering me a little man. You've exploited my restraint, style, good taste. 'Oh, Gilberto Rossi—that's the one who keeps brooding over everything: the Regime, the Era, the faucet that doesn't work, the generals in the Great War, this and that.' Well, I want to tell you something: brooding over things means being a man, existing. And it means acting accordingly, in one's own small way, which must always be one's maximum way, whether a man of culture, or an electrician, or a publisher, farmer, mechanic, teacher, industrialist, policeman, senator, assistant director, doctor, actor—but *not* a priest, since in the conduct of political and administrative affairs the supernatural should not be brought into the picture, that's too convenient."

I was awakened by a rather frightful remark from my interlocutor: "Please tell me, then, why did you come back to work for me?" I was already awake and saw that I had not gone back to work for him.

So, the first time, Blatt did not reveal all his notions about the coming struggle for power at the Institute but there were many later occasions, created and used by him with ability, lucidity, kindness. Blatt let me blow off steam, in fact looking at me with a sympathetic little smile; then in the following weeks he took me on rides along the coast toward the north, and it was on such occasions that our dialogue and friendship began to solidify.

For the first time in my life I saw trees stunningly deformed by the wind, silhouetted against stretches of white beach and the ocean; these places appeared solitary and wild inasmuch as all the houses, made of wood, primitively and solidly structured, the timber painted in beautiful dark colors, were concealed among trees thousands of years old; some of the houses were perched on steep ground among precipices, with narrow and bubbling creeks running nearby and reaching the ocean through hidden ways. In the ocean there were remnants of shipwrecks, seals, sharks, occasionally even a whale.

It is the most beautiful spot in the world, and Blatt was born somewhere around there. His family lived originally in Pennsylvania, but his grandfather's generation had settled here. Especially after his divorce, Blatt had got into the habit of coming back often to this place, where his mother lived. She was still an energetic woman, though hampered in her movements by old age, but she was not afraid to live alone in that forest. When I asked how, for example, she managed to get her food supplies, Blatt enlightened me completely by saying simply, "The mailman brings her meat." She would prepare our meals, including homemade bread. Although Blatt fancies himself a good cook, his mother looked on her son's efforts with contempt. I have visual recollections of those trips north, but even more so, they are olfactory: the smell of saltiness and the smell of wood, fused by the smell of fog; and inside the house, smoldering embers, and meat and bacon smoke. We were indeed in the north, far from the semitropical climate of the Institute.

And all the while, Blatt gave me instructive talks. He is slightly younger than I am, yet he talked to me as to a kid brother. He claimed I was something of a fanatic, that even at the outset I would place every problem in a universal framework. I did not quite get what he meant but I let him speak on, and he was finally able to answer my question about the Issue in the struggle for power.

. . .

According to Blatt, the Issue will be presented by the anti-Alphonse opposition in the most practical and technical style possible. This style, Blatt adds typically, is apparent even from the simplest analysis of their lexicon. Example: the word "structure"; used also in the plural, as in the key phrase Renewing the Basic Organizational Structures. Again in the plural, the term is applicable also to "thought," as in the Basic Structures of Thought in Our Institute; those too must be renewed. All of this will have to be done in order to realize the idea expressed in Chuck's leitmotif: Full Use of Our Institute's Potential Resources so that it may be Functionally Integrated in the Life of the Nation and in Our Time.

Once decoded, these messages mean that the opposition wants to get rid of Alphonse and bring about a set of reforms—very undesirable changes in Blatt's view. "As you must have noticed," he says, "our Institute is conducting free research. Our idea of public service begins where that of the opposition ends, or vice versa. We exist inasmuch as we operate with a free mind, and this sense of freedom must be renewed by each of us every morning when we shave, when we confront ourselves face to face in the mirror."

"Precisely my opinion."

"Even when we accept young people who are still students at the university, for us they are already young free researchers. In a way they're guinea pigs, too, because they bring with them a reservoir of typical lexicons, and a fresh outlook on one of our research areas or another—as will be the case with this young Italian friend of yours who is due to arrive."

"I never saw him in my life. And say, you will take care of him, won't you?"

"I'm looking forward to it." Perhaps Blatt understands that I prefer to talk about it as little as possible. And that my reasons are inexpressible, or as we would put it here, pre-verbal.

"I imagine you have already guessed, from Chuck's and other people's talk," he continues, "the kind of thing they have in mind. They would like to turn the Institute into an academy, but watch out—not in the sense that we would use the word 'academy,' but rather in the sense it has when you say 'military academy.' A school to produce a corps of specialized officers, perhaps with governmental sanction. Just as there are schools for policemen or for diplomats, so this one would be a school for, let's say, propaganda officers. Specialized personnel for cultural agencies abroad, just to give an example."

"My friend Mary did some work for one of those," I mumble, not wanting to be heard. I have never talked to him about Mary, about my joys and sorrows with her.

"Generally speaking, they would like to have their say in every activity which aims—I'm using their lexicon—at Verbalizing the Image of Our Society in Our Time. Budd Rotondi has computed the recurrence of that expression, 'Our Time,' in many of their texts; he got to astronomical figures. And another thing. Their goal is not only the creation of an academy for propaganda cadets; they would be in seventh heaven if they could wrap its operations in thick veils of top secrecy . . ."

Here, because now I can see them, clear, recognizable characters on my own stage, I cry out with enthusiasm, "After all, they are madly envious of nuclear scientists and other categories of individuals chosen and processed through security filters and then living cloistered and aloof in their laboratories, far from ordinary mortals. In my junior year in school I invented—or at any rate, in conversation with myself—I started making wide use of an adjective, 'mysteriosophic,' which has proved very useful on many occasions . . ."

"Now you can imagine Alphonse's reaction." Blatt is very good at reproducing all of Alphonse's oratory, voice and gestures; although he doesn't resemble Alphonse at all—Blatt being the lean Alpine type, the other a towering mixture of solemnity and jolly-good-fellowship—at some point Blatt becomes Alphonse on stage, in the midst of a panel or a kamiri miri:

"We are attempting by all means to refine our techniques for the analysis and—why not?—for the exposure of verbal confusion and falsification; these gentlemen are actually proposing that we study new techniques for creating confusion and falsification, and on top of it, open a school for young confusionists and falsifiers. The curious thing is"—Blatt now reproduces the famous Alphonse smile with an imperceptible wink, which makes each listener feel singled out, even in an audience of a thousand—"that in making such proposals they use the lexicons and mannerisms of science while they're actually behaving like someone trying to convert a chemical research institute into a factory to produce weapons for chemical warfare."

"My feeling is that Alphonse will stay in the saddle," I interject.

"The others are better politicians than he is," Blatt shoots back, his head lowered. Then, raising it: "And do you want to know why they're better politicians? Because they are firmly capable of inconsistency, unshakable in their ability to contradict themselves."

"For example?"

"You have your example right there: their idea of an academy, the very definition of the word within their frame of reference. You must always remember that these people are forever preaching in favor of individual autonomy against interference from a mammoth government, and all that. On the other hand, they would be delighted if their academy for propaganda agents, and their work in general, received an official seal of approval from that very government; they already dream about trips to the capital, they look forward to memberships in important government kamiris. Apparently it doesn't even vaguely occur to them that there may be some contradiction between those aspirations and their anxieties about the individual being crushed by the state. Or take, for example, their attitude toward electronic equipment. You know very well Alphonse's position on that score: 'Electronic brains, according to the only communicable use of the verb, do not *think*. But for a varied and increasing number of functions they are wonderful, splendid, very helpful.' Generic but consequent.

"The others, however, without ever realizing it, give their simultaneous and massive support to two irreconcilable positions. On the one hand, they criticize the fact that the Institute uses computers only in a desultory, disorganized way; they'd love for us to have machines of our own instead of using those at Business Statistics. Thus, they think, we could probably obtain important financing, like industry getting government contracts, which is what Chuck wants for his military dictionary; and anyway, they are sure that that would raise our prestige wildly, putting us right into the big politico-electronic orbit.

"On the other hand, you see some of these same men look around with dismayed and threatening faces, propounding the tenet that the Individual, enslaved by the Machine, is going to the dogs. They want to monopolize everything, including Alienation and *Angst*."

Blatt's words strike me with the shock of perfect focus, of the bull's-eye: I recognize Chuck, but better yet, Louis Pickford. There are attitudes that Pickford takes when he speaks about the problems of Man in Our Time, and I mean attitudes in the physical sense, which can only be compared to a crucifixion. There he stands, his arms wide open, his neck swaying loosely in the air; that's his way to represent Anguished Man in Our Time, the Martyr of the Machine. Watching him perform that act one evening, I found myself murmuring, "He's the kind of person who would be wrong even if he were right."

Nadine, his wife, worships him, albeit with occasional matriarchal irony; she seconds him, she is continuously handing him an invigorating little dish or drink, to sustain so much intellectual & moral weight. The Pickfords are a very happy couple. They are well off, and they have an only son, slightly *grand puceau* and still covered with pimples, who at nineteen has already finished college with phenomenal grades and who is engaged to be married. I don't know why, but I often imagine that Tava, Jr., may be something like that, and I laugh bitterly to myself.

Blatt concludes epigrammatically, "They are fascinated by politico-electronic power. They are individualists and pioneers, but if some political big fish arrives from the capital and strokes them with his fins, they start purring immediately. Those are the people who will try, probably with success, to hang a rope around Alphonse's neck, as you put it."

Blatt is rather good at articulating his views on situations, with pedagogical clarity. In the months I've spent here—rather eventful months, intellectually and psychologically—I have had, besides Blatt, other useful sources of information about what is being prepared at the Institute. All of this concerns me because I belong to the intellectual immigration wave (I believe that's the expression), which means I'll probably end up a permanent employee here—provided that I can make a tolerably useful contribution to the Institute and at the same time continue to discover as best I can the reasons for my existence.

Items toward a clarification and complication of the picture have emanated from Beatrice Clinton and her milieu, including her remarkable father. With her blond round head and that air she has of a taciturn, observant girl, full of sensuality and wisdom, she had immediately made an excellent impression on me, never replaced or faded when we met subsequently. Putting down notes about her somehow brings me back to the talk of the women in my life, a talk which was nipped in the bud. Little by little I might manage to talk about all of them, with only the exception, I imagine, of Norma.

A few days after I met Beatrice, I received a note from her in fractured Italian: "Dear Professor [during the whole evening at Alphonse's she had used that title, making it sound like a slightly mocking nickname], you remember me? Can I come steal you, and we go chez my friends Epstein? 7:30 P.M. tomorrow? B. Clinton."

I insisted on following custom and went to pick her up in my Dodge; those were the days when I had just bought my second-hand car—which, by the way, continues to run well. I found Beatrice chatting with her father, who was having his dinner. He was just finishing a huge steak, very rare. An old man of the highest quality. A long time ago, when he was professor of English literature, he refused to recognize the existence of the Institute and considered it superfluous at best; to train the young for effective verbal communication, weren't English composition courses already sufficient? But later he changed his mind entirely. Clinton was born somewhere around here; however, he studied at Harvard around the end of the century. Having retired from teaching at sixty-seven, he was spellbound by Alphonse; finding himself with massive energy and very little to do, he embraced the Institute like a new fatherland. I knew he had begot Beatrice after sixty, but considering his by now venerable age, at the first kamiri miri I had expected he would have to be picked up and lowered into his chair with a crane; instead, he walked in straight and fast, casting fulminating glances all around. Stone-deaf. With a very old-fashioned hearing aid. He wore it with such authority and dash that you instantly felt that deafness was the right, heroic, picturesque thing for an old man of that caliber.

It is very difficult for me to describe the degree of fondness I can feel toward certain people. The most worthy of mankind; for a moment you think that if everybody were like them, many disasters of manifest and identifiable human origin would be avoided. If in the Institute's internal discords we ever reach the black-and-white breaking point, cards on the table, naked Issue, I know already that Clinton will be on the side which I shall consider the right one. I saw him in action at the kamiri. This kamiri had already been formed at the time of Alphonse's predecessor, Horace Buterweg, and was based on the Dialogue Principle; its slight raison d'être was to promote a Dialogue between the Institute (humanists) and the university scientists. The latter, before Clinton became chairman, had clearly shown their indifference colored with contempt. With Clinton everything changed. When the old man started to deliver sermons to them with key expressions like the Reading of the World and the Reading of Man furnished by great writers, to be favorably compared, in his view, to the interpretations of the same World & Man offered by science, the scientists would listen to him rather stupefied and also take notes.

Finally, being more extrovert, richer and surer of themselves than the humanists, they had no difficulty in swallowing their past indifference and contempt; in fact, they asked the Institute if they could borrow that remarkable old man for a series of lectures and demonstrations for science students, where Clinton would present these Readings of the World & Man offered by artists and poets. This opened a new period in Clinton's life, raising his pedagogical passion to a pitch he had never reached in his youth.

Beatrice conceals her love for him under a veil of sarcasm dictated by good taste. "He worked like a madman, he looked like an assistant standing for the first time on the firing line in the classroom. In time, his lectures became an institution; even professors attend them with their wives. At the end they ask him questions; he's too deaf to hear them clearly, so there is actually no relation between question and answer; whoever asks the question knows he's turning on the water tap of his voice again, and whatever comes out is good enough."

In Beatrice's life story there are two men besides her father who surpass all others in importance—a husband and a brother. She is divorced from the husband, and the brother is dead. Her relationship with the former is still friendly and urbane, though gradually fading, mainly because it has left no trace, such as children, or anything. The memory of her brother is still deep; he died of cancer of the throat just about the time of her divorce; Beatrice often speaks of the young man's quiet, efficient preparation for his death, once he knew that he was a terminal case. More exactly, he was a half brother. Son of old Clinton's first wife. Since his second wife, Beatrice's mother, is dead too, the aged father and the daughter of his late years, left alone, decided to live together. There is harmony and vitality in their relationship because each of the two has separate activities, friendships, memories to cultivate.

Even at the start, a relationship between a man and a woman does not necessarily grow well if the two are always by themselves. My curiosity about and attraction for Beatrice were evident in a flash the first time I found her at Alphonse's; they solidified when she brought me among her friends. She brought me to meet the Epsteins, whom I did not know at the time, although he, Harold Epstein, works partly for the Institute; to Beatrice these friends represented a normal, almost daily anchorage. Epstein is mainly a composer; at the Institute he has worked on elocution and sound values in oratory. He has also attempted original analyses of so-called exhortative music, like marches, anthems, combat songs. He doesn't live in one of the canyons but in the small town below, in a Spanish house blazing white on the outside and shaded inside, with high beamed ceilings, shiny brown tiled floors. Epstein's name is Harold not by accident but for the specific reason that his father and mother, who married very young, were both infatuated with Byron's hero.

Actually, in his youth Harold had a very scattered education; he finally settled in Paris, where he grew and developed as an artist. He lived and worked there until 1940, when he had to escape, leaving nearly everything behind; he escaped on a bicycle, with his persecutors practically on his heels. They did not manage to murder him, but they did murder some of his closest family and friends. Now here by the Pacific about twenty years later, some of those people appear in photographs, preserved intact God knows how, with their original frames and everything.

Every time you go to the Epsteins', as soon as you get out of

the car and stop in front of the small castle-style door of polished natural wood studded with iron nails, you immediately
see Harold's head framed within the small window, in the middle of the door, behind glass and wrought-iron bars. He has
large, protruding ears, the ears of a great absorber of sounds.
His sparse reddish hair is very light, almost like an infant's, on
his high, shiny pate. However vivacious or even mad his eyes
may appear, Harold's smile is always controlled by deep inner
restraint. Except that every now and then he will burst out into
roaring, deafening laughter, somewhat resembling my own for
its apparent untimeliness, but much more outgoing and propul-
sive, really liberating.

As a composer he is excellent, and he is also an important
human being; hence Beatrice's importance grew for me after I
saw her against Harold's background. *Significant datum:* I
never felt paralyzed in front of Harold or any of his relatives
and guests. The relatives are two: his wife, Natalie, whom he
married here (in Europe he had been a bachelor), and their
daughter, Sophie, thirteen, whose greatest interests in life seem
to be, first, skating, followed immediately by basketball.

The guests are usually few in number and all very close to Beatrice and to the Epsteins. I feel I have always known them,
even if I often forget their names. When I say I have no verbal
blocks in front of these people, I am not implying that when I
am with them I talk all the time—far from it. Beatrice and I
can stay all evening in a corner and listen, exchanging occasional comments between the two of us. This intensifies my relationship with Beatrice much more than if we took active part in
the conversation. And I always know that if from my corner I
opened my mouth to speak, I would do it spontaneously and
without giving it a thought. The general atmosphere may
change if, later in the evening, people like the Pickfords or the
Palmerstons arrive, because they always look as if they were
checking on the possible formation of alliances that would exclude them.

Harold Epstein's views go beyond Blatt's: according to him,
the inner struggle at the Institute is already on, in fact the re-
formers have already won from the beginning; the Institute has
already started to be an academy for propaganda technicians
employable in all areas of life in Our Time. "Do me a favor,"

Harold Epstein says, "and have a look at the histories of all those who over the years have passed one way or another through the Institute. Where do you find them? All of them correctly attired in dark suits, with beautiful well-oiled voices, each in his own way a professional verbalizer."

"What do you mean?" Beatrice asks from our corner.

"I mean that Alphonse may have thought he could turn this into a disinterested scientific institute, but the truth of the matter is something else. The men who come out of here are snapped up by industry to write brochures and beautifully streamlined phrases; others follow some politician to write his speeches or go around the world 'selling' the 'image' of the country. That is to say, they are excellent writers of literature in the sense that you attach to the latter word when you refer to reading material describing a new automobile or a new medication. And if it comes to that, where could they find more serious studies on propaganda jargon than those conducted here? You see, he agrees with me." He points to one of the friends present, a Frenchman by the name of Paul Lebournet.

Lebournet's main study area has been the Rhetorical Structures of Advertising. Primarily on his initiative, the Institute has collected whole chunks of advertising material of some of the industries from the beginning of the century to our days; that's very appetizing material for future public relations geniuses to study here.

"They come, they come," Lebournet declaims, "the way foreign spies sneak into a country, camouflaged as art-loving tourists. And they find a very efficient net of supporters among the local population. Why not? They are new men, useful, integrated in Our Time."

Lebournet writes novels; at first I thought he saw his personal refuge in literary art, so different from his work at the Institute —the way Harold, I believe, sees music. But instead, Lebournet finds that his verbal training at the Institute is very useful to him as a writer. He says he aims at what he calls the "compilation novel": "rigid, bookkeeperish, inventorial"; once he referred to what he called a "mineral novel." Who knows? At any rate, it's his problem.

One evening he read us a story presumably written according to these concepts, and it made you slobber with boredom. He is working on a huge novel which he will entitle *The Perimeter of Things*. Extremely likable man. Thirty-two, with a beautiful nineteenth-century beard, he already has his tenure. Married to an American girl from the South, a very affectionate and soft little pigeon who nevertheless has borne him four children, each one an absolute beauty. He is very affectionate at home, yet he goes on writing his hard, hostile stories.

"At the Institute the struggle for power has been going on for some time," he says in a hard, "mineral" tone, though smiling and sensuously caressing his beard, "and before it's concluded we may see blood."

I could go on describing Harold's entourage for hours, but instead I'll concentrate on Beatrice Clinton, as I said I would. She is a woman you become deeply fond of, and the reasons for this are mainly egocentric: you find it easy to talk to her about yourself and about your difficulties in life. From our very first encounters I let myself go considerably in that direction, without reticence or even awareness, mentioning also minute facts, seemingly stupid but very important to me, such as the upsetting irritation somebody like Fiorenzo Bocca can cause me (the man who makes faucets), or the shock I can experience in front of a newsdealer who instead of attuning himself interestedly to my talk, breaks in and asks bluntly, "Well, which paper do you want?" Any example will do; to me, everything goes down to the root of human relations.

I had no difficulty in also telling Beatrice that sometimes I feel I am losing my balance, in the physical sense of the term. Although I am neither very tall nor very large, on occasion my movements are clumsy, and I cannot say this is a limited and episodic feeling; rather, I would say that when I experience it, it extends to my general equilibrium in the universe, in the cosmos. I feel oblique, crooked, pulled around in all directions. "Believe me, Beatrice—the great enemy in human life is the force of gravity." And she understands me instantly.

Besides, when I go through such moments, I suddenly perceive the absurdity of my physical appearance as in a revelation —of the very ingredients, taken one by one, which comprise a man. I look at myself naked in the mirror, I see the navel, the neck, teeth, hair, testicles, veins; very odd stuff, all of it. Whenever I told Mary anything like this, she would start laughing; if I insisted, she would advise me to see a doctor. (Or perhaps a psychologist, like her present lover, that Ottorino!) Beatrice, however, listened to me from the very beginning with interest and participation, smiling attentively as if she were learning something and at the same time checking on a symptomatology already known to her.

Ever since the first times we met, Beatrice judged with simple and generous casualness my most doubtful and defective accomplishments, such as the way I dance, drive a car, speak English. So it was by way of contrast that it occurred to me to mention Mary, who never showed any generosity toward my insufficiencies: "She wasn't cruel; she was, in a most placid and natural manner, intransigent."

After giving Beatrice these definitions, of course I expanded my talk about Mary. To me it was hard to imagine, I said, that they both belonged to the same country, so different were they. "But then, why should two women from the same country resemble each other? In fact, let me tell you—not even a minimum of happiness and fairness will exist in the world until 'Nationality' is in the fourteenth or fifteenth place on the list of a human being's vital statistics. Actually one hopes that in time that datum will be eliminated from the record altogether. It would be ideal if someday the Institute, which deals with words, could produce some criteria to define a man, to replace the unreal nomenclature that is now entered in the passports."

Beatrice listened, then she said soberly, "But of course."

I told Beatrice that deep down, Mary had accused me of being against her country. To that I would object: "But, Mary, don't forget that I—and, for instance, my very good friend Corso Gianfranchi—are generally considered to be exactly the opposite." Hopeless. In fact, somehow, the more I expressed my attraction for this coast, where I have finally come, the more she would shake her head to indicate that that didn't have anything to do with it. In other words, certain things, whether attractive to me or not, were her exclusive business, and my point of view was always wrong. This attitude of Mary's was synthesized in a particular look she occasionally gave me, as, for example, during a dinner in Rome to which she had me invited, on the occasion of the visit of some eminent politician from her country.

At some point she got up, tinkled a glass with her knife to attract general attention, and proposed a formal toast; her look reached me from that detached, tense, ecstatic altitude. It was as though she had been officiating at a flag-raising ceremony; and the flag—that should be clear—was not mine. She seemed happier when in turn I hurled accusations at her, saying that when she was employed by certain agencies she was doing propaganda work. "There, you see, I was right," she seemed to be saying by her rigid smile, her mouth a straight horizontal line.

It should be added that Mary was often sick, or rather, sickly. Sometimes we would spend a whole week in bed together, but it was not so much to make love as because she was sick that I stayed close to her. She drew physical comfort from me. On the other hand, she made it more and more obvious that she would never marry me; and at the very first hint that I might leave and maybe settle here, it was evident that this would make our union even more difficult for her.

"But didn't you tell me that someday you'll go back to your own country for good?" Here again, it was hopeless—rigidity, mysteriosophic secrecy. And for that matter, at the time when I was making my arrangements with Alphonse for the future, she already had her new boy friend, Ottorino.

I undoubtedly experienced an Ottorino trauma. It may be difficult now for me to reconstruct my own self as it was during those days, but I know I wandered around Rome a lot, rapidly and deliriously. The union between us had been too organic for me not to feel as if I had received a stunning blow on the head —out of phase, lost, amputated, abased.

Finally, one afternoon I found myself wandering, apparently by accident, through streets with which I was unfamiliar. Meager newspaper stands, more similar to those of roasted-chestnut vendors than to the dear little kiosks stuffed with printed matter; a milk bar; half-blind basements. Some faint recollection of early-twentieth-century luxury. Even touches of *art nouveau*. I liked the intensely urban trees. I asked myself what I was doing there, but there was no need for me to answer; the answer was already brought into focus by the question itself. I was going toward the house where Mary's boy friend lived.

Ottorino is a kind of psychologist—I believe it is called *psychotherapist*—of Italian-American extraction. He received me without any surprise. He spoke Italian with an accent somewhere between Slavic and Spanish; he referred to Mary as Maria: "I've heard s-so much about you from Maria."

One of my first impressions, if not indeed the very first, was that Mary, per se, didn't matter to him much. He was dripping with what he called his love for her.

Seated in Ottorino's enormous high-ceilinged living room, on a sofa covered with thick hairy cloth with greenish Pompeian figures printed on a dark-red background, I said, " 'Love.' I see. You're still trying to make that kind of terminology work." Following one of my usual methods—that of saying one thing and meaning another—I told him that I once met a man named Empson, one of those Americans who become obsessively European, and that he collected old TV sets. They looked antediluvian, I told him, when compared with, say, a quattrocento table. Except that in Empson's case it was just a form of superficial and conscious snobbishness; in Ottorino's, with his Love, there was full confidence in the practical applicability of his method: hence the atmosphere of pure folly. I finally realized that Ottorino was not only fatuous but also far from amusing. He was, I thought, like one of those who still wanted to make the monarchy work in Italy; and thinking of this, I shouted point-blank in his face, "Long live the king!"

He did not seem bewildered; instead, he seemed co-operative, ready to "understand the oddities" of a man like me, to excruciate me with friendship and comprehension. There was no doubt that he had taken Mary away from me. Now, however, seeing with the naked eye that I wouldn't "do anything foolish," he wanted to offer me some masculine solidarity, as from one gentleman to another. Trying to get him off this nonsense and bring our talk to the level of real human relationships and affections, I asked about Mary's liver trouble and how she was.

"Well. Moch, moch betterr." He issued this verdict in haste, to block me at once, like someone pushing a door against an undesired visitor.

"Listen, Ottorino, what do you do?" I asked him. "How do you make a living? Do you have time to be with her, money to have her cured? Do you always know who the best doctors are?"

He let his gaze weigh on me for some long moments. He must have realized that in his capacity as a successful psychotherapist he was by no means necessarily going to be taken seriously by me. Finally he said, "Gilberto, I am rrich. I can sleep wherrever I want with my monny." Sleeping evidently meant living somewhere, also living without having to work.

I caught fire and started to address him with the familiar form *tu*, as he had been doing all along: "Then you know what you should do? You know what your task is going to be? You must build your own life around Mary's life." I pointed out to him that Mary had a real aptitude for organizational high life and for public relations. To her, happiness is just such an existence.

"You will be a kind of prince consort, she is one of those women who may someday become ambassador."

Although not infrequently sickly, Mary had always been able to show exceptional energy and competence in her work. To me, that had actually been one of the reasons for her attraction. At the same time, her line of work did not interest me; if anything, I found it rather repellent. Yet precisely these feelings had made me grow ever more attached to her.

I doubt that Ottorino grasped all of this, but he must at least have grasped the essentials. And as a matter of fact, mutual acquaintances later confirmed to me that in choosing between his life and Mary's, Ottorino, as he should, gives higher priority to hers.

After my interview with Ottorino I was sick. Even as I left his house I felt all disarranged physically. I went into a bar and downed three Fernet-Brancas in a row.

Here by the Pacific, every now and then in the presence of a new object, person or landscape, I feel Mary's flag-raising look suddenly upon me. And in the same instant I feel a quick and acute bite of nostalgia for her.

I told Beatrice all of this as we drove in the evening twilight through the canyons. Mountains were already made of shadow; the bourgeois communities in the opposite valley were carpets of lights spread out toward the desert. I said, "Beatrice, I can't find a way to thank you for your patience with me."

"I wish you had arrived early enough to know Peter." Her half brother, dead of cancer. "I'm happy you and I met, anyway." She had glimmers of tears in her eyes but she spoke in a monotone, practically.

"You can imagine how I feel about it," I said, unable to contain one of my spurts of laughter. "You have a capacity for understanding which is way above normal."

One evening after such a ride we ended up at my house, still talking on and on, then kissing each other, undressing, doing all possible things to each other.

And now I come to the World Symposium project.

During the months I have spent here, Alphonse's wife, Doris, has come to see me quite often. I have never known a woman like her. I am trying to imagine Aunt Luciana as a multilingual person instead of an essentially vernacular one. People say that without Doris, the Alphonse we know would not have existed, would not have occurred. When Doris comes to my house she always brings her own practical contribution, maybe simply a light bulb to replace a dead one, a jar to keep sugar in, or she even drags along a competent and swift workingman because she has noticed that a faucet is leaking. Depending on what hour of the day it is, she prepares coffee or a drink for herself, and she sits down and talks for a while. One time she even brought me vitamin capsules.

Up to the most recent of her visits she had never mentioned Alphonse once. She knew I see him every day and get his news live. Only the last time did she speak about him; she started right away, and Alphonse remained her one and only subject for the day.

"Have you heard about the international Symposium? You haven't? Evidently Alphonse hasn't mentioned the subject even to his closest associates; he may want to give you some sort of official announcement. Apropos of this, keep the sixteenth of this month free to have dinner at our house."

My heart started galloping at once. I now realize that after those very first words I anticipated practically everything. I hardly listened to Doris, I knew already. The idea of this Symposium had immediately fallen into place within the series of facts which I have so often discussed with Blatt and the others. Doris described the future Symposium as a project of large proportions: Africans, Russians, even an Italian senator, a friend of Alphonse's, would participate. Alphonse had already sounded out various people in different countries around the world, including territories behind the Iron and Bamboo curtains.

"I'm afraid he is dreaming about the behind-Bamboo countries," I said. "And probably about the behind-Iron countries as well."

Doris took a big swallow of beer. It was six o'clock in the evening. "Don't believe Alphonse doesn't know that. But he tries, anyway. All alone. He's so big and tall, and when he goes through a period like this, it's as if he were several men in one. But there's also another way to look at this whole thing." Doris put her glass on the table with a bang. She threw herself back in her chair and crossed her arms, supporting her bosom, then lowered her head and raised her eyes, keeping them fixed on me for a while. These are all typical gestures of hers. "There's another way to look at this whole thing," she repeated. "Alphonse is the way cats are." A pause. "Cats, when they feel sick, go away and hide somewhere all alone."

Elaborating on irrelevant images is a kind of nervous tic I have. "In a way," I said, "cats are always alone. They stretch out and lick themselves, each on his own." Doris didn't pay any attention, wasn't even looking at me. I changed register, said with fervor, "And then, please, Alphonse is not sick."

She raised her eyes again. "Oh no, he's in good health. As you undoubtedly know, he had cancer of the bladder, but there are cases of complete recovery and I'm sure his is one of them. But he's having a bad time, or rather, a difficult one."

Defiantly: "You mean because there are people trying to hang a rope around his neck?" I was trembling. Anger. Feeling of responsibility, fear.

She smiled like a woman of great experience at hearing a child use a dirty word. Before answering, she collected herself for a moment to arrange appropriate and simple sentences in her mind. "I'll give you an example. Before Alphonse and I got married, we had an affair for about six or seven months. I gave relatively little thought to marriage. One morning he came to pick me up and suggested without any preamble that we go and get married. That decision didn't seem abrupt to me but perfectly obvious. Why? Because, as he put it, the organically right moment had come. As this is true about positive actions, so it is about negative ones. Now, following a decision he has made all by himself, he will gather this Symposium in order to resolve whether the organically right moment has come for him to quit." Getting up, she concluded, "Mind you, that's where his real strength lies." The last thing she said was that the two of them were going to be alone that evening and she wanted to prepare a particularly enjoyable dinner.

As soon as she left, I phoned Blatt. We talked for half an hour, then we interrupted our conversation because he came to my house and we resumed our talk. We went on talking in his car going north, to his mother's house; we reached that precipitous forest by the ocean at the break of dawn. We went on talking, and by then we already had a regular routine of keylines.

One of us would open: "At any rate, Alphonse must win."

The other would object: "If he realizes his hour has struck, he won't fight."

"Then we'll run a regular campaign for him."

"We are a research institute. If we hold a symposium, it's not going to be a party convention or an election campaign."

"It will be, in this case. In fact, from the point of view of technique, it will be subtler and more interesting than a convention or campaign because we are L & C specialists; our Symposium will be like a house which a great architect builds for his own use, or like a wedding cake which a pastry cook prepares for his own daughter's wedding."

We slept for a few hours up there, in wood-paneled rooms, with those ancient trees just outside the window. I dreamed about the President of the United States. He rushed by me in a hurry, flanked and followed by notables, but he recognized me, so that the notables—Chuck Palmerston among them—gave me friendly and encouraging smiles. The President shook my hand rapidly but vigorously: "Come and see me, Rossi, any time. Door's always open for you." I thanked him with sober dignity.

Blatt woke me up, fully equipped for our return, a soldier ready for combat. I was full of boldness and tensions. I have a nervous heart and know how to distinguish between bad and healthy palpitations. On the whole, those flutterings were healthy.

And, of course, on the sixteenth we went to Alphonse's dinner. All of the predictable people were there, including Harold and old Clinton, Lebournet and also the electronics technician, Budd Rotondi. The only really unpredicted guest—proving the

exceptional quality of the historical moment—was Horace Buterweg, who had just arrived by air in order to accept, I understand, the honorary chairmanship of the Symposium.

Buterweg came in with his son-in-law, Chuck Palmerston, on
one side, and Louis Pickford on the other. They seemed to be
supporting him, not because he is old or an invalid, but because
like some of my successful friends of the Gabriele Crocetta type,
from his demeanor and from the cadence of his step it looked as
though the materials of which he is composed were of a specific
gravity higher than normal. He pressed the thick carpet deeply
with each step; he is also slightly flatfooted. But when he shook
hands with people his manner was not detached; in fact, it was
excessively solicitous, as though implying that we were all in
danger in the same boat.

In other words, the difference between a Crocetta and Buterweg is that when you meet the Crocetta type, he manages to put
a glimmer of slyness and conspiracy in his eyes, but the Buterweg look is completely different: it is the ingenuous, yet demo-
niac look of the professional Anguished Man in Our Time.

Through the whole evening his two supporters hung on his
words, repeating and divulging his sentences as soon as he emitted them, doing a sort of simultaneous vulgarization. He drank
a great deal, but even when his sentences lacked coherence, he
maintained an oracular tone in uttering them.

Alphonse talked a good deal; his bravura at mixing themes
reached new peaks; at the end of the evening everyone had captured the image of this coming international Symposium but
would have been unable to analyze at what moment Alphonse
had transmitted it. Also, everyone had the impression of being
the first to partake of a secret and to be engaged in an exciting
operation. He concluded by giving portable definitions, as
though he were handing out prefabricated mimeographed notes
to his listeners. "The Symposium," he seemed to be dictating,
"will have to be a review, before a qualified and participating
audience, of the present state and future plans of the Institute
—what in the lexicons of some European government classes is
referred to as 'verification.' "

At this point Chuck's exaggerated applause disconcerted us.
The first guests had hardly left and Lebournet, holding his
beard in his fist, was already saying, "He's giving his enemies

the royal treatment. All that he'll accomplish is to die with a flourish."

Alphonse had a special word for everyone. To me he said, "I count on you. You'll have to present a substantial paper."

I replied, unheard, "I won't be up to it." And that was the signal. I started counting mentally from one hundred up: one hundred and one, one hundred and two, one hundred and three . . . the way I do when, in bed toward early dawn, I realize I am still awake and I go on ticking like that in the night, in solitude.

As if he hadn't said enough, Alphonse went on, "I have news of your young friend Tava. He's just leaving. He'll stop in Paris to see his uncle Giorgio Partibon, then he'll fly here direct."

Later, in the car with Beatrice, who had been invited in the double capacity of her father's companion and mine, I talked to her for the first time about Ruggero Tava, Sr.; I tried to tell her in my bumbling way what friendship, memories mean to me. And now this boy was coming, with a whole set of ideas of his own, a stranger. I was not going to identify myself. He couldn't interest me.

But she said to me, "Gilberto, the ideas of a twenty-one-year-old are always interesting."

CHAPTER
FIVE

"Look, Ruggero, you're going to drink three quarters of this new bottle." Elena filled up her son's glass with Barolo. "Lucky you, who can drink as much as you want."

"That's not necessarily true. Each of us has a limit." Ruggero took the bottle, filled exactly one third of his mother's glass; he was an expert also at preventing the last drop from falling on the tablecloth. "By the way, Natasha has heard rumors that the doctor has forbidden you to drink."

"Heard from whom?"

Ruggero shrugged his shoulders ever so slightly, in his usual fashion.

"Bunk," his mother said. They looked at each other, suddenly quite serious. "You didn't tell me much about Kuntz. Does he suffer physically, too?"

"Excruciating pain. But then, when he feels well, he feels well. He's very happy about the way Irene plays. Irene is very fortunate."

"What about her father?"

"Enrico Fassola presumes he will have to spend some time in

prison. But Enrico's suppositions are not very exact."

"Not very exact." Elena produced a subdued howl, like a brief spurt of laughter behind closed lips.

Ruggero took a sip of wine. "This second bottle is even better than the first one."

Elena raised the glass to her lips, smelled the wine, put the glass down. To concentrate on her son, she pressed her elbows on the table, her fists on her cheeks.

Ruggero pointed to his mother's glass, one-third full: "For you as for everybody else, it isn't good to drink beyond your limit. But this side of the line, it's not only good, it's *very* good. Each of us has a limit, a line of demarcation."

Elena sighed. "Ruggero, I must have told you this many times: you can be a crushing bore."

Her son smiled happily; Elena was perhaps the person in the world with whom he felt most comfortable. "Yes, you've told me that many times." He raised his glass; his mother did the same. Both drank bottoms up and replaced their glasses on the table simultaneously. They remained immobile, looking at each other.

When her son made a motion, Elena grabbed his hand across the table: "Keep still. Right now you look exactly like your father."

"Too bad I don't have a mirror."

"When you're like this, a bit flushed and glowing from wine, or from the cold, you're identical."

"He was taller, though."

"Yes, but now you're sitting and it's not noticeable."

"Actually, I have short legs."

"Crooked rather than short, like mine."

"And then there are other differences."

"Between you and your father? You're more intelligent. And then, you were still a baby, or rather—no, a 'baby' would really mean one who doesn't talk yet, whereas you have always talked, and without making any mistakes, that's your oppressive side— anyway, up to the age of three or four you lived in a period of blackouts, and rationing, and every now and then bombs, but somehow, all of this must have made you immune. I mean, your father had an unhappy childhood and you didn't, in spite of the fact that he grew up in peacetime."

"In my case, it was a matter of your succeeding. He had become an orphan very early."

"His mother wouldn't have mattered, anyway. She was a sick woman who wouldn't have mattered. True, I'm sick too, but that's different."

"You have terrific stamina."

"At one point my stamina came from you."

"At one point? What point?"

"The moment you were born, obviously, the moment you had begun to exist, while your father was already dead, no longer there, nonexistent. And remember, his existence was more important to me than any other has ever been in my whole life. When he and I were together, the whole history of Venice became insignificant, or at least, whatever was significant in it had the two of us as protagonists. Even you become insignificant by comparison. But when a person ceases to exist . . . Even speaking of sorrow, of suffering, is ridiculous. There's the void, and it has to be filled, and you were there to do that, with facts, with precise, concrete objects. Food. Woolens for a winter without heating. And then, when you were one year old, you got enteritis. I restored you to health. In those days I was hard, heavy, an animal. And very efficient as a nurse. But you knew that, didn't you?"

"Yes, yes, I had all of those facts, but now that I'm leaving, it seems as if you all want to give me a sort of recapitulation. Enrico Fassola too. Only, I prevented him from lingering on the story of his love for you, an area he has already covered too often. I realize now that there is some analogy between Enrico's story and what you say about yourself and my father. In the case of Enrico too, as far as I could grasp, his relationship with you seemed more important than what you might call public affairs, historical events. There are relevant differences in detail but the general analogy is there."

"The general analogy." Having uttered this characteristic phrase, her son just stopped, looking serious but with his face radiating naïve contentment; courteous, natural, never pompous; with such complete self-assurance that it wasn't even noticeable any more. Elena found him attractive and ridiculous at the same time; she would have liked to shake him, hug him, pinch him. She did not feel tenderness but rather something stronger, a kind of carnal pride. She concluded, "At any rate, when you're like this, you resemble your father a lot." Then she changed the subject: "By the way, that Gilberto Rossi you mentioned—I believe he and your father were friends. Classmates. They must have seen each other, particularly during the time when your father and we were not on speaking terms."

" 'We' means who?"

"I and your Uncle Giorgio. Adolescents. As you know, your Uncle Giuliano is several years older than Giorgio, and in adolescence that kind of difference in age is very important. I and Giorgio were a pair; in fact, a lot of people used to say that there was incestuous love between us."

"I already have all of that. Only, I didn't know about my father and Gilberto Rossi."

"There you see, even you discover something you didn't know. Have you written to him?"

"To whom?"

"To Gilberto Rossi, to tell him you too are going to be at that place—what's the name of it?"

"No, I didn't write. Why should I write?"

"Correct. I'm sure if someday by accident I should meet Gilberto Rossi here in the street in Venice, I wouldn't even speak to him. You know how it is, especially in Venice, and most especially if you haven't lived here all the time. Somebody you haven't seen in twenty years you meet all of a sudden face to face—many streets are so narrow—and you immediately realize that it would be far too complicated to start explaining, reminiscing. Maybe you exchange smiles and that's all. At least that's the way I feel in my relationships with people."

"Really?" It never occurred to Ruggero to describe what his relationships with people were like. He poured a little wine into his mother's glass, much into his own. So they finished the bottle, in the exact proportions Ruggero had established, looking at each other with vague toasting gestures.

From St. Mark's they walked home arm in arm, close together, through San Stefano and across the Academy Bridge. There was fog on the Giudecca Canal and all was still. In the night they saw shadows of the huge boats that carried timber. For some time, for reasons of economy, Elena had arranged to live with her parents in an apartment which some friends, the

Krauses, rented out to them for a nominal figure. When Ruggero was in Venice he slept there too, on a sofa bed in the living room.

As they entered the apartment they found Paolo Partibon's wheelchair in the foyer. Ruggero observed, "Grandfather showed everybody to the door, then he went back to his room on foot." He made his mother sit in the wheelchair; coasting and curving nimbly among the furniture, he piloted her to her room, where he left her. "You go to bed. I'll go and pack, so I'll have everything ready tomorrow morning."

Returning to her room after a while, he found her in bed, a lamp lit above her head, above her thin hair the color of copper mixed with gray. She wore glasses with bluish lenses. Propped up by the pillows, she held a closed book in her hands, which rested on her lap. She was very pale and seemed extremely tired; through her half-open mouth her breathing was rapid and shallow. She looked for a long while at her son, with love and irony, then spoke as if ending a conversation: "The Barolo was very good, though."

Those were Elena Partibon's last words to her son before his flight to the Pacific. Actually, she had already asked him during the evening, in case she were asleep the next morning, not to wake her up for a last repetitious farewell.

No relatives but all of the Camentinis accompanied Ruggero to Marco Polo Airport on the Venetian mainland near the Lagoon marshes; he had discarded the idea of driving to Paris with the young Camentinis, in spite of their promise that they would let him take the wheel; so all they could do was accompany him to the airport in the motorboat belonging to Giovanni Camentini.

Giovanni himself was at the helm, with Ruggero sitting next to him; his brother, Piero, was in the cabin behind, with Silvio and Riccardo, their sons. The three of them sat in silence, visibly looking like blood relations, with very black, strong hair, clear skin, square faces and shoulders. Through the little glass door they followed every movement of their friend Ruggero, who appeared to them in profile; every now and then Ruggero was exchanging a few words with Giovanni, watching him steer, or else he would cast photographic glances around: he was going so far away, for such a long time.

They had coasted along the Zattere up to the water terminal, where, on the stone pavement of Venice, among old houses, automobiles are first encountered; from here, passing close to huge cranes and large ships that had arrived from Odessa, from Hong Kong, through new and old canals they had come out into the open lagoon.

As they were speeding over the Lagoon waters, the noise of the motor was deafening; Giovanni Camentini surpassed it with the sound of his own voice, shouting at Ruggero, "You'll see wonderful stuff in America. Bring me some ideas!" He was a man who wanted to keep well informed; through foreign magazines he followed the development of modern techniques in the areas that were most essential to him, such as market research and public relations. He had sent his son to an American university for a couple of months the previous summer. "Riccardo has seen a lot, but you are more accomplished."

"No, Giovanni, I'm not as specialized as he is."

"All right, but you are more accomplished; just think of the languages you know!"

Ruggero had heard similar statements from Piero, but coming from Giovanni, they seemed less empty. Though only three years younger than his literary brother, Giovanni Camentini looked almost as if he were Piero's son; his black eyes were still mobile and possessive; his lips tensed into something between a smile and the set grin of a runner, exposing small, perfect, cutting incisors. Rather than softening up, he had become harder through the years. He had kept his small mustache, lone concession to the memory of the conquering, musketeering male he had been in his youth.

For Ruggero the image of the youthful years of a man like Giovanni Camentini existed only as he had pictured it from tradition and legend; so he knew there had been times when men were able to look at women from the point of view of conquerors and collectors. Just as there had been the wits, raconteurs and quotable-phrase makers like the Massentis and Paleonas of *Milano Sabato,* so there had been sex athletes, the superdecorated champions of copulation, the technical experts at an activity which in those distant days must have been regarded as heroically sinful.

At twenty-seven, during an interval between military drafts, in a time of historical calamities, Giovanni Camentini had, in the fullness of his virile élan, descended upon the lands of the confectioners who had taken refuge at Visnago; here were the country estates of those people who, in Venice, exercised an art traceable perhaps to the twelfth century, the production of crystalline delicacies to be licked and sucked, an art destined to be transformed, with the passing of time, into a mass industry. Thanks to the acclaimed genuineness of the fruit essences employed, and the transparent beauty of the product, the future father-in-law of Giovanni Camentini had been able to merge the riches of the Venetian countryside with those of a city famous for its arts and its savoir-vivre. His mints were sublime. So much so that the local phrase makers, speaking of the old head of the candy factory, known for his illiteracy and for the simplicity of his mind, had played on the double meaning of *mente,* "mints" and "mind," and coined the phrase which had become proverbial: "That man, what *mente!*"

And he, Giovanni Camentini, known even in the anatomical sense as a man of singularly comely and ample means, had descended on those lands and on the freshest fruit of that genealogical tree, catapulted, launched missilelike by the very force of two syllables which had a vaguely Chinese flavor: *screw-ing.*

What is, Giovanni boy, your life occupation?
Screwing.

Those years of irresponsible ardor were long past; he was the chief candymaker, devoted to his duties, alert to the mutations of taste and to the new ideas of his competitors, his products widely distributed in foreign markets. *Giovanni B. Camentini, rio terrà Barba Frutarol, Venezia (Italy)*. His new private residence was the main floor of a cinquecento palace on the Grand Canal.

He was never tired, and he considered himself one of the most adroit men of his generation. Now accompanying Ruggero to the airport, he was steering the boat as an outlet for his always overflowing energy. And then, he loved to be surrounded by young people, but unlike his brother, not to satisfy some frustrated paternal urge, but because he felt, as he himself

[*166*]

would put it in the most elementary terms, that the future belonged to the young. Wounded, and later a prisoner of war in North Africa in the early forties, he had become, completely and forever, a pacifist; he was convinced that through his work he had contributed to social progress; higher standards of living had paralleled the spreading of his products to increasingly wider segments of the population; within these terms Giovanni Camentini visualized and grasped the sense of contemporary Italian history.

If he cast a glance at past history, then the Venetian in him would appear behind the Italian. From his historical angle, for instance, some Oriental threads in the texture of the Venetian Republic had contributed, on the level of taste, intriguingly perfumed sherbets and fruit ice creams; even the Austrian domination, which lasted for practically two thirds of the nineteenth century, had left a positive trace in making Venice sensitive toward *Mitteleuropa,* or more particularly toward certain simple, yet refined sweets, based on two elementary ingredients, flour and butter. The two areas for which Camentini now envisaged major developments in his industry were ice cream and a line of mass-produced and frozen cakes and tarts.

Good-bye, then, to the limited area of candy, sugar drops, mints. Giovanni's father-in-law, especially during his last years of arteriosclerotic fits of temper, had promised that if anyone ever mentioned *mente* to him with a certain little smile, he would slap his face till it swelled up, and kick his ass wide open, but Giovanni would have been perfectly willing to have a mint leaf engraved on his letterhead, in the same spirit as a builder of supersonic jets would keep a model on his desk of the first piston engine produced by his factory.

Giovanni's dialogue with Ruggero consisted of short phrases transmitted over the roar of water and wind around the speeding boat. He repeatedly urged Ruggero to bring back—or better yet, send him—all the literature he could find on the subject of frozen pastry.

In the past he had availed himself of the young man's collaboration in even more substantial ways. When Giovanni started thinking about expanding into new production areas, Ruggero had, with Riccardo at his side, prepared a series of slogans for him and even a plan for a suitable advertising campaign, including some suggestions for a possible television commercial. After the two young men punctually delivered the plastic-covered typescript, Giovanni shut himself in his study, and there in the silvery, water light that came through the cinquecento windows, he started to read those pages drafted in an impeccably lucid style, and he later reread them several times with increasingly warm interest.

That same evening he took the two young men to the country in his Jaguar to eat in a fish *trattoria* on the Romea Road. Over *scampi* and broiled sea bass he punctuated his speech the whole evening with the phrase "Boys, I swear, you've surprised me."

Ruggero had surprised him on earlier occasions, too. Even the boy's first appearance in his home, introduced at sixteen by Giovanni's son and nephew, turned out to be a surprise, so different was he from what Giovanni had expected. Ruggero's visit had been preceded by his considerable fame as a precocious boy who had spent a long time in England, and there he was now, looking like a serene, sly pussycat, with a quick mind and an affinity for practical jokes, by no means first in his class, a big eater. He and Giovanni were immediately on first-name terms, and theirs was not the nephew-uncle kind of relationship that boys often establish with their fathers' old schoolmates; Ruggero, for that matter, had never had a father; theirs, Giovanni had always felt, was a man-to-man rapport.

To put him to a test, Camentini had asked Ruggero once to act as his interpreter in a business call to England. After getting the essential data on the situation, Ruggero did not even turn to Giovanni again; he conducted the telephone conversation without further help while Giovanni listened, now and then nodding his astonished approval. At the end, after saying good-bye to his distant party, Ruggero handed the receiver to Giovanni, who took it as if hypnotized and hung up without taking his eyes off Ruggero, murmuring, "Damn good, damn good."

He would have liked to cultivate Ruggero as a future permanent aide but the young man was hard to keep up with; he never stayed put in Venice. One evening at dinnertime, new surprise: Ruggero on the phone. Giovanni had said to the maid, "But didn't you tell him that my son isn't in?" He and his wife were having dinner alone. The maid explained that the call was for him, Giovanni. He dried his lips with the napkin, and rising to go to the telephone, he had cast a pleased, intrigued glance at his wife, which failed to register on her.

Ruggero, calling from Rome, told him that during a protest demonstration conducted by young people, he had been arrested. He was among those who had soon been released, so, he added, in his case the proper term would be "detention" rather than "arrest."

"Screw proper terms, go ahead, tell me." But since there was a short pause at the other end, Giovanni pressed on, "Where are you? Do you need anything?" Meanwhile he was trying to gain some sort of perspective; he vaguely recalled that Piero, who followed such events, had told him about large youth manifestations with police intervention and everything, fights, people wounded, chaos; Piero had spoken at length, finally coming to expressions such as "engagement," "dissent," "generation gap," and now Giovanni was sorry that as usual, he had not listened to his brother when he was talking like that. Somewhat at random he asked, "These demonstrations are fomented by outside individuals of the extreme left, aren't they?"

"Is that your hypothesis?" Ruggero asked from Rome. "Or did you get it from the newspaper? Anyway, I doubt its validity. Here I am, an outsider, and I have been released, while others, who live here, have been booked. There is a Venetian friend of mine among them who studies biochemistry here, Ugo Momo."

"I know him, fellow with a beard; if they booked him he must have a record."

"Right. Exactly. And I'm coming to the reason for my call: if I remember correctly, you have a lawyer here in Rome."

"But did you call Fontana or Fassola?"

"Useless complication. Maybe Enrico would rush down here; you know how he adores my mother. Nor would I call my grandfather's house; they wouldn't even listen, they would do the talking. I thought of you as the right source of information. What's your lawyer's name and could you please give me his phone number?"

"Trinchieri. From Venice. I'll call him immediately. Then I'll call you back. Where can I reach you?"

"No, no, you give me the address and phone number. Or rather, I'll look him up in the phone book. What's Trinchieri's first name?"

"Angelo Maria—but wait, let me see, let me organize my thoughts. You never seemed to be that kind of young man at all. What did you have to do with—things . . . demonstrations? Are those your ideas too?"

"What ideas?"

There was a brief silence at the Venice end. Camentini was looking for the right words but for him it was like chewing air.

Meanwhile from Rome there came a simple "Thanks for the information, Giovanni, see you soon," followed by the click of the line being cut off. Back at the dinner table, he told his wife, "Nothing—he just wanted an address."

He had come back to the subject that night in bed. Speaking to his wife was like speaking out loud to himself to recapitulate his thoughts. It was already past midnight when he suddenly began to say, "Well, I know him, I regard him highly, I would be glad to have him work for me, but if they told me, 'He's a subversive, he has a cache of arms at home,' I wouldn't be able to reply, 'That's impossible, I refuse to believe it.' "

Propped up against her pillow, without taking her eyes away from the ladies' magazine she was reading, his wife said, somewhat dolefully, "Ruggero is so handsome. Not as handsome as his uncles, though. His uncles—mmm, such handsome men!"

Seeing the young man in Venice sometime later, and realizing that he wouldn't broach the subject himself, Giovanni finally asked him, "By the way, did you call Trinchieri?"

"Oh yes, he's awfully good, thanks again," Ruggero replied. Since Giovanni seemed a bit disappointed, Ruggero added, "He was very helpful to my friend Momo, and as you can understand, he may become helpful to me too if similar situations should develop, now that I have a police record. The next time they might book me too. Don't you think?" Judging from his tone, he could have been speaking of a dentist ("Excellent work, my molar doesn't bother me at all now, but if the filling should come out again, he might have to put on a crown") .

After a second bottle of dry Tokay that evening of their dinner on the Romea Road and of his enthusiasm over the advertising plan, Giovanni reverted subtly to the subject, or so he thought: "You're a practical young man, Ruggero, well organized, you're a smart fellow. You would do well to apply these assets to the right objectives. Are you asking me what objectives?" The young man, though attentive, did not open his mouth. Giovanni tapped the presentation with the back of his hand. "To build, Ruggero, to realize, to produce. I have never envied anybody in my life, but do you want to know what I must confess? There are moments when I would like to be you."

"What moments?"

Giovanni did not find a ready answer, and Ruggero, after one of his quick, nearly invisible shrugs, went on to say, "Giovanni, perhaps you can provide me with a correct item of information. By way of premise, you should know that I'll probably have a chance to go to America for a certain length of time. What with my police record, do you believe I'll have difficulties with the American visa? Do you know of any precedents?"

"No, I don't"—Giovanni tried to concoct some sort of smile —"but you don't strike me as an Interpol case yet; however, I'll talk to the consul—I know him."

"Don't do it yet."

After a pensive moment Giovanni was able to say, only "So you're going to America," without being able to add, "Now that I wanted to make you some definite proposals."

Well, it wouldn't have been the right moment, anyhow. In spite of the admirable work contained in that plastic cover, Giovanni had the feeling that Ruggero couldn't have cared less about his business, or about any other business in the world. "You'll go to America and then come back and get your degree, won't you?" he asked, and got as an answer, "Oh, that." Ruggero was studying philosophy, had taken only a few examinations, perhaps someday he would write a thesis in psychology on problems of communication with a view to turning it into a book.

Giovanni had later been very busy in Venice and elsewhere, including trips to Prague and Budapest, and he lost sight of Ruggero. He had no doubt Ruggero was still "retrievable" and he planned to keep an eye on the boy; when he heard that his departure was imminent he gave a big dinner for him. It was a very festive occasion, with people even coming from out-of-town, including Irene Berlocchi, to whom the Camentinis had grown very much attached. Ruggero never again mentioned legal or bureaucratic problems, and Giovanni did not touch on them either.

Not until now, after the motorboat crossing on the morning of Ruggero's departure, did Giovanni take Ruggero aside at the last moment in the main lobby of the airport. "Well, then," he asked, "about your visa—did everything go smoothly?"

The young man answered, apparently without having listened, "Really?" A private conversation was difficult because the other Camentinis were crowding around. They all kissed Ruggero on both cheeks. The Camentinis being four, there were eight exchanges of kisses.

A couple of hours later in Paris, Ruggero left his suitcase at the airport, took the limousine to the terminal; from there he moved on foot toward the brasserie where he was to meet his Uncle Giorgio. As in Milan a few days earlier, sunshine filtered through a light haze; the air was even more pungent. He first walked by buildings some of which must formerly have been aristocratic residences and now contained ministries, embassies; today there must have been some important visitor because flags were hanging at many windows, colorful and immobile as on a stage.

He wandered through narrow streets and cobbled, irregularly shaped little squares; here café awnings with their bright colors stood out against the gray background as earlier the flags; booksellers and perfumers exhibited their glorious merchandise in small windows wearing the patina of time. All his life the young Venetian had heard from his mother and his artist grandfather that "the Paris skies," along with those of their own city, were the best in the world, so he raised his eyes to watch the present sky and its subdued silver-gray splendor behind housetops with mansard roofs and wrought-iron balconies. In the autumn air he breathed odors of dry leaves, of coffee, of cooking. He was hungry, and as he passed by an attractive little bakery he strongly felt like buying himself a long thin bread to eat on the way, but he was dissuaded by the thought that his uncle would feed him more sumptuously.

Giorgio Partibon was for the moment sitting in a wicker chair on the sidewalk in front of the brasserie; when his nephew came he got up, and after the usual exchanges of kisses on both cheeks he took Ruggero by the arm. "Come," he said, "let's go in and have some boiled meat *au gros sel.*"

The place was packed. They had to wait for a few minutes. The lamps were in the floral *art nouveau* style but with glowing electric bulbs which made the old wood panelings, the dark leather, the polished brass and the china sparkle brightly. Standing face to face, they studied each other's appearance. They were about the same height. "With that padded jacket you look like a pilot at the beginning of the century," Giorgio Partibon said.

Ruggero barely shrugged, in his usual fashion, found a passage through the crowd and went to hang the jacket on a brass peg.

His uncle followed him, took him again by the arm: "Come, we have a table." They were slipped into two seats at a small corner table. Giorgio placed his nephew on the leather seat with his back to the wall, and himself on the outside chair. They didn't take their eyes away from each other. Physically they were like father and son. They ordered two large beers immediately. Both had voices that were not high but penetrating, so the thick buzz all around did not bother them. When the huge goblets of beer arrived, they raised them, toasting each other—"This is to you!"—and after taking serveral gulps, they replaced the glasses simultaneously on the table, drawing deep sighs of well-being.

"Now, in that pullover," said the uncle, "you look like a bicycle racer. But you look all right. I wish I could. If I wear something like that, or like that jacket you wore before, I look ridiculous; besides, I've put on weight again; when my wife and the girls are here, we eat too well, they're splendid cooks, all three of them. Now they're away for a couple of weeks, at my wife's home in Italy; but I told you that yesterday over the phone. I miss them, you know. Living alone is murder. Even when it comes to such a simple matter as not having somebody you can give freewheeling talks to. Now with you as a target I can go on freewheeling for a while."

He took another large gulp of beer and smiled brightly at his nephew. "Besides," he resumed, "you're someone people always talk to a lot. It's always been said that you had an isolated

[*173*]

childhood, but that's not true. There were always people around you who talked to you a lot, especially women. But as a rule, in those days children were less isolated than we had been, even when you were very small. Perhaps in your case certain practical necessities helped, like having to hide, or spend time in air-raid shelters." The uncle paused, concentrating, staring at his glass; the waiter startled him when he put the meat in front of him. Uncle and nephew ate the first large morsels in silence. "Good, isn't it?" They also took several draughts of beer.

The uncle pointed at Ruggero and resumed, "Now they write whole libraries about this business of the generation gap. But the gap between us and our elders was even wider than it is now. Only, now there's more free time for this sort of talk, and the communication media are incomparably more extensive, so problems are much better advertised. But anybody can see that the gap between the young and their elders in our time was much larger. All sensible people that I know agree with me, more or less. Don't you?"

Ruggero murmured, "Sure . . ." He found his uncle's talk even more inconsequential and rambling than Enrico Fassola's, but perhaps that was precisely why it aroused more curiosity; besides, his uncle was working for an international agency here in Paris, so in his own way he must have gone farther than his contemporaries.

"When I used to give lectures, I got along with young people even too well. Nevertheless, I'll tell you quite frankly, Ruggero, I wouldn't want you to be my son. You would make demands that my girls don't make, and besides, they are more fun. You're amusing too, mind you; among men of your tender age I rarely find anybody as amusing as you are. You've always been, with your pre-ci-sion of lan-guage. All of us Partibons, for that matter, have always had a tendency to pour ourselves out; rather Venetian in that respect, I'd say. I can still see you in the country at the Krauses'—you can't have been more than five —standing on a chair at the window facing the garden, acting your piece all by yourself, gesticulating: " 'Zzzz . . . zzz . . . zzz . . . From the balcony of the Palladian villa of his rich friends, Ruggero Tava Partibon is conduc-ting an orchestra of mosquitoes. Zzzz . . . zzz . . . zzz . . .' They let you go on, even though you might fall out the window; they brought you up right, so you wouldn't get any complexes, and you owe that mainly to my sister, your mother. How is Elena?"

"Pretty good. I took her out to dinner last night, to a place where they have a splendid Barolo."

"Hm, Barolo?"

"Splendid. But then she got tired, so this morning when I left I barely opened her door, and I saw that she was still sleeping very soundly."

"Very soundly, hm?" Uncle and nephew just looked at each other for a while, chewing in silence. Then the uncle left the fork and knife on the plate, dried his lips: "When we were small children, your mother and I planned to get married some-day."

"I know."

"You never had any sisters. I don't envy you; it's a great experience. You have a brother, or to be more precise, a half brother, your father's legitimate son. Do you ever see him?"

"I saw him a couple of times years ago. A very heavy fellow."

"Physically, you mean?"

"I'd say in all possible ways."

"I believe his mother's family are monarchists—can you imagine?"

"Excuse me, Uncle Giorgio, there's one thing I wanted to ask you. Do you by any chance remember somebody by the name of Gilberto Rossi, a fellow who used to live in Venice, a lawyer's son?"

"Of course. Very well. He had an aunt in Portogruaro. I went there with him once. One night."

"Do you have any recent data on him?"

". . . One night. New Year's Eve, something like twenty—no, wait a minute, twenty-five years ago. It's incredible how many times I have thought of that night, and the funny thing is, I don't believe I've seen him since. Like an idiot, I had taken the wrong train, and instead of arriving in Venice, I got to Porto-gruaro; he was on that train, and he said, 'Good. So you'll spend New Year's Day with us.' Which meant at his aunt's. She was a blonde, full of vitality; incidentally, I happened to meet her here in Paris not many years ago. Her husband had just died —his name was Bartolomeo Strigato, if you care to know—and that's why she took that trip, to try to get over it. It was she who recognized me and stopped me, although in the meantime I had grown much heavier, alas, while she was exactly the same."

"How long ago? Did she tell you anything about her nephew?"

"I think she said he was working for some newspaper. No, wait, a publishing house."

"Do you know where he is now?"

"Who?"

"He, Gilberto Rossi."

"No."

"He's at that institute in America where I'm going."

"Good for him. Give him my regards. I remember him perfectly. A man with the right ideas. A man who really existed. And so, off he goes, to America. He must be the kind of man who never settled down, and this doesn't surprise me. The temporary-employee type. Like myself. Right?"

"In other words, you don't know what he does now?"

"Didn't you tell me he's at that institute? Well, they are going to hold an international conference there in the spring. I've heard this from a friend, Senator Marchesan, who is apparently going to attend. Problems of information and communication. Electronic computers used for humanistic studies. Marchesan was telling me. Didn't you know they were having this conference? There, you see, sometimes even I can give you some useful information. Incidentally, Marchesan is here now and you'll meet him today. If I wanted to, and if I put my mind to it, perhaps I too could attend functions like that—conventions, round tables, symposiums, panels."

"Do you consider conventions useful?"

"Well, sometimes. Who knows?"

"I attended three of them as an interpreter; in Venice recently, we had a convention of Scientists for Peace."

"And what are you going to do in America?"

"Besides other, more obvious things, I intend to study Chinese."

"Really."

"They're experimenting with methods for teaching languages, and it seems they want to use Chinese as a model; this will make it possible for me to start learning Chinese."

"That will keep you busy for a while."

"At what time are we going to meet your friend Marchesan?"

"Well—now, in the afternoon."

"Good, because later on I'll have to leave."

"Where are you going?"

"Well, to America."

The uncle was silent for a few moments, scrutinizing his nephew: his rosy face glowing with health; his strong, stooped shoulders contained in that tight-fitting pullover; his fist, small and round like that of a strong child, brandishing the fork. He asked, "Say, do you have your luggage with you?"

"Oh, yes, I even have two regular suits, one heavy and one light. This friend of yours, Marchesan, what does he do? What's his line of work?"

"In Italy he is a senator, which may not sound like much to you, as I have a feeling you're interested only in pure technicians. Now he's here as a member of a cultural mission."

"In Milan the other day a man called Francalancia was referring to the two or three thousand people in the world who, according to him, are 'in circulation,' and these people, he said, all know one another. Do you believe so too?"

"No. I wonder, would you be interested in some *tarte aux pommes?*"

"Why not?"

"I want you to have some so I can sit here and look at you while I consciously and rationally perform an act of abstinence."

The apple tart came and Ruggero attacked it with gusto; then came the coffee and Uncle Giorgio got lost in his thoughts; Ruggero's words woke him up: "Mother says that Gilberto Rossi was a friend of my father's."

"That I don't remember."

"Perhaps it isn't true. My mother is not the most reliable of sources."

Now Giorgio Partibon was silent for a long while. There were moments, Ruggero knew, when his uncle, with shadows of despair in his eyes gazing into empty space, would distort his mouth in a wide, quick grimace, as if he were going to yell, to laugh madly, or to break into sobs. Ruggero observed these facial crises as if he had been following the preparation for a sneeze. This time, too, his uncle's face recomposed itself very

[*177*]

soon without exploding. When he talked he had that vaguely last-will manner to which Ruggero had grown accustomed after other farewells in the last few days: "Your father was my best friend and he was the person who least deserved to end the way he did. Courage, a sense of duty, a happy disposition—all of this wasted. We, the survivors, will never forget him."

A heavy silence followed. Ruggero put in, as if checking on a piece of information, "Enrico Fassola says you are the men of 1945."

"You say that as if you were giving me a phone number."

Ruggero tried gain: "Judging from some brochures that Irene got, one of the subjects they deal with at the institute I'm going to is war. In fact, as specimens for their studies in communication, they use many texts which have to do with war."

Now the uncle was silent even longer, then he sighed heavily and resumed, "A friend of mine, by the name of Venturini, who is the district doctor in a village near Corniano, has all his life been repeating this phrase: 'We tend to forget, although we should always remember, that the dead are all dead—each, one by one, dead.' He used to say this after the Great War, the first. After '45, he added, 'It looks like a simple idea, but try to apply it to the second war too.' For one thing, Venturini has a kind of fixation about war cemeteries, ceremonies, wreaths, monuments, and there I don't follow him, but I quite agree that an idea like 'all dead, one by one' isn't simple. In fact, it's enormously complicated. Don't you think so? Am I right?"

As his nephew didn't react, he nodded to himself: "Quantities of naked corpses, thin, but thin in some unreal, crazy way, left there in a heap like spaghetti in the refuse. After this happened, I know, the human race should have finished, at the very least. But it didn't. I'll admit this may be worse, but there you are." He interrupted himself, watching Ruggero's eyes, clear and well-intentioned but obviously uninvolved; he added casually, "I suppose you've never even seen a dead human being."

After another long pause he went on, "So? Men of '45? When we were boys, Enrico Fassola and I were what you might call intimate enemies. Now we sometimes call each other on the phone on Sundays, when rates are lower, and we talk a little bit . . . about what we have done with our lives. He says he feels younger now than he did then. Same with Ovidio, his brother-in-law, his sister's husband, who has his university chair in modern history and everything. Frankly, I don't feel I'm any particular age. And I have no chairs. I have given numerous lectures, even in rather prestigious places, but nothing on a permanent basis. And in order to raise my girls I've done a variety of other things, lots of translations, for instance, newspaper correspondence, historical narratives for picture magazines, et cetera—but you know all that. My books, like *Psychology of the Political Act,* which you haven't read, never brought me one lira, but I want to tell you, that book was read by quite a few of the right people; what do you think of that? Some pages on the concept of 'nation' were already in my mind when I was seventeen, and perhaps you feel that, when you read them: youthful naïveté.

"At the time when I met your Gilberto Rossi I avoided even mentioning countries by name, so repulsive was nationalism to me; I thought of the war, which was then imminent, as of a civil war on the international level; you'll call me a deceived fool, or rather, you won't call me anything, because you don't quite follow me. At any rate, I was rather consistent later on. I remember that once you were talking about the people of previous generations and you divided them into categories; well, among your categories don't forget those who are consistent, they are the most scatterbrained of all, unfit for a political career, and as a matter of fact, my own was nipped in the bud. Right after the war I was on my city's municipal council, and later, when I ran for mayor of Venice, I didn't even—to put it in sports language—reach the semifinals; I was eliminated earlier. That was the time when I met my wife, the happiest time of my life. A man must start out with the idea of giving a certain importance to his life; hence it's quite clear that seeking public success would be fatal. I hope you have already understood me on this point and that you will act accordingly. I wouldn't like you to be my son, as I said before, but whenever we've met, especially since you were in your teens, I have tried to be educationally useful to you. In so doing, I, who began my career as a historian, did not insist on forcing large historical perspectives on you, as you may have noticed—or if you didn't, I'll have you notice it now; I'm convinced that you must find them by yourselves, as we did in our time. Rather than public events, I tried to put some private citizens into proper focus for you, even members of your own family, like myself, my father . . ." He stopped because he had seen their waiter and signaled for the check.

Ruggero took advantage of the brief pause to say, "Grandfather is an extremely agreeable man."

"Your grandfather was a painter by profession, so until we were old enough to take care of ourselves, he brought us up by the strokes of his brush. Creativity and common sense. A family who have never stepped on anybody's toes, whereas their toes have been stepped on rather frequently."

The check came, and while Giovanni waited for the change, he resumed, "Their toes, and sometimes their whole legs. You know, don't you, why your Uncle Giuliano walks with a limp?"

"They tortured him, didn't they?"

"When they arrested Giuliano some stupid idiot—a man from Corniano, incidentally—kicked him violently in the shins, rather than torture him in the technical sense of the word, and by this elementary method managed to break his leg. You can imagine what kind of medical attention Giuliano got after that, so he is not only lame, he occasionally also feels acute pain. Besides, from the blows he got on the head, his ear trouble got worse, so at this point he is completely deaf in the left ear. He can hear quite well with the other, though. But Giuliano will always be a Partibon, and you know what our public image is, and if you don't, I'll tell you now: privileged people, who hold themselves untainted by life; snobs; aristocrats; perhaps even quite well off. Now, really! Giuliano, who has never been particularly smart, is an accountant in a glass factory. I struggle along here. At any rate, I assure you my work is without any governmental sanction—any government's. I have a feeling that the Italian officials I know would encourage me if I wanted to get into that kind of circulation, but I tell them I am totally outside national patterns; they think I'm being facetious, whereas substantially it happens to be not only the truth but also precisely what I dreamed I would someday be able to say, practically from the time when I was a child. When I was a candidate in the municipal elections they must have seen through me at once, and flunked me even before I opened my mouth. All the same, I won't deny that I always go to Venice to vote, taking advantage also of the customary railroad discounts."

[*180*]

"Good for you, Uncle Giorgio. And I always check with Irene and Natasha, and with the Camentinis, to be sure that they go to the polls."

"I go because it interests me, and I tell you, during election time here in France I go insane because I can't vote. You wouldn't even need to vote in order to be considered a well-adjusted, integrated young man. I have the impression you'll be the first in our family to be acknowledged as such. But at this point I sound the alarm: You mustn't get confused. Arrange your own life with the utmost care. Anybody who doesn't feel intensely about his personal life doesn't feel intensely about historical life, either. I mention this to you just in passing. Perhaps historical life doesn't mean much to you. But take my advice: build up a system of supports, of attachments, for yourself. Don't end up like Enrico Fassola, who is still alone. I would have gone mad if I hadn't had my wife and the girls."

"However, Enrico is going through a period of euphoria. At any rate, I wanted to marry Irene but she didn't think it was such a good idea."

"Well, if she doesn't want to, stop thinking about it. Did you go to bed with her?"

"Yes."

"Didn't you satisfy her?"

"I thought I did."

"It may be that the physical side doesn't interest her, or it may be that she wants something other than what you did to her. How old are you?" The uncle picked up some of the change the waiter had brought; he got up.

"Twenty-one."

"There, you see? You still have time. You've always been considered a precocious boy, but I continue to consider you immature for your age."

The European Center for Cultural and Technical Exchange, where his uncle held temporary employment, was a new eight-story building, the size of a ministry or of the huge brain of a large industrial plant. There was a constant stream of people in and out through high glass doors, like the entrance to an airport or a movie theater. In the ground-floor lobby, facing the entrance, two telephone receptionists were sitting some distance apart behind a long desk—one French-, the other English-speaking. There were showcases all around, containing Center publications in a large assortment of languages.

Visitors waiting to be received in one of the building's numerous offices sat on chairs and sofas covered with a light-colored plastic material, or else wandered aimlessly among the showcases; judging from their attire, many of them seemed to belong to colorful African and Oriental nationalities; this, too, contributed to the airport atmosphere.

Uncle and nephew went up to one of the receptionists; she seemed to know Giorgio Partibon, yet she channeled her attention toward Ruggero, and after a moment she seemed to get along with him much better than with his uncle. She said she hadn't seen Monsieur Marchesan arrive or any other member of the commission to which Monsieur belonged.

"Well, then," Giorgio said, "we'll go up to my office in the meantime."

There was a row of elevator doors with red lamps, lighted arrows, soft bells, announcing arrivals and departures. These were large American-type elevators, usually known to Europeans only in hospitals. Uncle and nephew embarked with another dozen people of great linguistic variety. Ruggero felt comfortable in that huge building full of efficiency. In the elevator going up, his uncle shook hands and exchanged bows and amenities with a pleasant, lively young mulatto in a tweed jacket; he got off at the fifth floor after saying good-bye in Spanish to Giorgio and even more affably to Ruggero. "Poet from Haiti," Giorgio informed his nephew.

The two of them got off at the seventh floor and walked along a corridor without any visible end; there were doors on both sides, and in the spaces between them, great quantities of books, newspapers and mimeographed material on shelves, in display windows or piled up on top of long tables. On a door to the right GIORGIO PARTIBON was typewritten on a card, along with two other names.

Ruggero stepped into the office first and cheerfully greeted the only person who was there, sitting behind one of the three desks: a colored lady of subdued elegance, with silvery hair and silver-framed glasses whose lenses for hypermetropia immeasurably magnified her intelligent and melancholy eyes. Both from his uncle and from the lady herself, Ruggero learned that she dealt with the problems of *l'Afrique francophone;* she handed him several little volumes so that he might spend his time reading while his uncle looked through his mail and other papers on his desk.

Seated opposite his uncle, Ruggero was soon absorbed in the prose of a Senegalese writer, then works by other writers and poets. This way over half an hour went by; every now and then the uncle would throw a glance out the window at the gray courtyard far below; at one point, as his gaze turned back to the room, it met the eyes of his nephew, who in the same instant had looked up from his reading. "By the way," the uncle asked, "how is Kuntz?"

"Not well, or rather, well and not well; you know how it is with Kuntz."

"I would so much like to see him." The uncle was lost in his thoughts for a prolonged moment, then he abruptly picked up the phone, dialed four figures, asked for news of Senator Marchesan, listened to the answer and said, "As soon as you get hold of him, please let me know." And to his nephew: "You still have time, don't you? Then are you going to fly direct to the Coast?"

"Grandfather says we may make a stop at Winnipeg."

His uncle's gaze was lost for another moment as he looked out the window again at that small, inner, secret piece of the city. He said, "At any rate, in twenty hours or so you'll already be on the Coast." Ruggero glanced at the clock on the wall and resumed his reading. There was another long silence, interrupted only by the swishing noise of papers being shuffled, of pages turned. Then the uncle spoke again: "I see you're reading with interest. For one thing, French-African literature has the great merit of creating confusion in the very concept of nationalism, and that's what I keep harping on. If you were not leaving tonight, I would have you read some material in another field of mine: Uniform Presentation of History in European Curricula. You can imagine. A literally endless problem."

The silvery lady at the other desk listened to him sympathetically. Ruggero looked at the clock again. His uncle seemed oblivious. "Perhaps I'll go to Africa," he announced, "but I don't want to be pressed for time. Stay there no less than one year; two would be even better."

"Certainly," his nephew said.

The phone rang. After having listened for a moment, Giorgio replaced the receiver and got up. "Come, let's go; Marchesan is there already, listening to music."

They descended to the ground floor; through new lobbies and corridors they came to a felt-covered double door with an oval, thick porthole in either wing. They entered cautiously, as in a theater after the curtain is up.

In the center of the room was a large horseshoe table dotted with the standard features of international conferences: water glasses and pitchers, earphones for listening to simultaneous translation, signs with names of countries to indicate delegation seats. In the case at hand, the national distribution of the people present had not been respected: the place marked "Italy" was occupied by two elderly Japanese-looking ladies; a hefty, blond, curly-haired man was sitting at the place marked "Ghana." In the general silence and immobility, this man waved to Giorgio Partibon, who whispered to his nephew that that was Senator Marchesan. All had earphones on.

The opposite wall, facing the open end of the horseshoe, was occupied by a sort of huge showcase, or something like a small stage separated from the rest of the room by thick plate glass within a frame of insulating material. Behind the glass, Ruggero and his uncle saw five people, silent to them like fish in an aquarium, four men wearing pullovers like Ruggero's, and a woman in slacks. Two of the men in the background held in their hands huge sledgehammers with round, stuffed heads, which they were beating on long, sparkling metal sheets of various sizes, suspended like laundry hung out to dry. Toward the proscenium, on the left, another man attended to a huge electronic tape recorder. Finally, on the right, the fourth man and the woman, immobile, straight as the microphones before them, were opening and closing their mouths, apparently singing.

Uncle and nephew took the seats of two Asian nations; the moment they put on their earphones they were in the midst of extraordinary amalgams of sounds, clangors, thumps, powerful swishes; against that background the voices of the man and the

[*184*]

woman rose with cries and lamentations which had the power of sounding at the same time composed and wild, restrained and lacerating.

They listened for a long while in total absorption and ever-renewed tension. Oblivious to the passing of time, all listeners sat stooped and intent as if through their earphones they were receiving important and cryptic revelations. At the end there was no applause; each person slowly removed his earphones, and silently put them back on the table, rising.

From the opposite side of the horseshoe Marchesan, surrounded by a number of people, was transmitting a sign message to Giorgio Partibon. Quick circular motion of the hand toward the people surrounding him: he had to exchange a few more words with them. Index finger pointed upward: he would join Giorgio and his nephew upstairs. Cupped hand raised to lips: upstairs, at the cocktail party.

Ruggero and his uncle went back to the elevator; this time they got off at the second floor. The uncle said, "I had already heard that piece performed before, but I'm glad that now you've heard it too."

"Pity we haven't got Kuntz here with us. He, too, would have found it wonderful."

"Wonderful, isn't it?"

The cocktail lounge was on the second floor and it was already buzzing with people. After a very strong dry martini, uncle and nephew started moving about; every now and then Giorgio would greet somebody; there were some quick introductions with Ruggero, but on the whole the two of them preferred just to circulate arm in arm without committing themselves, exchanging brief comments or talking about their own private affairs. "Thanks for stopping to see me" was the uncle's refrain. After a second and third martini, Ruggero looked at his watch and laughed. "You know something? I have to go."

Just at that moment they saw Marchesan elbowing his way through the crowd, a powerful, Nordic structure, followed by a young man with glasses, his tense lips in a tight, ceremonious smile, dressed like a mannequin, all attention and efficiency. Having found Giorgio Partibon, Marchesan slapped him several times on the back with his large hand by way of greeting, then in a vague hint at an introduction he pointed to the young man with glasses. "Dr. Peritti. He's my lackey," he mumbled affably in a heavy Venetian accent; then, squeezing Ruggero's hand in a firm, warm handshake, he raised his voice solemnly: "Good afternoon, my friend; I knew your grandfather. You're the one who did a film on Venice, aren't you? I hear you're going to America now, to that institute Rossi's got there."

"You mean Alphonse Rossi, the director." In a state of slight inebriation, Ruggero laughed as if the coincidence with Gilberto Rossi's surname suddenly struck him as hilarious.

"Alphonse Rossi, of course," Marchesan said, himself very cheerful. "Tell me about him. He wants to invite me to a convention. Will you be there too? At that time I'll be going to America for other reasons too; perhaps we'll meet there."

Dr. Peritti was grabbing him by the arm, pulling him away; the senator was sucked into the crowd.

"Well, you'll have to say good-bye to him for me," Ruggero said to his uncle, "because it's really time for me to—"

"How did you come from the airport?"

"I took the limousine to the terminal, then I walked; now I guess I'll do the same. In reverse, of course." They both laughed with exaggeration.

"I'll stay here a little longer, but I'll see you to the elevator. Of course you're not going to walk. Here"—he squeezed some bills in Ruggero's hand—"you'll get a cab so there is no danger that you miss—"

"There is some danger, anyway. If so, I'll find you here."

In front of the elevator they embraced tightly, with no other words than " 'Bye, be good," and tears in their eyes.

In the city the soft haze was imbued with light, no longer gray but reddish, while the sky above was becoming a very dark, precious-stone blue.

So in the twilight Ruggero Tava Partibon's farewell visits were over; riding in a taxi to the airport, he was pervaded by a theatrical feeling of satisfaction, as from a practical joke that had come out right; he was deliriously amused by the idea of having stopped for a few hours in Paris for some idle chats with his uncle and a brief meeting with that other Venetian personage, and to listen to that extraordinary music. Once, talking to Irene, he had described himself as "after all, a specialist in holidays." Filling and enjoying the empty spaces between utilitarian occupations. Letting oneself go deeply into things, temperatures, sounds, colors, food, drink. A neon sign, its yellow glare looking liquid in the haze, became an uplifting vision.

The inside of the jet plane, with its electrified air, its sidereal lights, and music in the background, slightly sidereal too, immediately seemed to welcome him. His seat number was 18 B, and 18 A was occupied by a little girl, so young that he thought she might be one of those package-passengers entrusted by families to airlines.

Their conversation began immediately after they fastened their seat belts, and soon the child convinced him that she was as autonomous as any other isolated passenger suspended at that moment in the air above lands and oceans. In fact, she had a knowing and protective way of talking: "You speak English very well; British English, but at any rate, very well. Do you have friends in America?"

To make her happy, Ruggero said, "Oh yes, there's a man there who was a friend of my father's." But he knew very well that in his mental file Gilberto Rossi's card was still blank.

CHAPTER
SIX

GILBERTO ROSSI:

Now for a little while I believe I had better try to put down on
paper my position in regard to the present historical moment.
New paragraph.

The *quality* of historical facts has changed so radically that
the very expression, "historical facts," no longer fits. Don't try
to tell me that it always seemed so to those who lived through a
given historical period. Quite the contrary, my friends. Scores
of notorious and more or less recent historical protagonists
must have been only too convinced that they were living in History and manipulating it; in fact, never before has the world
witnessed such intense and impudent awareness.

Well, the reason I receive a salary here is also that I may
every now and then contemplate from above, through academic
eyes, Time and History flowing to and fro under the bridge;
playing with words a little, I might say I am again conducting
my meditations from the top of an Academy Bridge; but what I

wanted to say is this: I suspect that the above-mentioned protagonists, with their orgies of self-staging and self-mythifying,
have represented something like the last intense flare of an electric bulb before it goes kaput forever.

So we see their era being followed by an era of group leadership and of technicians. Great changes. And again, don't try to
tell me that every period has regarded itself as a period of great
changes. In thirty years, science has made more progress than in
the previous three thousand. This simple observa

Waking up in the middle of the night, I found these notes
and read them with bewilderment. Everything out of phase, of
course; wrong tone, to begin with. Hell of a way to prepare
notes for my contribution to the Superkamiri, i.e., the World
Symposium, expected to be a perfect model of its kind, executed and conducted by L & C specialists.

Alphonse told me, "Your contribution? The individual. History. Language. That's the area." So now I am completely at
sea.

Through these pre-Superkamiri weeks, Alphonse has been in
an excellent mood; he is isolated; he is isolated even if he is
among people because he doesn't listen to anybody, he goes
straight ahead like a horse with blinkers or like a missile. He
does all the talking. And he continues to correspond with half
the world, according to reports from our girl /dp. He announces
as already realized, projects which have been debated for years,
like the one about Chinese as guinea-pig language: "It's all
done. The experiment will begin at once. The Orientals at the
university are giving me at least two competent men." It should
be observed that he doesn't do this sort of thing as a display of
activity to foil accusations of inactivity from the enemy; on the
contrary, he does it knowing, for example, that the enemy dis-
approves of the Chinese experiment.

The news that the experiment would be conducted was given
by Alphonse almost accidentally: it came as a reply to a question posed by Ruggero Tava, Jr., this young nightmare recently
landed among us. Tava already knew all about everything, including the Symposium. Obsessively well informed. So well adjusted he looks unreal.

I met him the first time as we were "watching" a meeting of

the executive kamiri for the Symposium. Out of extreme naïveté or extreme political cunning, Alphonse had appointed
Chuck Palmerston chairman of that kamiri (a kind of organizational empyrean for the Symposium)—Chuck Palmerston,
whom even the cleaning help point out as his major antagonist.
Lebournet did not pass up the chance to remark that the kamiri is called "executive" because its aim is Alphonse's execution.

Chuck has decided that meetings of the executive kamiri
shall be public, held in a lecture hall, panel style. So you sit
there and watch the scene onstage, with Chuck in the middle.
So far they have been discussing, in a specialized language almost inaccessible to me, the formation and composition of
other kamiris, and subkamiris with special functions. Much
time was devoted to weighing of terms: for example, whether
the relationship between electronic brains and humanistic studies should be entrusted to a new ad hoc kamiri, or whether such
a body should not instead be regarded as emanating from the
already existing kamiri for relations with scientists, whose
chairman is old Clinton.

During the first hour this was the only topic they discussed.
They all spoke too well for me; after that first hour I didn't
even try to listen, the more so since Clinton himself, who is a
member of the empyrean kamiri, ostentatiously unplugged his
cumbersome hearing aid and shut himself up in marmoreal silence.

When Blatt and I decided that we would watch at least the
first session, we had arranged to meet in the lecture hall; as
soon as I came in, I saw he had brought Tava along; the young
man had been consigned to him by Alphonse upon arrival. But
Tava certainly didn't need any guide. He sat there, looking
around the room with a level gaze, his round, strong back filling up the curved back of the chair; he looked as if he had been
around that lecture hall all his life. A person's independence
can be judged by the way he sits. I saw him in profile; he was
the first person I saw as I came in and I had no doubt as to who
he was. Hair planted the same way as his father's. And that
solid, rosy cheek: he was made of the same dough as his father.
But reproductions can turn out to be vaguely frightening. This
was Tava, obviously. However, wholly different from his father,

and undoubtedly *older* than my friend was when he fell in the Alps over twenty years ago.

I sat down beside Blatt, who let some time pass before he asked, "But have you two already met?"

"Not yet," I said, and shook Tava's hand briefly behind Blatt's back. No names were mentioned.

Meanwhile Chuck and other kamiri members were exchanging ideas onstage. As I said, I listened only up to a point. I got lost in my own thoughts, not about my dead friend Tava exactly, but about my writing the Italian essay for him during our final examinations, or my telling him about my crisis on the Academy Bridge. I reviewed these and other memories which are still being developed in my mind, in my life.

When we got up at last, Tava came over to me. "May I come and see you in your office one of these days?" His manner was neutral, neither aggressive nor respectful, but he was studying me intently.

I rambled: "At Göttingen we used to visit older professors in their homes on Sunday morning. Here we all have our offices. Not that I'm an old professor, mind you, for the good reason that I am not a professor; but I have an office. Come next Tuesday, in the afternoon."

He pulled out a small diary and said immediately, "Quarter to four?"

"Well, come at four, it's a round figure, simpler to remember." I was beginning to laugh in his face a little bit.

This exchange took place on a Friday. The following Monday was a holiday. During this abundant weekend I met Tava no less than twice. One evening at the Pickfords' and another at the Clintons'. In both cases it was as though he had known those people all his life. Even the Pickfords' usual vassalage routine didn't apply in this case. Seen in their model kitchen, young Tava appeared as something already *there,* a domestic animal, a fixture.

By chance I had met Nadine Pickford at the supermarket; my cart bumped into hers in the aisle between jams and detergents, and she asked me to come up to the house for an apéritif (Pickford lexicon) . I first went to store ice cream boxes and other perishable stuff in my refrigerator; then, at the Pickfords', in the model kitchen where Louis was experimenting with sauces, I found Tava already settled and perfectly well oriented.

To drink our apéritif we went into the huge living room, and I allowed Pickford to prepare something very special for me, vaguely resembling what used to be called an *americano* in Italy, but with a robustness all its own, provided by a solid foundation of vodka. I drank three such apéritifs. Each time, Tava brought me the huge glass from the bar, where Pickford prepared the concoction, to the sofa on which I was ever more comfortably distributing my limbs. I never said anything to Tava other than "Thank you, my friend," hardly looking at him, while my mind's eye was fixed on Tava, Sr., machine-gunned "by a relative" in the Alps; Tava, Jr., was always around me, studying me, ready to catch a hint which, however, never came. When finally Nadine suggested that I stay on for dinner I simply groaned, to indicate how unthinkable that was.

In my car, speedily climbing Bitter Canyon, I realized what was happening to me: it was as if the scene in the Pickfords' living room did not exist while it happened; it took shape now, like a photograph being developed. As was my custom, the first thing I did was to judge myself unfavorably: my detached, haughty attitude, my going away disdaining the invitation—all wrong.

Fortunately I found Beatrice in my garage, feeding the cat. This was a cat who, however excluded from the inside of the house, would wait for me as I went out in the morning and came back in the evening, to welcome me and be fed. As a matter of fact, as the weeks went by I had got into the habit of buying, at the supermarket, cans of ever more specialized cat food, scientifically balancing his diet. He knew I wouldn't let him in the house; in fact, Beatrice and I had christened him *"Out."*

One rainy day when I opened the door, there he was, completely drenched, yet he didn't make the slightest attempt to force his way in; he actually looked wryly at me.

Beatrice distracted me from the thought of my recent visit; I didn't even mention it to her. We broiled two splendid steaks for ourselves and after dinner we desultorily watched TV in that atmosphere of unparalleled serenity which Beatrice always manages to create.

Only later on, when she was leaving, she surprised me by saying, "Monday is a holiday and we're going to take Ruggero for a drive to Mexico. You'll come too, won't you?"

"Ruggero? Mexico?"

"I thought he had told you. He so much wants to get to know you better."

The net was becoming larger. That boy Tava was already spreading out all over. I was still the person least accessible to him. "I don't know whether I'll come. The part of Mexico we've got near here doesn't mean much to me."

At this point we were already outside, by Beatrice's car. She kissed me tenderly and got in behind the wheel. "Monday you should at least come for dinner afterward; we'll be back from Mexico around seven," she said while she affectionately pressed the back of my hand against her cheek before starting the car.

Now I shall try to describe how I felt in regard to young Tava. I felt like one of those characters in stories with old British Empire background, when a new young officer arrives and presents himself to the superior officer who has been there a long time already, and is, in fact, slightly corrupted by local habits and customs. This superior officer usually has something in his past record, a shadow brought from his mother country, and it isn't clear how much the young man knows about it. The fact is, he looks at the older man with eyes in which a penetrating and questioning light is clearly perceptible, as if he wants to check in person on what he has heard, presumably in London, before leaving for this outpost.

That kind of look was always enough for me to shut myself up in my personal snail shell; every now and then, however, I would pull out a listening antenna and regulate it any way I pleased. To counter the young man's inquisitive manner I decided to adopt a similar attitude: I would study him, taking advantage of the occasion to broaden my observation of men born at a time when I was already a soldier, a cultural employee, *Universitätslektor,* Norma's fiancé.

Meanwhile, Blatt occasionally talked to me about Ruggero. He saw much more of him than I did. From the very beginning I realized that young Tava, perhaps also on account of my attitude toward him, was like a large plant thriving all by itself here on the Pacific Coast; at a distance I could maintain only a minimum of control over him through Blatt's reports. For instance, Blatt related to me that the young man came here with the intention of studying Chinese, and having learned from the chairman of the kamiri for guinea-pig languages (Alf Lundquist) how things stood, he had precipitately gone down to the old university campus, discovered a department of Oriental languages with a couple of Chinese teachers who were not of very recent origin but apparently still usable, and he presented Alphonse with a detailed project for an experimental course. He had also immediately made an agreement with Budd Rotondi for the use of a laboratory outfitted with tape-recording gadgetry for correcting pronunciations, et cetera.

It was hard to tell how large a part Alphonse had had in the long-delayed decision to get the Chinese experiment under way, and how much of it had been the work of this hyperactive young man; the fact is that Tava had done a lot of shuttling back and forth between the Orientals' office down in the village, and Alphonse's office up here; to do so he had used the same means of transportation that he chose the minute he arrived—a motorcycle.

I might add that he had already brought Alphonse a list of potential customers for the new course, most of them motorcyclists like himself, young characters wearing checked shirts or turtleneck sweaters, or leather jackets with pictures on them. I have often watched them in action, sometimes using field glasses to follow them from my observatory up here. These motorcycles far away would run like toys along the foot of the mountain; then, disappearing and reappearing on their tortuous course up the canyon, they would climb until they passed close to my window, speedily crackling away. They constitute one of my nocturnal background noises. Occasionally I have met some of these motorcycle riders through Beatrice, who knows them; in fact, I wouldn't be surprised if in the past she went to bed with one or two of them.

Tava wears similar garments, except for the pictures on the leather jacket; however, he is also apt to turn up wearing regular and very tight-fitting suits; apparently he has several particular fixations regulating the pressing, or rather, nonpressing, of his narrow, pipelike pants, the length of his sideburns, the height of his heels.

Blatt told me that one evening when he went to pick him up,

he found him knotting his tie, a tie that looked like a flower bed, persisting until the two ends came out perfectly even; and after having perpetrated this idiotic feat, he added with joy and pride, "Look at it—how perfect!"

That Monday evening I went to the Clintons' rather late; the party had come back from Mexico a couple of hours before, and they were sitting at the table eating. Old Clinton had retired already, and it was young Tava who told me about it: "He asked us to excuse him; he is intransigent about his sleep, and he's right." In other words, this new boy had all of a sudden become the spokesman for the house. My reaction was a brief snicker to myself without even looking at him. He was sitting at the head of the table, with Beatrice on his right. She and I exchanged kisses and I went to sit down at the other end of the table, so Tava was facing me; he never ceased focusing his large, gentle, all-absorbing eyes on me.

Beatrice was the only woman present. Besides her and Ruggero, there were two young men. One was Pickford's son, still with an adolescent's pimples on his face. The other was a motorcyclist with dark, shiny hair; from a distance he didn't look more than sixteen, while in close-up his face turned out to be a bit withered. He had on a leather jacket with pictures, whereas Pickford and Tava wore regular suits and even shirts with button-down collars.

"David, pass the meat to Mr. Rossi," Tava said to the boy in leather. David got up and brought me a large wooden platter with slices of broiled meat on it. I transferred to my plate a piece of meat, burned outside and bloody inside according to regulation. When I raised my eyes to thank the young man, I stopped midway: on the painted façade of his jacket I saw a swastika. I pointed to it: "That will have to go, you know."

Beatrice said, "Don't forget that it's also an old Indian symbol."

"Maybe so, but would you kindly remove that jacket?" I said and David promptly, acting rather sportive and amused, took it off. They were treating me as if I had said that a certain lamp bothered my eyes.

From his end of the table and without paying much attention to the scene, Ruggero asked young Pickford to pour me some wine. Pickford came over to me and poured the wine while Tava, as if to attune me to their company, pointed to David, who was now sitting at the table in his shirt sleeves, quietly nibbling corn on the cob, and said, "David is working with Lebournet on art terminology. He is posing this question: Is a jukebox as an object, not as a producer of music, a work of art; and if not, why not?"

I could smell a kind of discussion Lebournet is fond of. I said nothing. I tried to drain my face of all expression. I ate my meat in silence. They abandoned me and went on debating among themselves. I excluded myself from listening. An old daydream vision rose before me, as concrete as ever before: my friend Ruggero Tava, very pale, dead, with blood coming down from his nostrils, already coagulated. Now, here by the Pacific, I felt as if we were all abstractions, or images seen in a kind of aquarium. Then it struck me that Beatrice and Ruggero seated at the table were decidedly a couple, older than the other two and looking almost like parents; ultimately, however, this did not mean anything to me either, it was like something that had already happened and was now only being reproduced.

But then I found myself listening to them again, and cheerfulness suddenly erupted within me. It must have been some stupid thing Ruggero was saying.

I'll give one example: We are at the end of the dinner, fresh fruit is being passed around, he hesitates between apple and pear, chooses pear, explains hesitation: "When they are good, pears are better than apples; but a good pear is much more difficult to find than a good apple."

"A good pear is then," I say, displaying intense interest in the matter, "preferable to a good apple."

"Absolutely," he says in all seriousness. Fallen into the trap.

I proceed: "An apple a day keeps the doctor away, so you can imagine what a pear will do. However"—I raise my voice and look at him with eyes wide open—"vitamin capsules are better, as even Dr. Fetucinetti knows by now."

"Who is that?"

"Who knows? Don't you ever invent anything?"

Still staring at me, he shrugs his shoulders, but barely, as a well-mannered young man.

I go on: "For a long time now, Dr. Fetucinetti too has been vitamin-conscious."

"Oh?" he says, dazed.

"Yes. But let's speak about our own affairs. You already seem to be quite well adjusted at the Institute. Well, which side are you on?"

Now he makes an effort to come up with a minimal answer.

I urge him on: "I see. You too are in an ambiguous position. And you probably feel that makes you up to date, a Man of Our Time. Right? Three cheers for the politico-electronic system, three cheers for primordial individualism." Now I felt as if I were dealing with the Ottorino type. "Well, you can be as well adjusted as you please, but you're still a newcomer here. So I warn you that any position is preferable to the fictitious modernism and fictitious up-to-dateness of Count von Buterweg-Palmerston-Pickford, president of the Superkamiri." I had forgotten that young Pickford was there but he didn't follow me, anyhow, nor did Ruggero or David. Only Beatrice understood me, elbow on table and cheek on her fist.

"Anything, my dear Tava, is preferable to that count's position, including, just to give you an example, some hoary formulas which used to make the lawyer Fernando Rossi's chords vibrate: *Avanti! Vorwärts! Forward! The new red sun is rising!* Such slogans are more modern and trustworthy than the ones propounded by the terroristic monopolizers of *Angst*, Anxiety, Anguish, who then turn out to be beautifully smooth characters, well-oiled, magnificently vitaminized. You don't follow me. What are you planning to do here? Blatt tells me that you're already chummy with Budd Rotondi, our electronics technician."

He replies immediately, "Yes, he's very good, he offered to teach me programming on the computers they have here. But I have a different idea about that." He coughs briefly. "My idea is: there are these specialists, like Budd. Well, you save time letting them do the job. I'll devote about forty percent of my time here to Chinese—"

"Those Chinese people you fished up are small fry; they strike me as people with a folkloristic view of China."

"Well, anyway, all the information we get on China is totally inadequate, isn't it? So, there you are. Chinese forty percent, add to that another thirty percent for other kinds of work and I'm left with thirty percent free time, not much." He concludes, "As for the problem of being or not being able to do computer programming, I have an analogy: we all use airplanes, even though we are not able to pilot them ourselves." A longer silence. Beatrice smiles at him, he smiles at her; then, finding nothing better to say, he asks me, "You, for instance—can you fly a plane?"

"I? I flew over Vienna with Ermete Fassola in 1917."

His smile fades out.

That is the moment when the newly arrived young officer superimposes the image brought from London on the image before his eyes and sees that the two match: it was all true, the man has gone to pot, destroyed by the tropics, probably drugged.

On my way home, driving up Bitter Canyon in the starry night, I began my self-accusation at once: I had done everything wrong, I had behaved irresponsibly, betraying Alphonse inasmuch as I had turned our deepest professional and moral interests into a puppet show. Perhaps I had inflicted conscious punishment on myself by going away abruptly, leaving young Tava there alone with Beatrice and those two sons of theirs. I was sure a night of insomnia awaited me, although I knew that in such cases sometimes the opposite happens.

Actually, as soon as I hit the bed I fell asleep and started to dream. I dreamed of Alphonse as a child. He was plumpish, dressed up, unhappy. Chuck Palmerston, bearing for the occasion a close resemblance to Signora Lezze-Adorno, was his mother.

"Fight her," I said, but my voice had no sound. "She's one of those ladies who go to funerals wearing the lackluster black uniform of the Regime, with a fur coat on top of it." But it was impossible for me to transmit this or any other image to Alphonse, to that unhappy child—the more so since his mother, with protean ease, was also a high officer of a German regiment with black attire and the death's-head insignia on the forehead; the uniform hung loose and flabby on her, like a sack; no doubt she was a military person but she was a woman, as was quite obvious from her wide hips. Then things got mixed up and at the same time they became clearer. A scene from my usual oneiric repertory took shape. I realized that the chief aim of that military person had been my arrest; I recognized at once the cell in which I was a prisoner while I could feel the presence of the football field in the tepid sun outside where my execution was being prepared. Deep within me I experienced also a sense of relief because I felt safe about Alphonse, deceiving myself into thinking that since he was a child, he would be excluded from capital punishment.

I have trained myself rather well to remember dreams, but I have never believed that they can be interpreted; all attempts in that direction have always appeared to me to be a little frivolous. Dreams have beauty and significance because they are what they are; reading abstract messages into them means creating mysteriosophic distortions. Et cetera. Et cetera.

Young Tava kept his appointment, coming to my office the following day at four o'clock sharp. I had given instructions to myself to receive him without any show of curiosity, and I succeeded perfectly. After having the secretary announce him, he came into the office with a respectful air. However, I was disturbed by the fact that he did not wear a suit, as he had the previous evening, but his motorcycle outfit. I remained seated behind my desk, pointing to a chair in front of me; he sat down. We looked at each other. I let the pause continue. How well I was conducting myself! From down the hall you could hear a typewriter breaking the silence.

Then the right opening line occurred to me: "Go on, Tava, tell me."

"I bring you greetings from Paris, from my uncle, Giorgio Partibon." First thing: he immediately used the familiar *tu* form of address as I had done.

"Good. Good. Thank you."

"Piero Camentini remembered you too."

"Well, good for him. Who is he?"

I soon realized that Ruggero had a way of mentioning his friends as if everybody should know them; that's the way children talk about their playmates to a visiting uncle. He indulged in this habit to the point of appearing insane.

"Piero Camentini," he explained, "is the one who writes.

Brother of Camentini the candymaker." He recited some commercial slogans of that firm, and he said that one or two of them had been his suggestions. He informed me that the candy tycoon had offered him a job in his public relations office. I looked at him with more interest than suspicion. I asked him whether he had accepted. "Of course not," he said. "Don't you see I'm here?"

Was that why he hadn't accepted? To come here? Wouldn't it have been better to settle down comfortably in business, especially now that the economy of the Western world was blessed with the Miracle? He thought about that for a moment, then he spoke just as precisely as when he had discussed the matter of the apple and the pear: "No. Even if only one of the two possibilities—working for Giovanni Camentini, or coming here—had presented itself, my decision would have been the same in either case; namely, negative in the former, positive in the latter." Brief cough. "When I realized that Giovanni was going to offer me a position and I spoke to Kuntz about it, Kuntz said nothing; he simply burst out laughing."

That's when I thought he was insane, also from the way he lit up when he mentioned Kuntz's name. I asked him who he was.

"He's a friend of mine and Irene's."

"Good, so you're all friends. And who is Irene?"

"She's a good friend of mine. She's great. She did magnificently at the school for interpreters, and she also plays the cello. If she concentrated on the cello for five years, she would become a concert player. Kuntz thinks so, too. Not a concert player of the highest order, but a good concert player. Irene Berlocchi."

"Berlocchi. Wasn't somebody named Berlocchi mentioned recently apropos of . . .?"

"Yes, yes, her father is involved."

"You mean the Berlocchi who is involved in that scandal is your friend's father?"

"Bravo. That's right."

"Do you know what he's guilty of, if 'guilty' is the word?"

"I don't believe even Irene knows exactly."

"Didn't you try to form an opinion?"

"Enrico Fassola, whose aviator uncle you were mentioning last night at Beatrice's, and who, incidentally, remembers you too, believes that Berlocchi will get a two-year sentence. More or less. So Enrico says."

All of his friends remembered me. Nevertheless, I couldn't quite figure him out. To put it in a few words, I am a serious and thoughtful person; for example, I have been following some big scandals that exploded in Italy during the Miracle era as if somehow they concerned me personally. But communicating this notion to Tava, Jr., now sitting in front of me, was like trying to climb up a mirror.

We were both silent for quite a while. I decided to fill this void by cultivating anything that might come to my memory or my imagination. Isolating myself in the presence of others doesn't bother me at all; in fact, I am extremely well versed in that operation.

I don't know why, but the image of a girl named Elvira Conti came to mind, and a conversation I had with her, perhaps in '34 or '35, at a tea dance of the Goof. Elvira was the younger, diminutive sister of Alessandra Conti, who a few years later was to become the legitimate wife of my friend Ruggero Tava. Perhaps even at that time the Conti family were aiming at a union between Ruggero and their Alessandra. And they must have known that Ruggero had always been in love with Elena Partibon. What happened was that Elvira, who was just then talking about Elena, whispered in my ear, "You know what she is? She's a viper. Just because she doesn't care whether she lives or dies —she's very ill, you know—she thinks that others are the same way. In fact, she wants that, she demands it. I hate her I hate her I hate her."

It wasn't as if I, then or later, necessarily agreed with this small girl or with that statement, delivered in a tone which is typical of some Venetian women, calm and frenetic at the same time; but at any rate, after nearly thirty years I could still perceive the whisper of her words in my ear, while with my antenna cautiously emerging from my snail shell I was studying young Tava and trying to capture any similarities between him and Elena Partibon, his mother. All things considered, I couldn't find any.

Then my memory turned to his uncle, Giorgio Partibon, and our New Year's trip to Portogruaro entered into the picture. I have already marked down in these notes my simple observation that a human event *begins* to exist the moment it occurs; then it goes on developing, intermingling in countless combinations with other, subsequent events. From what I remembered of all the messy events in which my friend Ruggero Tava was involved with the Partibons—love, hurt, death, illegitimate birth of a son unknown to him even as a possibility, a potential, a larva—I had come to the conclusion that he, Tava, Sr., had held the role of the victim in that mess. This feeling was strengthened as I observed the junior larva, who had in the meantime become a fully developed organism, independent, wholly new and ignorant. I confronted him in a way that I imagine seemed unusual to him:

"I know from examining your papers, which I did at Alphonse's invitation, that you were born in 1941. In a sense, in some important respects, you make me laugh. Although I'm a bachelor and have no children, and have been a teacher only sporadically, I have nevertheless had some experience with young people, as I have with people of all ages, inasmuch as, my dear Tava, by natural inclination I am well informed, concerned, committed, involved. You may safely count on my always knowing two or three times as much as you assume I know on a given subject—education, electronics, ethnology, sports, politics, jazz, semantics, life in general. And I take a stand. I discuss. I participate. I always participate, wherever I can, from morning to night, and in a sense, also from night to morning, inasmuch as I am a person who has significant dreams. My continuous participation is enlivened by my whole past, which is forever changing and being enriched in my mind. In other words, by the varying and fascinating light of experience. From this angle, you make me laugh; you all make me laugh." I went over to the collective pronoun because other cases were crowding my mind, Arrigo to mention one, my cousin Gianluigi Strigato's son.

One day just before I left Italy, when I was visiting them at Portogruaro, my Aunt Luciana, Arrigo's grandmother, was abandoning herself to evocations of a time even before Arrigo was born, during the defunct Regime, with its continuous and general sense of asphyxia, its ever more unbridled and tragic stupidities. And how did grandson Arrigo react? How did he listen to his grandmother? He listened with a faint smile; it was all foreign to him. But then, he knew everything. Moreover, he was a man of today. Now, just a minute, boy. "Granted, Arrigo," I said, "you're not guilty of anything. In fact, we have borne the guilt in even larger measure than would have been strictly necessary. But, you see, Arrigo, you did not inherit asphyxia; if anything, you inherited freedom, served to you on a silver platter. Do you follow me, Arrigo?" He switched off his little smile, not so much because he had accepted my words as because he is polite; they are polite, they have good manners.

Tava, Jr., has excellent manners. Self-confident, serene, completely at ease, a fish always swimming in the right water, at the right temperature and salinity. I had a suspicion that precisely those qualities constituted his menacing aspects, and that it was up to me to identify them. I resumed, "You all make me laugh. You believe you're automatically in the know, sources of pure modernity. Get that out of your heads. There is no modernity without experience, and your lack of moral and historical preparation would make everybody shudder, if it weren't for us watching over you." Perhaps he thought I was crazy, what with my subsequent peroration; I was actually carried on a wave of specious but effective oratory: "Like my cousin's son, Arrigo—I can just smell it—you too visualize the time when I and my contemporaries were young as being filled with historical events that seem practically Assyro-Babylonian to you, and furthermore, you suspect that those events were largely invented by us. I can place you without difficulty—I know some of your relatives and I know your native region, Venetia. I can just see you: pampered when you grew up, fed with a golden spoon. Like Arrigo and so many others. Until you find me. You've bumped into the wrong man. You've found your nemesis. The jig's up. *Finie la rigolade.* Good-bye to the cornucopia. The frolic's over. Would you like some good advice? Stay away from me."

Well, that's what he did—he stayed away from me. Blatt had put him to work in the area for which he was responsible, on the processing of a lot of material in Italian and other languages, the kind of work which is eventually channeled toward "up-to-date comparative definitions" of certain words (e.g., he put him to work on "radicalism," "liberalism," "dialogue," "alienation") . Once in a while, since I was Blatt's closest associate,

[*203*]

Ruggero was advised to ask me for directives too, and then he made an appointment through the secretary. When I saw him come into my office I first experienced a stab of joy, immediately followed by a stronger jolt of irritation. Hope followed by disappointed awakening. For friendship is indeed hope, and his head was the same shape, his cheeks the same color as my friend Tava's; to some extent he even had the same way of looking at you. But this was not my friend, this was a stranger, and the similarity, if anything, was an aggravating circumstance.

One day I said to him, "Hurry up, Tava, you're such a bore," and he broke into merry laughter, saying that his mother always told him that. He was in excellent health. His skin was getting darker as he got suntanned motorcycling up the canyons, and when I asked him why he didn't go surfboarding he replied, again laughing happily, that he wasn't much of an athlete.

It became common knowledge that we didn't get along. In this milieu there grows a sense of respect, underscored by small attentions, around two people who don't get along; first of all, they are never invited together. I continued to see Beatrice, but never with Ruggero, while I knew, or rather, I guessed that they saw each other often. Finicky and unpleasant as I can be in human relationships, I did not fail to tell her sarcastically, "Nothing I like better, Beatrice, than being excluded from nice cozy dinners where I have to meet some characters with swastikas."

She squeezed my wrist; by now she had taken to kissing me on the forehead, smiling and without really knowing what to say. But Beatrice's smile is unforgettable; her upper lip juts out and partly covers her lower lip, so her smile remains hidden underneath, which makes it deeper and more important; meanwhile she frowns, with an air of intense concentration. She doesn't concentrate only when she is deep in thought, but even more so when she is savoring physical pleasure, as anyone knows who has held her in his arms at certain moments. I have sometimes tried to describe to her the way she looks; somehow I wanted to put into words my affection and gratitude toward her.

The last time she came up to my house, she left earlier than usual, making it quite clear that she had a date with Ruggero. She had come up in her own car. We had hardly spoken the whole evening. Usually, silence between us was light and pleasant, a sign of our harmony, but this evening there had been a heavy feeling of tension. I accompanied her to the door and was following her outside when I heard her exclaim with surprise, "Gilberto, look!"

I have already spoken of this cat who was our friend. Now he was lying stretched out, dead, near the streetlight in the middle of the road. He seemed completely untouched. I used a tree branch to push him to the side of the road. I explained to Beatrice, "Otherwise they come with their motorcycles and make a mess of his body." Dragging the cat like that, I had the impression that he was all broken inside. But then at the roadside I rearranged his body exactly as we had found it; there he lay as I went to the car to open the door for Beatrice and she got in behind the wheel. She was saddened by the sight of that poor creature but capable of practical suggestions; before starting the engine she informed me that there was a municipal office which took care of removing dead animals from the streets. Actually, I discovered later that you just call this office and then a big truck arrives, with a robust and friendly driver who even knows how to smile with sympathy and understanding if he realizes you have lost an animal dear to you. By means of huge pincers operated by a crane, the animal is gripped and hoisted, then thrown through a hole into a kind of tank at the rear of the truck.

All of this happened the next day. At the time, the cat was lying on the roadside, where he would remain for the night. After Beatrice left, and before going back alone to the house, whose entrance had always been closed to him, I returned to look at him stretched out there in the lamplight, in a dejected, dignified position. Then I started to cry. Partly this was caused by the sight of that dejection, dignity, composure. Besides, it is now clear that I was entering a period of crisis, and my confused emotions were a sign of it. Later I undoubtedly sobbed even in my sleep, although I had no dreams that I recall.

The next day the weather was extremely dry, with a desert wind blowing; and under the violent sun, in that arid and agitated air, I witnessed the departure of the cat with all the maneuvers I have described.

The next time I saw Beatrice, Ruggero was with her. This happened in a church where a memorial service was held on the anniversary of Peter Clinton's death. Beatrice had told me with detachment, without adding any comment of her own, that Peter's widow was very keen on this kind of ceremony. I got mixed up about the time and arrived an hour late at the church, which was freshly painted and had stained-glass windows with bright, modern color combinations. The ceremony was over, everybody was getting up to leave. There were young, tall priests who moved like athletes and smiled showing rows of extremely healthy teeth. There were also some of those nuns who usually teach in comfortable immaculate schools, swishing through wide, well-ventilated corridors over shiny linoleum floors. I recognized a nun who attended my course in modern Italian *Kulturgeschichte;* she smiled at me protectively, she seemed to know that I didn't feel well.

I asked myself why I had come; lucky that I was late. I stood at the church door, which to me was an entrance, but since everybody was by now coming in the opposite direction, it simultaneously became an exit. Beatrice and Ruggero walked toward me, their elbows touching slightly. Before stepping outside, they, like many others, turned back toward the inside of the church for a last-farewell gesture. Beatrice bent her head in a quick bow that reminded me of one of my Aunt Luciana's movements when she laughs. Ruggero added a jerky sign of the cross, a purely muscular reflex of the arm.

Perhaps it is appropriate that I insert a brief parenthesis here on my attitude toward religion. It is by no means an original one, and I shall try to describe it in the simplest terms. So let me say that no concept of the supernatural has ever been a fount of consolation to me. Therefore I find that those who possess such founts are not very fair, or even polite, in flaunting them. If they have such hidden resources they should at the very least pretend that they don't, and be in the same boat with us. Now I must add, however, that Tava, Jr., though making that gesture, did not give me the impression of possessing those secret founts, for the simple reason that he must have felt no need of them. On the other hand, one of my fixations is to discover some significance in any gesture made by people who, in one way or another, are important to me.

So when we were all out in the sun on the cement square in front of the church, I spoke excitedly to Ruggero, with Beatrice there listening and nodding pensively, smiling, but with gravity; there was a note of anxiety in my voice: "To make certain gestures, precisely because one doesn't believe in them? To deprive them of meaning, to corrode them from the inside? Am I right, Ruggero? You mean that it is of so little importance to you that doing or not doing it is all the same? Hence your strictly mechanical reflex movement? That's it, isn't it? I think I understand."

"Is that so?" he says, smiling with gentle curiosity. With the air of a slightly imbecile child too, come to think of it.

He found other friends, so Beatrice took me by the arm and we walked away, isolated. I accused myself: "When I get rid of my verbal block I talk too much, and always out of perspective. I'll never cure myself; in fact, in time I'll get worse. Then I regret it, and come back to it at night. But you mustn't think that my nocturnal brooding is necessarily a negative quality, quite the contrary. It's very demanding, however; it consumes considerable energy. One needs a lot of energy."

"How is your nasal infection?"

"Bad. But it will pass. It's nothing." Actually it had been a torture for many days, but I imagine I meant that it was nothing compared to what Peter had experienced, her half brother just commemorated. For instance, before the final agony and liberating death, they had amputated a large part of his tongue, piece by piece. As a boy Peter had suffered from sinus infections, but that condition, compared with his later trouble, took on an almost cheerful aspect. Beatrice had sent me to the same specialist who had taken care of Peter's sinuses; he had also removed Peter's tonsils. And now, evoking these episodes with her, I felt as if I too had been here when Peter was a little boy and suffered from sinus trouble and underwent tonsillectomy.

Talking about him, Beatrice and I walked arm in arm, up and down along a row of parked cars. By now it was just as if I had known him too; I admired his vigor, his cheerfulness, his courage; I lived the memory of his pains intensely.

Then I spotted Ruggero far away, standing among a group of people. I made a motion with my head in that direction; it seemed perfectly natural to bring Ruggero into the picture, as the latest addition to our domestic circle. "How are things going with Tava?" I asked.

"I believe Ruggero is becoming indispensable to me."

This phrase made no impact on me; I felt as if I had heard it before. It fit exactly with the impression Ruggero made, so well oriented, so like a fish in the right water; it didn't even remotely occur to me that Beatrice was several years older than he; he was such a young man, pink and naïve, yet he seemed timeless, as though the future had already happened to him. I felt a strong desire to be alone. I really felt sick.

When I was left alone, I went to the supermarket and stumbled on Nadine Pickford with Lebournet. Nadine cultivates Lebournet, who reads to her, in French, parts of his future novel, *The Perimeter of Things*, and also theoretical essays. While we waited at the meat counter with one hand on the bar of our metal cart and the other holding on to the plastic card with our number, Lebournet entertained us on the subject of a new series of TV commercials he was studying, and of their rhetorical structures. He said he was preparing "first-rate stuff" for the international Symposium.

A moment before, I had wanted to be alone, but when Nadine left us (the great Horace Buterweg, Alphonse's predecessor at the Institute, was her house guest) I accepted Lebournet's invitation and followed him in my car to his house, then followed him inside to his study.

I felt as though I was going to have some kind of revelation. A TV set of very recent model occupied a central position in the room; facing it, at the right distance, was an equally low leather chair which had an element in common with highchairs for infants, a kind of movable tray, only this one was not to place food on, but to be used as a small desk. It had hinges on one side, so it opened like a door and the televiewer could shut himself in. Obviously Lebournet used that contraption to take notes while watching commercials.

I sat down in that place; he asked me whether I wanted to watch something on TV. No, no, I said, I was there simply to think. Think about what? he wanted to know. He was my friend. A sturdy friend, bearded, with keen eyes. He urged me to let off steam. He asked me how my nasal infection was.

"Not all right, but that's not it. It's rather something . . . It isn't the first time in my life . . ." I shrugged. "Well, I see objects and people, and I feel I'm dreaming them up."

"But what has this to do with a nasal infection?" With a firm grip on his beard, he studied me with solicitude.

"I don't know. Nothing, I suppose." Now I wanted to be alone again; to isolate myself, I got him to talk about his collection of TV commercials and about their rhetorical structures. He spoke at length; I listened to his talk occasionally and even found it rather interesting. He picked up a plastic-covered manuscript from his desk, it was the first part of his new essay; he stroked it fondly, saying, "This, my friend, is real work." The trouble was that he, Lebournet, was not real. I was dreaming him up.

Ostraden, Megafol, Astaril, Dinosan, Sympathil, et cetera, et cetera. I am making up the names. They are equipollent to those of remedies prescribed by a Dr. Wood. Nathaniel B. Wood. Suggested to me by Nadine Pickford, who calls him "Woodie." Each crisis has its own nadir, then you come up the slope again. I am now making these notes while on my way up the slope. Let me also say that once you touch bottom, you can find useful things there to take up with you. It would be ideal if one could always arrive at the conclusion that such useful acquisitions have not been too terribly expensive.

There were these long hours in total emptiness, during which I cried a lot. Crying is generally an obvious relief, letting go, clarification—vaguely, I would say, the way sneezing is. But my crying during those long hours was not like that; it was no liberation, because there was nothing that could be liberated. My crying would start and then go on all by itself; it left no trace, except muscular fatigue in the face, in the throat; not a beneficent and relaxing fatigue, though, but rather like the pain from a blow you aren't aware you have received.

I modified some practical notions about myself. Basically I have always enjoyed perfect health. Malnutrition in periods of war and poverty seemed on the whole to do me good. I have never known exactly where the liver is located. I can drink considerably and hold my liquor well. As for my nervous heart, after all, I have always considered it a useful thermometer. Even in Nordic climates I never had even as much as a sore throat. Always managed to breathe well, through the nose. This solid physical foundation has permitted me to bear psychic disorders. Or rather, this is what I had always believed. During my recent disorder that idea was practically subverted.

What I mean is, it probably was a lucky thing that I felt so bad physically, first with an infection of the respiratory tract, then with a more general one. For one thing, I ran a very high temperature. This was fortunate; it represented something one could get hold of and try to subdue by practical means. Through rare sporadic moments I even managed to find solace in a vision that Blatt has suggested to me concerning medication: "There isn't only the sinister, clinical concept of these matters, there are also other possibilities: there is comfort and a sense of opulence in the idea of being able to procure all that beautiful stuff for yourself, those potions, those sedatives, those soothing lubricants up your nose." Blatt once told me of a friend of his who stands in front of a pharmacy window "exactly like a gluttonous child in front of a candy store."

I seem to have come a long way in this respect; a couple of times I even tried certain drugs. My conclusions on the subject are worthy of a professional rationalist like myself, not so much cowardly (actually I have pretty good physical courage) as opposed to mythomania; not easily enchanted, hence perhaps a bit dry. At any rate, my idea is that the drugs I tried make you see the same things, the same knots of problems that you had before, except that you see them in pleasant, colorful versions. At some point you may feel you understand everything, but in the end that is of no use. You have to content yourself with what you get to understand in, as it were, an atmosphere of grayness; it isn't much, but at least it's the real thing.

Nadine's Dr. Wood completely replaced the nose specialist of Peter and Beatrice inasmuch as the locus of my problems had become immeasurably larger, and he subjected me to various kinds of tests; from the very little he allowed to transpire even to a keen observer like myself, he seemed decidedly confused and worried. Difficult to evaluate. He would measure, inject, do this and that, without ever saying a word. Even when he took my temperature, he would stick the thermometer in my mouth, then pull it out and look at it without telling me what it read.

I adapted myself to this style, so different from the method of my father's friend, Dr. Giulio Levi, who during the long, happy years in Venice, before the nefarious rulers drove him to commit suicide, would describe the slightest disorder to his patients in a nasal and solemn tone of voice, vernacular and Ciceronian at the same time. But let's not awaken memories of *that* Academy. It seems certain that Dr. Wood's worries, however tacit, proved contagious to others who are apparently fond of me, because when I saw their faces, in a circle around my bed, they looked apprehensive. Then I summoned Blatt for a confidential talk and gave him the address of my Aunt Luciana Strigato, and other data as well, in case I should die. I tried to give him a few instructions, with a minimum of rhetoric and a maximum of efficiency, and I am happy to say Blatt understood me very well, which makes me feel safe for any future eventuality.

Having settled bureaucratic matters, so to speak, I rambled on a little longer about my aunt and also about the place where she lives; it came to me now as a vision, more intense and lucid on account of my high fever. The façade of my aunt's house, I told Blatt, is, in its simple, no-nonsense way, one of the most beautiful I know: Renaissance, but comfortable, something for everyday living; solidly planted on its three low arches, it immediately inspires a feeling of serenity, never of awe. When I said things like that, Blatt would look at me with a clinical eye, as if collecting symptoms. Then he would come out with a phrase like "That's what you're missing. You're missing that kind of harmony."

I tried to make him understand that that kind of harmony had helped me in its day; I told him about my crisis when I was fifteen, and how my Aunt Luciana had helped me overcome it. But now, I went on, with one of my outbursts of laughter, the crisis I was going through was more commensurate with my broadened experiences and interests. He laughed too; Blatt and I have become real friends.

My worst attacks, as is right and natural, came during periods of nocturnal solitude. New kind of insomnia, caused not only by thoughts but also by physical pain. Dreams of a new kind, too; I would say there was a pretty radical change in my oneiric system. I mean that in happier times, the system had worked like this: I would fall asleep, fluctuate toward a timeless region where dreams fully held the status of dreams, recognizable as such upon awakening, to be isolated, remembered, noted down;

now, however, it was all like mush, where sleeping and waking were mixed up. And this mush, like an enormous swamp swept by winds, was swept by words. Fragments, remnants, of all the talks, all the voices that have always been invading my moments of silence were sliding toward this dark, disfigured plain; my head was filled with words; powerful ear buzzings (due also to medication) became like personal kamiri miris, private panels.

It might be useful at this point to insert the information that during my crisis I always continued to work. On a small scale, to be sure, but I did, for example, attend a couple of pre-Symposium meetings of the kamiri for relations with scientists, and I went on giving my lectures on modern Italian *Kulturgeschichte;* I missed only one of those. I developed certain ways to be up and around in spite of physical pain and fever, and to reduce the fever by taking the proper number of the right kind of pills, meanwhile budgeting what little energy I had at my disposal and keeping a bed ready on which, after completing my work, I would collapse.

Once in bed, as I said, I was visited in the night by these semi-dreams, more auditory than visual: I would find myself with my head swept by words; a concert of giant frogs over interminable marshes; mutilated and distorted talks as in a phantasmagoria kamiri, an obsession panel. Often I could discern, deeply hidden, the usual Institute with the usual Chuck, Pick, Blatt, except that now my infection was flourishing, or rather, it had come to the fore; I took the part of a walking disease in the aisles of the electrolibrary, a one-man epidemic.

"By now, Gilberto, the poisoning of your old brain is too far advanced. You must make room for the new brains—the electronic, antiseptic kind."

"But they can't think!"

"Well, as far as you're concerned you have no choice, Gilberto, you must let them take over. Your mind is out of commission, filled only with ghosts."

"But I worked today even! I always work, my boy." This "my boy," this phantasmagorial interlocutor, was often recognizable as Tava, Jr. This may seem interesting, but when it is prolonged and extended during long feverish nights it isn't that at all, it becomes only obsessive. But what I wanted to say is, the fact that I continued to work helped my capacity to endure, because through that, even in the black, deranged swamps of the night, I maintained a connection with daily, colorless, dutiful reality; however disproportionate my effort, I was still in the game.

Except that sometimes total exhaustion produced the completely obliterating type of sleep; this did not last long and was succeeded not by a sense of relief, but by fear from having known that abyss and having in fact at least one foot still in it. If I say that these were terrible moments I am not exaggerating, but to say that in such moments one desires death seems to me a banality for at least two reasons: first, one has no capacity to desire anything, hence not even the end; second, even assuming one had the strength to desire something, one would then channel it in that direction, as is proved by the fact that any Dr. Wood would be ready to provide sleeping pills; after storing up a goodly quantity of those, a pill suicide would be the simplest thing in the world, yet one doesn't even vaguely dream of arranging it.

On the contrary—I am aware I am emphasizing my personal case, but it's the only one on which I exercise any authority— the feeling you have is that you must not die, that that wouldn't be licit (in other words, "must" in the sense of Ger. *dürfen*), that actually you should stay alive whether you want to or not. And as a matter of act, you feel that your being alive does not make you a privileged being who has escaped an adverse fate, but rather, one who has been left here by chance to get along by himself, and who has got to stay on, no fooling around, to keep his pledge and for a number of other reasons, including precisely the obligation of thinking of the others, the already dead, remembering them, keeping them in mind.

Such an experience entails an incomparable feeling of solitude, and here my semi-dreams, conducted along kamiri and panel patterns with Pick and Chuck, would give way to other formations; other voices of frogs and wind would sweep those night swamps. To replace the predictable and more recent apparitions, the characters out of some ancient, fragmentary Venetian tales would erupt from my deepest memories—the heroes of fascinating, stupid, mysterious rhymes, like Mister Intention or Count Canaille. Fever would pulsate in my temples to the rhythm of "This is the fable of Mister Intention" (*Questa xè la fiaba del sior Intento*), "which lasts a long time" (*che dura tanto tempo*), "which never gets going . . ." (*che mai no la se destriga*), or of the celebrated "Count with the dirty pants" (*Conte, da le braghe onte*), "with a straw hat, Count Canaille" (*dal capel de pagia, conte canagia*) . . . The most indecipherable visitor of all was a dog, whose factotum career from one o'clock to midnight had so often been recounted to me as a child by the lawyer Fernando Rossi, who drew it from his atavistic sources: "At one o'clock, the dog works" (*A la una, el can lavora*), "at two, he stops" (*a le do, el mete zò*), "at three, he makes himself king" (*a le tre, el se fa re*), "at four, he goes mad . . ." (*a le quatro, el deventa mato*).

To remember and then to trace and retrace all of the stations in this enigmatic dog's life until midnight, when bells tolled for his last agony and the devil carried him away, became a vexing duty. It seemed imperative that I recall, recapture and investigate the lives of these creatures, who presented themselves to me thusly—manifestations without development, mutilated subjects, obscure, not registered, not perceived by History; and little by little along the way I would find others who in the course of my later life had replaced those erstwhile characters; they too were mutilated, victims, with no historical countenance: the Rossis with their wooden smile; Tognon, number nine, hence safe but right next to an executed comrade in arms; and so on and so on to my own Tava in the Alps; to Carlo, Alphonse's brother, killed before he was able to leave a message about what the word *patria* had meant to him; and all of those who had been evoked by my Uncle Bartolomeo in the long nights of talk and wine with his brother-in-law Fernando, my father: "You can't even imagine, Fernando, so many dead, an orgy, a bacchanal of killing . . ." Our voices at Portogruaro, including the harmonizing, including the song about Alpine soldiers marching to the train ready to leave for the front: "At the Feltre railroad station, a black flag" (*Alla stazione di Feltre, bandiera nera*) . . . "The best of our youth going under the earth" (*La meglio gioventù che va soto tera*) . . . We should have been with them, Gilberto. Under the earth, that was the sensible, dignified place to be. Survival is always something of a freak of nature.

On the other hand, it was in my half sleep, and close to the dead for whose sake I carried on, that I felt I was finding my protection, my strength. Protection from what? From the audio-visual material, from the perforated cards, from antiseptic history, from the deluxe morgue?

In the end, at the moment of supreme solitude, I could even talk to myself about my fiancée, Norma. Norma will always be part of me, so how should I talk about her? I would try to define her; such factual items as these would come to mind: Norma was a demanding person, an exclusivist, incapable of compromise. Born in Paluello, a rustic locality in the full Venetian countryside; as trees, she admitted only poplars. She excluded supernatural aid to the point that not even the village bells at sunset would delight her. Dead during a bomb raid, killed by people who for many reasons would have been her natural friends, a destiny similar to that of Tava, Sr. Those rare times when I'll talk to myself about you, I promise, Norma, I shall always do it as now—a few precise facts, with my eyes dry.

It is quite possible that in the notes I am about to make, I shall be cheating a little, playing with loaded dice. I mean that now I feel I am in a position to see in perspective the whole curve of my crisis, from the moment when the light changed and all things revealed themselves to me as fictitious, reality had no depth, Lebournet was somebody I dreamed up, to the moment when Blatt was here and I gave him to understand that I had discovered the positive aspects of my rather protracted disorder (it lasted quite a few weeks) , or the useful things I had brought up from the bottom of the abyss.

My mind was lucid, relieved and agile as I reported to Blatt. "I believe I have perceived this: everything is precarious, an apparition; in other words, *la vida,* of course, *es sueño,* yet precisely because life is a dream, one has to go on, get involved, be on the ball, soberly and correctly."

That's more or less what I was telling him; as he listened to that and other formulas, he frowned and smiled. We were delighted with the fact that something in my recent experience could now be captured and expressed through words, through the very tools of our study—which means, of some of our hopes. It even seemed as though it was the words that healed me, insofar as one can ever be healed. Hence the suspicion that I may be cheating, playing with loaded dice, because I seem to forget that physical healing was running its course, footing a major part of the bill, as it were—something that could be registered, measured: no fever, normal blood pressure, clean urine.

Blatt often came over to see me and we talked at length. Naturally the preparation for the Symposium and the strategies around it were one of our main topics. According to analyses conducted especially by Lebournet but largely accepted now also by Blatt and almost everybody else, opposition to Alphonse was deepening and solidifying, the Issue was being enriched with larger cultural and political implications; the opponents' public relations forces devised ever more damaging slogans; through media of persuasion, both overt and hidden they managed to elaborate and project an image of Alphonse's Institute as a gathering center for technicians without ideals, stateless intellectuals, and of course also godless.

Frequently Blatt and I discussed Tava, Jr., and now I want to dwell on this subject for a moment. Ruggero was on very confidential terms with Blatt and they often talked about me. The young man, according to Blatt, knew that his father and I had been close friends. I, who with my complicated animosity had described Ruggero as "a moral illiterate," now listened avidly to Blatt's words, and finally exploded with mordant satisfaction, "You see? He knows that, and it leaves him completely indifferent. You will probably remind me that his father died before he was born. And I'll counter with the observation that among human beings there have been some who practically went mad, foundlings for instance, trying to find out something about their fathers; that's not sentimentality, it just takes a minimum of imagination and human curiosity. But not Tava—when he meets somebody here who knew his father when his father was younger than he is now, he doesn't feel even a shade of curiosity, he just sits there, rosy and ingenuous; he's a big plastic doll, that's what your Tava is."

"If he became 'my' Tava, it's because you gave explicit orders to that effect."

"So you see," I went on, ignoring the interruption, "in the struggle for power, I'm sure which side he'll be on, I can al-

ready see him: Pick's pet, highly esteemed by Chuck . . ."
Here the way Blatt was looking at me made me stop.

He was looking at me as he had done for many weeks now, with a clinical eye, but a special sort of gloom was added now; with this gloom in his eye and in his voice he said, "Gilberto, you make me laugh." He calls me by my first name, the American way; I call him by his surname, as we did with our schoolmates.

He elaborated: "You're completely wrong. You're much closer to Pick and Chuck than he is. Because, you see, in that particular sense he's not close to anybody. There is a rapport between you and those people, which might be enmity, but a rapport it is. As far as he is concerned, there is no 'pro' or 'con.' The issue does not exist."

"You see? Irresponsibility? Moral illiteracy?"

"I don't believe your terminology can be of any use in this case. And at any rate, even if he were illiterate, what have you done to educate him? You kept him at a distance. Ruggero told me that before coming here, he was continually asking everybody, friends and relatives, whether they knew you, what you did, what kind of person you were. His uncle in Paris told him you were *a man who really existed;* Ruggero remembered the exact phrase."

"Think of that," I said with clenched teeth. With clenched teeth because I felt my chin tremble and I had to make a certain effort to contain myself; there was a running contest between me and this boy, who had tormented me even in my dreams. However, I spoke very dryly: "He doesn't seem to need anybody's help."

"Right. The help he gives is much more than the help he gets. Beatrice Clinton once told me, and I grant you it may sound banal, 'I have never met a more human person.' Just the opposite of the plastic doll." Blatt grabbed the gallon jug by the handle, poured some of the red wine, drank, cleared his throat, spoke like a panelist: "The young man belongs, rather, to what may become known as the neo-human era. The problem of man vs. machine—whether the mechanization of our world is a nightmare or a salvation—has never existed for him. He has found the great electronic equipment all nice and ready, neither more nor less astonishing, mysterious or agonizing than a telephone. This is his right element; you might say that people like him vegetate in automation. And this, curiously, doesn't make automatons of them, but rather, as individuals, the contrary. Ruggero is very good at his work, but that done he is absolutely adamant—always in his efficient and courteous way—about observing his vacation and leisure time. He has no career jitters; key formulas like 'a good position' don't belong in his lexicon. Yet he gives you the impression of knowing exactly what he wants from life. Beatrice is a few years older than he, but in many thing she is now dependent on him. You know, of course, that they plan to get married and I'm sure they'll do it very soon."

"I known I know," I said while Blatt continued to study me clinically. It wasn't entirely true that I knew. My heart started galloping, but that was my business. I am very much accustomed to a life made up of surprises and solitude. The question of Beatrice and Ruggero had presented itself to me both in daylight and in dreams. Synthetic phrases like "This boy has taken her away from me" had, after I pondered them awhile, definitely appeared useless, unrelated to reality.

Blatt went on with verbal gusto, "Ruggero is an intensely normal man, vertiginously well balanced. He has made his conquest of Beatrice, if 'conquest' is the word, sweeping her away into a whirlwind of serenity. They knew each other intuitively at once. You might say that the moment they first looked at each other, they got married."

Quite right. Bravo, Blatt. Our young Ruggero, after all, has even the physical appearance of the solid, Nordic husband, sitting there quietly in the evening with his pipe. Considering his extreme youth, he should actually look like an amateur acting the part, but it doesn't turn out that way. He's marrying a divorcée with more years of age and more experience than he, but the scene doesn't come out at all wrong; once more that appalling young man seems to master the situation completely.

"I imagine Beatrice's marriage will make you even lonelier," Blatt said in passing, without looking at me.

"Certainly." But I also observed that seeing those two get settled like that gave me a feeling of relief. We tried to find the reason for that. Old man feels he's finished and leaves his place to young one? No, not at all. Gilberto on his deathbed, opening his arms, fluttering his withered hands like tiny wings and emitting with a thin voice the classic "Children, come close, I want to bless you"? Let's not be ridiculous.

The contrary, then, perhaps? A residue of malice toward the chosen one, on the part of defeated Gilberto, who feels, deep underneath, that the young man is getting himself into something of a mess? From bad to worse.

Blatt and I were silent for some time. The moments of silence are the thermometer of the seriousness of a conversation. Then I said, "Well, let's say it's something like this: he is my friend Tava's son, and since Tava is absent, I've got to show some concern for his son; hence I feel relieved seeing him fixed up with someone I know well."

Deep in thought, Blatt drank some wine, then he said, "One day Ruggero was talking about you; he said you had rebuffed him by telling him that he might as well not come and see you; and as a matter of fact, he saw you only occasionally. Then it occurred to me to remark, 'You are avoiding each other because you are seeking each other. Deep, deep down, your coming here has been a voyage in search of your father.' Of course he didn't understand me, my words probably didn't even register on him, but that's natural; people like him never analyze the things they do."

One of the actions Ruggero has performed without analyzing was to come and see me a few days ago; Blatt was here too. I am still recuperating, so when friends come here in the evening I frequently receive them already in bed. The way Ruggero turned up here irritated me. Why should he choose the moment, arrive unannounced?

He had done that once before, while I was in the thick of my crisis. In a chair by the bedside he lit his pipe and launched a series of questions: "How are you? Are you still taking drugs? What kind of doctor is Wood?" He gave me a detailed description of a complete physical checkup he had had in Milan, and along the way we embarked on a discussion of the tremendous possibilities of electronic computers in the clinical area, for the gathering and prompt transmittal of each individual's data, a kind of medical identification card which someday might be obtained anywhere in the world, perhaps via satellite. Blatt was right: when people like him or me discussed that kind of subject, we did so with caution on the one hand, and on the other even with considerable enthusiasm; Ruggero never lost his equilibrium but always sounded as if he were discussing a new washing machine. I finally answered affirmatively his question about my taking drugs, adding that therefore he shouldn't be surprised if he lost me somewhere along the way in our conversation. After that he kept quiet, watching me with professional attention to see whether I would burst out in a mad delirium or whether I would fall asleep. When he saw that I was dozing off, he went away without a word, on tiptoe, letting me fall back on my semi-dreams.

Now on his latest visit he found a man more or less in a state of repair, a Gilberto propped up on the pillows, his bed covered with polyglot newspapers, showing some stamina in discussion and generally in the L & C area.

The topic of conversation between Blatt and me had again been the Institute; Blatt had exposed a theory which had recently been gaining ground concerning the tactics the opponents would devise in order to eliminate and submerge Alphonse. No frontal attack, but a wide encircling maneuver. During the Alphonse regime, the Institute had become practically autonomous, whereas it was actually part of the university; so the reforms necessary to integrate it in Our Time would confirm and reinforce its dependence upon the larger Structure. It so happened that the current president of the university was due to retire in a few months, and there was a strong movement in favor of appointing the pre-Alphonsean director of the Institute, Horace Buterweg, to that post. Whether the movement succeeded or not, it was clear that in the reapportioning of authority, the post of Institute director could no longer appeal to a man of Alphonse's caliber; he would therefore undoubtedly resign.

When Ruggero came in, I was reacting eloquently to Blatt's news. Since I had got rid of even the slightest trace of superlaryngitis and supertracheitis, I spoke with a clear voice, in an easy, rhetorical vein. I greeted young Tava with a simple wave of the hand, pointing to a chair, and I went on, addressing Blatt, "More than once, Blatt, you have described the Institute as a microcosm in which bloodless machinations and contests take place, comparable within their narrow framework to the fierce and bloody battles which occur in the tragic macrocosm of the politico-historical scene. Well, that scene—as we know, studying samples from the L & C point of view—abounds in foul plots, hits below the belt, murders, actually inspired by a mania for destruction and a gluttony for power, but adulterated through language and presented to the soldier and the voter as crusades and holy wars. It is not by accident that the ghosts of the masterminds of verbal falsification wander at night through the aisles of our electrolibrary—the crusaders with their retinue of billions of words and billions of corpses . . ." But suddenly I stopped because Ruggero's attitude made me curious. This wasn't the usual Ruggero. He seemed unresponsive and down-cast. I tried to shake him up by bringing him into the discus sion: "And how do *you* see the situation? How are you preparing yourself for the Symposium clashes?"

He looked at me without expression. "The Symposium. Yes. They're assigning some interesting work to me. You see, more than once I've done simultaneous translation at conventions."

"The pure technician. At night you don't see ghosts, do you?"

He barely shrugged, still looking at me with a blank face.

Suddenly, watching that face, the shape of that head, those pink cheeks, I lost control: my whole life with its memories started to dance in a ring around me, so I grasped the closest thing, the most immediately transmissible; I shouted, "Would you like me to tell you, Tava, how your father died?" My cry fell upon total silence.

Then he asked very quietly, "Were you there?"

"No, you silly fool, but I can describe it perfectly. I can stage it for you." I was almost looking around for Sergio and Gian-luigi Strigato to help me. "There's this little blockhouse here, bolted and shuttered, like those electric chambers charged with death. Your father is advancing on a green plateau toward this blockhouse. The blockhouse is like a head, the enormous ce-ment head of a cretinous giant; his sole facial feature is the lips, the horizontal cut, a thin stripe of darkness from which a gun barrel emerges, moving fanlike, spitting fire. And from behind it comes the voice: '*Roger! Fais attention! On va te tuer!*' That's the voice of one of his relatives. And even as the relative shouts like that, he goes on machine-gunning him. Have you ever seen a machine-gunned man? He doesn't necessarily break into pieces and die at once. It can be a long, complicated scene."

Silence. The three of us look at one another without saying anything. Sometimes I turn everything into puppets, especially things that lie too deep to be reached by tears. Naturally I regretted having talked as I did, I deserved no friendship, no consideration from this young Tava.

But I don't think he even heard me. Again it struck me that he was withdrawn, unreceptive. I offered him some wine. With his face flushed after the wine, he resembled his father even more. We spoke again about the Institute, the Symposium, I let him expatiate on simultaneous-translation techniques, but he spoke automatically, he did not light up.

Blatt said to him, "You're so absent-minded. What's the matter? You've been like this for days."

I asked, "Are you tired? Perhaps you work too much? All that Chinese?" I realized I asked him that without a trace of irony. He was an admirable young man, that's what he was—just over twenty and already a systematic, adult worker, all in all very desirable to have as a son, someone to be proud of.

Then he spoke in that childish way he has of mentioning friends nobody else knows: "I've heard from Irene. Then I talked to her on the phone. Meanwhile I also got a letter from her." He kept it all in his pocket. A cable and a letter. To simplify explanations, he showed them to me. The cable was a few days old. It said only: KUNTZ DEAD—IRENE. The letter was very short, one small airmail sheet with a newspaper clipping attached, from the obituary section: "Irene Berlocchi, Ruggero Tava Partibon and Piero Camentini announce that their dear friend Osvaldo Kuntz died yesterday after a long illness." In her brief note Irene said: "No one ever called him Osvaldo. Reading his whole identity is like seeing him in Sunday clothes, clumsy. You also feel tenderness because you think his mother must have called him Osvaldo, and when he was a small boy his schoolmates probably made fun of him because of that name." Only the closing followed.

Beatrice was away; she had gone with her father to a cabin they have up in the mountains. Obviously Ruggero had not wanted to be alone, and since Beatrice was absent, I represented second choice. He spent the night at my house. First the three of us had dinner here; he and Blatt prepared steak and salad. We finished the whole gallon of wine.

About his dead friend he spoke little and intermittently. He told us that in the past, in Venice, Kuntz would come to their house to tune the piano. "But he also came simply to visit us. Then he moved to Milan. It was I who brought Irene to him."

"I gather he was a composer, wasn't he? Did you ever talk to Epstein about him?"

"No, nobody knows Kuntz as a composer. No one knows him in any way, for that matter."

"But you knew him well?"

"Oh yes, and Irene too, lately." He looked at me. "Yes," he repeated, "of course."

I tried something like "He must have meant a lot to you," but he stared at me as though he didn't understand the language. We talked about other things, and then suddenly, as if he remembered a piece of information he must give us, he said Irene had been present during Kuntz's last moments. "Irene told me over the phone that at the very end he repeated several times, in a very clear voice, 'I'm strong, I've always been strong.' And as if to give evidence of that he raised himself, sat up in his bed, and he died in that position." At this point Ruggero and I looked at each other, and I burst into laughter. He smiled with a friendly, contented expression.

When Blatt was gone, Ruggero and I stayed up awhile to talk. He spoke of Kuntz's death only a few more times. It was clear that confronted with this fact he, verbally so well equipped and precise, became practically a stammerer. Example: "Perhaps it will seem odd to you, but I don't know . . . somehow I wish . . . I'd like—I'd like to have been Kuntz."

I would ask him very general questions: what kind of man Kuntz was, how often they met. Ruggero tried to express himself with his hands too, as if he felt at a loss for the right words. This is another of his phrases: "You see, Kuntz was always *there*." He also said, "A man who really existed." I recognized that phrase; it was what Giorgio Partibon, according to Blatt, had told Ruggero about me. I am sure Ruggero didn't realize that. Very good. It was best not to analyze anything.

We exchanged stories; I told him about the night on the train and New Year's at Portogruaro with his Uncle Giorgio.

He listened tensely, but this was a superficial kind of tension, with lips half open, like someone waiting for the punch line in a story, as a signal to liberate his laughter. Actually we did laugh quite a bit. Our talk was relaxed and zigzagging, so naturally I thought of the times I had spent with his father in Venice, Bergamo, Milan. He also talked about his mother, saying that she remembered me very well, having met me more than once "on the Academy Bridge, your hair blowing in the wind." Ruggero utters a phrase like that, which absurdly makes my heart leap, in a flat, lucid manner, as pure registration of a fact.

By himself he made his bed in the living room, one of those wide comfortable American beds you pull out of a sofa; he knew all about the way they work. Before we retired he asked me, "Do you by any chance have one of those sleeping pills Dr. Wood used to give you?" He swallowed the pill, drinking a glass of milk, and thanked me "very much for everything."

In bed, I stayed awake for a long while, reading; from my room I could hear him snore evenly and powerfully. At dawn, between sleeping and waking, I heard noises from the garage; he was pulling out his motorcycle and riding away, but he waited until he reached the curve below here before starting the motor, evidently in order not to disturb my sleep.

CHAPTER
SEVEN

GILBERTO ROSSI:

Later on Ruggero and I did not meet often, but not for the old
reason that we avoided each other, rather because we all here
have been very active, burdened with duties. Ruggero has been
busy organizing a simultaneous-translation service for the Symposium; he has proved himself very able and clear-headed, to
everybody's satisfaction.

To give some idea of the atmosphere prevailing here, it may
be sufficient to say that even before it got under way, the Symposium had its own press bureau, where Budd Rotondi plays an
important role, due to the electronic nature of so many communications media. This office not only sends out news items but
gathers newspaper clippings concerning the Institute; their
number is considerable.

Alphonse has not been much in sight. Blatt and I have had
moments of anxiety, asking ourselves whether our director is

abandoning the game and whether his speech at the Symposium may turn out to be his swan song.

The executive empyrean, under Chuck Palmerston's chairmanship, has been very active, holding panels in a language largely incomprehensible to me, and also sending out packages of mimeographed material, written in that same language on paper of different colors according to various classifications of the Institute's activities, such as historical research, public service, relationships between computers and cultural life, et cetera.

Tackling this mimeographed material, I am sure, would be to me like plunging into a world with which I had a fleeting contact at the time when my course in modern Italian *Kulturgeschichte* was being organized, and when, incidentally, an evaluation of my Italian was set at eighty-five percent. At the time, I had the immediate feeling that that world operates on a level of reality different from mine, and I lost, or rather, I forgot to resume, any contact with it.

Generally, in Chuck's communiqués, a bureau-enigmatic language alternates with a language of another kind, equally perplexing to me: the one based on New Structures and Values, Great Complexities of Our Time, Necessity for Concrete Dialogue, just to give some elementary examples.

As for my personal misfortunes, more than once now I have dared label the last few weeks a post-crisis period. For example, here is a good symptom: more than once I have had lively and amusing dreams, in which I encounter characters such as very tall, high-spirited ladies in furs who, meeting Blatt and me in the street, shout, "This is for renouncing God and your country!" And they smash us over the head with their umbrellas. One awakens from such dreams feeling refreshed and clarified. Our meetings with these umbrella-wielding ladies occurred in a small square, which was a narrow plateau up these canyons and at the same time San Salvador Square in Venice.

Not by mere accident did my oneiric antennas capture from the night of time and space the image of the latter place; there is a kind of analogy with a real scene of about forty years ago. That's the scene where Adriana Rossi, née Strigato, my mother, chatting away with her friend Giuseppina Lezze-Adorno about the current Italian situation, expresses an inadequate and naïve opinion of the new leaders of the fatherland, something like "I kind of feel they are a bunch of rascals."

Giuseppina replies with something predictable, like "You are blaspheming the saviors of your country," and after that, without umbrella blows but even more dramatically, she takes one step backward, and at that right distance she extends her arm, points at her friend and utters the vaguely Biblical key line, "Punishment will fall upon your children."

There is a silence, during which my mother assimilates that line, and then she says in a solicitous tone, "But, Pina, I have only one child, you know."

And by the way, this only child, not older than nine, is present, quite perplexed, of course; he doesn't know what to say. Now, forty years later, perhaps it's time to ask whether he has been punished, but here, too, I wouldn't really know what to say. Anyhow, a meeting like this one between the two ladies, as I evoked it in my post-crisis period, was not at all nightmarish, in fact it had something festive about it, as if the two ladies in the long course of years and in the continuous reshuffling of events, had been able to be reconciled, to meet, in a calm, unpoisoned air.

Something similar happened to my memories of my father as well; I could see him in situations that were even frivolous. Remembering him had been of little use to me during my crisis, on account of the permanent, routine quality of his despair. Now he appeared before me smiling, dressed in white, as I saw him one day when I happened to pass in front of the old Pilsen restaurant, where he was sitting with one of his Austrian lady friends. Just at that moment the lawyer Augusto Fassola, who had his office nearby, was also walking past the restaurant, in the opposite direction; out of the corner of his eye he had undoubtedly seen the Austro-Venetian couple, yet in returning my greeting he said, significantly underlining his words, "And by the way, do remember me to your father, will you?" My reply was dignified, antivenomous: "You can do that yourself; surely you must have seen him sitting there. Good-bye, Mr. Fassola." Even the memory of this brief exchange, in its small way, indicates harmony with the world, balance, a limpid and well-ventilated view of human relations.

I have a feeling that Tava, Jr., has contributed to the establishment of this state of affairs within me, or rather, it was Tava, Sr., who actually did it, the noblest and most antivenomous human being I have ever encountered in my life. I have finally recognized some of those traits in the son, who carries these signs but is entirely unaware of them, born with the prefabricated mark of freedom and independence, being a bastard even.

I am now coming back for a moment to my umbrella-twirling viragoes because I simply want to say that that's not just a scene out of a farce; those figures, though in a farcical key, do personify certain forces and instruments through which a serious attempt is being made at dealing blows to the head of the Institute in its present, Alphonsean version.

To give some idea of these situations I'll have to turn back and first take a look at the general picture, then come to specific points, particularly to one of Blatt's theories, the one concerning zero words.

The main purpose of the Institute, whenever Blatt and I try to describe it in language accessible to me, is to do something so that human discourse may be less like a series of dialogues between the deaf than it is now. That's obviously why we train ourselves to analyze the language of influential historical figures, especially if they appear to have been clearly pernicious. Even more obviously, we must keep refining the instruments with which we keep the protagonists of the current historical scene continuously under control. The most evident principle of all, the true pivot in Alphonse's position as compared to that of his adversaries, is that our work must be conducted outside any directives from governments or from other potential prefabricators of opinions & judgments; on the contrary, every morning (when we face ourselves at shaving time, as Blatt has correctly suggested) we must renew our pledge of truthfulness and perspicacity. Et cetera, et cetera.

Let's keep in mind that the Institute has been processing great quantities of material in the area of political oratory of the last fifty years; from this, a whole technique has been developed for the compilation of lexicons typical of a given period, or even of a particular historical figure in his relationship either with the people of whom he was the leader or with other historical figures by virtue of coevality, of a mutual desire for destruction, of complicity in crime, or whatever.

As a great systematizer of lexicons in various languages, Blatt has arrived at the rather obvious conclusion that many of the principal words in the normal vocabulary of international political exchange have been so completely abused, torn apart, pulled in all directions, that they have long ceased to have "usefully communicable meanings," in the same way that those who utter them have long ceased to assume any true responsibility for them. This situation is quite evident to the average newspaper reader, TV watcher, frequenter of political assemblies, et cetera, but Blatt and the Institute in general have undertaken to expose it more amply and insistently than has been done before. And since Blatt has a fixation about signs and symbols, he has sought one that will indicate, in the respective lexicons, the completely meaningless and empty words; he has decided to mark them with a small empty circle; those are zero words.

Blatt has also observed that nowadays cardiograms or urinalyses of political leaders with great responsibility and visibility are being publicized—and rightly so—as matters of public concern; by the same token, he advocates the establishment of a "verbal clinical record" for persons who, within a given linguistic area and in the exchange between areas, have borne or are bearing the responsibility for the destiny of populations. The clinical record of a public figure whose speech is cluttered with zero words would of course have to be regarded as an extremely poor one.

This Blatt formula probably would not have had greater resonance than many others used in projects and publications of the Institute if something hadn't happened; one day as Blatt was preparing some conclusive notes on a number of martial-patriotic oratorial texts (which Lebournet had helped us analyze), he stated incidentally, and without thinking he was doing anything extraordinary, that "in such texts and probably in the general average lexicon of political life, God should be considered a zero word."

Lebournet once wrote a highly technical essay entitled *Gott mit uns: The Reference to the Godhead in the Politico-Military Peroration,* but it turned out to be too abstruse, dull and difficult to grasp for the general public. Now, however, some reporters covering the Institute jumped at "zero word God," as they immediately saw a chance for exciting headlines such as GOD SCORES ZERO AT LANGUAGE INSTITUTE, or even, GOD'S NONEXISTENCE "PROVED" BY COMPUTERS.

This kind of news was made to order to stir certain areas of religious and civic opinion, and sound the alarm in regard to Alphonse's Institute. I say "religious and civic" because if we broaden our outlook for a moment and consider the pair, "God and Country," we should never forget that the Institute presents a "stateless" image; by its standards, the national origin of its individual components couldn't matter less, or if it does, it is for purely technical reasons: Italians, say, have been engaged for studies on Italy, but even so, things have actually gone from bad to worse, from the patriot's point of view, since texts and images and even anthems (Harold Epstein) have been subjected to cold scrutiny and analyses—operations the patriot naturally feels suspicious about. The patriot, I have often noticed, possesses a basic esprit de corps linking him to all other patriots, whatever their origins. Patriotism for him can have any name, shape, color or taste, provided it does exist and is always kept at the right temperature. I'll observe in passing that the nocturnal ladies who smashed us over the head with their umbrellas had the generic aspect of gendarmes without any particular nationality.

One morning Blatt announced, with an incredulous but tense laugh, "I have the impression that things are taking a rather serious turn." There had been various letters to the newspapers, plus other written & oral activities on the part of individuals & groups; an idea was spontaneously taking shape that the Institute should become the object of an investigation by some outside, superior kamiri. Meanwhile, even some internal trends called for at least a reassuring word from the director. There was an atmosphere of verbal tension; in such moments, people on the inside speak of nothing else, and the most casual remarks uttered by a central character enjoy immediate circulation and acquire the L & C weight of historical phrases; this was the case with Alphonse's remark when it was made clear that a statement from him would be in order, to soothe public opinion: "What would they like me to do? Announce a press conference about God?"

A problem arose naturally among Institutologists: To what extent was the anti-Alphonse opposition fomenting present criticism of the Institute, or at least proposing to turn it to its own advantage, "instrumentalizing" it? An indication was given at the moment when it became clear that Alphonse would hold no press conference or anything of the sort; and then Chuck Palmerston, though showing complete understanding for Alphonse's abstention, immediately took it upon himself to announce that criticism recently aimed at the Institute would be discussed in public during a special meeting of the executive kamiri for the Symposium. In other words, he took the public image of the Institute in his own hands. As usual the debate would be in the form of a panel. Invitations to speak would be extended to people who were not regular members of that conclave. But however well conceived Chuck's idea may have seemed, his whole planning collapsed when the man who should have been the main outside speaker on the panel, Blatt, declined the invitation. Here again Chuck Palmerston expressed his understanding.

Chuck Palmerston's attitude, either in Alphonse's or Blatt's case, was not wholly clear; it wasn't clear whether his understanding was prompted by respect for those two eminent colleagues, or whether it didn't rather imply the notion that the two were done for, anyway, and there was no reason to have them make one final useless effort. But there was one palpable consequence of Chuck's initiatives: with typical élan, old Clinton submitted his resignation from the executive kamiri. He did so in a speech, and before announcing it, he ostentatiously unplugged his hearing aid to make it clear that he would not acknowledge interruptions and objections. He expressed disdain for "Dr. Palmerston's implication that we should offer excuses for our work as though we were on trial," and with evident delight he used the loose language of a political campaigner, as when he said, "We shall never allow our activities to be in the least controlled by the illiteracy of reactionaries."

Even during this public scene, Chuck affected understanding. He even applauded Clinton, like a young champion applauding the last marathon of an old one. He no longer felt there was any need to hold a special panel. He had already made himself sufficiently visible to the public as the new man, a symbol of order and wisdom. Meanwhile he had already replaced Clinton on the kamiri with a man as new as himself, Alf Lundquist, who was already chairman of the kamiri for guinea-pig languages and a member of dozens of other kamiris. Lundquist is tall, neat, alert—the vigorous and disinfected athletic type. He also has a passion for dancing. Another passion he has is gardening; in his lapel there is often a flower he has grown himself. He is a very active extramural speaker; he gives lectures to religious societies in various communities.

For me this has been a rather happy period. Apparently, to be happy I must have reality displayed before me like a show—a demanding show, with a chance for me to take part in it; in fact, to plunge into it with conviction and vigor. Although I am rather new to this place, I believe I have managed to participate, to expose and to impose myself, to get involved, to get implicated, all of which are to me deep needs, at least when I am in relatively good form. Insistent, precise and—to call a spade a spade—unpleasant as I can be, I have always held myself available any time & any place, especially when circumstances seemed to make my talk particularly inopportune. I would touch upon the subjects regarded as most sensitive and dangerous, and of course I would not be on the defensive; on the contrary, I would do my level and lucid best to aggravate the situation. Basically, every single word expressed the feeling of admiration & loyalty I have for Alphonse. To his critics and to those who thought they smelled sulfur emanating from the Institute, I said that our activities were but the beginning; larger and more complex results could be expected from us in the long years ahead, naturally under the direction of Alphonse, who had to be considered, for all practical purposes, the founder of the Institute. Since I preferred to use this kind of language with people of the Budd Rotondi or Alf Lundquist type, and their respective circles, who had considered Alphonse's demise a sure thing even before the most recent criticisms and complications, I would be viewed with astonishment, impatience, alarm, contempt. Having been acquainted all my life with this kind of reaction to what I say, I was not in the least disturbed and continued to perform what I considered a limited but useful didactic function.

In the history of any micro- or macro-community, I have noticed that during a struggle like this, the most polemical and pointed exchanges occur among the small fry; the big fish, who are playing for the really substantial stakes, find occasion to treat one another very pleasantly. Minor figures are much more intensely partisan and may sometimes feel that they have been fooled when, at a party, for instance, they watch great antagonists exchange confident smiles and firm handshakes, caressing, greasing, massaging each other with their looks; however, I must also add that after half an hour at the most, they all—standing there clutching their drinks—finally look unreal; then, way down below that colorful, unreal surface, you sense the presence of silent underwater torpedoes.

During this pre-Symposium period, the Pickfords have done nothing but give cocktail, dinner and after-dinner parties. The most enlightening was an after-dinner party to which Nadine had invited me. "Just a few of us. We wanted Alphonse, too, but he's busy. We adore Alphonse." Then Blatt called, urging me not to miss the soirée. We went together, and were the last to arrive.

As soon as we came into the living room (large, low-ceilinged, sprawling—with many sofas, large, low and sprawling as well) we noticed that we were not so few. In front of a group of people Blatt behaves in the same way as when he is analyzing a text, only instead of key words he instantly spots the key people and the structures they form. He whispered immediately, "There's the whole shadow government." That means the group of people who already have their eye on the positions they will occupy when the opposite group are defeated and replaced by them. In the context of the other stars, some of them endowed with a strong light of their own, the design of the Shadow constellation had immediately been evident to Blatt the astronomer.

I was far short of knowing all the people present. I lead a rather secluded life, and besides I am bad at connecting faces with names. However, not only did I distinguish the main characters with my naked eye, but it was also quite easy for me to imagine them onstage, in a parliamentary chamber seated on the government bench, and to assign them the positions they would occupy after the fall of the present Alphonse government. I saw Pickford as Premier, holding perhaps also the portfolio of Foreign Affairs; as Vice-Premier and Minister of the Interior, I sensed Alf Lundquist; Chuck would get Defense; the important and modern Ministry of Technology would go to Budd Rotondi; Lebournet would be Minister of Culture.

Among the guests, in fact in a central position, there was also Horace Buterweg, the Great Predecessor, surrounded by his adherents. I had met Buterweg one distant evening at Alphonse's, when Alphonse had apparently offered him the honorary chairmanship of the Symposium. At any rate, Buterweg had turned it down, but he had lingered on here and later had come back several times, always received with particular attentions and courtesies, like a cardinal visiting his original parish. I have already noted that Buterweg was spoken of as the next president of the university; therefore in my vision of a post-Alphonsean future he was a supragovernmental figure on my inner stage, head of state, President of the Republic.

My designations of the Shadows seemed decidedly right to Blatt as well. We found Lundquist a particularly happy choice for Vice-Premier and Minister of the Interior. As I said, he is an excellent dancer and gardener; occasionally he produces huge belly laughs; but above all, he is a towering compiler of mimeographed communications and questionnaires to be filled out. At first sight, the immediate inclusion of Lebournet in the new government may seem less clear. But Lebournet has certain assets whereby he fits in beautifully: in the first place, he is very young and already a capital paterfamilias, well integrated in the social order; then, with his sound studies on Rhetorical Structures and with the abstruse but imposing reputation of his "mineral stories," he has managed to create an aura of specialist, of technician around himself; that makes him one of those men whom a new government can incorporate without worrying about what party or wing he belongs to.

Whole volumes could be written about a single evening; here I shall confine myself to essentials. We were in the presence of great reorganizers of the Institute, advocates of Basic Restructuring. My first discovery of the evening was that they did not at all look like people hatching a more or less secret plot. Maybe they had looked that way earlier; now they didn't. They looked like winners, with their appointments already in the bag. They could permit themselves to look at members of the previous government with admiration & reverence.

Clinton was present, too, and he was an object of worship. Nadine Pickford was delighted to tell me that Beatrice and Ruggero had accompanied and deposited him there, and that they would come and pick him up later on; meanwhile the canonized old man sat in the most comfortable chair, silent and impervious. But up to a point.

Actually, while a long drink was being served from pitchers —a drink with lots of fruit in it, looking innocent but based on vodka and champagne—old Clinton, who possesses the sensory antennas of the really deaf, got up as if he had been summoned to a debate, and went straight to the corner where Buterweg was sitting in a circle of his aficionados. Buterweg, by the way, though strongly built, usually speaks with a thin and emotional voice as if he were exchanging advice & help with his interlocutors at a time of great crisis. As a matter of fact, "exchange" is not the word. When the person he is talking to puts in a brief remark, he immediately reacts by lowering his eyelids as if to assimilate it and then whispers, almost whines, "Yes, yesss . . ." as if he meant, "It's so true it hurts." But then he doesn't really give the impression of having listened and goes on with his own talk, which is followed with solicitous deference.

Now, through his antennas, Clinton had got the idea that in the Buterweg area of the room they were debating, in some fashion or other, the relationship between Man and Machine, Humanity and Technology, et cetera. The issue had occupied a considerable part of Clinton's flourishing old age, both during kamiri miris and in the classroom. In particular, with the frenetic self-assurance of the deaf, he assumed that in the Buterweg circle they were discussing problems of moon exploration. He stopped in front of the group, and naturally all the eyes of those low-seated people were raised and converged on him hovering high above them, out of their voices' reach. He spoke in a quick, practical manner, like a schoolmaster summarizing grammatical rules already explained: "There are hundreds of other activities open to the technologist, compared to which a trip to the moon is nothing but the indulgence of a childish whim." He paused, as if to allow them time to take notes. Without the slightest trace of rancor, in fact in an affable, persuasive tone, he resumed, "And at any rate, your approach is wrong. You are pernicious people. You throw human intelligence into the mud. You exploit some of its most spectacular and pleasing achievements to get political publicity out of them." He shook his head; and not in a tone of reproach, but in a kind of cheerful singsong, he concluded, "Shame–on–you—shame–on–you."

Three handclaps, three in number, came from the other end of the room. It was Chuck Palmerston. He also said, "Bra-vo."

At that point I was sitting next to Nadine Pickford; she squeezed my arm with a stifled cry: "Ideas . . . ideas . . . Always talking about ideas."

On my other side I had Harold Epstein, who followed Clinton's talk with the kind of smile he might have had listening to a tolerable performance of some of his own music. In the face of any human exhibition, Harold always takes the right attitude; you can use him as a very exact moral thermometer. That can be irritating, too; but then, his thermometric precision is always redeemed by human touches of folly. Now he raised his glass full of vodka-champagne, shouting, "Sputnik *sí*, Chuck *no!*," and gulped it all down.

"Always ideas," Nadine went on lamentingly.

Clinton was going on too; in fact, he had started playing one of the favorite records in his repertory, the one about the Airports Level. I had heard him play it more than once at kamiri miris and elsewhere. I recognized the opening: "While you're playing around with the moon, the technological gap, the real one, is expanding." The real technological gap, according to Clinton, is not the one between developed countries and countries that are less- or under-developed, it is the gap between human beings and the technical means they themselves invent and produce. People let the machines get out of hand, they use them but they fall behind, in the sense that they are unable to accept them emotionally, to experience them fully and vitally, and, incidentally, to turn them (Clinton's words) into culture & poetry. "And meanwhile," he went on, "you happily allow yourself to be guided by prime ministers, foreign ministers, ministers of this and that, all of them people whose gap is even worse than your own because they usually live on the Airports Level."

[*236*]

I haven't traveled much and I have only a limited and recent experience of jet planes, but here I follow Clinton very well; all you need is to be an ordinary reader of weekly magazines. What he means to say, or rather, what he does say all day long even without the slightest encouragement, is that the lives of Our Leaders largely consist of arrivals & departures, climbing & descending airplane ramps, or equivalent comings & goings through accordion funnels; entrances & exits into and from hotel rooms or official residences or halls for international meetings, summit or otherwise, equipped with the same conditioned air as airport lobbies or jet cabins, same temperature, same proportion of oxygen, same light, same voices conditioned through filters, through simultaneous translations, through earphones, and immediately printed on magnetic tape, fragments of which are bounced in turn to us through new filters, satellites, TV screens, et cetera. I, Gilberto Rossi, am formulating some ideas on these subjects, not all white or all black; in other words, to me it is an open question, while to Clinton, at the present stage, life at that level of conditioned air & light evidently seems a hopeless unreality.

When he had finished playing his record in that vein, again it was Chuck who applauded him. It is easy for Chuck to applaud him; all avenues are open to Chuck, he being the man of the technological era and of the forest, of electronics and of the prairie; he can plug in one or the other of his personalities the way you change the attachments on your vacuum cleaner.

"Ideas, ideas." Nadine Pickford did not change register. But this time she concluded: "Whereas what really matters is the people, *the peo-ple.*"

"You're right, Nadine." She yearned for the triumph of those Human Values which she was promoting by giving one party after another in order to cultivate her husband's political game and alliances. Meanwhile old Clinton went back to his chair, more canonized than ever. The whole thing was like a minuet. Genius of the party: to turn everything into minuet. In the meantime, people like Clinton were done for; the New Order would keep them around only to listen to them every now and then, as to old carillons. But I was also asking myself, "These various characters, Pick, Chuck, Budd, Alf, with their respective spouses, what satisfaction did they get from life?" In a sudden change of scene on my mental stage I saw them all coupled, naked in bed, but the vision lasted only an instant.

Since there had been some place rotations, I found myself seated next to Buterweg; I realized that this tête-à-tête was the reason for my presence, planned and prearranged, part of the minuet.

For the first time I was getting a comfortable close-up of Buterweg. Noble and momentous nose, piercing eyes, thin lips with the quiet smile of the sage: a caricature of Erasmus. I began to find him much more acceptable when I discovered, behind that façade, a man evidently capable of practicality and toughness.

"What will you be doing at the Symposium?" he asked me. "I've heard very good things about your work. I hope you'll also participate in the discussions on the use of computers in relation to language and on the regulation of that use, a regulation which in Our World and in Our Time has become an urgent necessity. Palmerston is very hot on the subject and will deal with it at the Symposium. Of course there's no reason why we should all agree with Palmerston."

It shouldn't be forgotten that Chuck Palmerston is his son-in-law. I got one of my impulses to laugh. I suffocated it and said with detachment, en passant, "No . . . listen, my paper for the Symposium has nothing to do with the use of electronic devices; my subject is 'Some Aspects of the Use of Pronouns in Political Oratory.' "

He looked at me and whispered with fervor, "Good, good," but I wasn't sure that he had been listening. At that moment I realized he has dark, luminous eyes, and that he slightly resembles a bishop I have sometimes watched here on TV. He also has a beautiful head of straight, thick gray hair. He is a man of utmost elegance, preserved with the greatest care. Speaking face to face, he abandoned his whining tone completely. In my chest I felt my heart abandon its slow, comfortable pace and start to run off, finally settling on tachycardia. This was a signal indicating that we had come to a decisive moment in the evening, perhaps in my life. Why had the Shadows invited Blatt and me? Their messages must be decoded quickly: Had they invited us to sound us out and to suggest between the lines that we stay on here, collaborators in the post-Alphonsean New Order?

"What are your plans for the future, for the next few years?" Buterweg put the cards on the table just like that.

Careful now. Appropriate reply needed. My exordium was more or less verbatim the way I am putting it down here: "Buterweg, there is no point in being ambiguous. If our talk is to be at all useful, we must somehow go back to our conception of life and of relations between human beings. Of course it would be impossible for me to tell you my whole life story in just a few words, but let me give you some examples." I briefly described the nature of my crises, which over the years have tended to increase in frequency and variety. I sketched some key figures in my professional life, such as Ceroni or Di Gaetano. As Buterweg seemed to be genuinely curious, I went on to some illustrations drawn from my dream world: how, not infrequently, I found myself in a cell, waiting, while outside, in a soccer field in the sun, everything was being readied for my execution by shooting. "A problem which can become vexing for me is, for instance, this: at the last moment, before falling in the pool of blood, I would shout Long Live what? I always wake up before I have decided."

He nodded knowingly. But Buterweg is also a good moderator, not a sublime one like Alphonse, but really good; he can soberly bring a conversation back to the main track. He spoke about our present cultural-historical time, and particularly about academic careers, titles, publications. He hinted at the possibility of drawing up five-year contracts, not with the Institute, but direct with the university; at the end of that period a research associate in my category could become eligible for life engagement, tenure. He quoted regulations; he defined my bureaucratic position better than I would know how. I was sufficiently determined & able to deviate the talk to more substantial themes.

"Buterweg," I said, "my coming here is the result of a series of events, the most significant of which is that something clicked between Alphonse Rossi and me. I shall not mention other clicks which have occurred here on the spot, with Blatt, with Clinton. In professional life, such rapports should be safeguarded above all. Our L & C studies indicate that even in the most vertiginously high summit meetings, the human factor I'm referring to is essential. I suppose this is even more true of situations like our own which are not subjected to the dehumanization process implicit in what our illustrious friend Clinton calls life at the Airports Level; such situations, in fact, thrive in their independence of that Level. The 'clicks' I've mentioned are like sparks of pure reality; any life arrangement that didn't take them into account would be contrary to the organic nature of things. For instance, any guarantee of permanent employment with a retirement plan, any form of tenure that did not produce those sparks would be something unreal; in fact, there would be something sinister, evil-eyed about it. We must do all we can, Buterweg, to stick to reality, somehow or other." I paused. Come to think of it, I wouldn't be surprised if my words were sufficient to block any Concrete Offer from the Shadows. I resumed in a more confidential tone, the tone of a casual chat after the formal part of a meeting is over, "This may seem strange to you, Buterweg, but to me the true sign of reality is if it presents itself as a show, as a performance of some sort. I have several forms of mental staging, the technical details of which I shall spare you. The essential point is that there be a performance, and that my role in it may satisfy me, as long as it lasts, may keep my conscience at peace as a man, as a citizen, and if you wish, as a potential poet."

I must say that this time he seemed rather flabbergasted; I didn't get a chance to analyze his reactions more thoroughly because suddenly old Clinton appeared. He stooped over me, preceded by the microphone of his cumbersome hearing aid, which he proffered to me as if it were something to eat, meanwhile whispering with urgency, "Could you please repeat the first part of what you said? I was off the air."

Then Clinton pulled me away, for one reason because Chuck Palmerston was leading Buterweg over to a small sofa where he deposited him beside Blatt; evidently there was a preordained series of person-to-person interviews. Before the one with me, Buterweg had had a talk with Harold Epstein; I had overheard nothing of it, but I had seen Epstein at some point start humming a tune for Buterweg in a low voice, beating time with his forefinger, and shortly after that the interview had come to an end.

Alone with Clinton in a corner, I reconstructed my speech to Buterweg as well as I could, and he absorbed it with lively and critical curiosity. Then something else occurred to him; he came closer to me with his microphone and all, laid his strong ancient-mariner's hand on my arm and whispered in my ear, "Would you do me a favor? Could you tell me something about my future son-in-law?"

The question made me feel elated and proud. Somehow I have a great need to breathe family air, and for some time now I have felt about Ruggero and the Clintons as if they were my relatives. I gathered my thoughts and tried to give a clear and well-organized report. I didn't mention Ruggero, Sr., because I felt that would introduce an autobiographical note, whereas Clinton simply wanted an objective opinion of Ruggero, Jr. I told him quite openly that at first I was inclined to consider the young man an efficient and insensitive monster made of plastics. Later on, using my experience of other young men, and having obtained enlightening help from conversations with Blatt, my perspective changed considerably. With the new perspective, I came to the conclusion that Ruggero did not lack what some vague lexicons describe as Thoughts & Feelings, but that he had no need to take cognizance of them, place them, frame them, catalogue them within a *Weltanschauung*. Individuals like him never have a troubled conscience. And even if they perform, say, what according to ancient, familiar lexicons was referred to as a Good Deed, they do not recognize it as such, they do not accompany it with propaganda, and even less do they present it within the framework of a philosophy. Their actions are not disturbed by the shadow of a *Problematik*. One reason for that may be that they grew up in a period which did not necessarily compel them to take unequivocal stands on one side or the other, and at any rate, they are not conscious of this, either, because the idea of living in History frankly does not concern them. I spoke a little along these lines.

The old man smiled happily. He asked, "These young people don't know anything, do they?"

I thought about that for a while, then I replied, "It seems to me that in this context, the verb 'know' may be considered a zero word."

"Bravo!" He was even happier. I was happy too. We communicated well. Clinton's mental agility is almost wild. I pointed at him: "Now, for example, take the Clinton Theory about the technological gap; well, it doesn't apply to Ruggero. For him that gap has been filled in the only way possible—by never having existed. To him, electronic resources, automation, et cetera, are natural, organic facts of life." Here I was more or less quoting Blatt.

He grunted, but at bottom he was tickled to hear me refer to a Clinton Theory, because he is actually rather vain. "Good," he said. "You reassure me. You must understand, my daughter is the only family I have left." He added in a lower key, "She'll always be devoted to you. You were too old and demanding for her, but she'll always be devoted to you."

For some time now Blatt, who had finished his talk with Buterweg, was signaling to me that we should go. I agreed. I was in excellent form; my dialogue with Clinton had been enough to give me a sense of reality in human relationships, which the previous talk with Buterweg had partly elided. Premier Louis Pickford accompanied Blatt and me to the door. During long handshakes he looked each of us in the eye, with his "European" manner—confusing in a man who has the face of a Mexican idol. "Thanks for coming." Did he perhaps imply "Thanks for your vote"?

Blatt and I had arrived in my car; I did not need to tell him that I was now driving to Alphonse's house; it was instinctive for both of us to do just that. The windows were still lighted when we got there. We rang and Ruggero came to the door.

In the living room we found Alphonse in a dressing gown, uncombed, with the white percentage of his hair much in evidence, his eyes fixed and shiny but curiously cheerful: for our purposes, hardly a receptive Alphonse. Doris, immersed in the sofa beside him, waved her hand to greet our entrance. Ruggero went over to a card table in a corner where he evidently had been sitting before we came, with Beatrice and someone not familiar to us. He remained standing, and the other two also got up; Beatrice came forward and kissed me on the cheek. Raising my voice so everybody could hear me, I said to her, "Your father is waiting for you to rescue him from the Pickfords', where he is trapped by the Shadow government."

No one paid any attention to me. Ruggero came toward us with the unknown gentleman, first turning to him: "Senator, I'd like to introduce two senior colleagues of mine, Hugh Blatt and Gilberto Rossi." Then, turning to us, he said more rapidly, "Senator Angelo Marchesan."

As usual, seeing Ruggero the guide, always perfectly at ease with everybody everywhere, I felt torn between irritation and paternal pride. I found out later that Ruggero and the senator had met in Paris, where, according to Ruggero, they had listened to "some magnificent music," while the senator added, "if 'music' is the word." At any rate, this was the famous senator friend of Alphonse's, invited by him to the Symposium. From the Venetian province. It was the first time I had ever touched with my hand a senator of the Italian Republic, odd that it should happen here on the Pacific Coast. I look less impressive and not as old, but later I discovered that he is my age. It was obvious right away that he is the type who knows everybody. No sooner had I finished informing him, at his request, that in Italy I had been employed by the publisher Di Gaetano than he was saying, "Marcellino Di Gaetano? We're old friends." Even actresses. "Paola Imperatore? A dear, dear friend of mine. Paola is quite smart and a very serious girl." All in all, I was rather impressed. It was evidently possible to lead a life in Rome that was quite different from mine. If I examined my acquaintances thoroughly, I would probably come to the conclusion that the most important person I knew in Italy was Di Gaetano himself, and it would never have occurred to me to call him Marcellino. Yet the senator did not look like the fatuous, bragging type; he spoke slowly and with precision, pondering his words; he sounded like a self-taught man of peasant origin.

Now he sat down on the sofa between Alphonse and Doris and chatted with them in an easy, informal manner; he was trying to persuade them to spend next summer in Italy. They talked about new speedways, restaurants, wines, this and that. At one point they looked crazy to me. Ruggero joined the conversation, and somehow it turned to the technique and industry of deep-frozen foods. Ruggero, the infuriating monster, possessed a lot of information in this area, about which I unfortunately know very little.

Silently, I was studying Alphonse. Storm clouds—let's use the conventional image—were gathering over his head, and there he was, discussing frozen foods. Where was the Alphonse once described by Doris? *He's so big and tall, and when he goes*

through a period like this, it's as if he were several men in one.
Now he made me feel pity and anger instead. I thought of the
time when I dreamed of him as a child. My heart was agitated
by apprehensive tenderness. And at the same time I could have
choked him. I jumped to my feet. Everybody's eyes converged
on me.

I turned to the senator and asked him point-blank whether
he, who had come here to attend the Symposium, knew anything about the Institute's present situation and its significance.
"This may look to you like a serene and happy realm, but on
the contrary, a deep struggle is going on." I summarized the
terms of the struggle, I animated the scene with various characters, from Pick to Chuck to Buterweg. In conclusion I said that
the final purpose was to overthrow Alphonse, and that if for no
other reason than that, I could not understand how they could
sit there discussing frozen foods. Blatt interrupted me, seemingly trying to pour oil on my troubled waters. Then my voice
rose to a high pitch, and I enlarged my presentation by going
from micro to macro: "Senator, you know what? Three cheers
for open revolt, for unbridled rebellion, arson, looting." Everybody was looking at me and I laughed, in my peculiar way.
They kept on looking. I lowered my voice: "Better that sort of
thing than to keep up appearances and manners and courtesies
while actioning the torpedoes." Evidently I had grown very pale
because Alphonse got up abruptly; with vigorous strides he
went to the bar, fixed a strong Scotch and soda for me, placed it
in my hand and returned to the sofa.

For a long while you could literally hear only the gurgling of
my whiskey, the clinking of ice in the crystal glass.

Then, serene and reliable, Beatrice and Ruggero rose together and said they were going to pick up Papa to take him
home to sleep. Beatrice kissed me again, this time on the forehead. After they had gone I said to Blatt, "Perhaps it's time for
us to go too," but Doris got up and fixed nightcaps for both of
us. We drank while the other three resumed their talk about
next summer in Italy.

It was hopeless. As so often in my life, I was inopportune and
out of phase. I stopped talking. I didn't talk even when Blatt
and I were outside, alone under the starry sky. I drove in silence
along the Pacific Highway at the legal speed limit. The en-

trance to Blatt's house is right on the highway. In the rear there is a stretch of sandy beach a few yards wide, and stones, and then immediately the ocean; when I stopped the car we could hear the crashing noise of breakers behind the house. Before leaving me, he said, "Try to sleep. Take one of the pills Wood gave you." He shook my hand firmly and added quickly, "You have really learned nothing." Blatt is perhaps the closest thing to a brother I have ever had. His words were rather cryptic but I didn't feel like starting a discussion. And then, perhaps I understood him well enough and he may have been right.

I drove away fast, but before taking the turn up my canyon, I stopped at an open space between houses, a kind of terrace overlooking the ocean. I got out of the car and stood there for I don't know how long, watching and listening to I don't know how many breakers, maybe a hundred. Things of great beauty & vitality. Widely spaced and enormous, they rise like walls of water and then fall with a crash; for a while there is the furious turmoil of foam and finally the backward surge, just as powerful, like a cascade in reverse.

I resume several weeks later and try to organize my notes on the Symposium

It's astonishing to see how well known the publications of the Institute are in various parts of the world. I found an Englishman and even a man from Japan, delegates to the Symposium, who knew Blatt's work and mine and asked detailed questions. It occurred to me to use the term "delegates" because it is used at international conventions, but come to think of it, it doesn't apply to at least ninety percent of the people who have come here. Who is supposed to have delegated them? Actually their presence here is the result of happy accidents and of invitations extended by the most diverse sources. It is perhaps possible to distinguish rather clearly a backbone of Alphonse invitations, but then, just to give one example, there is a group of advertising people interested in electronics, who are constantly together with Budd Rotondi. Great friends of his. Rotondi is a superb cook, although in a different key from Louis Pickford, and he has these friends in for dinner, receiving them bare-chested amid kitchen smoke, in front of his pots and pans.

From the very start we realized not only how popular the Institute is around the world but also how many different notions there are concerning its nature. That is shown by the heterogeneous quality of the participants and of their professions & origins. There are about fifty delegates, and I have spoken with fifteen or twenty, which is quite sufficient. They span a wide range, from those who had apparently thought of the Institute as a kind of wealthy empyrean or the quintessence of all international cultural agencies, to those who seem to have considered it a school where languages are taught fast. In my view this variety of images is a sign of the Institute's strength and of its potential vitality, which they all, without exception, evidently sense correctly and instinctively. There are quite a few men of letters.

The Englishman I mentioned before is a poet named Jason Jones, unknown as a poet but who says very sensible things in the L & C area, expressing them with concision and fine humor. The man from Japan is a writer too, a friend of Lebournet's, Uruki by name; one of his aims in life is to publish stories in which the quality and choice of typeface and paper, peculiarities of the design, and even the binding, would be integral and definite components of the work. During the war Uruki was a kamikaze, or at any rate he says he was, but he was not sent on a suicidal mission because in the meantime at Hiroshima *tout était finito, Schluss,* as Uruki himself says, his L & C instrument being a European medley drawing on various sources. The Hungarian representative could perhaps be considered a proper delegate; by profession he is director of the government tourist agencies. A wild polyglot, he is on familiar terms with convention members of all origins, by whom he likes to be called George. He laughs all the time. Very muscular, and bathes in the ocean every day, although he is a very bad swimmer. He is extremely interested in electronic devices insofar as they are used in booking airline reservations, hotel rooms, et cetera. In his way he is a man of letters, too, a loud reciter of poems in various languages; he has explained a couple of very interesting things about Hungarian folk songs to me.

These and many other convention members don't seem to have asked themselves exactly what form the Symposium would take; they came here in a festive mood and open-minded. We all know that there is a stereotyped image of conventions which presents them as nothing but an excuse for fun & games, dinner parties and excursions. Nothing could be more false in our case. If there is anything the visitors here seem to have been hungry for, it is not food and drinks but the Institute's collections and study materials. Many of them, especially Europeans but also Afro-Asians, spend hours in special booths poring over remote yearly sets of newspapers and magazines on microfilm, and when they finally emerge they look dazed and inebriated.

Besides lectures, presentation of papers, panels, round tables in the various theaters and lecture halls, there is a kind of permanent exhibition, a fair open around the clock and equipped to offer samples of the products and demonstrations of the machines. There is enormous interest in the prodigious collections assembled by Alphonse, especially in the war posters and placards with ferocious images and slogans, now rigid and frozen in the fluorescent light and in the silence of wall-to-wall carpeting, hanging on the walls like pictures at an exhibition or mounted in showcases like flags from ancient battles, cleaned and pressed, or like huge venomous spiders now embalmed and kept behind glass. Equally well preserved are the voices of demagogues, of national leaders, especially the most rabid; naturally, some of the voices are very familiar. They come through the electronic filters soft and limpid, and go on practically day and night from auditoriums and projection booths; there are convention members in their fifties who wander from room to room like somnambulists, hunting these voices in this assembly of phantoms from their past. Perhaps, I told myself without having to spell it out more exactly, perhaps this is what Alphonse wanted above all.

Blatt's success; Lebournet and TV; Chuck-Pick-Alf panel

Part of the nourishment that a convention offers its participants is, of course, a number of more or less formal speeches called papers, contributions, or whatever. Each of the designated speakers is too preoccupied with his own presentation to feel much like going to listen to the others; at least this has been the case with me, but of course I didn't miss Blatt, Lebournet or the Shadows. Blatt is a good speaker. I didn't understand all he was saying, but in spots I found him deeply moving. His domain was again war oratory but his particular subject was rather new, namely, "The Heroization of Neutrality." Blatt, as everybody knows, has a great reservoir of knowledge on the vocabularies and images used by demagogues in their calls to arms, to bloodshed, to death. As of now, I doubt that there is anybody on the market who can top Blatt when it comes to knowledge of the diction and methods used in hero mythification of the great carnages of our century. Since he is very much interested in Italy, he has frequently conducted his analyses on material chosen from that area. There he has found, for instance, excellent illustrations of a well-known argument of militant orators, the one according to which a Blood Tribute permits and sanctions a nation's entrance into History. There is an essay by Blatt on the mystico-political use of the word "blood" which we consider exemplary.

Naturally, this time he wasn't giving a report for specialists in the narrow sense, but rather a speech prepared for the occasion. So he was a bit rhetorical too, not really histrionic but speaking with feeling and sometimes with personal vehemence. He always knows how to train his flashlight on the key phrase in a given text. The superb key phrase, the *consommé* phrase was extracted this time from an inflammatory speech by an Italian "interventionist" who had said during the Great War: "It matters little who wins." In other words, the prospect which that leader presented to the people was possible defeat, and certainly desolation & death, but what mattered, in his view, was the fact of taking part in the great historical drama, treading the tragic stage with spurred boots.

This is, in simple words, what I have retained of Blatt's conclusive statements: the talks which incite people to take neutralist positions, however convincing, will always have a hard time if they try to sound like calls to heroism, especially in comparison to great war exhortations, which always maintain a high L & C temperature. But there can actually be more heroism in the former than in the latter. My memory at this point turns briefly to the lawyer Fernando Rossi. Passion is heroic, reason is not? That is sloppy and pernicious thinking.

Preacher Blatt ended with a flourish: "Let us then try to work on the opposite hypothesis. Those two words, passion &

reason, are in the vast majority of contexts zero words, but if we are going to do something with them, let us go about it in the right way. Let us then try to say that reason is vitality, imagination, élan, and that passion is sterile tragedy, enslavement, falsification—well, impotence, masquerading as virile aggressiveness."

Nothing new in that, but Blatt's tone and spiritedness effectively hit the audience. Bravo, Blatt. Many congratulated him while clasping both his hands or slapping his shoulder, especially some Afro-Asian members.

Now for a moment I'll go over to Lebournet. On the podium Lebournet makes a tremendous impression, not so much on account of his mustache and beard—which actually look a bit false on such a young face, with its fresh, well-fed lips opening up behind those thick bushes—as on account of his bearing and the way he talks. The shoulders, the fists pressed on the lectern, the head, the voice—everything about him is rigid, monotonous. It's hard to tell whether his attitude is a sign of impervious aloofness or of unsuspected timidity.

Practically everything he said was what he read from a folder in a transparent plastic cover. The title of his paper was "The General Rhetorical Structure of the Television Commercial." He provided a lot of examples, causing some nervous laughter among those in the audience who recognized several commercials he was analyzing, for beer, deodorants, or whatever. He did hear the laughter, yet he maintained a straight face; in fact, his speech became ever more technical and monotonous. A couple of times he went to the blackboard to draw diagrams, using lines, arrows, letters, numbers. I was sitting between Jason Jones and Uruki; they both seemed excited when Lebournet, somewhat in the manner of the New Critics, drew a comparison between the structures of some TV commercials and certain scenes in Shakespeare and eighteenth-century opera.

This is the idea, in simple terms: many of the advertising documents analyzed by Lebournet consist of a song followed by an explanatory part; more specifically: choral voices, sometimes of little or adolescent girls, would lyrically describe a given industrial product; then a male voice would interrupt the chorus and music to give its authoritative approval ("Yes . . ."), followed by a talk on the subject, in expository prose recited in a mellow baritone. In Shakespeare, on the contrary, the lyrical *summatio*—to use Lebournet's terminology—does not precede but instead follows the discursive part; and also in eighteenth-century opera, for instance, the little aria comes after the recitative, offering a kind of short verse summary of it.

At the end of Lebournet's speech there was a debate; many asked questions, among them one of Budd Rotondi's advertising friends who turned out to be extremely smart; he astonished everybody with his knowledge of literary works.

This advertising man's name is Humphrey Dodd and he is president of the Humphrey Dodd Agency. I heard it's a small but excellent agency. Dodd himself is rather small too, very thin, made of vibrant wire, with a shiny black tight-fitting suit and a green-and-black striped necktie; he smokes small, thin, dark cigars. I approached him at the exit; being overwhelmed by one of my irresistible attacks of intrusiveness, I nipped in the bud a private talk between him and Lebournet in order to confront him with some urgent questions.

I told him how tremendously worried I am by the problem of commercials interrupting television news: "When the announcer is telling us about some disaster or giving us the latest information on the agonizing crises of the day, he will at some point interrupt himself and let us know that he will resume 'after this message'; the message is a commercial; the talk on grave issues yields to the exaltation of beer and deodorants. Thus the tragic fact of world-wide importance and the small item of domestic comfort are placed on the same level; in fact, the latter is allowed more importance and authority than the former. Are you aware of this? Are there any remedies? Am I crazy? Am I being delirious when I say that 'We shall continue after this message' is one of the most pernicious key phrases in our civilization?"

In a calmer tone I pointed out that I am not at all opposed to industrial products; for example, my automobile, though second-hand, gives me varied and ever fresh pleasure. I attempted a verbal sketch of sunsets seen driving down my canyon, with the light sparkling on the hood and on the faraway ocean. And much simpler things too: the other day I bought myself a new pair of shoes and I keep looking at them all the time.

There was a short silence, then Dodd explained to me that

his agency specialized in building public images of people rather than of industrial products; however, his attitude was opposite to the one that under similar circumstances would have been taken by, say, Fiorenzo Bocca, my friend from the faucet factory: Dodd said that my talk interested him very much and asked me whether we might resume it after the Symposium; he gave me his card, which looked like a very expensive piece of engraving, and assured me in the most genuine of manners that he would like to take me to lunch someday.

But at that particular moment both he and Lebournet were in a hurry. "You're in a hurry too," Lebournet said to me. "I'm sure you don't want to miss it?" I remembered then that it was time to go to the major production staged by the Shadows, a five-man panel formed by Chuck Palmerston, Louis Pickford, and Alf Lundquist, with the addition of Dr. Mario Peritti, Senator Marchesan's assistant, who, it turned out, never talked; and the poet Jason Jones, who did talk—as a matter of fact, quite well.

Alf Lundquist was the first speaker. In fact, he spoke twice as long as all of the others put together. Flower in his lapel; friendly toward everybody; exuding well-being. The room, the table, the water pitchers, everything glittered. This was the biggest and best-equipped of the lecture halls. Earphones at every seat, both onstage and in the auditorium. Up above, all around the room a kind of balcony was suspended, as in eighteenth-century ballrooms, except that this one was divided into booths, where simultaneous translators were kept behind glass and could be seen busy at work by their microphones. Ruggero, for instance, was up there translating into Italian; his was the voice that both the senator in the audience and Dr. Peritti onstage heard through their earphones. Occasionally I have listened to Ruggero too; to me he sounded prodigious, with the absolute evenness and flatness of tone of the real expert.

Crackling noise of sheets of paper came through Alf Lundquist's microphone. A swallow of water and a little cough to feel his vocal cords before the attack. A frank, athletic smile, a display of teeth: the flag of friendliness and efficiency. Meanwhile the eyes, up above, are busy taking in a panoramic view of the audience.

After these preliminaries you might have expected a sonorous, vibrant speech from Alf; instead, it was a massive bore. For at least half an hour he spoke about the linguistic preparation of secondary-school students and about various methods to evaluate their preparation, grade them, make a classification for the time when the best among these hypothetical students would be ready for admittance to the Institute, cadets at the new Verbal Academy. Mimeographed copies of reports had already been distributed, consisting of many pages of statistics and numbers, and then many more pages in which the statistics and numbers were discussed. While we were leafing through this material Alf's speech on the podium was going on; both the mimeographed material and the speech were evidently intended to produce, and did produce, an impression of great significance. By their very presence, for that matter, both that solid and well-organized man and those magnificently typed and mimeographed sheets symbolized the new Institute, the new Structures.

Yet I couldn't concentrate either on him or on the pages. Deep down I felt—and I suspect many of the others felt the same—something like "If this is life, then death is preferable." And strangely enough, this raised my spirits.

Since the topic for the panel discussion was the relationship between electronic computers and the structure of cultural life, Lundquist spoke of the use of computers in evaluating grades, titles, assets & liabilities of the people who would be considered for admission to an institution like our own. Questions of this sort interest me and I think about them, but when Lundquist presented them, somehow I did not recognize them any more. I stopped listening. After Lundquist, Chuck Palmerston spoke, more briefly and to the point.

Chuck is definitely phonogenic. He used his beautiful voice in a relaxed way, conversing with all of the others (except Dr. Peritti) seated onstage with him, and also with convention members in the auditorium. He picked up the subject which Alf had treated in a way that made it unrecognizable to me, and he made it recognizable by coming to the essential points at once. The proposition is: How much authority should the computer eventually be allowed to exercise? Can we conceive of a world in which it would be installed as the supreme authority, and in which agreement would be reached to accept its judgments and its choices as irreversible? Naturally the problem applies not only to the selection of personnel for a firm or of students for an institute; it will present itself, with increasing forcefulness, in such situations as legal decisions, medical diagnoses, et cetera, et cetera.

Such speculations are interesting; they can even be alluring. To give a banal example, I'll admit I would rather be chosen or judged by an electronic brain than by the brain of a man like Lundquist.

After a good start Chuck, in my view, went from bad to worse. First the poet Jones, then other people in the audience argued that in the future as he saw it, enormous authority and responsibility would be conferred not so much on the machines, which of course could neither assume authority nor feel responsibility, as on the (human) programmers, the technicians who are capable of using the increasingly complicated machines and conducting a dialogue with them. Would the functioning of community life fall into the hands of those technicians? Wasn't that an agonizing vision?

On the stage, in the line-up of panelists' faces, immediately after Chuck's there was Pickford's. In the past Pickford had been a great connoisseur of Man's Agony in Our Time; now, however, he was Premier Pickford, resembling a locked safe: "no comment," *au-dessus de la mêlée.* Then I looked up at Ruggero, who was translating with total technical detachment in his glass booth. I recalled that in his opinion, computer specialists weren't agonizing at all; he placed them on a par with jet pilots or telephone operators. For a moment I plugged in Ruggero's voice and heard him translate with the usual efficient flatness. I put the earphone down, since I always try to understand English through direct effort.

Answering the questions raised by the audience, Chuck began in the classic manner, stating that he was happy that those particular questions had been asked. He expressed his gratitude and moved on to the more substantial part of his talk. I took rather disorganized notes on what he said; it seems to me there were three main points:

First, the Institute ("We up here") proposes to contribute in an increasingly active way to the training of "verbal technicians," experts in the formulation and transmission of words.

Our Time needs them in enormously growing numbers and wants them to be efficient and well equipped, not mere dilettanti, as has often been the case until now. They are needed in all areas, from industry to politics, from diplomacy to science.

I have already said that Chuck wasn't giving a formal speech, and as a matter of fact, these ideas came out in the form of a dialogue between him and Louis Pickford. Bouncing the conversational ball between them, they said that all important organizations, firms, large embassies, government offices, agencies, political and military units, et cetera, et cetera, needed "verbal attachés," technically up to date in the fullest meaning of the term. The ordinary writer of speeches and messages, and the ordinary interpreter, are inadequate. Pickford's phrase: "It's as though dentistry were still practiced by tooth-pulling pharmacists." Instead, as an academy for the training of these new odontologists, as it were, the Institute will be equipped with the most up-to-date superelectronic drills.

And here we come to the second point. You only had to watch Chuck's head onstage, and the two heads that were lined up on his right and left, to know that the idea he was now going to propose was the one they had cooked up with the utmost care. It is the idea of a simplified, or "computable," language. What does that mean? It means that in order to facilitate human discourse, international, intercommercial, intercultural, interindustrial relations, to lubricate the very joints of the body politic and ultimately to advance life and progress, what you need is a simplified language, clarified, disciplined, insured, patented, schematized, a verbal main track for political, diplomatic, industrial and commercial exchange, a lexicon and a grammar capable of putting any conceivable message in a foolproof semantic strait jacket. This would be a "computable" language, i.e., transferable *in toto* into the codes with which computers are fed, manageable by them with absolute certainty, agility, authority. Chuck expressed his concept in much more technical terms, but that is the general idea. Applause from the Budd Rotondi group.

Thanking them, with a magician's flash in his eyes, Chuck announced, "The material you are holding in your hands is all written in easily computable language." For the first time I took a rather substantial sampling of that mimeographed prose. It gave this impression: it was at the same time simpler and less clear than normal prose.

After the idea had been launched, various people spoke in disorderly fashion. Clinton made a brief comment from the auditorium, sensible as usual and a bit out of phase: "Scientific papers too should have style. It is erroneous and unscientific to think that scientific language shouldn't have its richness, its nuances." He got up, waved his hand in a gesture at once cordial and regal, said, with a good Italian accent, *"Arrivederci"* and left the room.

Others were speaking at the same time. The one most people listened to was Jason Jones, who was able to use an excellent microphone at the panel table; nothing is more effective than a hugely amplified whisper: it drips individually into each listener's ear. With much elegant reticence and a bit of stammering, Jones said, "I was just thinking . . . It seems that my mind can't help turning over this idea, so forcefully put forward by Dr. Palmerston, this idea of the attaché, of the verbal attaché . . . Right? Well, somehow I can't help imagining this character a bit like the political commissar attached to an industry or an army unit. Don't you? This idea of handing out diplomas for —" He coughed briefly and ended with greater firmness: "I am not at all convinced that the whole affair, especially the distribution of the—well, working permits and licenses wouldn't become a big racket." (Applause from various sectors.)

Chuck resumed his talk, more self-assured than ever, with his third point. It is hard to say whether the poet Jones gave him the immediate inspiration; a clamor from the audience was probably even more decisive. Many were still lingering on the alarming image of the future Technician or Attaché or Commissar with his enormous power; to reassure them, somebody had to come up with a suggestion on how to protect whole populations from such power. Now somebody from the audience— I'm almost sure it was George, the Hungarian—cried, whether seriously or ironically no one will ever know, "Militarize them!"

As I have already noted here, Chuck is infatuated with the military. More than once he has tried to entice me, in a man-to-man tone, with stories about his experiences in Europe, where he knew prestigious personages in the military-diplomatic world. He quotes his conversations with them verbatim, to make it clear that they were on first-name terms. Whether irritated or simply spurred on by that voice ("Militarize them!"), Chuck the generalophile plunged into a spirited encomium of the military world. It was surprising, he said, that so many clichés on the subject could still be in circulation; they belonged to the times of the tooth-pulling pharmacist. To insist on certain hoary conceptions about military people was simply stupid. Among them are some of the best doctors, engineers, scientists in general. Also receptive to arts & letters. For a while Chuck trotted along this way, smiling, persuasive. And yet, my immediate impression was that by this finale, Chuck had got himself into a mess. Even the applause sounded stilted.

Actually the meeting had already come to an end; many in the audience were getting up and forming into groups. I joined Blatt and Lebournet, voicing my impression that Chuck had not ended in triumph and that Alf's opening talk had been a crushing and ineffective bore. Lebournet immediately told me I was wrong. He drew my attention to the fact that the audience included some distinguishable groups: just as there was an advertising group and a literary group, so there was a very important group of educators. These educators were all aficionados of the Shadows. Alf Lundquist's talk was poetry to them. They were the type of convention members who brought with them to the breakfast table the pack of mimeographed material from Chuck and Alf which they found in their mailbox, and didn't part from it all day as they wandered around the Symposium's halls and theaters. Quite a few among these educators were women—unanimous, incidentally, in judging both Chuck and Alf very handsome men.

My contribution and escape

Panic, at the thought of the speech I was to give, had intermittently overtaken me for several weeks. Now the moment had come. However, I slept well the night before. The dream in which I met the President of the United States turned up again, with new details. There was a brief conversation but I must assume it did not interest me, because unfortunately on waking up I could not even recall its general tone. When I entered the lecture hall, my head was completely void of ideas. I had, however, many notes. It was one of the smaller rooms, but it was chock-full. Among the people present I immediately noticed Horace Buterweg, and only then did it occur to me that he had not been on Chuck's panel. I hadn't seen him since the evening at the Pickfords' and my mind had totally erased his image. His activities must have been taking place at a rarefied level, *au-dessus de* the very *dessus de la mêlée*. What was he doing here now? Anyway, his presence didn't worry me. Very briefly, for a fragment of a second, I laughed openly at him. There were also other known faces; but in the same way that I felt completely free of ideas, I also felt free of any stage fright in front of people, known or unknown. There was the senator and there was his aide, Dr. Peritti; I find the latter extremely annoying. And of course, there was Blatt. Seeing him was what brought the first idea into my head, empty until then. I don't remember what I had planned by way of introduction, but it must have been the usual, conventional words; instead, I opened with a reference to Blatt.

I started, in fact, with an encomium of Blatt, of his mind, at once imaginative and systematic, of his capacity to wed intuition and method. Without Blatt—known, besides other things, for his now-so-popular definition of zero words—the Institute would be inconceivable. Without him, the very words I was going to utter, and the ideas I might express, could not be uttered and expressed. The research work on which I was about to report had been conducted in collaboration with him.

The subject of my report had been given simply as "the use of pronouns in political oratory," but it would have been more accurate to say that the paper also dealt with such uses of verb inflections (person and number) and, finally, with abstractions. Blatt and I had spent hours in painstaking research in books and microfilm of newspapers, especially those covering ante-bellum periods; we picked examples and pinned them like insects.

Almost every time I speak in public, the scene of which I am so prominent a part strikes me at first as totally absurd; and I get the impression that I must reconstruct within myself, starting from scratch, the very ability to articulate words. But I get my bearings in a short time; in fact, the danger eventually is that I may not be able to stop.

And now I had a large quantity of examples neatly entered on index cards, and I used them profusely. The main thread of the research Blatt and I had conducted was almost ridiculously simple. We had started from an observation of the forms used by leaders in addressing the often oceanic multitudes. How did the leader designate those multitudes in, say, Italian? By which pronoun and verb form? By a collective *voi*, second person plural, or by a symbolic *tu*, second person singular? And what about himself? What did the leader call himself? Very obvious observation: in the great majority of important clinical cases in our files, the leader doesn't say "I," he says "we"; in other words, he associates himself, with various degrees of ambiguity, and possibly without any right to do so, with the crowd he is addressing.

These may seem trifling matters, but Blatt and I had got into the thick of our research with increasingly intense curiosity; we actually felt that in a tangible way we might be establishing a factor, by no means secondary, in the dehumanization of relationships in the modern world, et cetera. The time period we explored coincided mainly with my youth, a period which offered a rich harvest of resounding examples. In urging the bewildered population toward the most sinister enterprise in its whole history, a leader of my native country—very notorious, at least among people now over forty—had suddenly used the form of address which in Italian can be both familiar and solemn *(tu)*, to exhort it to rush to arms *("Corri alle armi,"* second person singular) , but that's a rare case.

Actually, in general, in speeches of demagogues, especially when exhorting the people to sacrifices, grief and death, the approach through a direct verb form appeared to be rare and atypical. At the key moment of the invitation to kill, to get killed, or at any rate, to perform or submit to scarcely desired though somehow "mythicizable" acts, the direct "you" form is automatically replaced by a collective abstraction, and you have then *das deutsche Volk; il popolo italiano;* I suppose, also, "the American people."

In the leader's speech, the X people or the Y people "know," "believe," "will do," "will never allow" this and that; and the leader makes these statements while addressing members of that very people, each one with a head & mind of his own.

Thus the leader, in an infinite number of historical cases, has achieved his purpose: through that rhetorical artifice, his audience has become an abstraction. The orator's effort is precisely that of fostering in his public the ardent desire to belong to an abstraction. Mythicizing people & events. The single individual feels he is carried upward, he is becoming part of History. Et cetera, et cetera. I expressed this concept in several different ways, by using the great variety of insects pinned by me with the help of Blatt the entomologist.

Up to that point I was, so to speak, sailing in convoy with Blatt. From then on I flew off in a balloon of my own.

From this balloon I went on talking. Metaphorically speaking, I was holding in my hands, and reading here and there, a bunch of letters addressed by Tognon, the yokel, from his trench in the First World War, to his father back in the Venetian countryside. In this particular incarnation Tognon was a patriot, his king's soldier. I said to my audience that he too had been examined from the L & C point of view. And I said that voices like his were particularly pitiful—voices where patriotism existed as a small and exalting private icon, as the shabby illusion of the humble. And as listeners, these people are the dearest of all to their leader's heart. He feels maximum pleasure when he manages to enlist them for the Great Abstraction. The faith of the simple-hearted. And incidentally, that's also where you achieve the highest peaks of horror. I am reminded of the young man sentenced to death, to whom people and priests say, "You are among friends," administering final comforts to him. And then, he is the one who does the dying. Coming back to my pronouns, I attempted some conclusions about how little right the leader had to use a "we" in which Tognon & Co. were included.

That was the moment when I suddenly perceived an opening for an attack on Pickford. I didn't mention him by name, but I did say things which had stuck in my throat for a long time on account of my repeated verbal blocks in his presence. I made it plain that after rereading so many speeches by the manipulators of historical destiny we had to listen to in our youth, I was of the opinion that we had now almost forgotten those texts. Or we had done something even worse: we had fashioned beautifully polished images, sophisticated, psychoanalyzed, of those blackguards whose canned voices have so often resounded here within the walls of our beautifully equipped electro-auditoriums. (For examples of polished, psychoanalyzed images, see L. Pickford, *The Monsters Day By Day*.)

As my mind wandered over the simple area of the Institute, it conjured up the clear and after all relatively happy image of Harold Epstein escaping on a bicycle, beating by a few lengths the heinous, zealous, macabre and splendidly well-organized persecutors who wanted to destroy him, and in fact destroyed many of his family. No (no, Pickford), Harold's persecutors were not aberrant human specimens, to be studied in terms of current usage, not mysterious, not mediocrities with sudden attacks of bestiality; they were criminals who were perfectly conscious of, and satisfied with, the activities they pursued, systematically orienting their whole moral and cultural weight toward an ideal of power for themselves, wholly desired and savored, and of total human degradation or death for the others, equally desired and savored.

Therefore (therefore, Pickford), it cannot and must not matter to us at all—in fact, it gives us a distinct feeling of revulsion —if someone comes and tells us that the butchers (oh, the mysterious and fascinating complexities of the human soul!) were officials who in all other activities except butchery proved to be upright, ordinary citizens, as a matter of fact rather dull and commonplace, but sometimes sensitive too—pianists, doting homemakers, protectors of squirrels. These facts are irrelevant, and only a sick mind can perceive them, linger on them even for a single instant, let alone write whole books about them, in elegant prose, with the author's photograph on the back, his countenance adorned by the knowing smile of one who has penetrated the alluring labyrinths of the human soul. And by the way, let's have a look at this word, "soul." Along with "heart" and many others, it belongs to a category of zero words one must be particularly wary of.

Having delivered myself of this belated reaction to Pickford, I thought of Ruggero, and of other young men like him. Still without mentioning any names, I stated that I saw some hope in that direction; I dared believe that these young people might prove capable of thwarting the eventual macabre leader, of catching him in the act as he abusively says *"we,"* of balking his speech. We are contributing to the groundwork for that operation; indeed, ladies and gentlemen, our L & C analyses will play a limited but very definite, useful part in that process.

I am usually a poor speaker; in closing a speech I am even worse, wholly inadequate: at some point I realize that my time is up, I put together a couple of sentences which are neither here nor there, and when I finish I give the impression of having stopped halfway. I believe my memory went back to Blatt's conclusion, in which the word "reason" sounded a little less "zero" than usual; I spoke my final clumsy sentences and abandoned them there to fend for themselves: "Let us, then, pay affectionate homage to clear reason, to the little hope there is. Every day, every hour, searching for truth, with limited but firm hope. Renewing this resolution every single moment. It isn't much. There is nothing else. Therefore, to say that it isn't much is really useless, even false. It would be like asking ourselves whether an egg, per se, is small or large. Thank you."

Many applauded, and of course it is in my nature to believe that they did it as a joke. I didn't know which way to look. My great resource was remembering the door; I threw myself toward it and made a quick exit. I began to walk down the hall, with many people following me, but at a distance; some were still back in the auditorium. But then two single individuals caught up with me. I saw these apparitions, one on either side of me: the senator and his aide.

As I have already noted, this is the first senator I have ever known; it is odd that our dialogue should have occurred here by the Pacific. Agreeable dialogue. Marchesan gives an impression of credibility; and of being alert to the world, and capable of doubt. His Dr. Peritti, however, is one of those people who instead of saying "Yes" say "Precisely," and instead of saying "No" say "Irrelevant," their thin lips always stiff, their eyes always vigilant. In other words, a pernicious imbecile. Luckily he excused himself, he had to go, I don't know to what panel; it looked as if the whole Symposium depended on him.

Alone, Marchesan and I walked on more comfortably. He

said to me, "You speak well. I like the way you mix your personal affairs with general ideas. And what are you going to do now? Shall we have dinner together?"

I said, "I must go away for a few days, or at least for a few hours. Recently my nerves have been in rather bad shape. There has been an intensification of some of my usual troubles. One of the patterns is this: things I say in the daytime turn up again at night in the shape of shameful nightmares. This may possibly happen tonight, so I had better be somewhere else."

"Where do you want to go? I wouldn't mind moving around a bit myself."

I found myself saying to him, "Come for a ride somewhere," and I was already thinking of the right place, Calliope, a curious little town with gambling casinos in the desert a few hours away by car. The desert is very beautiful, especially after the rains, when fantastically colorful flowers burst out. To get to Calliope you go through hamlets in the middle of nowhere, with frame houses, sometimes quite old, and sometimes also with old men sitting outside, motionless in the dry air, as if they had been there since the old days celebrated in Westerns. You also go through mountain passes, in the violent sunshine, in a supremely light air, at the same altitude as that of mountain resorts in the Dolomites, only there is no resort here, only desert mountains and valleys, and then it occurs to you that no man has ever spent a night here. But Calliope itself is in a flat area and is very lively, especially at night. The great gambling houses are hotels whose styles generally look Afro-Oriental, Moorish, Assyro-Babylonian. In the perpetual, even penumbra of the casinos it's like living in a submarine or in a very modern A-bomb–proof air shelter.

We stayed there for about ten hours. I played roulette, always betting on number thirty-three. At first I won. I won six hundred and forty dollars, something incredible. Almost exactly four hundred thousand lire; I felt the way you feel when you dream that you are flying. Then I lost over half of my winnings, and I would have lost them all if my conversation with the senator hadn't kept me occupied.

Finicky researcher that I am, in that faraway place I learned with enormous interest various things about the work of a senator in Italy, a subject on which, I realized, I had unfortunately very little information. The way I brought him on to the subject of his profession and working methods was my rather inopportune opening; I asked him, "Could a man like me become a senator?"

"Why not?"

"If it's true that I could become a senator, I feel much less impressed by the senate."

"I wonder why?" He was sincerely interested.

"In Italy I don't think I ever met a man as important as you are."

"Really?" He seemed to imply: "Take your chance. Anything I can do?" Almost changing his pose so I could take a better picture.

But then, instead of photographing him, I took pictures of myself for a good deal of the time, forced to do so by his questioning. We came out of our deluxe bunker and sat outside on deck chairs in the dry sun near the enormous pool, whose transparent water showed the solid blue of the sky upside down. We drank the so-called planter's punch. The young woman in shorts who brought it to us from the bar wore on her right ankle a pedometer like a wrist watch. "In one day," I told the senator, "she covers ten miles carrying drinks." I had given him several bits of information during our trip, fabricating them, but within reason. Our conversation was very pleasant, here at such a great distance from our places of origin, a gratuitous and accidental dialogue, aided also by our alcoholic-vitaminic drink based on rum and fruit. I had mentioned my nervous crises to the senator and he asked for details with the interest of someone of my own age.

I tried to reply with utmost simplicity. "The crises are signaled by a feeling of emptiness, like a sudden lack of breath in human relations. There can be some good in them; they could even be interpreted as states of grace, inasmuch as they make you feel in harmony with the world; that is to say, with the disparity and incomprehensibility of the world, with the lack of balance of life. You feel like saying to yourself, 'It's hell, but it gives you proper vision.' Proper in the main lines. But you cannot live along main lines. You have to set limits. Coming out of the crisis means discovering mental & physical limitations. For example, now that I have watched so much historical and personal water flow to and fro under the bridges, now that I have discovered, that as it happens, I am older than the premiers of various countries—well, now I feel I can perhaps size myself up more clearly."

He followed me with genuine curiosity: "Go on, go on."

"There are moments when each of us makes impossible demands on himself. Such moments are neither lucid nor useful. Then I try to shift gears and say, 'I am a rational man, a simple man. I am a persistent and effective worker within the proper limits and with the proper people, and besides, I also have a great desire to have fun and to laugh.' "

After sunset we went to a variety show, with everything from dancing girls to acrobats, then we went back to the casinos and all the while we kept talking.

"Rossi, believe me, you are neither rational nor simple."

"It would be wrong to believe that rational & simple describes an adaptable little man, easy to please. Take for instance my years of work with your friend Marcellino. To me, they were neither useful nor pleasant; I look back on them as something to be forgotten, yet I'm sure it would be perfectly possible to polish them up and palm them off to myself and everybody else as years of above-average professional success, with constant chances for me to offer Cultural Contributions and to obtain Economic Advancement."

"When are you going back to work in Italy? Do go back and get a good position in Italy."

"No, no. Too easy. I wouldn't dream of it. Besides, in my old age it has become clear to me that each stage in life is a preparation for the next and more advanced phase. And I have known such extremes of sadness and loneliness that I believe they cannot easily be surpassed, and since I've known the worst, I feel rather secure and well equipped."

I am just giving the essentials; at any rate, my talk was rather incoherent, but it was he who had got me started, so he had better be content with the result. He was, I told myself, a senator on vacation who apparently wanted a chance to listen to members of the more private and less visible sector of the population.

Our talk turned to Venetian ground, and then, against that desert background, Portogruaro and Venice appeared like mirages, and the Rossis, the Strigatos, Dr. Levi, the Lezze-Adornos, more or less everybody, uttering their respective key lines, transformed into memorable stage figures. This was the way, from grammar-school age on, that I had trained myself to identify with others, to bring the "you" into the area of the "I," so that the "we" could make at least a modicum of sense.

"Some people haven't the faintest idea of how well I knew them—gestures, words, everything. That's how I gained some understanding, by mimicking them and their actions, their joys and sorrows, et cetera. There are others like me, observing, empathizing, and I suppose Dr. Peritti would consider us wretched fools; but I have news for him: my hunch is that we are the men of the future. Provided we know how to use and regulate our talents, channeling them toward the highest possible degree of understanding, of communicating. Some see our L & C research as a kind of fooling around with words, just nonsense. But they forget that, for example, 'key phrase' can be synonymous with a man's vital center, the crucial cogwheel in his machinery, what really makes him tick."

Senator Marchesan admired the Institute, and he spoke to me about his old friendship with Alphonse. Then he added, "Some people keep telling me that he is behind the times. That's not true, but in some instances the truth doesn't have any bearing. What is his position here really like?" At that moment I started looking at my watch and was choked by anxiety and remorse. In a few hours Alphonse would be giving his speech at the Symposium, and here we were in the middle of the desert, speaking interminably about ourselves amid roulette wheels.

Alphonse's speech, and final results of the Symposium

I drove as in a moonscape through the desert in the light of early dawn, with the senator dozing at my side. The complete deployment of the sun had already taken place sometime before we arrived at the Symposium theaters; in spite of the fluorescent light and the filtered voices, after Calliope they had an old, homey look. We felt as if we had been away for a month. We had missed many reports, such as Uruki's paper, which Lebournet had found the most interesting of all, on the relationship between poetry and information. We met Lebournet in a corridor and it was he who told us that Alphonse's speech had already started. Lebournet himself had arrived a little late and hadn't been able to get into the crowded auditorium. They didn't allow anybody to go in—as Lebournet said with a note of satisfaction in his voice—otherwise they might have trouble with the fire-insurance people. The senator noted this datum with intense interest.

We went to an auxiliary lecture room and here we found Alphonse's image and voice already switched on, on a closed-circuit TV screen. Reception was defective; half of his head was missing. "Symbolic amputation," Lebournet couldn't help commenting while I happened to recall Alphonse's telling me once that in 1917 on the Isonzo River, his elder brother, Carlo, at twenty-two, had been hit in the forehead by a bullet which took off the top of his head. We adjusted the image on the screen; now Alphonse's head appeared whole, but compressed.

I can now linger on these details with the greatest calm, but at the time they were nightmarish. There was considerable tension. Alphonse's old friend Marchesan and his new friend Gilberto Rossi felt that they were witnessing a decisive moment in his life. In a corner of the room there was also /dp, his secretary, staring at the screen with a gloomy face. Lebournet looked gloomy too, but with touches of sadism.

We listened to Alphonse; I translated for the senator as best I could, and this was useful to me: it compelled me to pick out the key phrases as I went along. What I write here is more or less what I was whispering in the ear of Alphonse's old friend.

Alphonse was thanking the people present. "Ours has been an open forum, unplanned, free." He expressed this in various ways, working on that idea while with his eyes he probed the audience to make it his own. It became clear at once which path he decided on: when the Shadows were presenting themselves well prepared, organized, planned, mimeographed, he had presented an Institute with doors wide open, a piece of ground where everyone could camp the way he wanted. "In the L & C area there is so much to be done yet that any project, however small, may have its point; therefore our work will always be, by definition, fragmentary and uncharted."

Typical of Alphonse's speech: its sober tone; even extreme statements were made in a routine way. He answered his adversaries, but between the lines, as one would brush off a fly with his left hand and a casual "What a nuisance," while with gestures of the right hand he would go on underscoring the main points of his speech. He didn't even dream of spelling out some controversial items—the concept of zero words, for one; his idea was that such evident & elementary truths were always implicit. As a matter of fact, he said, in the contemporary world there was an increasing tendency on the part of leaders to perpetuate their useless vocabularies, thereby camouflaging their unwillingness or inability to make decisions, their irresponsibility and moral apathy.

"Nowadays the voter is often asked to choose between equally undesirable alternatives. To put it in our own terms: each candidate resorts to a vague and inadequate vocabulary, stammering or rambling syntactical structures, conscious dishonesties, odious approximations.

"The current language in political relations, et cetera, is so inadequate that any work of the kind we do is useful, in any area; practically everything still remains to be done; and no part of our work is ever to be considered complete. Maximum vigilance on current usage must be exercised continuously. Authoritative, up-to-date dictionaries should be issued biweekly and sold at the newsstands. With electronic devices continuously multiplying, it shouldn't be inconceivable to have word centers run along the lines of census bureaus, registering the birth of new terms, checking on their health, following the ambiguous careers of the old ones."

Incidental items, noted at random: "Of course we do not accept the notion of a simplified, computable language. We must carry the burden of language as a whole. Ours is a word clinic, and the proposal made would be like asking us to admit only patients with uncomplicated ailments. . . .

"Instances of violence, subjugation, injustice, unlawful arrests, rhetorical exhortations to butchery, coercion, torture—we try to get at the root of such facts in the verbiage of those responsible, and in the verbal exchange between them. To be sure, they will never speak a hypersimplified language just to please us and the computers. Far from it. They will be stubborn and confusing, their rhetoric will be nothing but duplicities and evasions. . . .

[267]

"In order to practice on texts belonging to the historical past, we have assembled a certain amount of diversified material, as you have seen for yourselves . . ." (Here there was isolated handclapping, then applause broke out at various points.) "This material is at everyone's disposal; it is a public service, as is our work on contemporary texts resulting from our vigilance on current verbal exchange, on the stream of words flowing under our bridges. . . .

"An institute such as our own had two possibilities: to analyze and teach the methods of verbal persuasion so that increasingly astute technicians would apply them to politics, industrial publicity, et cetera; or else to conduct our analyses in order to sharpen the minds of the people exposed to those methods. I cannot say that we chose the latter road. I simply say that there have never been any others. We have never considered any alternatives. . . .

"The primary result of our meeting in these canyons has been the realization that groups like ours exist in many parts of the world; alarm is general, disgust is widespread." (Several "bravos" around the hall.) "The purpose of such observatories is to subject every relevant oratorical text to continuous, honest, pitiless L & C analysis. The present speed in communications must be used for this purpose: here is the text; a half-hour later, the clinical analysis follows. . . .

"If we should lend our work to power groups of whatever kind and dimension, and train our youth to conduct verbal campaigns in the service of such groups, then the function of our Institute would cease. Or at least, I can assure you, any desire on my part would cease, to be its director or to be in any way associated with it. . . ." (The last phrase was uttered in a quick, flat tone, as one reads an oath formula. But it was underscored by an ovation.)

"Now, we frequently see not men in eminent positions of leadership but public images which are almost entirely the product of publicity manipulations. Naturally, our purpose is not to give aid to such manipulations, but the opposite: to analyze the mechanism, disassemble it, leave it there, open, so that everybody may clearly see all its component parts. We shall devote the rest of our lives to this task exclusively. Thank you."

Even this final pledge was uttered by Alphonse with the utmost flatness. He seemed simply to be giving some information, like, say, announcing what time the buses would leave for the afternoon trip to Mexico. The Symposium had come to an end. There were ten seconds of absolute silence. Then applause broke out; there was a standing ovation. So we discovered we were left with a simple assertion, which was already secondary and incidental, so obvious was it: if there was a struggle for power at the Institute, Alphonse had won it comfortably.

Meanwhile the TV camera, properly to illustrate the long and general ovation, was scanning the auditorium and at some point stopped on an old acquaintance: small and compact, absolutely unchanged, with a flower in his lapel—perhaps Alf Lundquist had given it to him—I recognized James Audubon Halleck, who at the *trattoria* Dal Pignolone in Rome, in the small, ancient Piazzetta del Cordaro, had shared *spaghetti all'amatriciana* and *abbacchio al forno* with Corso Gianfranchi and me. Clapping his small, hard hands like the two halves of a shell, he produced his own distinctly sonorous applause in a slow, regular rhythm. Quickly the camera moved to other known figures, including Chuck, Pick, Buterweg; finally, total darkness.

We found all of those public images moments later at the exit; to us they seemed to be picking up their tridimensional bodies like coats they had left in the cloakroom.

At lunch I happened to be seated at a table with Halleck, plus Pickford and Blatt. There I learned that Halleck, during a meeting of an obscure financial kamiri, had delivered a little speech in his eighteenth-century style, giving Alphonse his complete support & confidence on behalf of the Newton Ash Foundation, which he, Halleck, represented. On that same convivial occasion I also had an intuition, more lucid than any in my life, about the workings of politics. It was by now taken for granted that Alphonse had won and would stay on as director. Clearly, Pickford and the Shadows would have preferred to see Alphonse removed. Now, however, being born politicians, not only did they avoid expressing resentment, but they were actually, sincerely in favor of Alphonse, who had given clear evidence of his stamina and ability to win. In this sincerity, and in the ensuing loyal collaboration with the winner—never excluding the possibility of crucifying him later on, should the occa-

sion arise—Rossi (Gilberto) seems to recognize a basic ingredi-
ent in the make-up of the Politician.

We did not see Alphonse until later in the afternoon. Blatt
and I went to his house and found him on the phone; he was
talking to his sixteen-year-old daughter, who is now in Italy.
When he was through, he came up to me and spoke in a normal, workaday tone, though what he said seemed rather exciting: "I was talking to my daughter. This summer you will come
to Italy too. Come to my office tomorrow morning and we'll talk
both about your new contract and about this trip to Italy.
There is a chartered flight; your round-trip ticket won't cost
you much more than your roulette winnings." I had told him
about my short lucky streak at Calliope.

I am not going to deny that I felt tears in my eyes. When I
analyzed these pleasant tears, the primary reason for them that
occurred to me was that I would be able to talk to my Aunt Luciana again and obtain from her, viva voce, a simple, down-to-
earth interpretation of recent events in my life.

CHAPTER
EIGHT

·

Later, toward June, Natasha went from Milan to the Venetian province and took Irene Berlocchi along with her. Before they left, Irene had been running a temperature, and Natasha told her, "A change of air will do you good," but during the train ride Irene's temperature went up even visibly. She sat in a corner of the compartment; her flushed face and shiny eyes made her look lost and humiliated.

Especially during the years when she was Elena Partibon's domestic help and friend, Natasha had become familiar with the world of pills and medicines, learning how to take extreme care of her physical well-being, while Irene's negative attitude was due not so much to distrust as to ignorance.

"You can't live like a wild flower, it isn't smart," Natasha said to her. "Look at Ruggero, who always gets a complete checkup."

Irene shrugged and extended her hand, palm up. Natasha placed two pills in it; Irene chewed and swallowed them. "They work faster that way, don't they?" she asked, with sadness in her darkened eyes. Natasha poured mineral water in a paper cup, and Irene obediently took a few sips.

Studying Irene seated opposite her in the compartment, Natasha reflected that since Kuntz's death she looked transformed. On the other hand, Irene hardly seemed to have noticed the events in her father's life, which had recently culminated in his arrest and imprisonment. But Natasha's purpose was not to reason things out; she tried only to be of help. In this she felt she resembled Ruggero, whom she missed very much and tried to replace. Irene, however, said that she did not miss Ruggero at all, even though, she admitted, hearing his voice over the telephone a few days after Kuntz's death, she had wept; the tears had just come to her eyes, then streamed down her cheeks; they somehow did not seem to belong to her and they had neither heightened nor lowered her spirits.

Of Ruggero, she said, "That boy, my dear, is perfectly happy where he is now, and I bet you he'll stay there longer than he had planned. He will be very popular, because he has a straight mind; he is, as everybody says, a well-organized young man." After a pause she resumed, "There have been certain events in my life, rather relevant ones too; for example, the way my mother died—well, it never occurred to me to talk about things like that with Ruggero. We got along well together; there never was anything wasted. Sometimes when he told me that he and I ought to get married, just for fun I would describe what our relationship would be like, the place each of us would have in the arrangement: 'You, always self-assured, successful, and I, more intelligent than you, following you and understanding everything but remaining somewhat in the shade. Success,' I would tell him, 'entails a certain kind of mediocrity, which you possess and I actually don't.' When I said things like that, we would both laugh. I tell you, we got along very well, Ruggero and I, and now I realize he left at the right moment."

"He'll be back soon."

"Soon or late doesn't make any difference."

"I used to envy you," Natasha said in her slow, accurate manner, which added weight even to the most ordinary remarks. "What was between you and Ruggero must have been very beautiful."

Irene gave her a smile, short and hard like a bite, and for a while she did not say anything. Natasha insisted that they go to the dining car, and Irene followed her obediently and with skepticism. It was an old dining car of uncertain national origin, with hard leather seats and table lamps with silk shades. Natasha had an authoritative, man-to-man tone in dealing with the waiter and getting him to bring things different from what was listed on the menu. For Irene she got some very hot bouillon, boiled rice and a baked apple. Without reacting, Irene drank the bouillon, ate the rice and the apple; her only initiative was to order a strong, sweet cherry liqueur afterward. She drank it with intense delight, she licked it, she breathed it, whispering, "God, how I like this." Natasha watched her closely with restrained satisfaction; she was sure she could help her, make her get better.

They got off the train at Mestre, where they went to a modern hotel whose owner was a good friend of Natasha's and charged her a ridiculously low rate. She helped Irene get into bed, then gave her a sleeping pill and made her drink a cup of hot camomile tea. With Natasha sitting at the foot of the bed, Irene, as she was drifting off to sleep, kept evoking distant episodes she had heard about, belonging to the period of Natasha's "trouble." The next part of the story was the "rescuing" of Natasha through the good offices of Enrico Fassola, who had been pressured by Ruggero—Ruggero, toward whom Fassola entertained, as Irene put it, curious paternal feelings—curious, because Fassola was after all not Ruggero's father; he had only been passionately in love with Ruggero's mother "in an old-fashioned Venetian manner, so that now Fassola lives alone with his mother and the cats." Irene said all this in a monotone as if she were reading it. Natasha laughed, not because she agreed, but because behind that monotone she sensed a touch of cheerfulness. "But you," Irene went on, "married quite well in Milan; even if you don't live with your husband, you're very good friends, and that's something I find most enviable."

"My husband will be here for lunch tomorrow. He's in Venice to make purchases in the glass factories—for his shop in Milan, you know."

For the moment, the sleeping pill was giving Irene a relaxed and euphoric loquacity: "All things considered, even your life as a maid when you were a young girl, your quarrels with the

Countesses Dall'Olivo, whom you managed to enrage so that they got a liver ailment, and then your carryings-on with men —it all looks as if it must have been something really free and happy."

"The Dall'Olivos were no countesses. And the spinster daughter died before her mother, who now lives alone—she, too, with cats. When I heard that the signorina had died, I sent flowers."

"Good for you, Natasha."

"Why do you say that?"

"I don't know. Nothing can change anything, that's true, but certain things are like . . . like the solution." She was silent. Suddenly she fell asleep. She added later, as in a dream, "Kuntz always knew how to find the solution."

Natasha nodded: she had heard that phrase before. She got up. Standing by the bedstead, she touched Irene's forehead lightly with her hand, then let it rest for a moment on her closed eyes. She knew she had given her a potent sleeping pill. She left the room on tiptoe.

Everything was in order, tomorrow Irene would feel much better. Everything also seemed to be in order because she was at Mestre; these were her places, and now she returned to them with a visitor's detachment. Her places: the Venetian mainland, the countryside mingling with the new, productive, anonymous city, with a breeze blowing from the Lagoon, from that vast, flat expanse of water which at other, faraway points mirrored Byzantine churches, fishermen's houses, picturesque skies, gardens, church towers, while here its oily water mirrored vast silvery oil tanks, puffs of white smoke, industrial flames. Natasha felt delighted as she let herself down slowly into the bed, alone and serene, between fresh, slightly starched sheets, in her hotel cubicle filled with comforts. Soft, reassuring sounds reached her ears; she thought she could distinguish, besides those from the city streets, the noise from industrial plants always ablaze, even at night. Before turning off the light, she switched on a transistor radio she had brought along, lowering the sound to a most tenuous degree. Then in the dark she abandoned herself to a relaxed drowsiness; she didn't want to shut herself up in total sleep and miss the sensations she was savoring now.

For the next day she had planned lunch at a restaurant in

that rural-industrial area, managed by a cousin of hers who brought in excellent seafood every day from Chioggia, across the Lagoon. Besides her husband, she had invited Enrico Fassola, the lawyer, and two young men, Silvio and Riccardo Camentini; the two boys had eagerly accepted as soon as they heard that Irene Berlocchi, whom they avidly admired, would be there.

Natasha's morning seemed to start very favorably. Irene told her over the phone from her room that she felt stronger and practically free from fever. The cousin called from the restaurant, his voice trembling with pride as he announced that he had really exceptional things ready for lunch. Natasha left the hotel before Irene to go and see that everything was in order at the restaurant. On her way out she passed by Irene's room and found her in black underwear, over which she would put a skin-tight, soft red woolen dress. "You'll drive them insane," Natasha commented. She had decided that Irene, after Kuntz's death and her father's arrest, should stay away from Milan for a while, and she saw Venice as the right choice; she herself was prepared to return to that city to be near her. Besides, during the summer it shouldn't be difficult for a person with Irene's background to find work as an interpreter. In these projects, Silvio and Riccardo Camentini's function was to create contacts for her among the young. By telephone Natasha had consulted with Enrico Fassola on this point too.

Natasha's invited guests were leaving Venice. Her husband was isolated from the rest; he had satisfactorily concluded his glass buying, and after the stop at the Mestre restaurant he would go back direct to Milan. The young Camentinis had borrowed the Jaguar from Riccardo's father and would have been happy to have Enrico Fassola ride with them; he declined; the boys were not offended but genuinely disappointed. Enrico preferred to use his own car, much smaller and shabbier; he had kept it ever since the time he had been in the diplomatic service. He brought along his old friend and daily companion, Giuliano Partibon, Ruggero's lame uncle. Riding across the Lagoon bridge, the two men, both fiftyish, were savoring an identical, tranquil, deep feeling of contentment. They had had a full morning, accomplishing work which was, within its limits, useful; they were hungry, and that signaled physical health; they were moving toward excellent fish dishes and bottles of wine; and they were looking forward to the company. Huge, heavy, squeezed in the small car beside his friend, Giuliano spoke for both of them, drawing a deep sigh, "How happy I am to be seeing Natasha again!'

"She and her husband don't live together but they are very good friends."

"They are very good friends."

Over the years, between the two of them and in their family circles, they had frequently repeated exactly the same lines. Part of their contentment in life consisted in listening to themselves say the same things over again. They completed, in unison, "And mind you, he's nobody's fool." On the contrary, they elaborated, Stefano, Natasha's husband, had a keen business mind, and lively interests outside his work. He had attracted Natasha because he was a man of "cultural curiosity" and because he knew how to express himself.

At the restaurant they found that all the others except Irene had already arrived; and Natasha's husband was indeed being eloquent. He had a strong, cheerful face; his well-chosen necktie and his smooth, well-trimmed moustache proclaimed his subtle attention to his person. He interrupted his talk for a moment to greet the two newcomers quickly but with intense friendliness. "Here we are," he whispered to Giuliano Partibon, winking: he had seen him a few hours earlier at the glassworks, where Giuliano was employed. He resumed his talk, and the two got ready to listen to him with alert smiles.

Stefano held a glass of wine in his left hand, while he pointed with his right forefinger at young Riccardo Camentini: "Your father, I'm sure, was a furious fornicator in his days, and God forbid you shouldn't follow his example. I don't mean that; I mean, one thing doesn't exclude the other. There are different types of men."

"What doesn't exclude what?" Enrico asked.

Stefano turned to him: "We were discussing abstention, chastity. I'm telling you, Mr. Fassola, and I mean this seriously: with some individuals, and in certain areas, in our time and especially in our country, chastity has represented and still represents a force which must be taken into account, even, I daresay, from the historical point of view."

The two fifty-year-olds listened to Stefano with delight, exchanging significant looks; they could taste the kind of juicy topic which would become part of their repertoire and to which they would come back in interminable talk during their restful evenings together after work.

"And look, Mr. Fassola, I'm not referring only to prelates or Vatican leaders. On this point, all I have to do is remind you of the average longevity of cardinals of the Church. Right? I'm also referring to unmarried laymen and political leaders. If you take, for example—"

This talk was suddenly and permanently interrupted. Irene had arrived. The apparition of little red-dressed Irene, solid, with her strength back, yet vaguely languid, caused a prolonged silence, and on the part of the men, looks of total, precise, acute desire, which in the young Camentinis' eyes mingled with something like despair. One by one, Irene kissed everybody. She sensed that this meeting was for her, even though she had never really accepted the idea. She had followed Natasha with incredulous curiosity. In her kissing round she left Giuliano Partibon until last; they embraced for a long while.

When they sat down, lunch started immediately; Natasha's cousin had arranged things so as to give the occasion a certain theatricality. During the fish soup, total silence fell over the scene. The two friends, Enrico and Giuliano, raising the spoons to their lips, exchanged looks which meant, "This is the real thing." Natasha's cousin had prepared five or six times as many dishes as usual, not because he wanted his guests to gorge themselves, but because he wanted to offer samples from the whole wide range of his piscatory cuisine; for instance, some spoonfuls of fish risotto were distributed here and there while the first swallows of a white, dry, icy wine were being taken. Not all the guests faced a whole *granceola;* with her own fork, Irene picked up little bits of crab meat from the large half shell that Giuliano Partibon, sitting next to her, had let the waiter place in front of him; at first Giuliano had restricted himself to staring fixedly at the multicolored beauty of the seafood in it. The various table operations, the crossings of platters, of little dishes with lemons cut in quarters, of oil cruets, at first left little room for conversation, which largely consisted of such formulas as "Would you please pass . . ." and at any rate remained desultory and disconnected.

Long after the basic choice had been made between broiled fish and mixed fried fish for the main course, and after the unchosen dish had also been sampled, a feeling of contented lassitude spread over the scene; now the main reason for the meeting was finally broached. Giuliano Partibon, known from childhood for a kind of honest clumsiness even in the way he talked, provided the opening with no other preamble than "Oh, by the way," which went practically unnoticed. Only Natasha, at the head of the table, seemed to receive the signal. With her motionless round face and round eyes, she could appear slow and simple-minded, but she was always a sharp listener, registering everything. She put down her fork, raised her full glass to her lips and drank the wine to the bottom, her gaze remaining fixed on Giuliano.

He went on, "Enrico was telling me that there are regulations, procedures, what have you, whereby Irene's *papà*, it seems, could be transferred, if so desired, from the Milan jail to the Venice jail. Now, I should think . . ."

Irene, sitting next to that vast, clumsy man, raised her eyes toward him with curiosity; she smiled and seemed both amused and pained at seeing him so mixed up.

Giuliano stopped, and looking around, seemed to seek a conclusion to his own talk in the others' eyes, now focusing on him. Evidently he also feared he had used the wrong tone, almost as if he had been speaking of a relative's corpse to be transferred from one cemetery to another. He tried to remedy: "My sister, who is very clever about things like this—"

Enrico Fassola intervened: "Elena apologizes for not being able to come. Anyway, Natasha, you talked to her over the phone and you'll see each other in the next few days; needless to say, Elena is really looking forward to it." He concentrated for a moment, gathering his thoughts. "Well, I discussed the subject with Elena at length; to tell the truth, it was she who first brought up the question. In other words, as has been the case more than once in the course of our old friendship, this too was her idea. And it's true, the thing is feasible; we could probably obtain a transfer."

[278]

Giuliano corroborated affably: "So, if Irene now comes to Venice to stay, as we all hope she will, she can keep in touch with her *papà* . . . bring him things, you know?"

Natasha nodded. Among those present, she was the one who had had most experience with prison visits; she remembered them as very uncomfortable affairs but knew that they were better than nothing. She had not really envisaged Irene's departure from Milan as a way to keep her far from her father; actually, Mr. Berlocchi's eventual transfer to Venice was part of the plan that was now taking shape with the special support of those two middle-aged Venetians, Enrico and Giuliano. They were people of a kind she knew well, with their prolixity in casual conversations and sobriety in practical discussions; she felt closer to such men than to someone like her husband, who in the early days of their acquaintance had attracted and enveloped her with talk that was to the point, instructive and brilliant, but then in a practical sense left things more or less unchanged. Her husband had told her once, referring to people like the Partibons, "Venetians, you know, are all schizophrenic." To such statements she would reply, "I doubt it. But maybe that's because you're in business, whereas I was do-mes-tic help." She seemed to relish, between tongue and lip, the very taste of the expression, and to charge it with new meaning.

Although the two young Camentinis were only cousins, they looked like twins. Now they exploded together in an invitation to Irene to come and live with them any time she wanted.

Irene became the center of attention and there was a prolonged silence. Then she spoke, in the same tone she might have used in giving an opinion on the fish just eaten: "All of these seem like very good ideas to me."

Giuliano took her small hand in his: "Ruggero too would like it this way."

"Really? Good, good," she said in the same tone.

The conversation turned to Ruggero. First there was a confusion of assorted bits of news. Only Natasha's husband had really read his articles in *Milano Sabato* ("very solid, very technical") , and Giuliano said that the young man was conducting "electronic experiments" on the Pacific Coast. But, he added, he wrote very little, so obviously he was also having a good time.

"They had a big international convention," Irene said, "and

[279]

he's a first-rate interpreter, absolutely the best in simultaneous translation." This statement was caught on the rebound by others who went on extolling Ruggero's virtues, his seriousness, his future in Italy, but Irene had ceased to listen. She had ordered her beloved cherry liqueur and was enjoying it by herself.

In various sections of the Venetian province, from Castello to Dorsoduro and to Cannaregio, and extending from the Lido to Mestre and even to Portogruaro, single individuals or groups of relatives and friends, or even people who had simply heard about him from others, were talking about Ruggero Tava Partibon, or thinking of him with intensity. Way ahead of everyone else, at considerable distance, was Paolo Partibon, the young man's grandfather.

He had received many clear and concise communications from Ruggero by aerogram. The old painter received those featherweight, bluish messages, and he was vexed by the fact of not having discovered a foolproof method for opening them; as he inserted the point of the letter opener and cut along the top he would murmur, "Now, let's see," always in fear that he might be amputating the typewritten message inside by a line or two. He was over eighty but managed to read without glasses; besides, Ruggero used a typewriter with large letters, well-spaced. Through one of these messages, probably destined to be the most memorable, Ruggero informed his grandfather that he was going to marry a young lady named Beatrice Clinton, adding that they would then leave for the Orient; their final objective was to get to China, one way or another, and stay there as long as possible.

Paolo sensed immediately that he was the only one to have received this information about Ruggero's plans; it had been the same way on previous occasions. Once more, therefore, it was up to him to decide on the procedure and on the limits within which the information should be permitted to become a topic of discussion within the family and throughout the city in general. At first he remained circumspect, he even cast vigilant looks around, pressing the aerogram to his chest, guarding it as a cat would a piece of liver or kidney. Reassured that he was alone, he savored the text slowly. His heartbeat quickened. He felt tears begin to come to his eyes.

China. Marco Polo, a Venetian. He shook his head to dispel this wholly outdated image. Instead, curiously, he happened to recall his wife as a young woman . . . his mother . . . those days; a China more visible, more palpable then, the distant people, immeasurably great and always in a state of commotion, in ever larger, vital upheavals, glories, disasters. And now Ruggero would go there with that young lady, almost without letting anybody know, with perfect ease, well oriented. The old man nodded, saying to himself, "I can *see* it all." Then he was overwhelmed by furious feelings of regret and remorse.

He felt he must somehow move around, and he easily convinced his brother Marco to accompany him in whatever little walking he could do, now no longer in the country but on the Lido, along deserted sections of the beach. Here he removed his shoes and socks, rolled up his pants; he bent down with some effort to gather shells, hold them in his hands and feel them, rediscovering their shapes; then, extending his arm, he would hold them at the right distance and observe them at length, in the light reflected by that greenish, empty sea, with little waves rolling in lightly to touch his naked feet. Then he and Marco would sit far back, both of them huge and solid, their buttocks firmly planted in the dry sand; well sheltered among inland brushwood, they gazed at the sea, exchanging few words between long pauses.

At some point Paolo started simply, "Time flies," and he reported on what Ruggero had written in his recent aerogram. So Marco was the first to get Paolo's news about the former golden child, who during the war and the bombings had been suspected of being deaf-and-dumb, the one whom Marco had once held on to as to a "living good-luck piece."

Marco's reaction was quiet approval: "I said to him myself that he should have gone to the Orient. And do we know anything about this Miss Clinton? Who is she? Is she pretty?" He repeated, "You remember I told him?"

"Yes, yes, I remember," his brother mumbled, his mind already elsewhere. It seemed so stupid not to have thought of that himself—of immediately getting a picture of this Miss Clinton. Regret and remorse seized him and he tried confusedly to express his feelings, define them: "It's not because of old age. That's not it, by any means. Age doesn't have a set, preordained

meaning. It's something else—the dullness, the stagnation . . ."
He used words like these during his solitary debates with the
TV set, which was "working again." "To think that in these
past few years I have busied myself with antiques, with auc-
tions, with things of that sort. Buying and selling *objets d'art*.
Can you imagine?" He didn't even have to formulate his decision to resume painting with vigor—the decision had, as it
were, already made itself. He would call his son Giorgio in
Paris to discuss his plans and tell him, "I certainly could not
tolerate the ignominy of ending my life as a dilettante." He
would speak with Vittoria, his wife, tell her about Ruggero and
have her get several photographs of Miss Clinton from the
young man. Somehow he did not feel like making the request
directly.

In bed with his wife, in the midnight silence, he opened with
the usual filler, "Time flies," but he had not gone beyond the
first few sentences when she interrupted him. "I already know
everything. Ditto your sisters. This evening while you were
reading *Le Monde* and then swearing in front of the TV set,
your sisters spoke of nothing else in the kitchen. I believe they
also telephoned several people."

"And what did they say?"

"They criticize your attitude."

"Really? And what is my attitude?"

They were both big, a regal old couple, propped against the
raised pillows as on comfortable thrones, and now they looked
at each other in silence with sly smiles. Vittoria Partibon was
not a loquacious woman; generally she would make brief comments and leave them hanging in the air, without bothering
whether anyone would catch them; however, as her husband
knew, every six months or so she might come out with a longer
speech, so well organized that it sounded prepared, in perfectly
apt language which she must have got out of nowhere, since her
reading was next to nothing.

"It stands to reason that your attitude is one of enthusiasm,
as evidenced by the fact that you keep it all to yourself and
hardly mention the subject. You wouldn't mention it even with
the protagonist himself, Ruggero, were he here and not ten
thousand miles away, or whatever the distance may be. But to
realize how much you think about it, one only has to observe

[282]

how you save his articles, heavily annotated by you. Now you've heard that he will go to China, and moreover, that he's going to get married to a girl from Ca-li-for-nia, probably attractive and full of intellectual and sexual vitality; so this, in short, is your attitude: rapture and envy."

"Now that you've described my attitude, describe that of my —my critics."

"Your sister Delia—quite probably after talking on the phone with some of her friends who go to lectures and concerts with her, and influenced by them—has come to the conclusion that Ruggero, by planning to go so far away, as if—I'm quoting —the place where he is now weren't far enough, and to prolong his absence maybe for years, is showing—I'm still quoting—irresponsibility and lack of feeling."

"Why?"

"Because for one thing, according to them, Ruggero runs the risk of never seeing his grandparents again."

"In other words, they wouldn't want him to miss our deaths? They would be inviting him to a lovely show, I'm telling you."

"Then Elena came too and they told her, 'Since you're his mother, you should write to him, make him understand.' "

"What did she say?"

"According to Elena, the prospect of death in the family in the next months or years is most unlikely. 'And anyway,' she says, 'why should it happen to them?' Meaning you and me."

"Age."

"You can imagine Elena's conclusion. 'Of course not,' she says. 'If anybody, it will be me; I'm worse off than anybody as far as health is concerned.' However, she added also that the health factor is not much of an indication, considering that the only relatively premature death she could think of among her blood relations was that of your cousin Odo, who enjoyed perfect health except for his teeth."

"His kidneys were in rather bad shape too. At any rate, I see Elena agrees with my point of view. And what did Giuliano have to say?"

"He wasn't there. Perhaps he was still at Mestre with Natasha."

"I asked him to invite both Natasha and the little Berlocchi girl to come and stay with us."

"We have no room."

"Very well, then, the Berlocchi girl can go to the Camentinis, who would love to have her. I'm planning radical changes in my way of life. Natasha will be an ideal companion and organizer to have in the house. I have much work to do. Marco, who apparently has told you everything, no doubt told you also that I'm going to start painting again full time."

The two old people went on talking long into the night, with growing animation.

The news spread that Irene was running a temperature again; both Enrico Fassola and the young Camentinis went to Mestre to see for themselves. They found Natasha and Irene not at the hotel but at the cousin's restaurant. They decided they might as well order some of those excellent fish dishes, and while they were eating they observed Irene closely and with anxiety. The Camentinis looked confused, even though they were solid, muscular young men, euphoric with wine and desire. Enrico Fassola, with his dark eyes, the eyes of an alert dog, was observing their maneuvers.

Silvio Camentini finished drinking a glass of wine, dried his lips and said in a choked voice, "Listen, Irene, we'll take you to Venice with us at once."

Fassola cleared his throat like a lawyer in court, and said quietly, "Of course not. Now Irene must return to the hotel and go to bed. Today is Tuesday, the day Aurelio Moscato sees patients here in his Mestre office. I've already asked him to stop by the hotel in the afternoon to examine her before he goes back to the office."

The young men looked at him as if he had said something extremely upsetting. Irene listened to Enrico's plan with a docile smile. They all went back to the hotel; Irene went up to her room with Natasha, to undress and get ready for the doctor's visit. Sitting in the lobby downstairs and thinking about Irene undressing, the two Camentinis thought they'd go out of their minds: with her figure both firm and soft, her flat tone of voice, her quiet, level gaze, Irene was disturbingly attractive to them. Sitting opposite them, Enrico studied them silently; then, seeing the doctor enter, he got up to meet him. On his way back he went by the two young men, who rose mumbling greetings to the doctor, and Enrico said to them, "There's no reason why we all should wait here, is there? Besides, Irene should have some rest. You go back to Venice; you have some examinations to prepare for, haven't you?" He patted their shoulders affably and left them; he accompanied the doctor to Irene's door. When he came down to the lobby again, the young men had already disappeared.

He admitted to himself that he had consciously wanted to get rid of them. He sat down again in a comfortable armchair and looked around. The clock behind the concierge's desk, the golden window curtains, the flowers and ashtrays on the tables, every object, every vision, had an important and precise relief. Perfect focus. Suddenly it seemed to him as though all of his past life had tended toward this moment. The world was free of banality or meaningless detail; every apparent trifle mattered deeply. He trusted Dr. Aurelio Moscato, who was now examining Irene; Aurelio was the nephew and heir of an old and, in his time, very popular Venetian doctor. Enrico intended to listen to his verdict with care, then he would go up to Irene, to be with her a while longer before going back to his office in the city. He felt he had reached a peak of quiet and mature vitality. Doing things for other people, even seemingly minimal ones. A different lighting seemed to illuminate one's finite world, and every detail emerged looking essential and irreplaceable.

He leafed through the newspapers while his ear was following the motions of the elevator. Every time he heard it come down and the doors open, he turned around to see who was coming out. Almost an hour went by, with only strangers appearing; and finally, a surprise: Irene, alone, in her red dress, handbag and all. Enrico had hardly got up before she was by his side, taking him by the arm.

"Natasha thought Moscato might as well examine her too," she said. "They are great friends. So now Moscato is examining Natasha."

"But what about you?"

"Nothing. He gave me some excellent new pills."

"Did he tell you to get up?"

"No. But come, let's go and listen to some records; maybe you can buy me one."

They walked arm in arm through the main streets, mostly in

silence, looking at shopwindows. In the beginning, days earlier, when she started to observe Enrico closely, it had occurred to her that she might want to shock him with childish suggestions, like "I'll tell you everything I did with Ruggero, and you'll tell me everything you did with his mother." But the way their relationship actually turned out had been totally different; it had acquired an aura, a blend of dignity and tenderness, something quite new to Irene; therefore she decided to take advantage of the situation and explore this novelty in full. She was used to living among people who more or less minded their own business and who did not usually talk about one another. Now, however, she sensed that among these Venetians there was a great deal of talk about herself, perhaps initiated by Natasha but then definitely controlled by Enrico Fassola; it came natural to her to keep close to him.

Irene seemed to be already known in the record shop; she picked half a dozen records and retired with Enrico to a rear booth to listen to them. The following hour was destined to remain in Enrico's memory as the one in which, for the first time in his life, pieces of music sounded to him like compelling and revealing forms of discourse. This happened to him from the very first moment; to feel that way, all he had to do was watch Irene as she listened, frowning, biting her lower lip; every now and then she would put one hand on his arm and point with her other toward the music as if to warn him that something was going to happen; and when finally the musical event erupted and began to develop, she would squeeze his arm tightly and cast a quick glance at him, which gave him a feeling of revelation, of giddiness and of uneasiness.

When the records were finished, they got up in silence; they found themselves face to face, scrutinizing each other as if it were the first time. Enrico asked, "Which records do you want? Why don't you let me get them all for you?"

"No, wait till Natasha and I are settled in Venice."

"An old friend of my mother's has a lot of connections with all sorts of cultural events and international conventions they have in Venice, especially during the summer. I'm sure that with your background—"

Irene interrupted him with a nod. "I'll find work. But first

Natasha and I are going to the mountains for a couple of weeks. It's off-season now and Natasha knows of some inexpensive places."

"I too have been planning to take my vacation now."

"Where are you going?"

"If it wouldn't annoy you, I was thinking of going wherever you go." He caressed her hair; he delicately forced her to press her cheek against his chest. Irene seemed curious to see what his next move would be. Enrico cupped her face in his hands and kissed her lips; she returned the kiss. They left the shop with their arms around each other. Irene was still running a temperature and would go back to bed at once. Enrico left her at the elevator.

He crossed the Lagoon bridge and drove slowly through the industrial landscape at sunset. In Venice, he went immediately to his office and remained there until past midnight to finish the work he had neglected in the afternoon. Impulsively he called Giuliano Partibon and asked if they could get together; they went to a *trattoria* that was still open, to have something to eat and drink some wine. Enrico spoke about his afternoon with Irene. Giuliano cocked his one good ear but didn't quite grasp the full significance of his friend's words; however, he knew he had been summoned there to give Enrico a chance to talk. After he had finished his tale, Enrico did not say much, either. "I don't deserve it," he kept repeating, "I don't deserve it."

Although Paolo Partibon had been advised by his son Giuliano that Irene's and Natasha's affairs would be "settled in unexpected ways," he nevertheless continued to manage them in his authoritarian manner.

One morning he called Piero Camentini, the man of letters: "You have nothing to do; why don't you ever come to see me?"

This decrepit painter could apparently still arouse sparks of curiosity and awe. Not only did Piero Camentini accept the invitation, but his busy industrialist brother, Giovanni, took advantage of it too; and they brought along their sons.

What old Partibon considered the "business side" of the occasion was summarily disposed of. Since the Camentinis lived in an old palace, they asked for nothing better than to have Irene as their houseguest; that would leave Natasha free for the "organizational" functions that Partibon was planning to assign to her in his own home.

Irene being thus settled, the talk turned to her father's situation and became heated. The Camentinis vehemently agreed with Partibon that if Irene's father was sentenced to a prison term, then a "whole class" should follow him behind bars. The enthusiasm and genuine warmth the Camentinis displayed in harmonizing with him put them in a new light. Until now, whenever old Partibon spoke about them to his sisters, who valued them highly as Ruggero's faithful friends, he had used such characteristic definitions as "Very confused people—biologically too. You can say what you want, but they are people whose hands are always perspiring."

Now he took a new look at them; he decided he would summon them often to his house, especially the boys, to get to know them better, direct them, explain them to themselves. He had always considered Piero Camentini a rhetorician without any talent, and Giovanni, as maker and seller of candy, a "thief"; now, though his basic attitude remained unchanged, he was ready to take a broader view; he listened attentively to a long discourse by Giovanni Camentini on the subject of frozen foods and came to the conclusion that even though the fathers were more or less what they had always been, the children could still be saved.

He felt especially attracted to Giovanni's son, Riccardo: clumsy in his speech, with a probable hyperthyroidism which seemed to choke his voice, always with a questioning look in his eyes, he was, perhaps unconsciously, capable of thinking and suffering. Quite clearly his father, in wanting him to take over the management of the candy industry, did not know what he was doing. He had sent him to England and America to study, with imperceptible results. In that young man everything was still to be discovered; he needed to be piloted, liberated. "Riccardo," old Partibon asked, "why don't you try to get to China, now that Ruggero is going there?"

Partibon's broad view embraced many generations of Venetians; he could, on command, evoke their gestures, traits, voices. Sustained by the strength of this nearly century-long perspective, he wanted somehow to be of help to the newer ones, he sensed that that was his way of loving the city and the world, his duty as an old man. "Why don't you go to China?" Seeing both exaltation and stupefaction on the boy's face, he went on in a simple, offhand tone, "Trust my vision of things, even though it's true that I haven't traveled much. My brother, Marco, has been around a lot in his life; I went only a couple of times to Paris, and to Germany, in my youth. But what difference does that make? My sister Ersilia, for instance, is a virgin; yet if you were in some erotic mess, I would suggest that you go to her for advice; she will tell you very sensible and practical things. You'll get much greater satisfaction from her than if you went, say, to the rich lady who lives near here, direction northwest— I'm not mentioning any names—in whose bed, especially in the twenty years between '36 and '56, there was an incessant coming-and-going."

"Why do you set '56 as the terminal date?" asked the young man who, as an adolescent, had dedicated very advanced dreams to the lady in question.

"Never mind, I know what I'm talking about. And your Uncle Piero here"—he pointed to Piero Camentini, who made a little bow—"knows it very well too. I don't know about your father, who has been too much taken up by industry and commerce, after the hurricanes of his early youth." He rambled on a while in the same vein, then abruptly faced Giovanni Camentini. "I shouldn't want to give you the impression," he said, while Giovanni stared at him, his eyes popping, "that I feel obliged to take an antagonistic view of a man of your breed—an industrialist, and so forth. In the first place, I have never in my life considered anything obligatory, and in the second place, however little I may have followed your life and your work, you strike me as being better than some of the magnates who were fashionable at the time when I was the age you are now, if for no other reason than that you have to be better informed and shrewder than they were. I don't like your candy, but my daughter, for instance, whose judgment I respect, finds that some of your products have what she describes as exhilarating flavors. And my grandson Ruggero . . ."

Giovanni Camentini's eyes were glued to the old man, whose talk he followed with fascinated irritation. At one point he felt he was wasting precious time by being there, but immediately afterward he was sure that this was an extraordinary occasion and that none of it should be lost. He felt almost as if in a labyrinth. When the old man mentioned Ruggero, Giovanni recognized more familiar ground and said expansively, "Oh, that boy is a genius."

"I was discussing him recently over the telephone with my son in Paris, and I agree with Giorgio when he says Ruggero is a rather immature young man. I won't keep from you"—he looked around, gathering everybody's attention—"in fact, you are the first to hear me say this: when Ruggero announced his plans *to me* about matrimony and China, I drew a sigh of relief; there's more to him than we thought. He couldn't have chosen a more opportune moment to travel in that direction. Besides, from the little he told me about the young lady, I immediately sensed she must be a woman of great qualities." He nodded, as if putting a stamp on his own words, making it clear that the Ruggero topic was settled; without pausing, he turned again to Giovanni Camentini: "Listen, is it true that you plan to transfer your firm to the mainland, to Mestre?"

"Not at all; in fact, we believe—"

"Once upon a time," Partibon interrupted, "Ersilia was one of those who firmly believe that Venice is destined to be submerged; now she has gone over to the opposite theory. In my opinion, she has embraced the notion of survival precisely because, deep down, she feels it's absurd. I'm sure that without realizing it, she finds analogies between her city and her family. We are longevous by mistake. In other words"—now he stopped, with his large clear eyes fixed on his listeners—"survival is the curious accident, not death."

He sent Riccardo Camentini to the dining room to get a bottle of wine, and they ended the visit drinking and toasting. Before taking leave, Giovanni spoke for all the Camentinis: "Thank you, thank you, maestro, thank you; talking with you is always—how shall I put it?—refreshing."

However, after the four Camentinis had closed the door behind them and walked a few steps on the Zattere, and after they had embarked Giovanni's motorboat and settled in the cabin as in a familiar little parlor, they started to have doubts. A few hours yet, and the first news connecting Irene to Enrico Fassola would begin to circulate, through meetings and phone calls, opening the possibility for developments of which old Partibon, with his air of dominance over the local scene, did not seem to have the vaguest idea. So what was Partibon, then? An old sage ranging with his still-sharp eyes over the sea of time, or perhaps somewhat like a discarded admiral, a bit off his rocker, playing with paper flotillas in his tub? For most friends and observers in the city, the dilemma was destined to remain unresolved forever.

Elena Partibon and her few women friends often met in a café at the foot of the Academy Bridge on the Dorsoduro side. When Irene phoned her from Mestre and asked to see her, Elena agreed to meet her at the café. They sat outside, at the edge of the Grand Canal, with the cumbersome wooden arch of the bridge high above them; from the very beginning of their conversation Elena realized that Irene wanted especially to talk to her about Enrico Fassola.

Keeping her slightly sad hazel eyes fixed on Elena, Irene started giving details about Enrico's visits to Mestre; how he had taken care of her; Dr. Moscato's visit; the intense way they had been listening to music. Irene's report was given in her absolutely flat tone of voice, but with a questioning insistence, as though she expected from Elena some sort of clarification.

Presently Elena cut in: "All right, my dear, all of this seems very good to me, very promising." Women of Irene's age bored her; she felt no impulse to do anything for them. And besides, Enrico Fassola himself had come to see her a few days earlier, with the usual excuse of some papers to sign, and had spoken at great length about Irene in an emotional manner.

"This may seem strange to you," he said, "but you're the only person I really wanted to talk to. I spoke with Giuliano, but you, somehow . . ."

"I quite understand," she had encouraged him; "there is really no need for long explanations between us. Are you thinking about what there was once between us, for so many years? Are you trying, somehow, to justify yourself?" She remembered his visiting her, more than ten years before, in the English countryside, drenched with rain. Now she was again asking questions, to try to help him come out of his futile vacillations.

But Enrico evidently wished to keep the talk at a level of emotional eloquence: he was too happy to be able to deny himself that. "Elena, you know what you represent, what you have always represented to me, and not only to me, to many others . . . You're a woman for whom I can't find a better adjective than this: invincible." Then in a lower, more cautious voice: "What is your advice?"

"You would do well to marry her if you can. She's much younger than you, but she already looks like a middle-aged little woman." Yes, this was certainly the best that Enrico, whom she had known so well for at least thirty years, could hope for. "Oddly enough, I even believe she wouldn't be unfaithful to you. Besides, you can be useful to her professionally, what with the trouble her father is in now."

But this was not enough: Elena saw clearly that Enrico's eyes, those doglike eyes, demanded something less positive and immediate—words that would permit him to evoke the present scene later on, to caress it with feeling in his memory. Since Elena was incapable of that kind of talk, she had only whispered, in passing, some rather ordinary phrases from her repertory, "You know, Enrico, that there is room for everything, that nothing is ever wasted."

Now, with Irene sitting opposite her, she would have wanted to repeat the same words, meaning that there was room for this union between Irene and Enrico, as there had been room for the association between Irene and her son, Ruggero, or for the encounter in England between herself and Enrico—Enrico, who, so long ago, through her rejection of him and her union with Ruggero's father, had learned the meaning of pain: everything could always be kept alive and functioning; everything, including pain, had its charge of vitality. But seeing Irene's face, small and so still, Elena did not even try to communicate what she was thinking. She felt that of all the people she knew, the only one who would understand, even without words, was Natasha; it would certainly be cheerful to have her in the house, if Paolo managed to convince her.

As there was not much more to say, Elena had a feeling of relief when they saw Enrico Fassola appear, high on top of the bridge; already from up there he greeted the two women with exuberant gestures, then he descended upon them, sat at their table, suggested that they have another round of the sparkling wine they were drinking.

Elena accepted, settling down to observe Enrico and Irene as a couple. They were even better matched than she had expected. They had a detailed schedule of practical occupations, they went shopping together; Enrico said he had "spoken again" to this or that key person in the cultural organizations of the city, so that after their return from a mountain vacation, there would be work for Irene as an interpreter or something of the kind. Now Enrico had to go to Piazzale Roma, the vast city garage, to check on some repair work on his old car, and it went without saying that Irene would accompany him. Two ladies, friends of Elena's, turned up; Irene and Enrico gave their places to them. "We'll find you here when we come back," they said to Elena as they left.

They always used public transportation. Enrico had some fixed ideas about seats: in one of the smaller motorboats he would sit in front; in a larger boat, or *vaporetto,* he had to have a seat in the back. In this, as well as in other idiosyncrasies, Irene went along with him, with curiosity rather than impatience. At the garage she listened intently to the long discussion between Enrico and the mechanic; she was not bored, in fact she knew enough to be able to check on Enrico's familiarity with motors, and was happy to discover that he was quite an expert.

On their way back he didn't take her to the boat station; they proceeded on foot. Irene, who had grown up in Milan, had never walked on these streets; she had seen them only from below, from the canal. There was a bridge and then a long embankment, or *fondamenta,* along the canal through which the boat had come. They did not get to the end of the *fondamenta.* Suddenly, pressing her arm more strongly than ever, Enrico made her turn and led her into a wider road, lined with trees, dusty; he told her that that was a *rio terrà,* a former canal filled in with earth. She had not imagined that there could be a road in Venice looking so rural and so abandoned. "Where are we?" she asked.

The street was flanked by houses, low and all of a piece as on some fishermen's islands, with narrow doors, and laundry hung out to dry; in the middle of the street were two rows of trees, between which wild, dusty grass grew freely. On the grass, farther on, an old boat was lying in the weak sunlight, upside down.

On the right-hand side, the low dwellings continued to the end of the street, while on the left the line was interrupted where a high brick wall began, fortresslike. Immediately beyond the wall, very high, they could see, from the waist up, a guard in military uniform marching up and down on top of the parapet. The edifices within that kind of citadel had the anonymous, deaf-and-dumb aspect of warehouses.

They walked along under the wall; at the end, just before the corner, there was a door, not large but well proportioned and solid, its white stone frame standing out sharply against the brick background. That door with its frame, the two white stone steps, the little watchtower at the corner suggested by their style a maritime rather than a military building.

Turning the corner, they found themselves in a small square, bordered at the outer edge by a canal; a bridge across the canal led to buildings which reminded Irene of abandoned customs houses; here, too, the grass was growing wherever it could, blindly. They stopped at the foot of the bridge and turned around to look at the façade of the citadel's noblest building, in that old-Venetian-shipyard style that the side door had announced: orderly, compact brick, firmly contained within the white stone of the merlons; cornices shaped like rows of blind little windows; and the strong frame which marked and isolated its central part: here, up high, was the emblem of the Venetian nation, it too sculpted in white stone, the winged lion holding an open book in its claws, its face bearing the usual expression of enigmatic hauteur, and under it, carved in the stone, the suitable Latin motto, CUSTODIT PUNIT MONET, the humanistic touch, cultured, aloof, ancestral, indifferent, overlooking from its vast and vacuous altitude the ordinary oval metal plaque above the mundane door, with the emblem of the present Italian Republic encircled like a postmark by the inscription CENTRAL JUDICIAL PRISON.

Cautiously, with restrained fervor, Enrico whispered, "Well, this would be the place."

Irene measured him with a look; she was curious to know what else he would find to say.

In the long hours they had spent together, they had also mentioned Irene's mother more than once and the automobile accident in which she had died. Irene's father, at the wheel, with wife and daughter in the car, had been the only one of the three to come out practically unhurt from the crash. Irene had told Enrico, "People may not be aware of it, but one of my legs is shorter than the other; I walk with a slight limp. Maybe that's why Giuliano Partibon seems to be so fond of me."

Now, in front of that building, Enrico resumed the subject; as if concluding a long and complicated series of thoughts, he asked, "Don't you think he must have got a tremendous guilt complex, something like a need to expiate . . . ?"

"No. I don't think so."

After a long pause she reported, "I had that dream again, where Dr. Moscato comes to see me in a thick fog after visiting my father, who had thrown himself, head-on, full speed, against a wall in his prison cell. This time Moscato was smiling, the way you're doing now, and saying, 'Your father is doing nicely.' Actually," Irene went on in her monotone, "we will bring him baskets of food, he will grow fatter and flabbier, his face gray, unshaven. He'll be contented if they let him listen to soccer games on the radio."

"You despise him. You despise him very much, don't you?"

"No, I don't. Why should I?"

Enrico spoke with effort, feeling his ground with each syllable: "You're very strong, and you don't know it; this I find deeply touching."

Irene indicated the prison façade with her chin: "Of course, really to get some idea, one should visit the cells. But anyway, I too have the impression that he would be more comfortable here."

They started on their way back through the Carmini, Santa Margherita with its fish market, San Barnaba, where Enrico stopped to point out a house. "That's where Ruggero's great-grandmother died; and there"—indicating the church—"they had the funeral; I was there; before you were born." They went through the Toletta, through part of San Trovaso, they were again at the foot of the Academy Bridge on the Dorsoduro side;

Elena was no longer sitting at the café. Enrico led his companion to the top of the bridge and stopped there, looking in the direction of St. Mark.

They leaned on the wooden balustrade as if looking from a balcony. It seemed as if Enrico had chosen that high, central point to tell his companion something important, something conclusively true and certain. He found at first only the sober tone of a guide: "There used to be only one bridge in Venice, the Rialto Bridge. Venice is divided into six sections, *sestieri;* the Rialto Bridge joins the St. Mark *sestiere* to the San Paolo section. Then, during the last century, two more bridges were built across the Grand Canal, the one at the railroad station, and this one. They were iron bridges, of the same material and color as lampposts, or if you wish, as the Eiffel Tower. I remember this one as an iron bridge; the very name, *il Pòn-te dell'Acca-dèmia,* to me has an iron sound, that's how it resounded when we were children and trotted over it. Then both iron bridges were torn down and the one at the railroad station was rebuilt in stone, whereas here they placed this wooden structure, looking like a scaffolding to be removed later on, except that though it looks like something temporary, this is it, this is the bridge. And mind you, it's a very important bridge, joining St. Mark to Dorsoduro; but this temporary appearance is its real quality, and another quality it has is that it isn't beautiful; that's why I love it. I too, like Giuliano, love gray, ordinary, useful things.

"You will probably tell me that the Rialto Bridge is the real one, and in fact, that one is a monument, a work of art, but what is important about the Academy Bridge is the way it endures; it endures as it changes. The view from here changes too. For instance, that Gothic palace there in the background on your right near the Salute Church strikes me as absolutely uninhabitable and outside of reality; and it happens to be the house where I lived most of my childhood and early youth. Now I live near my office, on an inner, narrow gray street, to me very beautiful, called *Calle degli Avvocati,* Lawyers' Lane, and that's precisely why I came back here, to be a lawyer in my city before it got too late.

"Once upon a time we were a prominent family; now fortunately we are no longer that. I haven't much to offer. I know only that I can offer all that I have. Perhaps men like Giovanni Camentini are prominent now, but I know that while his products are being spread all over the world, the electronic brain of his firm stays here; his office windows overlook a canal and a bridge with the swishing of footsteps and the silly chatter like those I hear from the small square under my office when I am busy handling the affairs of, say, a Hamburg or a Rotterdam shipowner. Law offices in our city are generally located in old dilapidated palaces. Important business is transacted in rooms exuding ancient domestic smells of risotto, of cat excrement, of tobacco kept in eighteenth-century snuffboxes, and of saltiness and humidity.

"This is not a picturesque little town flooded with sunlight such as you find on the Mediterranean; this is a vast, complicated, foggy city, or at least that is the way I like it. And if I managed to convey to you what I feel when I say that in this foggy labyrinth, resounding with soft, endless chatter, I have my precise place; if I managed to tell you what it means to me to be able to call myself, and to feel like, *a Venetian lawyer,* then I believe I would feel the same as when in music, as you taught me, the essential theme is liberated from the tangle of sounds— the unique, incontrovertible statement which cannot be replaced, changed, transposed; and then I perceive, like a flash, or perhaps better, like a glimmer, what you mean when you speak about a man I never even knew and say to Natasha or me, 'Kuntz, he always knew how to find the solution.' And now I can only tell you that never in my life have I managed to talk the way I'm now talking to you, my dear, and that's because of the way you look at me, frowning pensively, serious, calm . . ."

Irene had listened to him, nodding every now and then, finally smiling; she took his hand in both her own: "I understand what you say. I really understand everything very well."

The departure for a brief offseason mountain holiday was set for the following morning. Irene went to spend the night with Natasha at the Mestre hotel. Enrico was going to pick them up at ten with his newly repaired automobile.

That evening Enrico dined with his mother, who retired early to bed; then he went out to join Giuliano Partibon at one of their usual meeting places, where they drank wine until midnight. Nothing could have been more customary and relaxed for the two old friends; usually they could spend as long as half an hour in complete silence, exchanging looks and smiles of mutual understanding as if they were conversing. But this evening Enrico evidently was bringing news; yet he remained uncertain until Giuliano encouraged him: "Did you ask her to marry you? What did you say to each other?"

Enrico looked at him as if he didn't understand the words, or even the language. Then, hurriedly, clearing his throat: "Yes, yes, sure, sure, and she answered in the most normal way. 'We can very well do that,' she said. 'I'll find work here in Venice and I can also go on with my music; Milan without Kuntz is no good, anyway.' "

"And then?"

"Then what?"

"Aren't you happy?"

Enrico leaned toward his friend as if he were offering secret advice: "When you feel like this, you wouldn't mind dying."

"But you look very happy."

"Happiness perhaps means feeling like this—prepared to die."

For a long while Giuliano looked in silence at his friend, the oldest friend he had in this city of their birth, of their attachments, of their joys, of their agonies, of their harmonies, of their burials.

CHAPTER
NINE

GILBERTO ROSSI:

Now I don't even know where to start. I am back here, at the Institute. Blatt is being considered as the new director, in fact he says he has received a firm offer. All the eligible candidates, except him, are people from outside. Apparently Chuck Palmerston has a candidate of his own, a general who was once ambassador somewhere in the Far East. Blatt, Lebournet, Epstein and I have a kind of kamiri of our own, not actually clandestine but certainly very unofficial; we meet regularly and discuss everything.

Ruggero and Beatrice are in Japan; from there they plan to go to China, I don't know whether by way of Hong Kong or by some other route. When I was in Europe I was in touch, also by telephone, with old friends from the time I spent at Göttingen as *Universitätslektor,* and I was able to reconstruct rather accurately the biography of my friend and former colleague Teh for these past few years; it is confirmed that he is a librarian in Peking, so I trust he and Ruggero will meet.

Also in Europe, and more exactly in Venice over dinner at a restaurant in the Dorsoduro section, I met several friends of Ruggero's, among them one by the name of Ugo Momo, who is extremely intelligent; he knows all about the police and police headquarters through his experience with arrests as a dissenter, especially in Rome, where he studies biochemistry. He confirmed that Ruggero was indeed going to China; Momo himself had given him names & addresses of biochemists there. Momo, who in some areas is so much more of an expert than I am (I don't mean biochemistry, that's obvious, but police and judicial procedures, for instance, on which unfortunately I have considerable information gaps), confirmed an old notion of mine concerning relations between human beings. I have always sensed that there exists, on a world-wide or cosmic scale, a network of relations between real people, individualized and not bound by any official ties; people, in other words, for whom the Airports Level of our friend Clinton not only does not exist but is a priori excluded from any form of rapport or acceptance, let alone utilization; and it would so remain, even if it were to undergo radical reform, which is highly unlikely. Meanwhile this cosmic network goes on operating without any general awareness of it; in fact, without even self-awareness, since it exists without definition. Indeed, I suspect that for such a network, definitions and labels would mark the beginning of the end.

I'll add a brief note about the person in whose company I met Ugo Momo. He was with another friend of Ruggero's, and at first the pair struck me as rather implausible, since the other young man was the son & heir of Camentini Candies. Actually, however, he showed total detachment from his father's industrial interests. Since everything, unfortunately, interests me, I was all set to sound him out on the degree of progress made in frozen foods in particular (the Camentinis are involved in this field) and in the supermarket idea in general, an idea which has become so familiar to me during my U.S. period; but this young Camentini, Riccardo by name, did not seem to appreciate my curiosity; he wanted me to talk about Ruggero instead, and when I did, he listened intently and murmured every now and then, "Me too, you'll see . . ."

At some point he called the restaurant owner and his daughters so they could listen to my stories about Ruggero; and now I certainly won't deny that finding myself like that, in a world which had been Ruggero's when I didn't know him yet, I felt a strange mixture of curiosity and emotion. To the subject of other encounters in Venice and in the Venetian region I shall naturally have to come back, and I shall do so as soon as I feel the right style coming to me.

Of course I see friends of Ruggero's here, too; in fact, more of them and more often than when he was here. Most of them are motorcyclists and they follow my course in modern Italian *Kulturgeschichte*. I have resumed the course with increased intensity and more documentary material, not only books but also films and tapes, recordings of speeches, including recent ones, TV-like newsreels, and so forth. They follow me diligently but deep underneath they are always mistrustful. Every now and then they come up with questions, not so much on particular points, but actually on such sweepingly wide subjects as the Position of the Individual in History, his Place in the Present Cosmos; and they don't seem to want answers, but rather to get me into a trap.

"You are being simplistic," I told them the other day, "and I shall be simplistic too. It seems to me that the first practical thing I can do to meet your demands is to attempt, for instance, a simple definition—a portable definition, so to speak, of Evil. Or at least an illustration, something about which we can agree that it indisputably constitutes Evil."

Imitating Lebournet, who goes to the blackboard and draws diagrams and little arrows, I drew a kind of double doughnut with chalk, i.e., a small circle in the center of a larger circle, which was in turn contained within an even larger one. In my hypersimplification the small, innermost circle represents us, taken one by one, the community of solitude, which means each one is alone but closely linked to every other human being. I demonstrated this by a simple formula: "I"—small arrow— "you"—small arrow—"n" ("n" being, let's say, a newly encountered person, a potential "you") .

Running all around us is a ring of the Saturn type, divided into two lanes: inner circle (red, if the diagram should be drawn in color) and outer circle (opaque black) . The inner circle is the one in which we operate; being our own, it is the ground on which we can somehow try to find some agreement in order to regulate it, to understand one another, to give help. The outer one is the zone which cannot be regulated, grasped, comprehended, defined, qualified—the often-cited tragic mystery surrounding our lives.

"Maximum Evil, in my opinion," I said, tapping my chalk on the various points in my diagram, "is represented by those men who, while necessarily operating, like all of us, in our inner circle—here—yet presume themselves to be the possessors of special knowledge, and to be representatives, interpreters, prophets and bonzes drawing authority from this other circle—here—the mysteriosophic outer circle, opaque black; and they claim this authority in dealing with matters of the inner circle, implying that their actions are thus justified, sanctioned, sealed, patented . . .

"You can try to apply this pattern to obvious daily situations, down-to-earth, national, civic, political, administrative on all levels; in such cases, you will be able to recognize with the naked eye the manipulators and occult prophets through the simplest L & C analysis; you will find them in the usual nuclei of power with their governmental labyrinths, secret kamiris, et cetera, where true orgies of zero words are being concocted, et cetera. A supreme example is the Men of Destiny, self-appointed vessels of the Right Vision . . ."

I spoke awhile along these lines, more clearly, I think, than in these quick notes; I saw signs of surprise and some interest even among the motorcyclists. I had had a certain amount of experience in this area, having given this kind of talk to my former boss Di Gaetano when I saw him again in Italy during the summer.

"You shouldn't publish only books," I had told him, "but also posters with diagrams like this one, in color, with symbols, with mottoes—easy schematic tables to be hung behind the teacher's desk in all primary schools of the republic." I scarcely need to add that Di Gaetano took the entire project to be one of my jokes.

In contrast, Lebournet liked it when I mentioned it during one of our accidental and informal kamiri miris, in which Harold Epstein also participates. Harold, incidentally, has just finished an extensive and significant new symphony. Lebournet made it clear that he and other specialists in "signs" have long been thinking along these lines in a very comprehensive way. We did a more sophisticated drawing of my doughnut and improvised several other sign tables, and we came to the conclusion that they should be displayed not only on classroom walls but also in public offices, cafés, clubs, and perhaps also on the roadside like traffic signs.

Lebournet looks at the future with justifiable seriousness. He foresees violent shake-ups, increasing revolts by downtrodden minorities, which may well turn out to be majorities; he expresses his easy prophecies in a rigid tone, with streaks of sadism toward excessively unaware citizens. He doesn't include among these only people fed on the rhetorical TV patterns he himself has analyzed, but also people adorned with serious classical studies, like his father-in-law, who is a tall, sportsmanlike gentleman with thick gray hair, a native of I don't know which Southern state. He comes here occasionally to visit his daughter and he seems to admire his French son-in-law but to understand little of what he says. On the other hand, he is on very friendly terms with Palmerston & Lundquist, for one thing because they play golf together.

Meanwhile, as far as Lebournet is concerned, his obscure and "mineral" fiction goes on flowing, like his happy family life with his devoted and competent wife, his ease, his tenure, and with a fifth son, even more beautiful and chubbier than the others. Curiously, Lebournet and I would sometimes lean out of the window of his or my office, and in the presence perhaps of a watchfully silent Blatt we would start on the usual Old World meditations about the "virginity without history" of these mountains, which have never echoed the sound of cannon or known tunnels and secret passages within their bowels; and of these canyons, never run over by armored cars. I had just come back with fresh visions of the Venetian countryside, a land famous for invasions and battles, where I had spent hours of sober but lacerating meditations in the late summer . . .

I'll put down some random data on the people I found again here. Blatt, as I said, is the most plausible next director of the Institute. By the way, he has got engaged. He lives with his fiancée. Naturally, on my return he was the first to provide me with a quick bird's-eye view of the situation. Of the former Shadows, Chuck Palmerston and Alf Lundquist have found ways to keep themselves busy organizing, planning, mimeographing; they produce useful, dull lexical work. Horace Buterweg did not become president of the university; the new president is somebody quite nondescript whose name I do not recall. "What about Louis Pickford?" was of course one of my first questions.

"He had a series of bronchial attacks but now he's well. He's working hard on a new book, which I think he intends to be, in substance, a rehabilitation of Rasputin. His son has lost or has at least camouflaged his pimples by growing his hair long, and a beard, and has transformed his engagement into a bucolically sexual relationship with Paula. Both he and Paula wear bright-colored shirts and corduroy pants, and they often hang beautiful huge brass chains around their necks; they have that savage and yet meek appearance which is becoming fashionable. All of this doesn't seem to displease young Pickford's father because it makes him feel he is in orbit too—*au courant.*"

There is general agreement on the necessity to intensify the Institute's work more than ever; this is the one truly essential point, which permits me to look at the immediate future without too much fear of crises. Alphonse's precepts are still very much alive. We are not only an institution for historical studies centering on language, but we intend to sharpen our points, multiply our antennas, perfect our radar, which are switched on day and night over the current verbal panorama: the media transmit a speech, a press conference, a treaty, a declaration, a memorandum, and half an hour later there is the clear, detailed, pitiless semantic analysis of the text, which is usually characterized by pernicious and fradulent vagueness and may presently be followed by casual butchery and indifferent carnage.

As things stand now, Blatt was saying the other day, not even the International Red Cross would be able to tell you what constitutes war. So the impression is that there is work to be done here, as well as in other centers similar to our own; according to Blatt, they are sprouting all over the world. Of course everything is relative, and one's external and inner situation should be re-examined, as always, every morning during the useful, thoughtful quarter of an hour while shaving, questioning one-self face to face in the mirror.

Now let's go into reverse. Some notes on past events are in order, starting from the time when I left here to go to Italy shortly after the Symposium and Alphonse's victory.

Alphonse left before me, and we had agreed to meet in New York; from there we would fly to Europe together. When I first came here I flew direct to the Pacific, so I had never been to New York. I saw only a small part of it, what was easily available. You get your bearings immediately. Avenues north–south, streets west–east: in the central part of this network you can do everything on foot. Very tall buildings, as everyone knows, sometimes splendidly rocklike, crystalline and metallic in the sun.

Inside the buildings, however, or at any rate inside the one where I was meeting Alphonse, you often find lobbies with the kind of furniture, mirrors and ornaments that you'd find in an old hotel in Vienna or Monaco. I stopped for a moment on the ground floor of this apartment building. Besides the mirrors and the rest, there were the gilded brass portals of the elevators in the background. Very deep carpeting. Shut-in sunbeams, hot and dusty. Silence. Nobody around. Then a deep sense of peacefulness descended on me. In a moment I would see Alphonse again, in this place which already looked familiar.

But when I went up to the apartment, a man I didn't know came to the door; tall, thin, with rimless glasses and sparse reddish hair; he checked on my identity by saying my name in an inquiring tone and with a good pronunciation, adding in turn, "My name is Willie Hatch."

He started to talk to me about the Rossis, Alphonse and Doris, as if both he and I were their relatives. He made me sit in the living room and drink sherry, and then started speaking in a measured tone, as if reading from notes: "Our dear Doris went ahead, she is in Rome already, with her daughter. Alphonse has been staying with us. Right now Melanie is up in the country with him. I can't leave my work." Melanie was his wife. "We have a piece of land up the Hudson, at Harmon, and a summer house. Alphonse can rest there. Because, you see, Gilberto," he concluded, looking at me with gentle but insistent, demanding eyes, "Alphonse has been rather ill."

Alphonse's message to me through Hatch was that I should join him at Harmon immediately, so I went there by train. At first you go through small stations which are still in the city, with names like "138th Street" or "University Heights." Brick buildings, with hundreds of apartments inside each one of them; close-ups of garbage heaps, or a discarded old bus, of a smoke-dirty shack with broken windows; dozens of equally abandoned objects; the sun, already fully summerlike but with a brightness like after a snowfall, putting sparkles on the windowpanes. Stretches of water like oily little lakes, and then the river, very wide, with wooded banks still looking to me like virgin timberland in spite of industrial smoke. Here, close-ups of floating river birds, and in the distant background, a steel bridge, pale-gray, almost white, feather-light, with tiny automobiles crossing it like shiny, multi-colored ants. Oil tanks. Freight cars with the name of the railroad company written in the old-fashioned typographical style of the adventurous days when they began.

Melanie was waiting at the small station in her car; we recognized each other immediately, and immediately started calling each other by our first names. Soon we came to the house, white and comfortable among old trees, with a view of the river in the distance; marvelous. Alphonse was in bed; an enormous bed covered with papers, books, newspapers, even a typewriter. Melanie just showed me into the room and went away; I was evidently relieving her; later I learned that Alphonse had spent hours dictating letters to her.

Alone, Alphonse and I shook hands tightly for a long moment, observing each other. As if to prevent any comment from me on his physical appearance, clearly marked by pain, he began, "You look tired. Funny, because lately at the Institute you had slowed up a bit. After your trip to Italy, that sort of laxness will definitely have to go." Then he answered the questions that had been in my eyes from the first moment; he pointed to his chest: "I've had some trouble here. Nerves. They may tell you there are traces of some old coronary, but don't

[306]

you believe them." I was much relieved; I remembered his cancer of the bladder, but that had evidently been filed away and forgotten.

However, before me was a new Alphonse. New York, even if not geographically and by actual measurement, is closer to Europe than to the Pacific Coast. Here Alphonse was speaking as if he were already in the midst of activities at home; he had all sorts of appointments and relatives. "I've already called Luigina over the phone." His sister. I never knew of her existence.

"In Italy you and I will meet a little later," he decided. "We both have reservations to Paris. I'll stop there for a couple of days; I have a Paris–Venice flight booked for you. Or would you rather fly to Rome?"

"Oh no, I'll go to Venice. Imagine, my old friend Corso Gianfranchi is coming to Venice just to meet me. He gets big discounts on railroad fares because he's a newspaperman."

Melanie wanted to take us straight to the airport but Alphonse decided to go to Manhattan, where he had some errands and shopping to do. Melanie deposited us in midtown; he and I walked for a couple of hours on Fifth, Madison and other avenues; he bought a lot of things, I bought some unusual and practical gifts for my aunt and for others. Every now and then Alphonse stopped in the middle of the sidewalk to take a deep breath. "What a splendid day," he kept saying. Actually it was too warm and he stopped because he was exhausted.

When we joined Melanie again for the ride to the airport, I sat with her in front and he sprawled in the back in his usual position, as though the car were a gondola.

During the Atlantic crossing he drank champagne and ate little; instead of watching the film, he had a long sleep. Very resourceful man also physiologically; his breathing, in sleep, was deep, quiet, comfortable.

At Orly he accompanied me to the particular gate lobby where I was to wait for my flight to Venice a couple of hours later. He left only after he had provided me with French and Italian papers to read; when we said good-bye we exchanged a tight embrace with kisses on both cheeks. After the embrace he turned around abruptly and walked away at a quick pace. Suddenly each of us was alone, full of old things of his own; he went to the cemetery in Montparnasse where his first wife was buried; I would fly to Venice, my heart beating with joy, with fear.

I found Corso Gianfranchi at Tessera, where the Venice airport is located. After more than a year on the Pacific Coast I felt somewhat lost, I was out of phase in my sense of proportions. Here by the Lagoon of Venice, for instance, each airplane had its own identity, was a clear, distinguishable fact. I experienced such a shock of delight at seeing Corso, smiling, waiting by the exit gate behind customs, that I couldn't say a word to him. He, on the contrary was perfectly poised, balanced. "Welcome back," he said. "How are things?"

He had come from Rome by train and had borrowed Enrico Fassola's car to come and meet me at the airport. In Rome he was a friend of Enrico Fassola's sister, married to a contemporary of mine from Venice, now professor of modern history. Again that's something I had lost: the sense of connection between people; here everybody was within easy reach, Corso knew the Fassolas, the Partibons. I also realized, during the following days, that I myself knew those people better now than when I used to see them—rather fleetingly, come to think of it —in the old days. Time goes on milling memories all by itself, keeping them in motion.

Corso looks absent-minded, as if he never did anything in particular, whereas without making any fuss about it, he is an enormously hard worker, well organized without making a production of it. He appears to be living in seclusion, yet he knows everybody. "If you want, I'll drive you to your aunt right away," he said. "But I would prefer that you spend the night here in Venice. We'll dine with some friends. Tomorrow you can go to Portogruaro; I'll have to go to Milan for my newspaper."

Anything was all right with me. He had already reserved a room for me at a *pensione* near the Academy. I wasn't tired at all from the trip. Without even going up to my room, I went into a small bar on the ground floor, with an old Venetian-glass door opening on a small garden, and I looked at Corso, sitting there opposite me, this old friend who kept asking, "Well, how are things?" But it was clear that neither of us expected any answers to questions of that kind. All I said was: "Well, here I am. You see, there was a cheap flight . . ."

"I saw Jim Halleck when he was in Rome recently. He had some nice things to say about you."

Obviously one couldn't pick up a phrase like that, either. I continued to watch my old friend in silence. By starting a chain reaction, with Halleck-foundations-Alphonse, Corso Gianfranchi had, after all, changed my life. And now, there he was, a bit drooping and sad, the most complete portrait of doubt and uncertainty; that is, of honesty as a permanent fact, as an inner gnawing renewed at every instant. He was well informed about my work, he received and analyzed the publications of the Institute; he also knew the senator. He knew all about Tava, Jr. "He's going to China," he said as if I didn't know, and added, "Good. Very good." It sounded almost as though he had planned that trip.

Don't fool yourself," I said. "He follows only his own inspiration. He has never read your articles on China. He doesn't even know you."

Corso nodded, smiling: "But I know him. He comes from a military family. I believe some of them were 'bersaglieri,' sharpshooters."

"That may well be. But it's you who know about them. To him they're total blanks."

"Are you sure? Good. Very, very good."

We had already had several whiskies and were talking inconclusively as you can when friendship is so old and safe that it transcends time and words. At some point, you may come up with a conversation you started mentally by yourself, and your friend picks it up midway and grasps it immediately. For instance, after I had been silent for a long while I realized I was suddenly switching to viva voce and was telling him animatedly, "So here I am, trembling with delight and anticipation at the thought of going to Portogruaro to see the widow and the sons of my Uncle Bartolomeo, which means finding again the spirit, the ghost, the unerasable and continuing presence of Bartolomeo Strigato himself, a man whom, on the basis of reason, I entirely disapprove of—his life was regulated by wholly ruinous patriotic principles—and to whom, nevertheless, I am viscerally . . ."

"Gilberto," he interrupted me, "most people have their Bartolomeo in some corner of their mind; wish to God they had only that."

Corso did not seem quite convinced about the quality of the restaurant where mutual friends had arranged our meeting for dinner. "But at any rate," he said, "you'll enjoy sitting right in the midst of the stones of Venice."

We did find ourselves in one of the spots where no water is visible, one of the inner squares, Campo San Fantin. Both the Fenice theater and the Ateneo Veneto are there; we ate outside; tables and chairs were set up on the old gray stone pavement, not far from those two huge stone cubes full of artistic & cultural history.

There were Giuliano Partibon and his younger brother, Giorgio, on vacation from Paris. And there was Enrico Fassola: he too treated me as if there had been a half-century of uninterrupted friendship between us; he even mentioned my father; our fathers had been colleagues and also, he added, great friends. I recalled meeting the senior lawyer Fassola in front of the Pilsen restaurant, sarcastically urging me to remember him to my father, whom he had very well seen sitting and eating there with one of his Austrian lady friends; now the chumminess of the junior Fassola made me laugh. And yet, and yet . . . I also found it restful, relaxing; and this somehow seemed to coincide with a sense, I mean a physical sense, of approaching old age.

Giorgio Partibon, as for friendliness and loquacity, was the same as that night long ago when he got the wrong train and came with me to Portogruaro; except that now he was more mellow and much heavier, just like our mutual friend, Ruggero Tava, Sr., when in my imagination I met him under the arcade in the rue de Rivoli and he told me, "Well, this is the way things turned out."

I hadn't seen Giuliano Partibon in perhaps twenty-five years, yet it was as if there hadn't been any interval; I knew he had been mistreated in '43 or '44 during a political arrest but I didn't remember that he limped. I brought up the subject, and Enrico Fassola seemed happy to be able to present for me, the newcomer, a sequence of scenes which were obviously well known to everybody else.

"It was a man from Corniano who broke his leg. Later, in the days of summary justice, Giuliano and I went to Corniano by makeshift means of transportation among the ruins. And one of the first people we saw, in the main square of town, was the man who had smashed Giuliano's leg. 'Look at What's-his-name,' we said and walked toward him as if to say hello; he was such a familiar figure, we had known him since childhood. Now, here's the catch: it was he, all right, but as it happened, he was lying there, stretched out on the pavement, killed already. For an instant, for a fraction of a second, our only impression had been recognition, and the idea of saying hello. Perhaps the realization that he was dead came to us simultaneously with the impulse, immediately contained because obviously superfluous, to smash his head."

The others went on eating, they knew the story. Enrico had his heart in it. "I don't know why," he concluded, "but that is one of the most important experiences I have ever had in relation to death."

This was the only relatively sustained talk of the whole evening. When Enrico Fassola noticed that I was listening to him, he took me into his confidence and told me about his love for a young woman, Irene Berlocchi, whom he had left a few days earlier at some hot-springs resort where he was having her take a cure; he visited her weekends, keeping alive an idyll destined to end in marriage. About this girl and her father, now in jail, there had once been a short and unsatisfactory exchange between Ruggero and myself; I would have been interested to hear more from Fassola but the others interfered, diverting the conversation, asking me about Ruggero, about work at the Institute, and a lot about women in that part of the world, all of this in a vague way, floating without direction, hardly anyone listening to answers. Then they wasted time because they had confused and complicated ways of ordering food and drinks; they kept bothering the waiter, who was apparently an old friend, however, and didn't mind.

"Are you insane? We don't want rosé wine."

The waiter took the rosé away and came back with red Merlot. When the Merlot had already been poured, somebody resumed, "Whoever wants to drink rosé?"

"Rosé is silly."

Then, to this little chamber concert a new theme would be added, "The bread is damp."

"Listen, the bread is damp, you know."

But after the waiter had come back with toast and they had already helped themselves to it, someone would nevertheless go on mumbling pensively, "Hm, damp bread . . ."

Giorgio Partibon was the youngest among us. Only later did his sister join us. Sitting down, Elena announced, "I've already eaten but I'll drink a little wine."

Between her and me there was a very intense exchange of glances, and I felt unreasonably certain that she had come because she knew I would be here. When she was fourteen or a little more, I used to see her on the Academy Bridge and I was never sure that she had recognized me. Now she had rings under her eyes, and some noticeable wrinkles; and the looks we exchanged were alert and steady. I decided I must see more of her. From the start she had addressed me with the familiar form, *tu*, which made it easier for me to say, "Elena, you should come to Portogruaro with me."

But like the others, she didn't listen much; she followed her own track: ". . . And then, I don't see how you can eat here. Do you see there where the pavement is all opened up? They are repairing gas pipes. You're eating gas. We're all going to be blown up or get asphyxiated."

The new theme went the usual round.

"There is a terrible smell of gas."

"Terrible smell."

"This gas smell is terrible," Giuliano said as if it were a fresh observation.

It was impossible to talk about less immediate things. I was hardly aware of this gas smell but I felt warm. I said, "I think I'll take off my coat."

Enrico: "I meant to tell you, take off your coat."

Giorgio: "Why don't you take off your coat?"

Giuliano: "Take off your coat, Gilberto."

I had crossed a continent and an ocean to land in the midst of this kind of talk, yet I drank it all in and took part in it, I drowned in the peace of non-thinking. Corso watched me, understanding.

Finally Elena answered, "I'll come to Portogruaro some other time, not tomorrow. Now let's go and catch a motorboat at St. Mark's, we'll get off at the Academy, you and Gianfranchi can take me home, and then you'll go to your *pensione*, which is nearby."

Of that evening in Venice, what remains engraved in my memory is not the important talk—which, for that matter, between people like Corso and myself can largely be left unsaid, implied—but rather the short walk through Calle delle Veste, Calle Larga Ventidue Marzo, San Moisè, and on to Calle Vallaresso, arm in arm with Elena. Midway in the crowded *calle*, a whiff of mixed odors hit me—fish, alcohol, face powder, sweat —carried by the hot, thick air. There we were: this was already the summer city, open, on exhibition, with foreign visitors roaming aimlessly. Caught among these wandering strangers, I stopped and looked Elena in the eyes; her eyes were still very shrewd but much less sarcastic and desperate than before. I said, "The city . . . this beast, which has survived all wars."

"Let's run, or else we'll miss our boat."

We caught that water bus practically on the fly, which then proceeded with its usual steady rhythm between the Salute Church and the hotels with their lighted, water-level terraces. After a brief stretch of the Grand Canal, there we were, under the Academy Bridge. I pointed my finger upward: "Sometimes I used to meet you here."

"I remember perfectly." This phrase gave me a definite shock of tenderness. Now I was enjoying my return, breathing it in deeply, as it were—my return to the city, not mine really, but where I had lived so long. We got off at the Academy Station and proceeded to Elena's home on the Zattere. She kissed both Corso and me on the cheek, saying, "Well, we'll see each other," and before we had time to arrange when & how, she had shut the door.

"She's not well at all," Corso remarked as we walked toward the *pensione*. "She must go to bed early and rest a lot. She came out this evening because she wanted to see you."

"Of course she probably wanted me to talk about Ruggero, but there was no chance."

"Oh no, she handles her relationship with Ruggero strictly by herself. Same as she does with everyone else, for that matter."

Corso had information about everybody, which could be

slightly irritating. "You're always acting the newspaperman, Corso, at all hours of the day and night. You know everybody —Venetians, Americans—much better than I do."

"I wonder what you mean?" He mentioned that Di Gaetano, my former boss, was ready to hire me again.

No reaction to that on my part.

"So, are you going back?"

"Where?"

"To the Pacific Coast."

"It depends on how we arrange things with Alphonse."

He knew all about Alphonse, too. After Paris, Alphonse would spend a short time in Bologna at his sister's, then he would go to Rome; finally he was going to be somewhere in the Venetian region, in a villa that friends were lending to him. "That's going to be the right place for the two of you to meet in quiet."

"I'll go to Portogruaro to my Aunt Luciana tomorrow; Alphonse knows he can always reach me there."

In the *pensione* there were long pauses in our conversation. We could hear oars beating on the water in the dark canal just outside; English voices at the concierge's desk, the tinkling of ice in our glasses, even the strong beat, as of a robust heart, of a nineteenth-century clock hanging on the wall. Between Corso and me there wasn't any need for the nervous, artificial exchange of news which is so typical of reunions; a few words at long intervals were sufficient; the words could even be simply "Who knows?" or, expanding, "Things are going from bad to worse"; yet somehow they always sounded a positive note. I am not saying it was a note of hope. It was actually something for which no definitions exist; but it proved that Corso and I, even far apart, had remained close.

What is essential? No use trying to answer that. For instance, my most relevant memories of my return to Portogruaro, curiously enough, are memories of sleep.

It was as though I had gone there to store up a good amount of sleep, and I was pleasantly visited by dream images which were generally quiet, well harmonized, interesting. Among these, a much-fattened Giuseppina Lezze-Adorno, rather tired, who realized by now that she had lost everything and laughed about it.

She says to me, in a weak voice, "You're an anarchist, an unpatriotic, godless man."

"So? Is that the description of a man like me? Good, Pina, good." Shortly after that, or before, or in dreamlike simultaneity, I cannot help reminding her: "Do you remember when you and my mother met in Campo San Salvador? You remember the words you uttered against your old intimate enemy, Adriana Rossi, née Strigato? You said to her, 'Punishment will fall upon your children.' Well, Giuseppina, my meeting you now can be useful to me because it gives me a chance to ask you, 'Have I been sufficiently punished?' "

She gives me a melancholy, yet vaguely ribald smile. Like a woman remembering old passions, her vigorous youthful sex. She says, "Gilberto, you have never loved me."

"Probably not, Pina, but if it comes to that, weren't you telling me yourself a moment ago that I am a man without feelings, without any of that sort of thing?"

"Oh, by the way," she goes on impulsively, "it isn't true that my son Oliviero was a virgin when he got married. He too used to go to the houses, like all of you pigs." All of this spoken good-naturedly, including "pigs."

"Nothing could be more natural, Pina. In fact, the defunct Regime did not recommend abstention but rather the opposite. Its chieftains were all men who, at least metaphorically, waved their sex organs as if they were banners & pennants, and who possessed, or at any rate claimed they did, testicles hard as fists. I still believe that Oliviero was a virgin, but I can't understand why you should take offense at that."

It should be remembered that Signora Lezze-Adorno has been dead for many years. Alive in my dream, she looked like a girl full of languid and desirous love for everybody. She spoke even of her son Oliviero as of an old lover capable of exploits which still made her proud.

I have given a random example of the dreams I had at Portogruaro; I had quite a few of them. Sometimes between dreams I would wake up and stay awake awhile, absorbing the silence with a feeling of beatitude until the new dream would come in like a slide inserted silently and smoothly into my nocturnal projector. Then in the morning my Aunt Luciana would come into the room and wake me up with *caffelatte* and everything.

"We can't go on this way," I said suddenly one morning, embracing her, kissing the top of her head, her white hair still thick. "I'll set the alarm clock and tomorrow morning I'll bring the coffee to you."

"If you wish. If it makes you happy. I'm so glad that you're here. Anything that makes you happy . . ."

At some point during the day, in the late afternoon after my siesta, we would talk at length. Here my Strigato cousins appear onstage too. Sergio has stayed on at Portogruaro; he has built for himself a simple, rustic villa and has followed in his father's footsteps, even to being a maniac about hunting and target shooting; he is a comfortable kind of doctor, well known even in the surrounding countryside.

Gianluigi, however, has moved to southern Italy, where he is a construction engineer in the Apulia province; I believe he came up to Portogruaro for a few days just to see me. He knows everything; the south has vitalized him; he would open a conversation with me by saying, "You people in America," and then display extremely accurate information by his remarks. He is much thinner and more muscular than his brother. Sergio and his most intimate playmates are generally fat, and so contented that by now they do very little talking. Years and years ago, after the disasters, they were, like myself, among the survivors, at that time still sharply distinguished from the dead. Hungry, and almost surprised to feel themselves breathing. But about the dead they knew little or nothing. I believe I would never have been able to accept the kind of life Sergio leads; yet if I question myself firmly in front of the mirror in the morning, I have to admit that I like him more than I do Gianluigi.

My plan to bring coffee to my aunt in bed did not materialize because of a sudden call from Alphonse. He asked me to join him at his friends' villa. Sergio knew the owners. In the Venetian region all villa owners know each other; I have no villa, so I don't know anybody. But I possess information of this sort: the section where this villa is located was occupied during the first war, in 1917, by Bavarian troops. The villa itself became a military hospital. Sergio assured me that no trace of this has remained and he was only mildly interested in my information. The villa is not very large but white and attractive, with its frescoes and its portraits of eighteenth-century ancestors and everything, surrounded by a shooting preserve "full of beautiful stuff," especially pheasants.

I had Sergio drive me, not only because he knew the place but because he is a doctor, and it had already seemed clear from the phone call that Alphonse was sick. This man was always calling me to country places where I would then find him sick in bed.

We found a suffering but loquacious Alphonse. Many multilingual papers were scattered on his bed, and he was interested in everything: he was delighted to meet Sergio, he asked him about being a doctor at Portogruaro, he requested details, figures; he became even more interested in Gianluigi when Sergio told him about this brother of his who was an engineer in the south.

Alphonse listened and commented avidly. Yes, this was Alphonse the orator; only his voice came out irreparably weak and slow: "Your brother, Dr. Strigato, has made a more significant life for himself than you have." He digressed: "It takes a lot of courage nowadays. And in fact, there is a lot of courage around, and of the right kind, especially among young people, but they are not aware of it; all they want to do is protest, denounce, ridicule . . ."

Sergio, even though without wanting to, looked at him with openly clinical eyes. Alphonse was perfectly aware of it and said, "My wife and daughter are in Rome. When I join them there, I'll be in excellent shape," but he didn't look convinced. His sister had come from Bologna to be with him; every now and then she came in to say, "You're much better already, you have a good color," and then he looked at her incredulously: "Let's hope for the best, Luigina."

There were too many things I would have liked to tell him, so I was silent most of the time. I am bound to remember the moment when, just to fill the silence and loosen my tongue, I brought up what I thought was an innocuous subject and I told him of the time the villa was a military hospital.

He looked at me with a fury that was purely instinctive, pitiless, like a wounded animal. He uttered some heavy curses.

Then it was strange to hear him fall back on the same weary voice as before: "A person comes here to rest, to get better, or at least that's what they want him to believe. Well, no! History! War! History! War!"

Granted, I should immediately have remembered that forty-five years ago his brother, Carlo, had his skull smashed by a bullet, about an hour away from here by car, but I was surprised nevertheless. And I was angry myself, torn inside as I closely observed his face; his grief, his childish stubbornness, his pathetic and confused emotion. Was he really thinking of Carlo Rossi and of the damned patriotic lexicons which had urged him to his death? I was nearly exploding with one of my laughs; I swallowed violently and went out of doors.

There were several tiers of hills all around, of extraordinary softness, but far away; the villa was in the middle of a widespread plain, of flat cultivated fields. Frequent gunshots were heard at various distances. I know so little about these matters that I can't say whether the hunting season was already open, or whether they were practicing on clay pigeons or even on live pigeons shut up in a box from which they explode, to be exposed quickly to the shooting of people like my Cousin Sergio and his friends. I stood there alone for a long while, straight like a scarecrow in the fields, with the hills and the shooting all around in the distance; it was like being in a war during a routine day.

And then suddenly, without any forewarning, on this landscape, which was crossed forty-five years ago by the victorious and confused lieutenant Hugo von Blatt, I saw projected the image of Dr. Giulio Levi; our last farewell on the Academy Bridge right after he had visited his friend, Fernando Rossi; and for the first time, perhaps absolutely the first time since then, I recalled the wording of the verdict he gave me, the dying man's son; I heard his voice, monotonous and solemn, yet stronger than the shooting, his ultimate, didactic, nasal, absurd key line: "Continue the therapy as prescribed, but of course there isn't any hope."

I ran back to the villa, fearing the worst. Alphonse didn't notice me. He was talking to Sergio. Unexpected subject: the world of espionage. "Never served any purpose . . . Ridiculous secrets . . . Never anything that may have won or lost a war

. . . So many people killed, guillotined, electrocuted, burned . . . Tragic stupidities . . . And in the end, everything draining into the popular magazines . . ."

"True, true," Sergio commented, completely captivated.

So, in spite of his low voice, Alphonse was still what I might call a verbal power. Only, he had to make long pauses. After one of these (he had sensed my presence without looking at me) he said, "You go back there, Gilberto, to the Pacific Coast; life is more difficult there."

"Of course, we'll go back together, won't we?"

Didn't he hear me? "Go back there," he repeated.

He did not hear us. We were standing on either side of the bed, and Sergio told me that Alphonse had spoken to him about his brother; not, however, Carlo on the bloody Isonzo River, but Carlo at home as a boy, or at school. More than once I had thought of telling Alphonse something like this: "After all, both of us Rossis, you and I, have lost a brother; you lost Carlo and I lost Tava, Senior. And over there, in our academic detachment, we were looking for the meaning of those deaths." Now it was too late for everything, he didn't hear me.

But he did have his moments. He was aware that Luigina had brought in a new doctor, and he observed, "They—the doctors—stand there and look at you. They ask *you* what's going on. But that's natural; I, who am living through it, know more than they do." He concluded simply, "And I am telling you that now I am dying." After the doctor had gone, he even said, "One must get ready to die with a minimum of dignity."

During those days (I don't remember how many; we measured time by the hour rather than by the day) he spent much of his failing breath summarizing his life, accusing himself of fundamental selfishness. "After the war they even offered to let me come back, settle down in Italy. How? Why? With what right? I had been away. I had lived as I wished." Then he said, "Of course the thought of Bologna always made my heart beat faster, tears come to my eyes, my mouth water, all kinds of things."

An emotional Alphonse pained and irritated me. I said soberly, "Of course. That's what Portogruaro is to me."

"The Italian cities," he went on. "The arcades. The town halls. This confused history, badly conducted, tragic and funny, which has produced these wonder cities and villages, each on top of a steep mountain. I traveled around a lot in the past few weeks before coming up here; I got exhausted but it was worth while. You're right, Luigina, one never ceases to admire, to love, to be moved and grateful. The spiritual and physical well-being that an Italian city can give. I know, Luigina." He seemed to recognize only his sister.

His physical suffering was indescribable. Even during the first few days, or hours perhaps, before he was almost constantly beyond all individual and direct contact, he had told me, "I don't even try any longer to describe to you how bad I feel."

Out of breath. *Out of breath.* "I'm out of breath" is a phrase one throws out nonchalantly, yet the thing itself can be overwhelming, cancel out of the whole world. He talked to me a lot (at least, I believe he was talking to me) about work done at the Institute, about his distant and resilient hopes. Echoes of early talks: "These dialogues between people who don't listen to each other, who purposely get lost in useless byways—years and years and years of this; and I wanted to do something, put them against the wall, force them to speak out clearly . . ."

"You've done a lot," I said.

Later, as if he wanted to assuage everybody's grief by presenting his by now intolerable pain on the level of a domestic fairy tale, he said, "I am rather happy to go, Luigina. I wonder if Carlo will recognize me."

Naturally Luigina had no voice, she was too choked up; so I said, "But of course he'll recognize you; you haven't changed a bit." In all of this there was something ridiculous, impossible, yet I couldn't contain my tears, I sobbed and laughed. Conversations of that kind are not easy to conduct. So I often went out into the fields.

I was out there, a lonely and stupefied scarecrow, when I heard Sergio come up behind me; he took my arm and squeezed it hard. Clearly it was the end. Alphonse Rossi had died. One did not cry any longer. One just stood and watched those fields, with the hills in the distance and the shots in the air. But then I turned to Sergio in childish, stupid, blind wrath. "What does this mean?" I asked, opening my arms wide, indicating and encompassing that land all around us. "What does this mean? What is it? Sergio? Sergio? What is all this? What is Europe?"

He cleared his throat, then he said with an inviting smile, "Come see Alphonse."

On our way back I asked him whether Alphonse had gone on talking to the last. Sergio explained calmly, "As far as I could tell, he was conscious and quite coherent the whole time. The last phrase I remember is. 'I already see myself at my own funeral, surrounded by deep sorrow.'" My cousin and I looked at each other in a daze and raised our thumbs, repeating the gesture which at the time of our puppet shows meant the "booking" of a key line to be brought onstage.

My recollections are rather confused; I know other relatives came from Bologna, besides Doris and daughter from Rome, of course. The girl had brought some of her friends, who said things like "Let's go to the Big Weep." But they were serious young women, quick, with lively eyes. The meeting point was Venice. From there, two or three close relatives would follow Alphonse to Paris because he had expressed a wish to be buried next to his first wife.

Among the relatives from Bologna was a little lady all handshakes and rhythmic little bows, dependable, alert, useful in funeral duties; she had brought along her young son, perhaps out of a dutiful feeling of family piety, or perhaps because she couldn't find a baby-sitter and leave him at home. In his turn, the boy had not been able to part with a beloved object: he carried, like a miniature valise proportioned to him, a small cage with a tiny bird inside. His mother would tell him, "There, hold him like that so he doesn't cry." Since the child himself cried, she would say, "Oh God, I've done everything wrong." I remember senseless details like that.

In Venice, at some point, Halleck turned up. Jim. James Audubon Halleck. He comes from New Hampshire originally, and I hear that's why he's so reserved; but he looked literally desperate. It was apparently he who had wanted to hold a ceremonial service in Italy before Alphonse was transferred to Paris. So what we may call the Alphonse Rossi obsequies took place in Venice.

I was told it was a ceremony with all the trimmings. I wasn't there. I wandered around the city instead. Several Camentinis turned up too—relatives, uncles or I don't know what, of that

Riccardo Camentini I had met at a Dorsoduro restaurant. Along with Halleck and the little lady from Bologna, they became natural organizers. Several other ladies were there too, tall ones, Italian friends of Doris' or something, looking rich and intellectual; before going to the ceremony, they were all gathered in the lobby of one of the large historical palace-hotels. It was then that I escaped, after greeting and kissing Doris several times with all the affection I feel for her. Doris was only giving directions. When she mentioned her husband and his eventual transfer to Paris next to his first wife, she seemed to be referring to a son and daughter whom she wanted to be together.

I hid for several hours in the neighborhood of San Trovaso, of the Academy Bridge, and around Campo San Vidal, where we had lived for many years. Strangely enough, I realized how happy those years had been, in spite of the Regime and everything. I see the friendly image of the lawyer Fernando Rossi floating in the background: a sensitive, first-rate gentleman; my relationship with him had always been outside the Oedipus complex. And the radiant calm of the long, never to be repeated season with Norma. Walks with her to the Murazzi, on the huge stones in the sun with the sea on one side and golden orchards on the other. And then home together. Norma as the perfectly fit place; love as protection found in her. I stopped with her by a marble well among the trees in Campo San Trovaso; I was just back from Milan and she was saying, "When you were here you spoke to me about books, and that was enough, but with you away, what could I do but read? Proust, for instance; I read the first three volumes while you were away, really sipped them." The marble well among the trees had seemed attractive and restful then; now it was funereal, like an urn or a sarcophagus. I fled toward the Academy.

At the foot of the bridge there is a café with chairs outside by the Grand Canal, and here I found Elena Partibon sitting alone. "Ah, there you are." She seemed to have been waiting for me. Through the various local networks, such as Camentini–Enrico–Giuliano, she knew all about the Alphonse obsequies, so it came natural to us to talk not only about him but about the dead in general. One of the first things she asked me about Alphonse was "Did you see him dead?"

"Certainly," I said. We both thought spontaneously of Ruggero Tava, hers and mine, whom we hadn't seen dead.

"Seeing them is better, much better," she said.

I hadn't seen Norma, either. It was the first time I mentioned Norma to anybody. She asked me, "What was her name? Norma what?"

I burst out laughing the way I do: "This may sound like a joke, but her name was a kind of nutshell history of opera, it was Norma Verdi." I realized that with this Partibon woman I could talk any way I wanted. At some point I said to her: "With Norma, the problem of the force of gravity didn't even present itself."

"What's the problem of the force of gravity?"

I began to explain my concept of "cosmic unbalance," but I had hardly opened my mouth before she got the whole picture. "Beatrice too," I told her, "your son's present or imminent wife, is quick at grasping certain things; yet there is no comparison with you."

"Really?" She held me tightly by the hand. She was enjoying herself. She enjoyed being able to understand, to help, even if her eyes did not seem to know, or to admit, hope. She got me to talk about my crises, but she seemed to know everything beforehand; she understood perfectly well that those experiences, in spite of their horror are ultimately also kind of a leaning point, a frame of reference, a company to which you return. She nodded with satisfaction, with faith in the words we said to each other.

She nodded in the same way when I reminded her that Ruggero, Sr., and I had been close friends. Perhaps she knew it already. I told her my fiction about our meeting in the rue de Rivoli, and that made her laugh. She laughed also at the story of my encounter—a real one, at a tea dance of the Goof—with that tiny shrew Elvira Conti, the little sister of Ruggero's legitimate wife, Alessandra, when Elvira had spoken to me about her, Elena Partibon: "She said that you were a viper, that because you were sick, you wished death for everybody."

Elena told me how after Ruggero was killed she had forestalled the ornate funereal-patriotic commemorations in honor of the fallen soldier. The soldier's widow herself, Alessandra

Tava, so young and fresh, in splendid mourning, had already planned the ceremonies. "But I went to talk to his parents. My brother Giorgio wanted to come along but I went alone. I spoke sternly to his father, and I convinced him. It was the last time I went to their house."

As we were talking along like that we became aware that along the waterway, under the bridge, a funeral procession was passing: the huge motor-barge hearse, all draped in black with embroidered silver crosses, trailed by a single file of motorboats, more usual but equally dignified in their slowness, full of people who seemed to me to be all women. For every conceivable reason of time & place this could not be the Alphonse funeral train; nevertheless I felt the fire of imaginative certainty surging within me, transcending reality; in such cases my mind doesn't compromise or give quarter.

"There he goes," I said. "My friend Alphonse Rossi is in there."

Elena looked at me with surprise, but then she understood at once and with her eyes urged me to go on.

"Let's use the conventional terms and say that to me he was a father, an older brother . . ." My voice trembled for a moment, but my mind kept on working by its own methods: it conjured up this morning's vision of the ladies in the lobby of one of the First Hotels of Europe, gathered there for a funereal apéritif and wearing with perfect know-how their Deep Grief faces, eyes already fixed on social engagements that would follow, after the ceremony, on this special day which they had to spend in the Pearl of the Adriatic. My mind quickly made up the scene, in fact, found it already there in its verbal and local context: I had not fled to the Academy but was still there, in a high-ceilinged *salone* of the palace-hotel with all its gold and stucco, and was choosing at random one of the ladies, whispering sadly to her, "Alphonse is alive. *You* are the ghost. You are on the wrong side of the ceremony."

As usual, I acted out both parts of the dialogue. Sour contralto voice: "Gilberto, what on earth are you saying? Do you really think this is the proper time to make jokes? Or perhaps it is Deep Grief—which would be understandable—that makes you delirious?"

[324]

I tried to wound myself, to disgust myself by my own calculated, vile language: "At one time your beauty was epoch-mak-
ing, and now you're all saturated with potions, pills, rays, mud
baths. In bed you wouldn't even be able to display, by your
movements, your erotic bravura."

"Gilberto, it's delirium, all right, but how dare you? I am
very much alive, and strong. I am a Cugumer-Palli, I am important, beneficient, compassionate . . ."

"Treachery! Fiction! Fraud!"

Other voices around me, all with hyphenated surnames: "I
am a Scosson-Tamberlini! I am a Lezze-Adorno!"

I could have cried with rage. Against whom? Who knows? Or
rather, yes: ladies at funerals, wearing fur coats on top of their
black uniforms, taller than I, heavily perfumed, rosy, flourishing, but tough, with the stiff lip of the masters, the crystal-hard
eye.

"Long live Ee-tally," I murmured.

Elena remained quiet, she said nothing, but she was important as a presence, observing me intently: me, swallowing my
sobs there in Venice by the bridge under whose arch, not only
now but for years in the past, the funereal boats, the cockroach
gondolas had passed. The lawyer Rossi had died a few yards
from the bridge; and Dr. Levi, on the opposite side, a few yards
away too, had committed suicide. No, those had not been happy
years. History all disjointed, incomprehensible, pitiless.

Elena's cool hand brushed my forehead; she said quickly,
practically, "You must calm down, you know, my dear."

Of course she was right. I accompanied her to her house on
the Zattere, and then she decided: "I'll rest for a few hours. You
too go and have a rest. Tomorrow we'll go to Portogruaro to
your Aunt Luciana."

I slept intermittently. I dreamed of Oliviero Lezze-Adorno's
wife. Not his mother, his wife. She was in a large double bed.
She too, like Alessandra Tava, whom she resembled, was a war
widow. She lay on her back, rigid, on her side of the bed; she always left Oliviero's side free. Unlike riddles, dreams have no solution, or there would be no point in having them; you can only
describe them. The main characteristic of this one was that it
turned reality upside down. In reality, Oliviero Lezze-Adorno is

[325]

not dead; he lives in the country, sixty years old, an orphan and a widower. In other words, besides his mother, his wife is dead too; she died in a bombing of Treviso. Not far from where Norma died in the same way. When Oliviero's wife was killed, she had been an active opponent of the Regime for some time, the same as Norma. But—obvious historical rule—the performers of the killing certainly cannot perceive subtleties of this kind; and their radio-commanding and button-pressing chiefs are not sensitive to them either.

I borrowed Enrico Fassola's car and before going to Portogruaro, we drove here and there around that country which Elena knows much better than I; she was driving, with sureness and very fast, as I had imagined she would. We looked into Treviso but never mentioned the dead or anything. Every now and then we stopped at some *trattoria* to get loaves of bread, cut in half, with prosciutto in between, and to drink a couple of glasses of wine.

Those were some of the happiest hours of my life, so there is no point in even beginning to try to describe them. To obtain any effect, I would have to draw on oversimplified lexicons, such words as "affection," "affectionate," whose value we perceived fully and calmly. We knew that from now on, for the rest of our lives, we would continue to feel this, and that we would want to help each other, whether we were close together or far apart.

We did not mention important events, not even the accounts of violent deaths which had been close to us; yet certain facts inevitably exist, e.g., that the First World War, the Great War, as far as Italy is concerned, was all fought in the Venetian region; so the blood of one war mingles here with that of the other; this is happening also in my Aunt Luciana's head, as I later realized when she said, "With the war, both you and Bartolomeo managed to pull through."

Bones, bones, bones. In the village squares, even stones and steles with the names of the fallen engraved on them seem to be made of bone. Huge ossuaries are among the most important monuments in the region. We drove around a lot, as far as the Piave, the fatherland's holy river; from the Vidor bridge we watched the riverbed, wide expanses of stones, clean and dry like bones too.

But then also: straight white country roads, and on them, weightless, incorporeal, blue, almost iridescent, the shadows of poplars. Norma's poplars. And also: low walls within iron gates and statues, domestic, artisanlike, but in elegant attitudes, kindly, welcoming in the sun. And behind the gates, richly cultivated fields, thick with vegetation, like orchards. Often I felt as if I were tasting the plants, the landscape.

At Portogruaro, my Aunt Luciana was sitting in her armchair, reading; she took off her glasses and got up to greet us. "You are the Partibon girl," she said affectionately to Elena. For some time all the talk was between the two of them. Aunt Luciana gave us Marsala wine with cookies. She didn't talk to me much at first, but of course from Sergio she knew all about Alphonse and she treated me with the small attentions one has for an orphan.

She asked me from time to time, "What are you going to do now?"

Finally I repied, "I don't know. I have a telegram here." I had received it in Venice and had been carrying it in my pocket. I read it out loud, with the two of them listening—associates, ready to consult with each other about my future. The telegram said: "PROVIDED WORDS POSSIBLE AFTER SUCH SHOCK PLEASE COMMUNICATE YOUR PLANS IF ANY AFFECTIONATELY—BLATT."

Elena and my aunt looked at each other, then the latter resumed in the same tone as before, "What are you going to do? Leave again?"

Naturally that made me laugh, so I now faced the subject squarely; I had to give them the right degree of information, clarification, enlightening shock. First I turned to Elena. "Recently," I said, "the real protagonist at the Institute has been your son. Nobody realized that, he least of all, but that's how it was. And why? Let me start by saying that the Institute, especially its famous electrolibrary, is filled with material concerning the key men of power, the star-leaders in the history of our century, in their wide range from tedious bores to unbridled criminals. Now, Ruggero is our specimen of a new type of protagonist, who can pass unobserved and who is not in the least interested in becoming a star and a leader."

By the way, my cousin Sergio was there too. He didn't say anything, just listened and frowned. I continued to orate, and I watched how Elena was following me: she obviously felt the absurdity there always is in anybody haranguing; yet by looking at me the way she did, she enchanted me, she brutalized me with tenderness, because I knew that in her own way she admired me.

I told them that a clear sign of the lack of interest, on the part of the Ruggeros of this world in achieving public stardom is the greater stress they place on their personal identities. This, I said, is indicated by developments in the language of emotions, which is now striving for utmost dryness & sobriety. I digressed, turning to my aunt, who has always been an avid reader of novels and poetry, and told her that poetic language, and literary language in general, is now better proportioned, more precise, altogether superior to that of only a few years ago. Hence, I added, the personal identity of an individual of the Ruggero type has a chance to be better defined and brought into sharper focus. This neo-human being will devote a proper part of his energy to community life and public service, and he may turn out to be excellent at it if his predecessors don't cut the ground from under his feet by destroying it; but he will manage to do so without sacrificing his own private interests and activities, including play, free friendships, idle talk, love affairs, vacations, et cetera, et cetera.

As soon as the star-leader is relegated to the scrap pile, some of the clever falsehoods of drawing-room historiography will be glaringly exposed, such as the dictum that no man is a hero in the eyes of his valet. The phrase is absurd not only for the obvious reason that valets don't exist any more, or if they do they are on their way out; the important thing is that that kind of hero is on his way out too. Or if you want to put it differently, let's say that the age-old drawing-room proverb should be turned around. In actual reality, verifiable individual by individual and face to face, instead of saying that no men are heroes in the eyes of their intimates, we should say that to their intimates there are only heroes. Our intimates can be scattered all over the world—let this be clear—and yet, form a network of which no one is aware; and even if someone—say, Dr. Peritti —should become aware of it, he would probably discard its components as people entirely unworthy of his attention.

My Aunt Luciana listened to me intently; then she replied in her own way, "I wish your mother were still alive and could hear you." She seemed to feel, I don't know why, that she had been surpassed by this nephew of hers, now nearing fifty. She continued with energy: "Me too, you know. I often feel I have seen enough." She had always read four or five papers every morning. Now, as she spoke, her mind seemed to be wandering a little, but her tone was more solid and vernacular than ever. She burst out laughing, somewhat the way I do. Then she started rather unpredictably:

"Menelik, Churchill, Crispi, Mikoyan, Sukarno . . . As you very well understand, I could go on like this for hours, making up lists of names at random." We followed her attentively. She went on disconnectedly, "I still read all I can, but I take much greater interest in myself than I used to. As a girl I got a real education, and you know that at that time this was a rather unusual thing for a girl to get. And, my dears, I don't feel in the least compelled to let my mind be dominated and ruined by any of those names that I could go on reciting for hours."

I asked, "What are you interested in? How do you keep busy?"

She shrugged. "Gianluigi's children, for instance. Sharp as arrows. They speak with a southern accent that's so funny it kills me."

I can't go on at this pace noting down everything. Aunt Luciana had us stay on for dinner, and I am sure both Elena and I haven't spent many days in our lives that were more absurdly serene, more inexplicably right. Going back to Venice I drove, in the darkness broken by reflections from oil refineries on the water of the Lagoon; we spoke little but in our silence we savored everything.

Later on, in Elena's house, I suddenly announced, "I'm leaving tomorrow. I have my return ticket. I'll arrive without having announced my return to anybody; that's the only conceivable way." She said nothing, so well did she understand me; that is, she knew that understanding could not be put into words. Only at the hour of parting did she resume in a plain, practical manner, "You're doing the right thing, and anyway, distances don't exist any more. I'll write to you. Thanks for the visit. For a long time no one has given me so much tenderness and enjoyment." We exchanged long kisses, holding each other tightly.

There were even tears in our eyes. Naturally I suggested, "Leave with me."

"No, Gilberto; but you'll see, it's like being always together."

Then there is another key phrase I want to put down: Elena's phrase, which others had noted, remembered, transmitted. Venice is full of people who go on talking for hours, mainly quoting other people, so the basic elements of their conversation are: He told me . . . I told him . . . Then she says . . . I say . . . She says . . . I told him to tell you . . . She told me that she told him that she told you . . . et cetera, et cetera. Elena's phrase, "There is room for everything, nothing is ever wasted," came to me by way of one of these bounces.

So I arrived here at night, full of energies which included the Institute and transcended it. I rented a small car at the airport and drove immediately to the familiar canyons. I stopped in front of that huge hut which looks like a mountain customs point where Alphonse and I, at the dawning of my Dodge, had stopped one evening to buy two bottles of whiskey. Naturally the place was closed, since it was nighttime. In the night sky there was a helicopter, perhaps one of those that carry mail. Having arrived like that, unknown, unannounced to anybody —in fact, with a sense of not knowing anybody any more—I looked for a place well encased among precipices and bushes and night flowers, and I got ready to sleep in the car as in a cozy bunk. In the morning I would decide what to do; meanwhile I wanted to spend the night in this place—both the place and I neglected, unnamed, unrecorded.

I don't know when a light at my back woke me up. A red, violent, rhythmic light. The flickering of the eye of a black automobile behind me. Police car. Its occupant came out, I heard his booted steps coming close to me from behind. Finally there he was, at my side, framed within my car window: a kind of TV Martian, except that he looked real rather than imaginary, with equipment, weapons, eyes, all made of authentic steel. Unfortunately, when he asked through the window for my papers, I realized I was bursting out into one of my laughs. Nothing could stop it; and since I was still in a semidormant condition, I semidreamed of myself in the usual football field where everything was being prepared for my execution by shooting. But that deputy sheriff did not seem to pay any attention to my laughter; it had no connection with his investigative duties. Instead he asked some trifling questions; for instance, what my profession was.

"Historical-linguistic research," I said and added, "Of course, I'm putting it in very general terms." Perhaps my idea was to create confusion in his mind.

But he simply asked, "Schoolteacher?" I shrugged, nodding. He noted it down. He was left-handed. He looked eighteen. Strongly built, with expressionless metallic eyes, he seemed unaware of the possibilities for violence & death which he carried in his muscles, in his armament. Then with a glimmer of curiosity in his voice he asked, "Where are you from?"

"Portogruaro."

Here I thought I had shaken him a little, but he proceeded in a regulation voice, "Where is Porogaro?"

"Northeastern Italy."

He was Italian too; anyway, of Italian descent. He even bore the name of a famous author, Artusi. Perhaps he had expected me to be a car thief and/or drug addict; it looked as if I had disappointed him. Like many people of my age & historical background, I am allergic to police and to uniforms in general. I imagine it was my surprise at hearing that name, Artusi, among the nocturnal canyons above the Pacific, that prevented me from starting on a trail of meticulous and irritating diatribe with my interrogator. I was overwhelmed by a feeling of quiet reasonableness. Not submission; in fact, the contrary. Basically the idea was: let's spare our energies, not waste them on trifles, if ever a day should come when quick and useful acts of violence are needed. And even this thought was enveloped in that feeling of reasonable calm which I felt spreading throughout my whole being.

Artusi asked me where I intended to stay, and I immediately gave him Blatt's address. After all, since my incognito had been broken so roughly, the best thing to do was to go to Blatt's, just like that, at three in the morning.

Blatt was asleep, and as I think I have said already, during the summer he had become engaged; when I rang his bell, both he and his fiancée were in the depths of sleep. He came to the door in his dressing gown; he recognized me, although thunderstruck and capable only of emitting a rattle which soundled like the follow-up to a just interrupted snore. When we put on the lights in the living room it was a dumb show at first because I was experiencing such an outburst of friendly delight in seeing him that I could find no words for it, and he remained in his somnambulant condition.

But then his fiancée appeared. I got up and she kissed me. I had never met her; I only knew her name, Alice Weaver. She was wearing a robe too, but she was very much alive and wide awake, her hairdo and make-up in perfect order. "Happy to see you, Gilberto. Heard so much about you. That's perfectly all right." It was perfectly all right for me to have awakened them.

It was at this point that Blatt surprised me. His rattle turned into a cry: "Gilberto Rossi!" He was suddenly awake, wide open. He added immediately, "Do you know what I feel like? I feel like having a beer."

He disappeared and presently came back carrying three bottles of Danish beer on a tray, and three colorful terra-cotta mugs. Then we set out in the night along the paths of talk and didn't stop till morning.

From the beginning, we talked more about Ruggero than about Alphonse. Blatt was by now lucid and didactic: "By the very fact of presenting such a wide, confused, incomprehensible picture, those countries are scoring an initial victory. Their reality cannot be reduced to fixed myths. That's why Ruggero is attracted to them as to a magnet."

I asked, "Did he talk about it in the same way that he used to talk about Kuntz?"

But Blatt didn't listen to me much. Either he talked himself, or his eyes were fastened on Alice Weaver in silent adoration. Now that I have seen them often, I realize that my first impression was correct: they were well matched because they were opposites. Blatt is full of activity and ideas, but after all, he is also Leutnant Hugo von Blatt, who, after breaking through the mountain front and charging down the valley slopes, starts to experience *Angst* and a feeling of void. Alice Weaver, on the other hand, is abstractly full of doubt and terror at the imminent destruction of the world, but one clearly sees that she feeds on more immediate worries: purchases to make, her love for

Blatt, the problems and comforts of everyday life. The threat of a nuclear apocalypse does exist, but she devotes only theoretical thoughts to it during leisure hours; and I could swear that her thoughts follow more or less this pattern: if mankind should go that far, well, then it will deserve what it gets. Man, in that case, would prove to have been a mistaken experiment. And good night, everybody.

She spoke of Beatrice and Ruggero with excitement. She told me that during the preparations for their departure, which actually took hours rather than days, Louis Pickford had tried to entice Ruggero into what he, Pickford, referred to as serious talk on the Themes of his voyage to China. He didn't get anywhere. The only subject on which Ruggero and Beatrice were at all definite was the matter of citizenship, and they reached their final conclusion immediately; namely, that it was more convenient for Beatrice to take the citizenship of Ruggero, her husband (they planned to be married "in Japan by some counsul") because at this time that would provide her with a passport which was more serviceable for purposes of admission and residence in the difficult Far Eastern countries.

Blatt said, "Ruggero and Beatrice spoke of citizenship as though the problem were a choice between different airlines." Old Clinton, they added, strongly approved of his daughter and son-in-law's travel plans. He will be rather lonely but he has innumerable friends, and besides, he will be busy with his ear operation. Ear specialists who have been among his students of poetry & letters are beaming with delight at the idea of restoring at least a fraction of his hearing to a patient they admire so much, subjecting him to a recently invented and exquisitely delicate surgery.

Of course I had to tell them something about my unannounced arrival, my stop in the canyons, Artusi. "Sometimes I feel a certain conventional nostalgia for so-called primitive freedom. The migratory life of Laplanders across frozen wastes, doweries computed in herds of reindeer, et cetera—you name it. I could sense a certain flavor of primitive freedom even up here, at a stone's throw from your house, before Artusi came."

Blatt asked from time to time, "What are your intentions about the Institute?"

I always answered at random, remembering Alphonse: any direction is good; everything is still to be done. "Just to give one example—these cosmic explorers. One should examine more clearly what they are all about. Hound them. Keep eyes and ears open. Same with the electronics people. I'll learn programming. Ruggero saw their machines on the same level as telephones, or as jets whose piloting was not his business; but I don't. I want a clearer picture, I am more demanding. I have always been a pedantic bore and I'll get worse. I have realized that when you feel even the slightest impulse to yield, then is the moment to shift to a higher gear. Would you like me to leave the Institute?"

"If you don't stay on, I won't accept the directorship."

This phrase irritated me but I didn't tell him. I resumed, "Everything here is too comfortable. The little house, the nice little metal desk at the library, the microfilm machine always ready, the air always conditioned. And in this air, Pick and his men elegantly discoursing on massacre & violence . . ."

"Irrelevant people," Blatt said in his unshakable equilibrium.

"Are you working on anything?"

"Various things. One is the problem of heroic deaths. Alphonse had already assembled a goodly number of letters, journals, reports on executions, and photographic material as well. The problem of heroization. The sensational, propagandized dead, already in the limelight of history. You remember, at the opposite end, the Decimation story. Number ten, not to mention number nine, will never be in the limelight of history. Whom do you feel closer to? These are questions we shall have to go on asking ourselves. But first you had better get into circulation again."

"Keep in mind that I haven't arrived here yet. If Artusi hadn't discovered me, I would still be in anonymous nature. You may consider that I have the same personality, citizenship, residence, as a codfish or a hornet. And even if, as a working hypothesis, we wanted to pretend that I have arrived, I am not here seeking my fortune or a settled position. For that matter, the emigrant looking for America-America has long ceased to exist, and anyway, the Institute certainly wouldn't be the most brilliant of goals for such a person. Pick-Chuck-Budd-Alf see in the new plastico-crystalline buildings an ever-more-concrete, future-directed reality; I don't; nor, I am sure, do you and Alice, or Clinton, or Epstein."

He insisted: "Tomorrow morning we shall start a series of completely informal kamiri miris of our own."

I said nothing. Then I laughed briefly, and went on saying nothing.

But Blatt talked: "As I said, I'll accept the directorship if you, Epstein, Lebournet, stay on . . ."

For a few moments I reveled in the game: "Naturally we must be sure that power is firmly in our hands."

"Power is quite a zero word, whose contents must be renewed every morning. As we have always said, this is true in micro- as well as in macro-dimensions. Whatever their size, all worlds have their weight and relevance. How do you see the future of the Institute?"

"It's a boat that leaks everywhere, and with a screwy helm and just as screwy navigation instruments. Like the country in general. Like the Western world in general. Like our globe in general. Like our solar system in general. Like our galaxy in general. And so forth. Thank goodness. That way life can be conducted with a minimum of pure courage, of dignity, at every moment. Without this, we wouldn't make any sense. We wouldn't make any sense without all the uncertainties, tensions, improbabilities, risks; and, I insist, all of these things not in small and occasional doses, but in large and permanent ones."

I was curious to see how he would react but he said only, with the Blatt poise, "Certainly, certainly; I understand, I understand."

Suddenly Elena Partibon came to mind, and they saw me smile. I spoke about her repeatedly even that first night: "I became very fond of a woman who gives me joy because, for one reason, she is absolutely incapable of hope. I feel I am always in her company. A while ago I started to tell you about the concept of an invisible network . . ."

"I understand, I understand." I don't know how much beer we had drunk; the fact is that dawn was breaking and finding us in a kind of acute half sleep, of lucid drowsiness. The ocean breakers, high as walls, were crashing almost up to the glass door; with their immense, slow rhythm they gave a feeling of well-being, truth, repose.

Blatt said, "That idea of the invisible network brought back to me, I don't know why, some images that were dear to Alphonse." As he mentioned Alphonse, we were silent for a long while. Then he resumed, "Do you remember when he talked about fish migrations? Or about time zones?"

I filled in, "Or about numbers, or musical notations."

Alphonse had simply wanted to say that all men were agreed on and adjusted to those regulating signs; all agreed and adjusted, even if only for the purpose of butchering one another. Carlo Rossi's leap from the trench at dawn, with a Hugo von Blatt leaping toward him from the opposite side forty yards away: a scene of carnage regulated by the same chronometer, same sun. And meanwhile, deep in the ocean, the fish were performing their natural and fecund motions. And so on, and so on. I talked and trembled: "The day navigating in space, always lighted. It is there for everybody, each takes his hour and it goes on there navigating high above the stale nations."

The fatigue of my journey was coming out now. I mumbled, "Numbers. Sounds. Whatever little one can understand. Kind of talk we had already with Norma, and again with Elena. Women who listen to you with patience." Now I felt like crying (repose, relax). "Don't ever be afraid to say things that seem too simple. We are only a few yet, or so we think. Every now and then you meet somebody, and you know it will last forever, wherever you may be, and then it occurs to you that there must be quantities of isolated people, a community of solitudes, all together one by one, spread out everywhere; the others don't look at them, or if they do look at them, they don't see them— as if they were transparent, immaterial, while instead those few are the most solid, the toughest of all."

Blatt has a way of saying things which sounds at the same time offhand and didactic: "Why, of course, from that point of view, you know, the history of the world has hardly begun."

Rome 1960–Venice 1968

ABOUT THE AUTHOR

P. M. PASINETTI was born and grew up in Venice. In 1935–37 he came to study in the United States, where his first published fiction appeared in *The Southern Review*. Mr. Pasinetti has since contributed to various literary reviews in this country, and since the age of eighteen has written pieces for magazines and newspapers in Italy, where he has also done occasional work on screenplays. His first book, three novelettes, was published by Mondadori in 1942.

Mr. Pasinetti first thought of teaching as a means of moving from his native country. After lectureships at Göttingen and Stockholm (where he spent most of the war years) he returned to the United States in 1946, taught briefly at Bennington and received a doctorate at Yale. He has since been associated with U.C.L.A., where he holds a professorship. He was appointed to the university's Institute for Creative Arts for 1964–65, and in 1965 received an award from the National Institute of Arts and Letters with a citation for fiction written in "the grand style of tradition but with a probing modern imagination." His first two novels, *Venetian Red* (1960) *and The Smile on the Face of the Lion* (1965), enjoyed a considerable international success. *Il Ponte dell'Accademia*, Mr. Pasinetti's Italian version of *From the Academy Bridge*, was enthusiastically received by Italian critics in 1968.